SIMON DALE

ANTHONY HOPE

1st WORLD
LIBRARY
Literary Society

Simon Dale

Anthony Hope

© 1st World Library, 2007
PO Box 2211
Fairfield, IA 52556
www.1stworldlibrary.com
First Edition

LCCN: 2007927700

Softcover ISBN: 978-1-4218-4504-3
Hardcover ISBN: 978-1-4218-4420-6
eBook ISBN: 978-1-4218-4588-3

Purchase *"Simon Dale"*
as a traditional bound book at:
www.1stWorldLibrary.com/purchase.asp?ISBN=978-1-4218-4504-3

1ˢᵗ World Library Literary Society

Giving Back to the World

"If you want to work on the core problem, it's early school literacy."

- James Barksdale, former CEO of Netscape

"No skill is more crucial to the future of a child, or to a democratic and prosperous society, than literacy."

- Los Angeles Times

"Literacy... means far more than learning how to read and write... The aim is to transmit... knowledge and promote social participation."

- UNESCO

"Literacy is not a luxury, it is a right and a responsibility. If our world is to meet the challenges of the twenty-first century we must harness the energy and creativity of all our citizens."

- President Bill Clinton

"Parents should be encouraged to read to their children, and teachers should be equipped with all available techniques for teaching literacy, so the varying needs and capacities of individual kids can be taken into account."

- Hugh Mackay

CONTENTS

CHAPTER I

THE CHILD OF PROPHECY

One who was in his day a person of great place and consideration, and has left a name which future generations shall surely repeat so long as the world may last, found no better rule for a man's life than that he should incline his mind to move in Charity, rest in Providence, and turn upon the poles of Truth. This condition, says he, is Heaven upon Earth; and although what touches truth may better befit the philosopher who uttered it than the vulgar and unlearned, for whom perhaps it is a counsel too high and therefore dangerous, what comes before should surely be graven by each of us on the walls of our hearts. For any man who lived in the days that I have seen must have found much need of trust in Providence, and by no whit the less of charity for men. In such trust and charity I have striven to write: in the like I pray you to read.

I, Simon Dale, was born on the seventh day of the seventh month in the year of Our Lord sixteen-hundred-and-forty-seven. The date was good in that the Divine Number was thrice found in it, but evil in that it fell on a time of sore trouble both for the nation and for our own house; when men had begun to go about saying that if the King would not keep his promises it was likely that he would keep his head as little; when they who had fought for freedom were suspecting that victory had brought new tyrants; when the Vicar was put out of his cure; and my father, having trusted the King first, the Parliament afterwards, and at last neither the one nor the other, had lost the greater part of his substance, and fallen from wealth to straitened means: such is the common reward of an honest patriotism wedded to an open mind. However, the date, good or bad, was none of my doing, nor indeed, folks whispered, much of my parents' either, seeing that destiny overruled the affair, and Betty Nasroth, the wise woman, announced its imminence more than a year beforehand. For she predicted the birth, on the very day whereon I came into the world, within a mile of the parish church, of a male child who—and the utterance certainly had a lofty sound about it—should love where the King loved, know what the King hid, and drink of the King's cup. Now, inasmuch as none lived within the limits named by Betty Nasroth, save on the one side sundry humble labourers, whose progeny could expect no such fate, and on the other my Lord and Lady Quinton, who were wedded but a month before my birthday, the prophecy was fully as pointed as it had any need to be, and caused to my parents no small questionings. It was the third clause or term of the prediction that gave most concern alike to my mother and to my father; to my mother, because, although of discreet mind and a sound Churchwoman, she was from her earliest years a Rechabite, and had never heard of a King who drank water; and to my father by reason of his decayed estate, which made it impossible for him to contrive how properly to fit me for my predestined company. "A man should not drink the King's wine without giving the King as good," my father reflected ruefully. Meanwhile I, troubling not at all about the matter, was content to prove Betty right in point of the

Anthony Hope

date, and, leaving the rest to the future, achieved this triumph for her most punctually. Whatsoever may await a man on his way through the world, he can hardly begin life better than by keeping his faith with a lady.

She was a strange old woman, this Betty Nasroth, and would likely enough have fared badly in the time of the King's father. Now there was bigger game than witches afoot, and nothing worse befell her than the scowls of her neighbours and the frightened mockery of children. She made free reply with curses and dark mutterings, but me she loved as being the child of her vision, and all the more because, encountering her as I rode in my mother's arms, I did not cry, but held out my hands, crowing and struggling to get to her; whereat suddenly, and to my mother's great terror, she exclaimed: "Thou see'st, Satan!" and fell to weeping, a thing which, as every woman in the parish knew, a person absolutely possessed by the Evil One can by no means accomplish (unless, indeed, a bare three drops squeezed from the left eye may usurp the name of tears). But my mother shrank away from her and would not allow her to touch me; nor was it until I had grown older and ran about the village alone that the old woman, having tracked me to a lonely spot, took me in her arms, mumbled over my head some words I did not understand, and kissed me. That a mole grows on the spot she kissed is but a fable (for how do the women know where her kiss fell save by where the mole grows?—and that is to reason poorly), or at the most the purest chance. Nay, if it were more, I am content; for the mole does me no harm, and the kiss, as I hope, did Betty some good; off she went straight to the Vicar (who was living then in the cottage of my Lord Quinton's gardener and exercising his sacred functions in a secrecy to which the whole parish was privy) and prayed him to let her partake of the Lord's Supper: a request that caused great scandal to the neighbours and sore embarrassment to the Vicar himself, who, being a learned man and deeply read in demonology, grieved from his heart that the witch did not play her part better.

"It is," said he to my father, "a monstrous lapse."

"Nay, it is a sign of grace," urged my mother.

"It is," said my father (and I do not know whether he spoke perversely or in earnest), "a matter of no moment."

Now, being steadfastly determined that my boyhood shall be less tedious in the telling than it was in the living—for I always longed to be a man, and hated my green and petticoat-governed days—I will pass forthwith to the hour when I reached the age of eighteen years. My dear father was then in Heaven, and old Betty had found, as was believed, another billet. But my mother lived, and the Vicar, like the King, had come to his own again: and I was five feet eleven in my stockings, and there was urgent need that I should set about pushing my way and putting money in my purse; for our lands had not returned with the King, and there was no more incoming than would serve to keep my mother and sisters in the style of gentlewomen.

"And on that matter," observed the Vicar, stroking his nose with his forefinger, as his habit was in moments of perplexity, "Betty Nasroth's prophecy is of small service. For the doings on which she touches are likely to be occasions of expense rather than sources of gain."

"They would be money wasted," said my mother gently, "one and all of them."

The Vicar looked a little doubtful.

"I will write a sermon on that theme," said he; for this was with him a favourite way out of an argument. In truth the Vicar loved the prophecy, as a quiet student often loves a thing that echoes of the world which he has shunned.

"You must write down for me what the King says to you, Simon," he told me once.

"Suppose, sir," I suggested mischievously, "that it should not be fit for your eye?"

"Then write it, Simon," he answered, pinching my ear, "for my understanding."

It was well enough for the Vicar's whimsical fancy to busy itself with Betty Nasroth's prophecy, half-believing, half-mocking, never forgetting nor disregarding; but I, who am, after all, the most concerned, doubt whether such a dark utterance be a wholesome thing to hang round a young man's neck. The dreams of youth grow rank enough without such watering. The prediction was always in my mind, alluring and tantalising as a teasing girl who puts her pretty face near yours, safe that you dare not kiss it. What it said I mused on, what it said not I neglected. I dedicated my idle hours to it, and, not appeased, it invaded my seasons of business. Rather than seek my own path, I left myself to its will and hearkened for its whispered orders.

"It was the same," observed my mother sadly, "with a certain cook-maid of my sister's. It was foretold that she should marry her master."

"And did she not?" cried the Vicar, with ears all pricked-up.

"She changed her service every year," said my mother, "seeking the likeliest man, until at last none would hire her."

"She should have stayed in her first service," said the Vicar, shaking his head.

"But her first master had a wife," retorted my mother triumphantly.

"I had one once myself," said the Vicar.

The argument, with which his widowhood supplied the Vicar, was sound and unanswerable, and it suited well with my humour to learn from my aunt's cook-maid, and wait patiently on fate. But what avails an argument, be it ever so sound, against an empty purse? It was declared that I must seek my fortune; yet on the method of my search some difference arose.

"You must work, Simon," said my sister Lucy, who was betrothed to Justice Barnard, a young squire of good family and high repute, but mighty hard on idle vagrants, and free with the stocks for revellers.

"You must pray for guidance," said my sister Mary, who was to wed a saintly clergyman, a Prebend, too, of the Cathedral.

"There is," said I stoutly, "nothing of such matters in Betty Nasroth's prophecy."

"They are taken for granted, dear boy," said my

mother gently.

The Vicar rubbed his nose.

Yet not these excellent and zealous counsellors proved right, but the Vicar and I. For had I gone to London, as they urged, instead of abiding where I was, agreeably to the Vicar's argument and my own inclination, it is a great question whether the plague would not have proved too strong for Betty Nasroth, and her prediction gone to lie with me in a death-pit. As things befell, I lived, hearing only dimly and, as it were, from afar-off of that great calamity, and of the horrors that beset the city. For the disease did not come our way, and we moralised on the sins of the townsfolk with sound bodies and contented minds. We were happy in our health and in our virtue, and not disinclined to applaud God's judgment that smote our erring brethren; for too often the chastisement of one sinner feeds another's pride. Yet the plague had a hand, and no small one, in that destiny of mine, although it came not near me; for it brought fresh tenants to those same rooms in the gardener's cottage where the Vicar had dwelt till the loyal Parliament's Act proved too hard for the conscience of our Independent minister, and the Vicar, nothing loth, moved back to his parsonage.

Now I was walking one day, as I had full licence and leave to walk, in the avenue of Quinton Manor, when I saw, first, what I had (if I am to tell the truth) come to see, to wit, the figure of young Mistress Barbara, daintily arrayed in a white summer gown. Barbara was pleased to hold herself haughtily towards me, for she was an heiress, and of a house that had not fallen in the world as mine had. Yet we were friends; for we sparred and rallied, she giving offence and I taking it, she pardoning my rudeness and I accepting forgiveness; while my lord and my lady, perhaps thinking me too low for fear and yet high enough for favour, showed me much kindness; my lord, indeed, would often jest with me on the great fate foretold me in Betty Nasroth's prophecy.

"Yet," he would say, with a twinkle in his eye, "the King has strange secrets, and there is some strange wine in his cup, and to love where he loves—"; but at this point the Vicar, who chanced to be by, twinkled also, but shifted the conversation to some theme which did not touch the King, his secrets, his wine, or where he loved.

Thus then I saw, as I say, the slim tall figure, the dark hair, and the proud eyes of Barbara Quinton; and the eyes were flashing in anger as their owner turned away from— what I had not looked to see in Barbara's company. This was another damsel, of lower stature and plumper figure, dressed full as prettily as Barbara herself, and laughing with most merry lips and under eyes that half hid themselves in an eclipse of mirth. When Barbara saw me, she did not, as her custom was, feign not to see me till I thrust my presence on her, but ran to me at once, crying very indignantly, "Simon, who is this girl? She has dared to tell me that my gown is of country make and hangs like an old smock on a beanpole."

"Mistress Barbara," I answered, "who heeds the make of the gown when the wearer is of divine make?" I was young then, and did not know that to compliment herself at the expense of her apparel is not the best way to please a woman.

"You are silly," said Barbara. "Who is she?"

"The girl," said I, crestfallen, "is, they tell me, from London, and she lodges with her mother in your gardener's cottage. But I didn't look to find her here in the avenue."

"You shall not again if I have my way," said Barbara. Then she added abruptly and sharply, "Why do you look at her?"

Now, it was true that I was looking at the stranger, and on Barbara's question I looked the harder.

"She is mighty pretty," said I. "Does she not seem so to you, Mistress Barbara?" And, simple though I was, I spoke not altogether in simplicity.

"Pretty?" echoed Barbara. "And pray what do you know of prettiness, Master Simon?"

"What I have learnt at Quinton Manor," I answered, with a bow.

"That doesn't prove her pretty," retorted the angry lady.

"There's more than one way of it," said I discreetly, and I took a step towards the visitor, who stood some ten yards from us, laughing still and plucking a flower to pieces in her fingers.

"She isn't known to you?" asked Barbara, perceiving my movement.

"I can remedy that," said I, smiling.

Never since the world began had youth been a more faithful servant to maid than I to Barbara Quinton. Yet because, if a man lie down, the best of girls will set her pretty foot on his neck, and also from my love of a thing that is new, I was thoroughly resolved to accost the gardener's guest; and my purpose was not altered by Barbara's scornful toss of her little head as she turned away.

"It is no more than civility," I protested, "to ask after her health, for, coming from London, she can but just have escaped the plague."

Barbara tossed her head again, declaring plainly her opinion of my excuse.

"But if you desire me to walk with you—" I began.

"There is nothing I thought of less," she interrupted. "I came here to be alone."

"My pleasure lies in obeying you," said I, and I stood bareheaded while Barbara, without another glance at me, walked off towards the house. Half penitent, yet wholly obstinate, I watched her go; she did not once look over her shoulder. Had she—but a truce to that. What passed is enough; with what might have, my story would stretch to the world's end. I smothered my remorse, and went up to the stranger, bidding her good-day in my most polite and courtly manner; she smiled, but at what I knew not. She seemed little more than a child, sixteen years old or seventeen at the most, yet there was no confusion in her greeting of me. Indeed, she was most marvellously at her ease, for, on my salute, she cried, lifting her hands in feigned amazement,

"A man, by my faith; a man in this place!"

Well pleased to be called a man, I bowed again.

Anthony Hope

"Or at least," she added, "what will be one, if it please Heaven."

"You may live to see it without growing wrinkled," said I, striving to conceal my annoyance.

"And one that has repartee in him! Oh, marvellous!"

"We do not all lack wit in the country, madame," said I, simpering as I supposed the Court gallants to simper, "nor, since the plague came to London, beauty."

"Indeed, it's wonderful," she cried in mock admiration. "Do they teach such sayings hereabouts, sir?"

"Even so, madame, and from such books as your eyes furnish." And for all her air of mockery, I was, as I remember, much pleased with this speech. It had come from some well-thumbed romance, I doubt not. I was always an eager reader of such silly things.

She curtseyed low, laughing up at me with roguish eyes and mouth.

"Now, surely, sir," she said, "you must be Simon Dale, of whom my host the gardener speaks?"

"It is my name, madame, at your service. But the gardener has played me a trick; for now I have nothing to give in exchange for your name."

"Nay, you have a very pretty nosegay in your hand," said she. "I might be persuaded to barter my name for it."

The nosegay that was in my hand I had gathered and brought for Barbara Quinton, and I still meant to use it as a peace-offering. But Barbara had treated me harshly, and the stranger looked longingly at the nosegay.

"The gardener is a niggard with his flowers," she said with a coaxing smile.

"To confess the truth," said I, wavering in my purpose, "the nosegay was plucked for another."

"It will smell the sweeter," she cried, with a laugh. "Nothing gives flowers such a perfume." And she held out a wonderfully small hand towards my nosegay.

"Is that a London lesson?" I asked, holding the flowers away from her grasp.

"It holds good in the country also, sir; wherever, indeed, there is a man to gather flowers and more than one lady who loves smelling them."

"Well," said I, "the nosegay is yours at the price," and I held it out to her.

"The price? What, you desire to know my name?"

"Unless, indeed, I may call you one of my own choosing," said I, with a glance that should have been irresistible.

"Would you use it in speaking of me to Mistress Barbara there? No, I'll give you a name to call me by. You may call me Cydaria."

"Cydaria! A fine name!"

"It is," said she carelessly, "as good as any other."

"But is there no other to follow it?"

"When did a poet ask two names to head his sonnet? And surely you wanted mine for a sonnet?"

"So be it, Cydaria," said I.

"So be it, Simon. And is not Cydaria as pretty as Barbaria?"

"It has a strange sound," said I, "but it's well enough."

"And now—the nosegay!"

"I must pay a reckoning for this," I sighed; but since a bargain is a bargain I gave her the nosegay.

She took it, her face all alight with smiles, and buried her nose in it. I stood looking at her, caught by her pretty ways and graceful boldness. Boy though I was, I had been right in telling her that there are many ways of beauty; here were two to start with, hers and Barbara's. She looked up and, finding my gaze on her, made a little grimace as though it were only what she had expected and gave her no more concern than pleasure. Yet at such a look Barbara would have turned cold and distant for an hour or more. Cydaria, smiling in scornful indulgence, dropped me another mocking curtsey, and made as though she would go her way. Yet she did not go, but stood with her head half-averted, a glance straying towards me from the corner of her eye, while with her tiny foot she dug the gravel of the avenue.

"It is a lovely place, this park," said she. "But, indeed, it's often hard to find the way about it."

I was not backward to take her hint.

"If you had a guide now—" I began.

"Why, yes, if I had a guide, Simon," she whispered gleefully.

"You could find the way, Cydaria, and your guide would be most—"

"Most charitably engaged. But then—" She paused, drooping the corners of her mouth in sudden despondency.

"But what then?"

"Why then, Mistress Barbara would be alone."

I hesitated. I glanced towards the house. I looked at Cydaria.

"She told me that she wished to be alone," said I.

"No? How did she say it?"

"I will tell you all about that as we go along," said I, and Cydaria laughed again.

CHAPTER II

THE WAY OF YOUTH

The debate is years old; not indeed quite so old as the world, since Adam and Eve cannot, for want of opportunity, have fallen out over it, yet descending to us from unknown antiquity. But it has never been set at rest by general consent: the quarrel over Passive Obedience is nothing to it. It seems such a small matter though; for the debate I mean turns on no greater question than this: may a man who owns allegiance to one lady justify by any train of reasoning his conduct in snatching a kiss from another, this other being (for it is important to have the terms right) not (so far as can be judged) unwilling? I maintained that he might; to be sure, my position admitted of no other argument, and, for the most part, it is a man's state which determines his arguments and not his reasons that induce his state. Barbara declared that he could not; though, to be sure, it was, as she added most promptly, no concern of hers; for she cared not whether I were in love or not, nor how deeply, nor with whom, nor, in a word, anything at all about the matter. It was an abstract opinion she gave, so far as love, or what men chose to call such, might be involved; as to seemliness, she must confess that she had her view, with which, may be, Mr Dale was not in agreement. The girl at the gardener's cottage must, she did not doubt, agree wholly with Mr Dale; how otherwise would she have suffered the kiss in an open space in the park, where anybody might pass—and where, in fact (by the most perverse chance in the world), pretty Mistress Barbara herself passed at the moment when the thing occurred? However, if the matter could ever have had the smallest interest for her—save in so far as it touched the reputation of the village and might afford an evil example to the village maidens—it could have none at all now, seeing that she set out the next day to London, to take her place as Maid of Honour to Her Royal Highness the Duchess, and would have as little leisure as inclination to think of Mr Simon Dale or of how he chose to amuse himself when he believed that none was watching. Not that she had watched: her presence was the purest and most unwelcome chance. Yet she could not but be glad to hear that the girl was soon to go back whence she came, to the great relief (she was sure) of Madame Dale and of her dear friends Lucy and Mary; to her love for whom nothing—no, nothing—should make any difference. For the girl herself she wished no harm, but she conceived that her mother must be ill at ease concerning her.

It will be allowed that Mistress Barbara had the most of the argument if not the best. Indeed, I found little to say, except that the village would be the worse by so much as the Duchess of York was the better for Mistress Barbara's departure; the civility won me nothing but the haughtiest curtsey and a taunt.

"Must you rehearse your pretty speeches on me before you venture them on your friends, sir?" she asked.

"I am at your mercy, Mistress Barbara," I pleaded. "Are we to part enemies?"

She made me no answer, but I seemed to see a softening in her face as she turned away towards the window, whence were to be seen the stretch of the lawn and the park-meadows beyond. I believe that with a little more coaxing she would have pardoned me, but at the instant, by another stroke of perversity, a small figure sauntered across the sunny fields. The fairest sights may sometimes come amiss.

"Cydaria! A fine name!" said Barbara, with curling lip. "I'll wager she has reasons for giving no other."

"Her mother gives another to the gardener," I reminded her meekly.

"Names are as easy given as—as kisses!" she retorted. "As for Cydaria, my lord says it is a name out of a play."

All this while we had stood at the window, watching Cydaria's light feet trip across the meadow, and her bonnet swing wantonly in her hand. But now Cydaria disappeared among the trunks of the beech trees.

"See, she has gone," said I in a whisper. "She is gone, Mistress Barbara."

Barbara understood what I would say, but she was resolved to show me no gentleness. The soft tones of my voice had been for her, but she would not accept their homage.

"You need not sigh for that before my face," said she. "And yet, sigh if you will. What is it to me? But she is not gone far, and, doubtless, will not run too fast when you pursue."

"When you are in London," said I, "you will think with remorse how ill you used me."

"I shall never think of you at all. Do you forget that there are gentlemen of wit and breeding at the Court?"

"The devil fly away with every one of them!" cried I suddenly, not knowing then how well the better part of them would match their escort.

Barbara turned to me; there was a gleam of triumph in the depths of her dark eyes.

"Perhaps when you hear of me at Court," she cried, "you'll be sorry to think how—"

But she broke off suddenly, and looked out of the window.

"You'll find a husband there," I suggested bitterly.

"Like enough," said she carelessly.

To be plain, I was in no happy mood. Her going grieved me to the heart, and that she should go thus incensed stung me yet more. I was jealous of every man in London town. Had not my argument, then, some reason in it after all?

"Fare-you-well, madame," said I, with a heavy frown and a sweeping bow. No player from the Lane could have been more tragic.

"Fare-you-well, sir. I will not detain you, for you have, I know, other farewells to make."

"Not for a week yet!" I cried, goaded to a show of exultation that Cydaria stayed so long.

"I don't doubt that you'll make good use of the time," she said, as with a fine dignity she waved me to the door. Girl as she was, she had caught or inherited the grand air that great ladies use.

Gloomily I passed out, to fall into the hands of my lord, who was walking on the terrace. He caught me by the arm, laughing in good-humoured mockery.

"You've had a touch of sentiment, eh, you rogue?" said he. "Well, there's little harm in that, since the girl leaves us to-morrow."

"Indeed, my lord, there was little harm," said I, long-faced and rueful. "As little as my lady herself could wish." (At this he smiled and nodded.) "Mistress Barbara will hardly so much as look at me."

He grew graver, though the smile still hung about his lips.

"They gossip about you in the village, Simon," said he. "Take a friend's counsel, and don't be so much with the lady at the cottage. Come, I don't speak without reason." He nodded at me as a man nods who means more than he will say. Indeed, not a word more would he say, so that when I left him I was even more angry than when I parted from his daughter. And, the nature of man being such as Heaven has made it, what need to say that I bent my steps to the cottage with all convenient speed? The only weapon of an ill-used lover (nay, I will not argue the merits of the case again) was ready to my hand.

Yet my impatience availed little; for there, on the seat that stood by the door, sat my good friend the Vicar, discoursing in pleasant leisure with the lady who named herself Cydaria.

"It is true," he was saying. "I fear it is true, though you're over young to have learnt it."

"There are schools, sir," she returned, with a smile that had (or so it seemed to me) a touch—no more—of bitterness in it, "where such lessons are early learnt."

"They are best let alone, those schools," said he.

"And what's the lesson?" I asked, drawing nearer.

Neither answered. The Vicar rested his hands on the ball of his cane, and suddenly began to relate old Betty Nasroth's prophecy to his companion. I cannot tell what led his thoughts to it, but it was never far from his mind when I was by. She listened with attention, smiling brightly in whimsical amusement when the fateful words, pronounced with due solemnity, left the Vicar's lips.

"It is a strange saying," he ended, "of which time alone can show the truth."

She glanced at me with merry eyes, yet with a new air of interest. It is strange the hold these superstitions have on all of us; though surely future ages will outgrow such childishness.

"I don't know what the prophecy means," said she; "yet one thing at least would seem needful for its fulfilment—that Mr Dale should become acquainted with the King."

"True!" cried the Vicar eagerly. "Everything stands on

that, and on that we stick. For Simon cannot love where the King loves, nor know what the King hides, nor drink of the King's cup, if he abide all his days here in Hatchstead. Come, Simon, the plague is gone!"

"Should I then be gone too?" I asked. "But to what end? I have no friends in London who would bring me to the notice of the King."

The Vicar shook his head sadly. I had no such friends, and the King had proved before now that he could forget many a better friend to the throne than my dear father's open mind had made of him.

"We must wait, we must wait still," said the Vicar. "Time will find a friend."

Cydaria had become pensive for a moment, but she looked up now, smiling again, and said to me:

"You'll soon have a friend in London."

Thinking of Barbara, I answered gloomily, "She's no friend of mine."

"I did not mean whom you mean," said Cydaria, with twinkling eyes and not a whit put out. "But I also am going to London."

I smiled, for it did not seem as though she would be a powerful friend, or able to open any way for me. But she met my smile with another so full of confidence and challenge that my attention was wholly caught, and I did not heed the Vicar's farewell as he rose and left us.

"And would you serve me," I asked, "if you had

the power?"

"Nay, put the question as you think it," said she. "Would you have the power to serve me if you had the will? Is not that the doubt in your mind?"

"And if it were?"

"Then, indeed, I do not know how to answer; but strange things happen there in London, and it may be that some day even I should have some power."

"And you would use it for me?"

"Could I do less on behalf of a gentleman who has risked his mistress's favour for my poor cheek's sake?" And she fell to laughing again, her mirth growing greater as I turned red in the face. "You mustn't blush when you come to town," she cried, "or they'll make a ballad on you, and cry you in the streets for a monster."

"The oftener comes the cause, the rarer shall the effect be," said I.

"The excuse is well put," she conceded. "We should make a wit of you in town."

"What do you in town?" I asked squarely, looking her full in the eyes.

"Perhaps, sometimes," she laughed, "what I have done once—and to your good knowledge—since I came to the country."

Thus she would baffle me with jesting answers as often as I sought to find out who and what she was. Nor had I better fortune with her mother, for whom I had small liking, and who had, as it seemed, no more for me. For she was short in her talk, and frowned to see me with her daughter. Yet she saw me, I must confess, often with Cydaria in the next days, and I was often with Cydaria when she did not see me. For Barbara was gone, leaving me both sore and lonely, all in the mood to find comfort where I could, and to see manliness in desertion; and there was a charm about the girl that grew on me insensibly and without my will until I came to love, not her (as I believed, forgetting that Love loves not to mark his boundaries too strictly) but her merry temper, her wit and cheerfulness. Moreover, these things were mingled and spiced with others, more attractive than all to unfledged youth, an air of the world and a knowledge of life which piqued my curiosity and sat (it seems so even to my later mind as I look back) with bewitching incongruity on the laughing child's face and the unripe grace of girlhood. Her moods were endless, vying with one another in an ever undetermined struggle for the prize of greatest charm. For the most part she was merry, frank mirth passing into sly raillery; now and then she would turn sad, sighing, "Heigho, that I could stay in the sweet innocent country!" Or again she would show or ape an uneasy conscience, whispering, "Ah, that I were like your Mistress Barbara!" The next moment she would be laughing and jesting and mocking, as though life were nought but a great many-coloured bubble, and she the brightest-tinted gleam on it.

Are women so constant and men so forgetful, that all sympathy must go from me and all esteem be forfeited because, being of the age of eighteen years, I vowed to live for one lady only on a Monday and was ready to die for another on the Saturday? Look back; bow your heads, and give me your hands, to kiss or to clasp!

Let not you and I inquire
What has been our past desire,
On what shepherds you have smiled,
Or what nymphs I have beguiled;
Leave it to the planets too
What we shall hereafter do;
For the joys we now may prove,
Take advice of present love.

Nay, I will not set my name to that in its fulness; Mr
Waller is a little too free for one who has been nicknamed
a Puritan to follow him to the end. Yet there is a truth in
it. Deny it, if you will. You are smiling, madame, while
you deny.

It was a golden summer's evening when I, to whom the
golden world was all a hell, came by tryst to the park of
Quinton Manor, there to bid Cydaria farewell. Mother and
sisters had looked askance at me, the village gossiped,
even the Vicar shook a kindly head. What cared I? By
Heaven, why was one man a nobleman and rich, while
another had no money in his purse and but one change to
his back? Was not love all in all, and why did Cydaria
laugh at a truth so manifest? There she was under the
beech tree, with her sweet face screwed up to a burlesque
of grief, her little hand lying on her hard heart as though it
beat for me, and her eyes the playground of a thousand
quick expressions. I strode up to her, and caught her by
the hand, saying no more than just her name, "Cydaria." It
seemed that there was no more to say; yet she cried,
laughing and reproachful, "Have you no vows for me?
Must I go without my tribute?"

I loosed her hand and stood away from her. On my soul, I
could not speak. I was tongue-tied, dumb as a dog.

"When you come courting in London," she said, "you must not come so empty of lover's baggage. There ladies ask vows, and protestations, and despair, ay, and poetry, and rhapsodies, and I know not what."

"Of all these I have nothing but despair," said I.

"Then you make a sad lover," she pouted. "And I am glad to be going where lovers are less woebegone."

"You look for lovers in London?" I cried, I that had cried to Barbara—well, I have said my say on that.

"If Heaven send them," answered Cydaria.

"And you will forget me?"

"In truth, yes, unless you come yourself to remind me. I have no head for absent lovers."

"But if I come—" I began in a sudden flush of hope.

She did not (though it was her custom) answer in raillery; she plucked a leaf from the tree, and tore it with her fingers as she answered with a curious glance.

"Why, if you come, I think you'll wish that you had not come, unless, indeed, you've forgotten me before you come."

"Forget you! Never while I live! May I come, Cydaria?"

"Most certainly, sir, so soon as your wardrobe and your purse allow. Nay, don't be huffed. Come, Simon, sweet Simon, are we not friends, and may not friends rally one another? No, and if I choose, I will put my hand through your arm. Indeed, sir, you're the first gentleman that ever thrust it away. See, it is there now! Doesn't it look well there, Simon—and feel well there, Simon?" She looked up into my face in coaxing apology for the hurt she had given me, and yet still with mockery of my tragic airs. "Yes, you must by all means come to London," she went on, patting my arm. "Is not Mistress Barbara in London? And I think—am I wrong, Simon?—that there is something for which you will want to ask her pardon."

"If I come to London, it is for you and you only that I shall come," I cried.

"No, no. You will come to love where the King loves, to know what he hides, and to drink of his cup. I, sir, cannot interfere with your great destiny"; she drew away from me, curtseyed low, and stood opposite to me, smiling.

"For you and for you only," I repeated.

"Then will the King love me?" she asked.

"God forbid," said I fervently.

"Oh, and why, pray, your 'God forbid'? You're very ready with your 'God forbids.' Am I then to take your love sooner than the King's, Master Simon?"

"Mine is an honest love," said I soberly.

"Oh, I should doat on the country, if everybody didn't talk of his honesty there! I have seen the King in London and he is a fine gentleman."

"And you have seen the Queen also, may be?"

"In truth, yes. Ah, I have shocked you, Simon? Well, I was wrong. Come, we're in the country; we'll be good. But when we've made a townsman of you, we'll—we will be what they are in town. Moreover, in ten minutes I am going home, and it would be hard if I also left you in anger. You shall have a pleasanter memory of my going than Mistress Barbara's gave you."

"How shall I find you when I come to town?"

"Why, if you will ask any gentleman you meet whether he chances to remember Cydaria, you will find me as soon as it is well you should."

I prayed her to tell me more; but she was resolved to tell no more.

"See, it is late. I go," said she. Then suddenly she came near to me. "Poor Simon," she said softly. "Yet it is good for you, Simon. Some day you will be amused at this, Simon"; she spoke as though she were fifty years older than I. My answer lay not in words or arguments. I caught her in my arms and kissed her. She struggled, yet she laughed. It shot through my mind then that Barbara would neither have struggled nor laughed. But Cydaria laughed.

Presently I let her go, and kneeling on my knee kissed her hand very humbly, as though she had been what Barbara was. If she were not—and I knew not what she was—yet should my love exalt her and make a throne whereon she might sit a Queen. My new posture brought a sudden gravity to her face, and she bent over me with a smile that seemed now tender and almost sorrowful.

"Poor Simon, poor Simon," she whispered. "Kiss my hand now; kiss it as though I were fit for worship. It will do you no harm, and—and perhaps—perhaps I shall like to remember it." She bent down and kissed my forehead as I knelt before her. "Poor Simon," she whispered, as her hair brushed mine. Then her hand was gradually and gently withdrawn. I looked up to see her face; her lips were smiling but there seemed a dew on her lashes. She laughed, and the laugh ended in a little gasp, as though a sob had fought with it. And she cried out loud, her voice ringing clear among the trees in the still evening air.

"That ever I should be so sore a fool!"

Then she turned and left me, running swiftly over the grass, with never a look behind her. I watched till she was out of sight, and then sat down on the ground; with twitching lips and wide-open dreary eyes.

Ah, for youth's happiness! Alas for its dismal woe! Thus she came into my life.

CHAPTER III

THE MUSIC OF THE WORLD

If a philosopher, learned in the human mind as Flamsteed in the courses of the stars or the great Newton in the laws of external nature, were to take one possessed by a strong passion of love or a bitter grief, or what overpowering emotion you will, and were to consider impartially and with cold precision what share of his time was in reality occupied by the thing which, as we are in the habit of saying, filled his thoughts or swayed his life or mastered his intellect, the world might well smile (and to my thinking had better smile than weep) at the issue of the investigation. When the first brief shock was gone, how few out of the solid twenty-four would be the hours claimed by the despot, however much the poets might call him insatiable. There is sleeping, and meat and drink, the putting on and off of raiment and the buying of it. If a man be of sound body, there is his sport; if he be sane, there are the interests of this life and provision for the next. And if he be young, there is nature's own joy in living, which with a patient scornful smile sets aside his protest that he is vowed to misery, and makes him, willy-nilly, laugh and sing. So that, if he do not drown himself in a week and thereby balk the inquiry, it is odds that he will compose himself in a month, and by the end of a year will carry no more marks of his misfortune than (if he be a man of good heart) an added sobriety and tenderness of spirit. Yet all this does not hinder the thing from returning, on occasion given.

In my own case—and, if my story be followed to its close, I am persuaded that I shall not be held to be one who took the disease of love more lightly than my fellows—this process of convalescence, most salutary, yet in a sense humiliating, was aided by a train of circumstances, in which my mother saw the favour of Heaven to our family and the Vicar the working of Betty Nasroth's prophecy. An uncle of my mother's had some forty years ago established a manufactory of wool at Norwich, and having kept always before his eyes the truth that men must be clothed, howsoever they may think on matters of Church and State, and that it is a cloth-weaver's business to clothe them and not to think for them, had lived a quiet life through all the disturbances and had prospered greatly in his trade. For marriage either time or inclination had failed him, and, being now an old man, he felt a favourable disposition towards me, and declared the intention of making me heir to a considerable portion of his fortune provided that I showed myself worthy of such kindness. The proof he asked was not beyond reason, though I found cause for great lamentation in it; for it was that, in lieu of seeking to get to London, I should go to Norwich and live there with him, to solace his last years and, although not engaged in his trade, learn by observation something of the serious occupations of life and of the condition of my fellow-men, of which things young gentlemen, said he, were for the most part sadly ignorant. Indeed, they were, and they thought no better of a companion for being wiser; to do anything or know anything that might redound to the benefit of man or the honour of God was not the mode in those days. Nor do I

Anthony Hope

say that the fashion has changed greatly, no, nor that it will change. Therefore to Norwich I went, although reluctantly, and there I stayed fully three years, applying myself to the comforting of my uncle's old age, and consoling my leisure with the diversions which that great and important city afforded, and which, indeed, were enough for any rational mind. But reason and youth are bad bedfellows, and all the while I was like the Israelites in the wilderness; my thoughts were set upon the Promised Land and I endured my probation hardly. To this mood I set down the fact that little of my life at Norwich lives in my memory, and to that little I seldom recur in thought; the time before it and the time after engross my backward glances. The end came with my uncle's death, whereat I, the recipient of great kindness from him, sincerely grieved, and that with some remorse, since I had caused him sorrow by refusing to take up his occupation as my own, preferring my liberty and a moderate endowment to all his fortune saddled with the condition of passing my days as a cloth-weaver. Had I chosen otherwise, I should have lived a more peaceful and died a richer man. Yet I do not repent; not riches nor peace, but the stir of the blood, the work of the hand, and the service of the brain make a life that a man can look back on without shame and with delight.

I was nearing my twenty-second birthday when I returned to Hatchstead with an air and manner, I doubt not, sadly provincial, but with a lining to my pocket for whose sake many a gallant would have surrendered some of his plumes and feathers. Three thousand pounds, invested in my uncle's business and returning good and punctual profit made of Simon Dale a person of far greater importance in the eyes of his family than he had been three years ago. It was a competence on which a gentleman could live with discretion and modesty, it was a step from which his foot could rise higher on life's ladder. London was in my power, all it held of promise and possibility was not beyond the flight of my soaring mind. My sisters exchanged sharp admonitions for admiring deference, and my mother feared nothing save that the great place to which I was now surely destined might impair the homely virtues which she had instilled into me. As for the Vicar, he stroked his nose and glanced at me with an eye which spoke so plainly of Betty Nasroth that I fell to laughing heartily.

Thus, being in great danger of self-exaltation, I took the best medicine that I could—although by no means with intention—in waiting on my lord Quinton, who was then residing at the Manor. Here my swelled spirit was smartly pricked, and sank soon to its true proportions. I was no great man here, and although my lord received me very kindly, he had less to say on the richness of my fortune than on the faults of my manner and the rustic air of my attire. Yet he bade me go to London, since there a man, rubbing shoulders with all the world, learnt to appraise his own value, and lost the ignorant conceit of himself that a village greatness is apt to breed. Somewhat crestfallen, I thanked him for his kindness, and made bold to ask after Mistress Barbara.

"She is well enough," he answered, smiling. "And she is become a great lady. The wits make epigrams on her, and the fools address verses to her. But she's a good girl, Simon."

"I'm sure of it, my lord," I cried.

"He's a bold man who would be sure of it concerning anyone nowadays," he said dryly. "Yet so, thank God, it is. See, here's a copy of the verses she had lately," and he

Anthony Hope

flung me the paper. I glanced over it and saw much about "dazzling ice," "unmelting snow," "Venus," "Diana," and so forth.

"It seems sad stuff, my lord," said I.

"Why, yes," he laughed; "but it is by a gentle man of repute. Take care you write none worse, Simon."

"Shall I have the honour of waiting on Mistress Barbara, my lord?" I asked.

"As to that, Simon, we will see when you come. Yes, we must see what company you keep. For example, on whom else do you think of waiting when you are set up in London?"

He looked steadily at me, a slight frown on his brow, yet a smile, and not an unkind one, on his lips. I grew hot, and knew that I grew red also.

"I am acquainted with few in London, my lord," I stammered, "and with those not well."

"Those not well, indeed," he echoed, the pucker deepening and the smile vanishing. Yet the smile came again as he rose and clapped me on the shoulder.

"You're an honest lad, Simon," he said, "even though it may have pleased God to make you a silly one. And, by Heaven, who would have all lads wise? Go to London, learn to know more folk, learn to know better those whom you know. Bear yourself as a gentleman, and remember, Simon, whatsoever else the King may be, yet he is the King."

Saying this with much emphasis, he led me gently to the door.

"Why did he say that about the King?" I pondered as I walked homeward through the park; for although what we all, even in the country, knew of the King gave warrant enough for the words, my lord had seemed to speak them to me with some special meaning, and as though they concerned me more than most men. Yet what, if I left aside Betty's foolish talk, as my lord surely did, had I to do with the King, or with what he might be besides the King?

About this time much stir had been aroused in the country by the dismissal from all his offices of that great Minister and accomplished writer, the Earl of Clarendon, and by the further measures which his enemies threatened against him. The village elders were wont to assemble on the days when the post came in and discuss eagerly the news brought from London. The affairs of Government troubled my head very little, but in sheer idleness I used often to join them, wondering to see them so perturbed at the happening of things which made mighty little difference in our retired corner. Thus I was in the midst of them, at the King and Crown Tavern, on the Green, two days after I had talked with my lord Quinton. I sat with a mug of ale before me, engrossed in my own thoughts and paying little heed to what passed, when, to my amazement, the postman, leaping from his horse, came straight across to me, holding out in his hand a large packet of important appearance. To receive a letter was a rare event in my life, and a rarer followed, setting the cap on my surprise. For the man, though he was fully ready to drink my health, demanded no money for the letter, saying that it came on the service of His Majesty and was not chargeable. He spoke low enough, and there was a babble

Anthony Hope

about, but it seemed as though the name of the King made its way through all the hubbub to the Vicar's ears; for he rose instantly, and, stepping to my side, sat down by me, crying,

"What said he of the King, Simon?"

"Why, he said," I answered, "that this great letter comes to me on the King's service, and that I have nothing to pay for it," and I turned it over and over in my hands. But the inscription was plain enough. "To Master Simon Dale, Esquire, at Hatchstead, by Hatfield."

By this time half the company was round us, and my Lord Clarendon well-nigh forgotten. Small things near are greater than great things afar, and at Hatchstead my affairs were of more moment than the fall of a Chancellor or the King's choice of new Ministers. A cry arose that I should open my packet and disclose what it contained.

"Nay," said the Vicar, with an air of importance, "it may be on a private matter that the King writes."

They would have believed that of my lord at the Manor, they could not of Simon Dale. The Vicar met their laughter bravely.

"But the King and Simon are to have private matters between them one day," he cried, shaking his fist at the mockers, himself half in mockery.

Meanwhile I opened my packet and read. To this day the amazement its contents bred in me is fresh. For the purport was that the King, remembering my father's services to the King's father (and forgetting, as it seemed, those done to General Cromwell), and being informed of my own loyal disposition, courage, and good parts, had been graciously pleased to name me to a commission in His Majesty's Regiment of Life Guards, such commission being post-dated six months from the day of writing, in order that Mr Dale should have the leisure to inform himself of his duties and fit himself for his post; to which end it was the King's further pleasure that Mr Dale should present himself, bringing this same letter with him, without delay at Whitehall, and there be instructed in his drill and in all other matters necessary for him to know. Thus the letter ended, with a commendation of me to the care of the Almighty.

I sat, gasping; the gossips gaped round me; the Vicar seemed stunned. At last somebody grumbled,

"I do not love these Guards. What need of guard has the King except in the love of his subjects?"

"So his father found, did he?" cried the Vicar, an aflame in a moment.

"The Life Guards!" I murmured. "It is the first regiment of all in honour."

"Ay, my lad," said the Vicar. "It would have been well enough for you to serve in the ranks of it, but to hold His Majesty's Commission!" Words failed him, and he flew to the landlord's snuff-box, which that good man, moved by subtle sympathy, held out, pat to the occasion.

Suddenly those words of my lord's that had at the time of their utterance caught my attention so strongly flashed into my mind, seeming now to find their explanation. If there were fault to be found in the King, it did not lie with his own servants and officers to find it; I was now of his household; my lord must have known what was on the way to me from London when he addressed me so pointedly; and he could know only because he had himself been the mover in the matter. I sprang up and ran across to the Vicar, crying,

"Why, it is my lord's kindness! He has spoken for me."

"Ay, ay, it is my lord," was grunted and nodded round the circle in the satisfaction of a discovery obvious so soon as made. The Vicar alone dissented; he took another pinch and wagged his head petulantly.

"I don't think it's my lord," said he.

"But why not, sir, and who else?" I urged.

"I don't know, but I do not think it is my lord," he persisted.

Then I laughed at him, and he understood well that I mocked his dislike of a plain-sailing everyday account of anything to which it might be possible by hook or crook to attach a tag of mystery. He had harped back to the prophecy, and would not have my lord come between him and his hobby.

"You may laugh, Simon," said he gravely. "But it will be found to be as I say."

I paid no more heed to him, but caught up my hat from the bench, crying that I must run at once and offer thanks to my lord, for he was to set out for London that day, and would be gone if I did not hasten.

"At least," conceded the Vicar, "you will do no harm by

telling him. He will wonder as much as we."

Laughing again, I ran off and left the company crowding to a man round the stubborn Vicar. It was well indeed that I did not linger, for, having come to the Manor at my best speed, I found my lord's coach already at the door and himself in cloak and hat about to step into it. But he waited to hear my breathless story, and, when I came to the pith of it, snatched my letter from my hand and read it eagerly. At first I thought he was playing a part and meant only to deny his kindness or delay the confession of it. His manner soon undeceived me; he was in truth amazed, as the Vicar had predicted, but more than that, he was, if I read his face aright, sorely displeased also; for a heavy frown gathered on his brow, and he walked with me in utter silence the better half of the length of the terrace.

"I have nothing to do with it," he said bitterly. "I and my family have done the King and his too much service to have the giving away of favours. Kings do not love their creditors, no, nor pay them."

"But, my lord, I can think of no other friend who would have such power."

"Can't you?" he asked, stopping and laying his hand on my shoulder. "May be, Simon, you don't understand how power is come by in these days, nor what are the titles to the King's confidence."

His words and manner dashed my new pride, and I suppose my face grew glum, for he went on more gently.

"Nay, lad, since it comes, take it without question. Whatever the source of it, your own conduct may make it an honour."

Anthony Hope

But I could not be content with that.

"The letter says," I remarked, "that the King is mindful of my father's services."

"I had thought that the age of miracles was past," smiled my lord. "Perhaps it is not, Simon."

"Then if it be not for my father's sake nor for yours, my lord, I am at a loss," and I stuffed the letter into my pocket very peevishly.

"I must be on my way," said my lord, turning towards the coach. "Let me hear from you when you come, Simon; and I suppose you will come soon now. You will find me at my house in Southampton Square, and my lady will be glad of your company."

I thanked him for his civility, but my face was still clouded. He had seemed to suspect and hint at some taint in the fountain of honour that had so unexpectedly flowed forth.

"I can't tell what to make of it," I cried.

He stopped again, as he was about to set his foot on the step of his coach, and turned, facing me squarely.

"There's no other friend at all in London, Simon?" he asked. Again I grew red, as he stood watching me. "Is there not one other?"

I collected myself as well as I could and answered,

"One that would give me a commission in the Life Guards, my lord?" And I laughed in scorn.

My lord shrugged his shoulders and mounted into the coach. I closed the door behind him, and stood waiting his reply. He leant forward and spoke across me to the lackey behind, saying, "Go on, go on."

"What do you mean, my lord?" I cried. He smiled, but did not speak. The coach began to move; I had to walk to keep my place, soon I should have to run.

"My lord," I cried, "how could she—?"

My lord took out his snuff-box, and opened it.

"Nay, I cannot tell how," said he, as he carried his thumb to his nose.

"My lord," I cried, running now, "do you know who Cydaria is?"

My lord looked at me, as I ran panting. Soon I should have to give in, for the horses made merry play down the avenue. He seemed to wait for the last moment of my endurance, before he answered. Then, waving his hand at the window, he said, "All London knows." And with that he shut the window, and I fell back breathless, amazed, and miserably chagrined. For he had told me nothing of all that I desired to know, and what he had told me did no more than inflame my curiosity most unbearably. Yet, if it were true, this mysterious lady, known to all London, had remembered Simon Dale! A man of seventy would have been moved by such a thing; what wonder that a boy of twenty-two should run half mad with it?

Strange to say, it seemed to the Vicar's mind no more unlikely and infinitely more pleasant that the King's favour should be bound up with the lady we had called

Cydaria than that it should be the plain fruit of my lord's friendly offices. Presently his talk infected me with something of the same spirit, and we fell to speculating on the identity of this lady, supposing in our innocence that she must be of very exalted rank and noble station if indeed all London knew her, and she had a voice in the appointment of gentlemen to bear His Majesty's Commission. It was but a step farther to discern for me a most notable career, wherein the prophecy of Betty Nasroth should find fulfilment and prove the link that bound together a chain of strange fortune and high achievement. Thus our evening wore away and with it my vexation. Now I was all eager to be gone, to set my hand to my work, to try Fate's promises, and to learn that piece of knowledge which all London had—the true name of her whom we called Cydaria.

"Still," said the Vicar, falling into a sudden pensiveness as I rose to take my leave, "there are things above fortune's favour, or a King's, or a great lady's. To those cling, Simon, for your name's sake and for my credit, who taught you."

"True, sir," said I in perfunctory acknowledgment, but with errant thoughts. "I trust, sir, that I shall always bear myself as becomes a gentleman."

"And a Christian," he added mildly.

"Ay, sir, and a Christian," I agreed readily enough.

"Go your way," he said, with a little smile. "I preach to ears that are full now of other and louder sounds, of strains more attractive and melodies more alluring. Therefore, now, you cannot listen; nay, I know that, if you could, you would. Yet it may be that some day—if it be

God's will, soon—the strings that I feebly strike may sound loud and clear, so that you must hear, however sweetly that other music charms your senses. And if you hear, Simon, heed; if you hear, heed."

Thus, with his blessing, I left him. He followed me to the door, with a smile on his lips but anxiety in his eyes. I went on my way, never looking back. For my ears were indeed filled with that strange and enchanting music.

CHAPTER IV

CYDARIA REVEALED

There, mounted on the coach at Hertford (for at last I am
fairly on my way, and may boast that I have made short
work of my farewells), a gentleman apparently about
thirty years of age, tall, well-proportioned, and with a thin
face, clean-cut and high-featured. He was attended by a
servant whom he called Robert, a stout ruddy fellow, who
was very jovial with every post-boy and ostler on the
road. The gentleman, being placed next to me by the
chance of our billets, lost no time in opening the
conversation, a step which my rustic backwardness would
long have delayed. He invited my confidence by a free
display of his own, informing me that he was attached to
the household of Lord Arlington, and was returning to
London on his lordship's summons. For since his patron
had been called to the place of Secretary of State, he, Mr
Christopher Darrell (such was his name), was likely to be
employed by him in matters of trust, and thus fill a
position which I must perceive to be of some importance.
All this was poured forth with wonderful candour and
geniality, and I, in response, opened to him my fortunes
and prospects, keeping back nothing save the mention of
Cydaria. Mr Darrell was, or affected to be, astonished to
learn that I was a stranger to London—my air smacked of

the Mall and of no other spot in the world, he swore most politely—but made haste to offer me his services, proposing that, since Lord Arlington did not look for him that night, and he had abandoned his former lodging, we should lodge together at an inn he named in Covent Garden, when he could introduce me to some pleasant company. I accepted his offer most eagerly. Then he fell to talking of the Court, of the households of the King and the Duke, of Madame the Duchess of Orleans, who was soon to come to England, they said (on what business he did not know); next he spoke, although now with caution, of persons no less well known but of less high reputation, referring lightly to Lady Castlemaine and Eleanor Gwyn and others, while I listened, half-scandalised, half-pleased. But I called him back by asking whether he were acquainted with one of the Duchess's ladies named Mistress Barbara Quinton.

"Surely," he said. "There is no fairer lady at Court, and very few so honest."

I hurried to let him know that Mistress Barbara and I were old friends. He laughed as he answered,

"If you'd be more you must lose no time. It is impossible that she should refuse many more suitors, and a nobleman of great estate is now sighing for her so loudly as to be audible from Whitehall to Temple Bar."

I heard the news with interest, with pride, and with a touch of jealousy; but at this time my own fortunes so engrossed me that soon I harked back to them, and, taking my courage in both hands, was about to ask my companion if he had chanced ever to hear of Cydaria, when he gave a new turn to the talk, by asking carelessly,

Anthony Hope

"You are a Churchman, sir, I suppose?"

"Why, yes," I answered, with a smile, and perhaps a bit of a stare. "What did you conceive me to be, sir?—a Ranter, or a Papist?"

"Pardon, pardon, if you find offence in my question," he answered, laughing. "There are many men who are one or the other, you know."

"The country has learnt that to its sorrow," said I sturdily.

"Ay," he said, in a dreamy way, "and maybe will learn it again." And without more he fell to describing the famous regiment to which I was to belong, adding at the end:

"And if you like a brawl, the 'prentices in the City will always find one for a gentleman of the King's Guards. Take a companion or two with you when you walk east of Temple Bar. By the way, sir, if the question may be pardoned, how came you by your commission? For we know that merit, standing alone, stands generally naked also."

I was much inclined to tell him all the story, but a shamefacedness came over me. I did not know then how many owed all their advancement to a woman's influence, and my manly pride disdained to own the obligation. I put him off by a story of a friend who wished to remain unnamed, and, after the feint of some indifferent talk, seized the chance of a short silence to ask him my great question.

"Pray, sir, have you ever heard of a lady who goes sometimes by the name of Cydaria?" said I. I fear my cheek flushed a little, do what I could to check such an exhibition of rawness.

"Cydaria? Where have I heard that name? No, I know nobody—and yet—" He paused; then, clapping his hand on his thigh, cried, "By my faith, yes; I was sure I had heard it. It is a name from a play; from—from the 'Indian Emperor.' I think your lady must have been masquerading."

"I thought as much," I nodded, concealing my disappointment.

He looked at me a moment with some curiosity, but did not press me further; and, since we had begun to draw near London, I soon had my mind too full to allow me to think even of Cydaria. There is small profit in describing what every man can remember for himself—his first sight of the greatest city in the world, with its endless houses and swarming people. It made me still and silent as we clattered along, and I forgot my companion until I chanced to look towards him, and found an amused glance fixed on my face. But, as we reached the City, he began to point out where the fire had been, and how the task of rebuilding progressed. Again wonder and anticipation grew on me.

"Yes," said he, "it's a fine treasure-house for a man who can get the key to it."

Yet, amazed as I was, I would not have it supposed that I was altogether an unlicked cub. My stay in Norwich, if it had not made me a Londoner, had rubbed off some of the plough-mud from me, and I believe that my new friend was not speaking wholly in idle compliment when he assured me that I should hold my own very well. The first lesson I learnt was not to show any wonder that I might feel, but to receive all that chanced as though it were the

Anthony Hope

most ordinary thing in the world; for this, beyond all, is the hall-mark of your quality. Indeed, it was well that I was so far fit to show my face, since I was to be plunged into the midst of the stream with a suddenness which startled, although it could not displease me. For the first beginning I was indebted to Mr Darrell, for what followed to myself alone and a temper that has never been of the most patient.

We had reached our inn and refreshed ourselves, and I was standing looking out on the evening and wondering at what time it was proper for me to seek my bed when my friend entered with an eager air, and advanced towards me, crying,

"Dear sir, I hope your wardrobe is in order, for I am resolved to redeem my word forthwith, and to-night to carry you with me to an entertainment for which I have received an invitation. I am most anxious for you to accompany me, as we shall meet many whom you should know."

I was, of course, full of excuses, but he would admit of one only; and that one I could not or would not make. For I had provided myself with a neat and proper suit, of which I was very far from ashamed, and which, when assumed by me and set off with a new cloak to match it, was declared by Mr Darrell to be most apt for the occasion.

"You lack nothing but a handsome cane," said he, "and that I can myself provide. Come, let us call chairs and be gone, for it grows late already."

Our host that evening was Mr Jermyn, a gentleman in great repute at Court, and he entertained us most handsomely at the New Spring Garden, according to me a welcome of especial courtesy, that I might be at my ease and feel no stranger among the company. He placed me on his left hand, Darrell being on my other side, while opposite to me sat my lord the Earl of Carford, a fine-looking man of thirty or a year or two above. Among the guests Mr Darrell indicated several whose names were known to me, such as the witty Lord Rochester and the French Ambassador, M. de Cominges, a very stately gentleman. These, however, being at the other end of the table, I made no acquaintance with them, and contented myself with listening to the conversation of my neighbours, putting in a word where I seemed able with propriety and without displaying an ignorance of which I was very sensible. It seemed to me that Lord Carford, to whom I had not been formally presented (indeed, all talked to one another without ceremony) received what I said with more than sufficient haughtiness and distance; but on Darrell whispering humorously that he was a great lord, and held himself even greater than he was, I made little of it, thinking my best revenge would be to give him a lesson in courtesy. Thus all went well till we had finished eating and sat sipping our wine. Then my Lord Carford, being a little overheated with what he had drunk, began suddenly to inveigh against the King with remarkable warmth and freedom, so that it seemed evident that he smarted under some recent grievance. The raillery of our host, not too nice or delicate, soon spurred him to a discovery of his complaint. He asked nothing better than to be urged to a disclosure.

"Neither rank, nor friendship, nor service," he said, smiting the table, "are enough to gain the smallest favour from the King. All goes to the women; they have but to ask to have. I prayed the King to give me for a cousin of mine a place in the Life Guards that was to be vacant, and

Anthony Hope

he—by Heaven, he promised! Then comes Nell, and Nell wants it for a friend—and Nell has it for a friend—and I go empty!"

I had started when he spoke of the Life Guards, and sat now in a state of great disturbance. Darrell also, as I perceived, was very uneasy, and made a hasty effort to alter the course of the conversation; but Mr Jermyn would not have it.

"Who is the happy—the new happy man, that is Mistress Nell's friend?" he asked, smiling.

"Some clod from the country," returned the Earl; "his name, they say, is Dale."

I felt my heart beating, but I trust that I looked cool enough as I leant across and said,

"Your lordship is misinformed. I have the best of reasons for saying so."

"The reasons may be good, sir," he retorted with a stare, "but they are not evident."

"I am myself just named to a commission in the King's Life Guards, and my name is Dale," said I, restraining myself to a show of composure, for I felt Darrell's hand on my arm.

"By my faith, then, you're the happy man," sneered Carford. "I congratulate you on your—"

"Stay, stay, Carford," interposed Mr Jermyn.

"On your—godmother," said Carford.

"You're misinformed, my lord," I repeated fiercely, although by now a great fear had come upon me. I knew whom they meant by "Nell."

"By God, sir, I'm not misinformed," said he.

"By God, my lord," said I—though I had not been wont to swear—"By God, my lord, you are."

Our voices had risen in anger; a silence fell on the party, all turning from their talk to listen to us. Carford's face went red when I gave him the lie so directly and the more fiercely because, to my shame and wonder, I had begun to suspect that what he said was no lie. But I followed up the attack briskly.

"Therefore, my lord," I said, "I will beg of you to confess your error, and withdraw what you have said."

He burst into a laugh.

"If I weren't ashamed to take a favour from such a hand, I wouldn't be ashamed to own it," said he.

I rose from my seat and bowed to him gravely. All understood my meaning; but he, choosing to treat me with insolence, did not rise nor return my salute, but sat where he was, smiling scornfully.

"You don't understand me, it seems, my lord," said I. "May be this will quicken your wits," and I flung the napkin which had been brought to me after meat lightly in his face. He sprang up quickly enough then, and so did all the company. Darrell caught me by the arm and held me fast. Jermyn was by Carford's side. I hardly knew what passed, being much upset by the sudden quarrel, and yet more by the idea, that Carford's words had put in my head. I saw Jermyn come forward, and Darrell, loosing my arm, went and spoke to him. Lord Carford resumed his seat; I leant against the back of my chair and waited. Darrell was not long in returning to me.

"You'd best go home," he said, in a low voice. "I'll arrange everything. You must meet to-morrow morning."

I nodded my head; I had grown cool and collected now. Bowing slightly to Carford, and low to my host and the company, I turned to the door. As I passed through it, I heard the talk break out again behind me. I got into my chair, which was waiting, and was carried back to my inn in a half-amazed state. I gave little thought to the quarrel or to the meeting that awaited me. My mind was engrossed with the revelation to which I had listened. I doubted it still; nay, I would not believe it. Yet whence came the story unless it were true? And it seemed to fit most aptly and most lamentably with what had befallen me, and to throw light on what had been a puzzle. It was hard on four years since I had parted from Cydaria; but that night I felt that, if the thing were true, I should receive Carford's point in my heart without a pang.

Being, as may be supposed, little inclined for sleep, I turned into the public room of the inn and called for a bottle of wine. The room was empty save for a lanky fellow, very plainly dressed, who sat at the table reading a book. He was drinking nothing, and when—my wine having been brought—I called in courtesy for a second glass and invited him to join me, he shook his head sourly. Yet presently he closed his book, which I now perceived to be a Bible, and fixed an earnest gaze on me. He was a strange-looking fellow; his face was very thin and long, and his hair (for he wore his own and no wig) hung straight from the crown of his head in stiff wisps. I set him down as a Ranter, and was in no way surprised when he began to inveigh against the evils of the times, and to prophesy the judgment of God on the sins of the city.

"Pestilence hath come and fire hath come," he cried. "Yet wickedness is not put away, and lewdness vaunteth herself, and the long-suffering of God is abused."

All this seeming to me very tedious, I sipped my wine and made no answer. I had enough to think of, and was content to let the sins of the city alone.

"The foul superstition of Papacy raises its head again," he went on, "and godly men are persecuted."

"Those same godly men," said I, "have had their turn before now, sir. To many it seems as if they were only receiving what they gave." For the fellow had roused me to some little temper by his wearisome cursing.

"But the Time of the Lord is at hand," he pursued, "and all men shall see the working of His wrath. Ay, it shall be seen even in palaces."

"If I were you, sir," said I dryly, "I would not talk thus before strangers. There might be danger in it."

He scanned my face closely for a few moments; then, leaning across towards me, he said earnestly:

"You are young, and you look honest. Be warned in time; fight on the Lord's side, and not among His enemies. Verily the time cometh."

I had met many of these mad fellows, for the country was full of them, some being disbanded soldiers of the Commonwealth, some ministers who had lost their benefices; but this fellow seemed more crazy than any I had seen: though, indeed, I must confess there was a full measure of truth, if not of charity, in the description of the King's Court on which he presently launched himself with great vigour of declamation and an intense, although ridiculous, exhibition of piety.

"You may be very right, sir—"

"My name is Phineas Tate."

"You may be very right, friend Phineas," said I, yawning; "but I can't alter all this. Go and preach to the King."

"The King shall be preached to in words that he must hear," he retorted with a frown, "but the time is not yet."

"The time now is to seek our beds," said I, smiling. "Do you lodge here?"

"For this night I lie here. To-morrow I preach to this city."

"Then I fear you are likely to lie in a less comfortable place to-morrow." And bidding him good-night, I turned to go. But he sprang after me, crying, "Remember, the time is short"; and I doubt whether I should have got rid of him had not Darrell at that moment entered the room. To my surprise, the two seemed to know one another, for Darrell broke into a scornful laugh, exclaiming:

"Again, Master Tate! What, haven't you left this accursed city to its fate yet?"

"It awaits its fate," answered the Ranter sternly, "even as those of your superstition wait theirs."

"My superstition must look out for itself," said Darrell, with a shrug; and, seeing that I was puzzled, he added, "Mr Tate is not pleased with me because I am of the old religion."

"Indeed?" I cried. "I didn't know you were a—of the old church." For I remembered with confusion a careless remark that I had let fall as we journeyed together.

"Yes," said he simply.

"Yes!" cried Tate. "You—and your master also, is he not?"

Darrell's face grew stern and cold.

"I would have you careful, sir, when you touch on my Lord Arlington's name," he said. "You know well that he is not of the Roman faith, but is a convinced adherent of the Church of this country."

"Is he so?" asked Tate, with an undisguised sneer.

"Come, enough!" cried Darrell in sudden anger. "I have much to say to my friend, and shall be glad to be left alone with him."

Tate made no objection to leaving us, and, gathering up his Bible, went out scowling.

"A pestilent fellow," said Darrell. "He'll find himself laid by the heels before long. Well, I have settled your affair with my Lord Carford."

But my affair with Carford was not what I wanted to hear about. I came to him as he sat down at the table, and, laying my hand on his shoulder, asked simply,

"Is it true?"

He looked up at me with great kindness, and answered gently,

"It is true. I guessed it as soon as you spoke of Cydaria. For Cydaria was the part in which she first gained the favour of the town, and that, taken with your description of her, gave me no room for doubt. Yet I hoped that it might not be as I feared, or, at least, that the thing could be hidden. It seems, though, that the saucy wench has made no secret of it. Thus you are landed in this quarrel, and with a good swordsman."

"I care nothing for the quarrel—" I began.

"Nay, but it is worse than you think. For Lord Carford is the gentleman of whom I spoke, when I told you that Mistress Quinton had a noble suitor. And he is high in her favour and higher yet in her father's. A quarrel with him, and on such a cause, will do you no good in Lord Quinton's eyes."

Indeed, it seemed as though all the furies had combined to vex me. Yet still my desire was to learn of Cydaria, for even now I could hardly believe what Darrell told me. Sitting down by him, I listened while he related to me what he knew of her; it was little more than the mentioning of her true name told me—a name familiar, alas, through all the country, sung in ballads, bandied to and fro in talk, dragged even into high disputes that touched the nation's fortunes; for in those strange days, when the world seemed a very devil's comedy, great countries, ay, and Holy Churches, fought behind the mask of an actress's face or chose a fair lady for their champion. I hope, indeed, that the end sanctified the means; they had great need of that final justification. Castlemaine and Nell Gwyn—had we not all read and heard and gossiped of them? Our own Vicar had spoken to me of Nell, and would not speak too harshly, for Nell was Protestant. Yes, Nell, so please you, was Protestant. And other grave divines forgave her half her sins because she flouted most openly and with pert wit the other lady, who was suspected of an inclination towards Rome and an intention to charm the King into the true Church's bosom. I also could have forgiven her much; for, saving my good Darrell's presence, I hated a Papist worse than any man, saving a Ranter. Yes, I would have forgiven her all, and applauded her pretty face and laughed at her pretty ways. I had looked to do as much when I came to town, being, I must confess, as little straightlaced as most young men. But I had not known that the thing was to touch me close. Could I forgive her my angry humiliation and my sore heart, bruised love and burning ridicule? I could forgive her for being all she now was. How could I forgive her for having been once my Cydaria?

"Well, you must fight," said Darrell, "although it is not a good quarrel," and he shook my hand very kindly with a sigh of friendship.

"Yes, I must fight," said I, "and after that—if there be an after—I must go to Whitehall."

"To take up your commission?" he asked.

"To lay it down, Mr Darrell," said I with a touch of haughtiness. "You don't think that I could bear it, since it comes from such a source?"

He pressed my hand, saying with a smile that seemed tender,

"You're from the country. Not one in ten would quarrel with that here."

"Yes, I'm from the country," said I. "It was in the country that I knew Cydaria."

CHAPTER V

I AM FORBIDDEN TO FORGET

It must be allowed that by no possible union of unlucky chances could I, desiring to appear as a staid, sober gentleman, and not as a ruffler or debauched gallant, have had a worse introduction to my new life. To start with a duel would have hurt me little, but a duel on such a cause and on behalf of such a lady (for I should seem to be fighting the battle of one whose name was past defending) would make my reputation ridiculous to the gay, and offensive to all the more decent people of the town. I thought enough on this sad side of the matter that night at the inn, and despair would have made a prey of me had I not hoped to clear myself in some degree by the step on which I had determined. For I was resolved to abandon the aid in my career that the King's unexpected favour had offered, and start afresh for myself, free from the illicit advantage of a place gained undeservedly. Yet, amid my chagrin, and in spite of my virtuous intentions, I found myself wondering that Cydaria had remembered; I will not protest that I found no pleasure in the thought; a young man whose pride was not touched by it would have reached a higher summit of severity or a lower depth of insensibility than was mine. Yet here also I made vows of renunciation, concerning which there is nought to say but

Anthony Hope

that, while very noble, they were in all likelihood most uncalled for. What would or could Cydaria be to me now? She flew at bigger game. She had flung me a kindly crumb of remembrance; she would think that we were well quit; nay, that I was overpaid for my bruised heart and dissipated illusion.

It was a fine fresh morning when Mr Darrell and I set out for the place of meeting, he carrying a pair of swords. Mr Jermyn had agreed to support my opponent; and I was glad to learn that the meeting was to be restricted to the principals, and not, as too often occurred, to embroil the seconds also in a senseless quarrel. We walked briskly; and crossing the Oxford Road at Holborn, struck into the fields beyond Montague House. We were first at the rendezvous, but had not to wait long before three chairs appeared, containing Lord Carford, his second, and a surgeon. The chairmen, having set down their burdens, withdrew some way off, and we, being left to ourselves, made our preparations as quickly as we could; Darrell, especially, urging speed; for it seemed that a rumour of the affair had got about the town, and he had no desire for spectators.

Although I desire to write without malice and to render fullest justice to those whom I have least cause to love, I am bound to say that my Lord Carford seemed to be most bitterly incensed against me, whereas I was in no way incensed against him. In the first instance, he had offended without premeditation, for he had not known who I was; his subsequent insolence might find excuse in the peremptory phrasing of my demand for apology, too curt, perhaps, for a young and untried man. Honour forced me to fight, but nothing forced me to hate, and I asked no better than that we should both escape with as little hurt as the laws of the game allowed. His mood was different;

he had been bearded, and was in a mind to give my beard a pull—I speak in a metaphor, for beard had I none—and possessing some reputation as a swordsman, he could not well afford to let me go untouched. An old sergeant of General Cromwell's, resident at Norwich, had instructed me in the use of the foils, but I was not my lord's equal, and I set it down to my good luck and his fury that I came off no worse than the event proved. For he made at me with great impetuosity, and from beginning to end of the affair I was wholly concerned in defending myself; this much I achieved successfully for some moments, and I heard Mr Jermyn say, "But he stands his ground well"; then came a cunning feint followed by a fierce attack and a sharp pang in my left arm near the shoulder, while the sleeve of my shirt went red in a moment. The seconds darted in between us, and Darrell caught me round the waist.

"I'm glad it was no worse," I whispered to him with a smile; then I turned very sick, and the meadow started to go round and round me. For some minutes I knew nothing more, but when I revived, the surgeon was busy in binding up my arm, while the three gentlemen stood together in a group a little way apart. My legs shook under me, and doubtless I was as white as my mother's best linen, but I was well content, feeling that my honour was safe, and that I had been as it were baptised of the company of gentlemen. So Mr Jermyn seemed to think; for when my arm was dressed, and I had got my clothes on again with some pain, and a silken sling under my elbow, he came and craved the surgeon's leave to carry me off to breakfast. The request was granted, on a promise that I would abstain from inflaming food and from all strong liquors. Accordingly we set out, I dissembling a certain surprise inspired in my country-man's mind by the discovery that my late enemy proposed

Anthony Hope

to be of the party. Having come to a tavern in Drury Lane, we were regaled very pleasantly; Mr Jermyn, who (although a small man, and not in my opinion well-shaped) might be seen to hold himself in good esteem, recounting to us his adventures in love and his exploits on the field of honour. Meanwhile, Lord Carford treated me with distinguished courtesy, and I was at a loss to understand his changed humour until it appeared that Darrell had acquainted him with my resolution to surrender the commission that the King had bestowed on me. As we grew more free with one another, his lordship referred plainly to the matter, declaring that my conduct showed the nicest honour, and praying me to allow his own surgeon to visit me every day until my wound should be fully cured. His marked politeness, and the friendliness of the others, put me in better humour than I had been since the discovery of the evening before, and when our meal was ended, about eleven o'clock, I was well-nigh reconciled to life again. Yet it was not long before Carford and I were again good enemies, and crossed swords with no less zest, although on a different field.

I had been advised by Darrell to return at once to my inn, and there rest quietly until evening, leaving my journey to Whitehall for the next day, lest too much exertion should induce a fever in me; and in obedience to his counsel I began to walk gently along Drury Lane on my way back to Covent Garden. My Lord Carford and Mr Jermyn had gone off to a cock-fight, where the King was to be, while Darrell had to wait upon the Secretary at his offices; therefore I was alone, and, going easily, found fully enough to occupy my attention in the business and incredible stir of the town. I thought then, and think still, that nowhere in the world is there such a place for an idle man as London; where else has he spread for him so continual a banquet of contemplation, where else are such comedies played every hour for his eyes' delight? It is well enough to look at a running river, or to gaze at such mighty mountains as I saw when I journeyed many years later into Italy; but the mountain moves not, and the stream runs always with the same motion and in its wonted channel. Give me these for my age, but to a young man a great city is queen of all.

So I was thinking as I walked along; or so I think now that I must have thought; for in writing of his youth it is hard for a man to be sure that he does not transfer to that golden page some of the paler characters which later years print on his mind. Perhaps I thought of nothing at all, save that this man here was a fine fellow, that girl there a pretty wench, that my coat became me well, and my wounded arm gave me an interesting air. Be my meditations what they might, they were suddenly interrupted by the sight of a crowd in the Lane near to the Cock and Pie tavern. Here fifty or sixty men and women, decent folk some, others porters, flower-girls, and such like, were gathered in a circle round a man who was pouring out an oration or sermon with great zeal and vehemence. Having drawn nearer, I paused out of a curiosity which turned to amusement when I discovered in the preacher my good friend Phineas Tate, with whom I had talked the evening before. It seemed that he had set about his task without delay, and if London were still unmindful of its sins, the fault was not to lie at Mr Tate's door. On he plunged, sparing neither great nor small; if the Court were sinful, so was Drury Lane; if Castlemaine (he dealt freely in names, and most sparingly in titles of courtesy) were what he roundly said she was, which of the women about him was not the same? How did they differ from their betters, unless it were that their price was not so high, and in what, save audacity, were they behind Eleanor Gwyn? He hurled this last name forth as though it marked a climax of iniquity, and a start ran through me as I heard it thus treated. Strange to say, something of the same effect seemed to be produced on his other hearers. Hitherto they had listened with good-natured tolerance, winking at one another, laughing when the preacher's finger pointed at a neighbour, shrugging comfortable shoulders when it turned against themselves. They are long-suffering under abuse, the folk of London; you may say much what you will, provided you allow them to do what they will, and they support the imputation of unrighteousness with marvellous composure, as long as no man takes it in hand to force them to righteousness. As they are now, they were then, though many changes have passed over the country and the times; so will they be, although more transformations come.

But, as I say, this last name stirred the group to a new mood. Friend Phineas perceived the effect that he had made, but set a wrong meaning on it. Taking it as a ground for encouragement, he loosed his tongue yet more outrageously, and so battered the unhappy subject of his censures that my ears tingled, and suddenly I strode quickly up to the group, intent on silencing him; but a great brawny porter, with a dirty red face, was beforehand with me. Elbowing his way irresistibly through the ranks, he set himself squarely before Phineas, and, wagging his head significantly enough, growled out:

"Say what you will of Castlemaine and the rest, Master Ranter, but keep your tongue off Nelly."

A murmur of applause ran round. They knew Nelly: here in the Lane was her kingdom.

"Let Nelly alone," said the porter, "if you value whole bones, master."

Phineas was no coward, and threats served only to fan the flame of his zeal. I had started to stop his mouth; it seemed likely that I must employ myself in saving his head. His lean frame would crack and break in the grasp of his mighty assailant, and I was loth that the fool should come to harm; so I began to push my way through towards the pair, and arrived just as Phineas, having shot a most pointed dart, was about to pay for his too great skill with a blow from the porter's mutton-fist. I caught the fellow's arm as he raised it, and he turned fiercely on me, growling, "Are you his friend, then?"

"Not I," I answered. "But you'd kill him, man."

"Let him heed what he says, then. Kill him! Ay, and spare him readily!"

The affair looked awkward enough, for the feeling was all one way, and I could do little to hinder any violence. A girl in the crowd reminded me of my helplessness, touching my wounded arm lightly, and saying, "Are you hungry for more fighting, sir?"

"He's a madman," said I. "Let him alone; who heeds what he says?"

Friend Phineas did not take my defence in good part.

"Mad, am I?" he roared, beating with his fist on his Bible. "You'll know who was mad when you lie howling in hell fire. And with you that—" And on he went again at poor Nell.

The great porter could endure no more. With a seemingly gentle motion of his hand he thrust me aside, pushing me on to the bosom of a buxom flower-girl who, laughing boisterously, wound a pair of sturdy red arms round me. Then he stepped forward, and seizing Phineas by the scruff of the neck shook him as a dog shakes a rat. To what more violence he would have proceeded I do not know; for suddenly from above us, out of a window of the Cock and Pie, came a voice which sent a stir through my veins.

"Good people, good people," said the voice, "what with preaching and brawling, a body can get no sleep in the Lane. Pray go and work, or if you've no work, go and drink. Here are the means." And a shower of small coins came flying down on our heads, causing an immediate wild scramble. My flower-girl loosed me that she might take her part in this fray; the porter stood motionless, still holding poor Phineas, limp and lank, in his hand; and I turned my eyes upwards to the window of the Cock and Pie.

I looked up, and I saw her. Her sunny brown hair was about her shoulders, her knuckles rubbed her sleepy eyes to brightness, and a loose white bodice, none too high nor too carefully buttoned about the neck, showed that her dressing was not done. Indeed, she made a pretty picture, as she leant out, laughing softly, and now shading her face from the sun with one hand, while she raised the other in mocking reproof of the preacher.

"Fie, sir, fie," she said. "Why fall on a poor girl who earns an honest living, gives to the needy, and is withal a good Protestant?" Then she called to the porter, "Let him go with what life you've left in him. Let him go."

"You heard what he said of you—" began the fellow sullenly.

"Ay, I hear what everybody says of me," she answered carelessly. "Let him go."

The porter sulkily released his prey, and Phineas, set free, began to gasp and shake himself. Another coin whistled down to the porter, who, picking it up, shambled off with a last oath of warning to his enemy. Then, and then only, did she look at me, who had never ceased to look at her. When she saw me, her smile grew broader, and her eyes twinkled in surprise and delight.

"A happy morning!" she said, clasping her little hands. "Ah, a happy morning! Why, 'tis Simon, my Simon, my little Simon from the country. Come up to me, Simon. No, no, your pardon; I'll come down to you, Simon. In the parlour, in the parlour. Quick! I'll be down in an instant."

The vision vanished, but my gaze dwelt on the window where it had been, and I needed Phineas Tate's harsh voice to rouse me from my stupor.

"Who is the woman?" he demanded.

"Why—why—Mistress Gwyn herself," I stammered.

"Herself—the woman, herself?" he asked eagerly. Then he suddenly drew himself up and, baring his head, said solemnly, "Thanks be to God, thanks be to God, for it may be His will that this brand should be plucked from the burning." And before I could speak or attempt to hinder him he stepped swiftly across the pathway and entered the tavern. I, seeing nothing else that I could do, followed him straightway and as fast as I could.

I was in a maze of feeling. The night before I had reasoned with myself and schooled my wayward passion to a resolve neither to see nor to speak with her. Resentment at the shame she had brought on me aided my stubbornness, and helped me to forget that I had been shamed because she had remembered me. But now I followed Phineas Tate. For be memory ever so keen and clear, yes, though it seem able to bring every feature, every shade, and every pose before a man's eyes in absolute fidelity, yet how poor and weak a thing it is beside the vivid sight of bodily eyes; that paints the faded picture all afresh in hot and glowing colours, and the man who bade defiance to the persuasions of his recollection falls beaten down by the fierce force of a present vision. I followed Phineas Tate, perhaps using some excuse with myself—indeed, I feared that he would attack her rudely and be cruelly plain with her—yet knowing in my heart that I went because I could do nothing else, and that when she called, every atom of life in me answered to her summons. So in I went, to find Phineas standing bolt upright in the parlour of the tavern, turning the leaves of his book with eager fingers, as though he sought some text that was in his mind. I passed by him and leant against the wall by the window; so we awaited her, each of us eager, but with passions most unlike.

She came, daintily dressed now, although still negligently. She put her head round the corner of the door, radiant with smiles, and with no more shame or embarrassment than if our meeting in this way were the most ordinary thing. Then she caught sight of Phineas Tate and cried, pouting, "But I wanted to be alone with my Simon, my dear Simon."

Phineas caught the clue her words gave him with perverse readiness.

"Alone with him, yes!" he cried. "But what of the time

when you must be alone with God?"

"Alas," said she, coming in, and seating herself at the table, "is there more still? Indeed, I thought you had said all your say outside. I am very wicked; let that end it."

He advanced to the table and stood directly opposite to her, stretching his arm towards her, while she sat with her chin on her hands, watching him with eyes half-amused, half-apprehensive.

"You who live in open sin—" he began; before he could say more I was by his elbow.

"Hold your tongue," I said. "What is it to you?"

"Let him go on, Simon," said she.

And go on he did, telling all—as I prayed, more than all—the truth, while she heard him patiently. Yet now and then she gave herself a little shake, as though to get rid of something that threatened to stick. Then he fell on his knees and prayed fervently, she still sitting quiet and I standing awkwardly near. He finished his prayer, and, rising again, looked earnestly at her. Her eyes met his in good nature, almost in friendliness. He stretched out his hand to her again, saying,

"Child, cannot you understand? Alas, your heart is hardened! I pray Christ our Lord to open your eyes and change your heart, that at the last your soul may be saved."

Nelly examined the pink nails of her right hand with curious attention.

"I don't know that I'm more of a sinner than many others," said she. "Go to Court and preach, sir."

A sudden fury seemed to come over him, and he lost the gentleness with which he had last addressed her.

"The Word shall be heard at the Court," he cried, "in louder accents than mine. Their cup is full, the measure of their iniquity is pressed down and running over. All who live shall see."

"Like enough," said Nell, as though the matter were grown very tedious, and she yawned just a little; but, as she glanced at me, a merry light gleamed in her eyes. "And what is to befall Simon here?" she asked.

He turned on me with a start, seeming to have forgotten my presence.

"This young man?" he asked, looking full in my face. "Why, his face is honest; if he choose his friends well, he may do well."

"I am of his friends," said Nell, and I defy any man on earth to have given the lie to such a claim so made.

"And for you, may the Lord soften your heart," said Phineas to her.

"Some say it's too soft already," said Nell.

"You will see me again," said he to her, and moved towards the door. But once more he faced me before he went, and looked very intently at me. Then he passed out, leaving us alone.

At his going Nell sighed for relief, stretched out her arms, and let them fall on the table in front of her; then she sprang up and ran to me, catching hold of my hands.

"And how goes all at pretty Hatchstead?" she asked.

I drew back, releasing my hands from hers, and I spoke to her stiffly.

"Madame," said I, "this is not Hatchstead, nor do you seem the lady whom I knew at Hatchstead."

"Indeed, you seem very like the gentleman I knew, and knew well, there," she retorted.

"And you, very unlike the lady."

"Nay, not so unlike as you think. But are you also going to preach to me?"

"Madame," said I in cold courtesy, "I have to thank you for a good remembrance of me, and for your kindness in doing me a service; I assure you I prize it none the less, because I may not accept it."

"You may not accept it?" she cried. "What? You may not accept the commission?"

"No, madame," said I, bowing low.

Her face was like a pretty child's in disappointment.

"And your arm? How come you to be wounded? Have you been quarrelling already?"

"Already, madame."

"But with whom, and why?"

"With my Lord Carford. The reason I need not weary you with."

"But I desire to know it."

"Because my lord said that Mistress Gwyn had obtained me my commission."

"But it was true."

"Doubtless; yet I fought."

"Why, if it were true?"

I made her no answer. She went and seated herself again at the table, looking up at me with eyes in which I seemed to read pain and puzzle.

"I thought it would please you, Simon," she said, with a coaxing glance that at least feigned timidity.

"Never have I been so proud as on the day I received it," said I; "and never, I think, so happy, unless, may be, when you and I walked in the Manor park."

"Nay, Simon, but you will be glad to have it, even though I obtained it for you."

"I shall not have it. I go to Whitehall to-morrow to surrender it."

She sprang up in wonder, and anger also showed in her eyes.

"To surrender it? You mean in truth to surrender it? And because it came from me?"

Again I could do nothing but bow. That I did with the best air I could muster, although I had no love for my part in this scene. Alas for a man who, being with her, must spend his time in chiding!

"Well, I wish I hadn't remembered you," she said resentfully.

"Indeed, madame, I also wish that I had forgotten."

"You have, or you would never use me so."

"It is my memory that makes me rough, madame. Indeed, how should I have forgotten?"

"You hadn't?" she asked, advancing nearer to me. "No, in truth I believe you hadn't! And, Simon, listen!" Now she stood with her face but a yard from mine, and again her lips were curved with mirth and malice. "Listen, Simon," she said, "you had not forgotten; and you shall not forget."

"It is very likely," said I simply; and I took up my hat from the table.

"How fares Mistress Barbara?" asked Nell suddenly.

"I have not waited on her," I answered.

"Then indeed I am honoured, although our meeting was somewhat by chance. Ah, Simon, I want to be so angry with you. But how can I be angry? I can never be angry. Why" (and here she came even a little closer, and now she was smiling most damnably—nay, I mean most delightfully; but it is often much the same), "I was not very angry even when you kissed me, Simon."

It is not for me to say what answer to that speech she looked to receive. Mine was no more than a repetition of my bow.

"You'll keep the commission, Simon?" she whispered, standing on tiptoe, as though she would reach my ear.

"I can't," said I, bowing no more, and losing, I fear, the air of grave composure that I had striven to maintain. I saw what seemed a light of triumph in her eyes. Yet that mood passed quickly from her. She grew pensive and drew away from me. I stepped towards the door, but a hand laid on my arm arrested me.

"Simon," she asked, "have you sweet memories of Hatchstead?"

"God forgive me," said I confusedly, "sweeter than my hopes of heaven."

She looked at me gravely for an instant. Then, sighing, she said,

"Then I wish you had not come to town, but stayed there with your memories. They were of me?"

"Of Cydaria."

"Ah, of Cydaria," she echoed, with a little smile.

But a moment later the full merriment of laughter broke out again on her face, and, drawing her hand away, she let me go, crying after me,

"But you shall not forget, Simon. No, you shall not forget."

There I left her, standing in the doorway of the inn, daring me to forget. And my brain seemed all whirling and swirling as I walked down the Lane.

CHAPTER VI

AN INVITATION TO COURT

I spent the rest of that day in my inn, agreeably to the advice of the surgeon, and the next morning, finding my wound healing well, and my body free from fever, I removed to Mr Darrell's new lodging by the Temple, where he had most civilly placed two rooms at my disposal. Here also I provided myself with a servant, a fellow named Jonah Wall, and prepared to go to Whitehall as the King's letter commanded me. Of Mr Darrell I saw nothing; he went off before I came, having left for me with Robert, his servant, a message that he was much engaged with the Secretary's business, and prayed to be excused from affording me his company. Yet I was saved from making my journey alone—a thing that would have occasioned me much trepidation—by the arrival of my Lord Quinton. The reverence of our tender years is hard to break down, and I received my visitor with an uneasiness which was not decreased by the severity of his questions concerning my doings. I made haste to tell him that I had determined to resign the commission bestowed on me. These tidings so transformed his temper that he passed from cold reproof to an excess of cordiality, being pleased to praise highly a scruple as honourable as (he added with a shrug) it was rare, and he began to laugh at himself as he recounted humorously how his wrath against me had grown higher and higher with each thing that had come to his ears. Eager now to make amends, he offered to go with me to Whitehall, proposing that we should ride in his coach to the Mall, and walk thence together. I accepted his company most gratefully, since it would save me from betraying an ignorance of which I was ashamed, and strengthen my courage for the task before me. Accordingly we set out, and as we went my lord took occasion to refer to my acquaintance with Mistress Nell, suggesting plainly enough, although not directly, that I should be wise to abandon her society at the same time that I laid down the commission she had obtained for me. I did not question his judgment, but avoided giving any promise to be guided by it. Perceiving that I was not willing to be pressed, he passed from the topic with a sigh, and began to discourse on the state of the kingdom. Had I paid more heed to what he said I might have avoided certain troubles into which I fell afterwards, but, busy staring about me, I gave him only such attention as courtesy required, and not enough for a proper understanding of his uneasiness at the dealings of our Court with the French King and the visit of the King's sister, Madame d'Orleans, of which the town was full. For my lord, although a most loyal gentleman, hated both the French and the Papists, and was much grieved at the King's apparent inclination in their favour. So he talked, I nodding and assenting to all, but wondering when he would bid me wait on my lady, and whether Mistress Barbara was glad that my Lord Carford's sword had passed through my arm only and done no greater hurt.

Thus we came to the Mall, and having left the coach, set out to walk slowly, my lord having his arm through mine. I was very glad to be seen thus in his company, for, although not so great a man here as at Hatchstead, he had

Anthony Hope

no small reputation, and carried himself with a noble air. When we had gone some little way, being very comfortable with one another, and speaking now of lighter matters, I perceived at some distance a party of gentlemen, three in number; they were accompanied by a little boy very richly dressed, and were followed at a short interval by five or six more gentlemen, among whom I recognised immediately my friend Darrell. It seemed then that the Secretary's business could be transacted in leisurely fashion! As the first group passed along, I observed that the bystanders uncovered, but I had hardly needed this sign to tell me that the King was of the party. I was familiar with his features, but he seemed to me even a more swarthy man than all the descriptions of his blackness had led me to expect. He bore himself with a very easy air, yet was not wanting in dignity, and being attracted by him I fell to studying his appearance with such interest that I came near to forgetting to remove my hat. Presently he seemed to observe us; he smiled, and beckoned with his hand to my lord, who went forward alone, leaving me still watching the King and his companions.

I had little difficulty in recognising the name of one; the fine figure, haughty manner, and magnificent attire showed him to be the famous Duke of Buckingham, whose pride lay in seeming more of a King than the King himself. While my lord spoke with the King, this nobleman jested with the little boy, who answered with readiness and vivacity. As to the last member of the group (whom the Duke seemed to treat with some neglect) I was at a loss. His features were not distinguished except by a perfect composure and self-possession, but his bearing was very courtly and graceful. He wore a slight, pleasant, yet rather rigid smile, and his attitude was as though he listened to what his master said with even excessive deference and urbanity. His face was marked, and to my thinking much disfigured, by a patch or plaster worn across the nose, as though to hide some wound or scar.

After a few minutes, during which I waited very uneasily, my lord turned and signed to me to approach. I obeyed, hat in hand, and in a condition of great apprehension. To be presented to the King was an honour disquieting enough; what if my lord had told His Majesty that I declined to bear his commission through a disapproval of his reasons for granting me the favour? But when I came near I fell into the liveliest fear that my lord had done this very thing; for the King was smiling contemptuously, Buckingham laughing openly, and the gentleman with the plaster regarding me with a great and very apparent curiosity. My lord, meanwhile, wore a propitiatory but doubtful air, as though he prayed but hardly hoped a gracious reception for me. Thus we all stood a moment in complete silence, I invoking an earthquake or any convulsion of nature that should rescue me from my embarrassment. Certainly the King did not hasten to do me this kindly service. He grew grave and seemed displeased, nay, he frowned most distinctly, but then he smiled, yet more as though he must than because he would. I do not know how the thing would have ended if the Duke of Buckingham had not burst out laughing again, at which the King could not restrain himself, but began to laugh also, although still not as though he found the jest altogether to his liking.

"So, sir," said the King, composing his features as he addressed me, "you are not desirous of bearing my commission and fighting my enemies for me?"

"1 would fight for your Majesty to the death," said I timidly, but with fervour.

Anthony Hope

"Yet you are on the way to ask leave to resign your commission. Why, sir?"

I could not answer; it was impossible to state my reason to him.

"The utility of a woman's help," observed the King, "was apparent very early in the world's history. Even Adam was glad of it."

"She was his wife, Sir," interposed the Duke.

"I have never read of the ceremony," said the King. "But if she were, what difference?"

"Why, it makes a great deal of difference in many ways, Sir," laughed Buckingham, and he glanced with a significance which I did not understand at the boy who was waiting near with a weary look on his pretty face.

The King laughed carelessly and called, "Charles, come hither."

Then I knew that the boy must be the King's son, afterwards known as Earl of Plymouth, and found the meaning of the Duke's glance.

"Charles, what think you of women?" the King asked.

The pretty child thought for a moment, then answered, looking up,

"They are very tiresome creatures, Sir."

"Why, so they are, Charles," said the King gravely.

"They will never let a thing alone, Sir."

"No, they won't, Charles, nor a man either."

"It's first this, Sir, then that—a string, or a garter, or a bow."

"Yes, Charles; or a title, or a purse, or a commission," said the King. "Shall we have no more to do with them?"

"I would desire no more at all, Sir," cried the boy.

"It appears, Mr Dale," said the King, turning to me, "that Charles here, and you, and I, are all of one mind on the matter of women. Had Heaven been on our side, there would have been none of them in the world."

He seemed to be examining me now with some degree of attention, although I made, I fear, a very poor figure. Lord Quinton came to my rescue, and began to enlarge on my devotion to His Majesty's person and my eagerness to serve him in any way I might, apart from the scruple which he had ventured to disclose to the King.

"Mr Dale says none of these fine things for himself," remarked the King.

"It is not always those that say most who do most, Sir," pleaded my lord.

"Therefore this young gentleman who says nothing will do everything?" The King turned to his companion who wore the plaster, and had as yet not spoken at all. "My Lord Arlington," said he, "it seems that I must release Mr Dale."

"I think so, Sir," answered Arlington, on whom I looked with much curiosity, since he was Darrell's patron.

"I cannot have servants who do not love me," pursued the King.

"Nor subjects," added Buckingham, with a malicious smile.

"Although I am not, unhappily, so free in the choice of my Ministers," said the King. Then he faced round on me and addressed me in a cold tone:

"I am reluctant, sir, to set down your conduct to any want of affection or loyalty towards me. I shall be glad if you can show me that my forbearance is right." With this he bent his head slightly, and moved on. I bowed very low, shame and confusion so choking me that I had not a word to say. Indeed, I seemed damned beyond redemption, so far as my fortunes depended on obtaining the King's favour.

Again I was left to myself, for the King, anxious, as I took it, to show that his displeasure extended to me only, had stopped again to speak with my lord. But in a moment, to my surprise, Arlington was at my side.

"Come, sir," said he very genially, "there's no need of despair. The King is a little vexed, but his resentment is not obstinate; and let me tell you that he has been very anxious to see you."

"The King anxious to see me?" I cried.

"Why, yes. He has heard much of you." His lips twitched as he glanced at me. I had the discretion to ask no further explanation, and in a moment he grew grave again, continuing, "I also am glad to meet with you, for my good friend Darrell has sounded your praises to me. Sir, there are many ways of serving the King."

"I should rejoice with all my heart to find one of them, my lord," I answered.

"I may find you one, if you are willing to take it."

"I should be your lordship's most humble and grateful servant."

"Tut, if I gave, I should ask in return," said he. And he added suddenly, "You're a good Churchman, I suppose, Mr Dale?"

"Why, yes, my lord; I and all my family."

"Good, good. In these days our Church has many enemies. It is threatened on more than one side."

I contented myself with bowing; when the Secretary spoke to me on such high matters, it was for me to listen, and not to bandy opinions with him.

"Yes, we are much threatened," said he. "Well, Mr Dale, I shall trust that we may have other meetings. You are to be found at Mr Darrell's lodging? You may look to hear from me, sir." He moved away, cutting short my thanks with a polite wave of his hand.

Suddenly to my amazement the King turned round and called to me:

"Mr Dale, there is a play to be acted at my house

to-morrow evening. Pray give me the pleasure of your company."

I bowed almost to the ground, scarcely able to believe my ears.

"And we'll try," said the King, raising his voice so that not only we who were close to him but the gentlemen behind also must hear, "to find an ugly woman and an honest man, between whom we may place you. The first should not be difficult to come on, but the second, I fear, is well-nigh impossible, unless another stranger should come to Court. Good-day to you, Mr Dale." And away he went, smiling very happily and holding the boy's hand in his.

The King's immediate party was no sooner gone than Darrell ran up to me eagerly, and before my lord could rejoin me, crying:

"What did he say to you?"

"The King? Why, he said—"

"No, no. What did my lord say?" He pointed to Arlington, who was walking off with the King.

"He asked whether I were a good Churchman, and told me that I should hear from him. But if he is so solicitous about the Church, how does he endure your religion?"

Darrell had no time to answer, for Lord Quinton's grave voice struck in.

"He is a wise man who can answer a question touching my Lord Arlington's opinion of the Church," said he.

Darrell flushed red, and turned angrily on the interrupter.

"You have no cause, my lord," he cried, "to attack the Secretary's churchmanship."

"Then you have no cause, sir," retorted Quinton, "to defend it with so much temper. Come, let me be. I have said as much to the Secretary's face, and he bore it with more patience than you can muster on his behalf."

By this time I was in some distress to see my old friend and my new at such variance, and the more as I could not understand the ground of their difference; the Secretary's suspected leaning towards the Popish religion had not reached our ears in the country. But Darrell, as though he did not wish to dispute further with a man his superior in rank and age, drew off with a bow to my lord and a kindly nod to me, and rejoined the other gentlemen in attendance on the King and his party.

"You came off well with the King, Simon," said my lord, taking my arm again. "You made him laugh, and he counts no man his enemy who will do him that service. But what did Arlington say to you?"

When I repeated the Secretary's words, he grew grave, but he patted my arm in a friendly fashion, saying,

"You've shown wisdom and honour in this first matter, lad. I must trust you in others. Yet there are many who have no faith in my Lord Arlington, as Englishman or Churchman either."

"But," cried I, "does not Lord Arlington do as the King bids him?"

My lord looked full in my face, and answered steadily,

"I think he does, Simon." But then, as though he had said enough, or even too much, he went on: "Come, you needn't grow too old or too prudent all at once. Since you have seen the King, your business at Whitehall will wait. Let us turn back to the coach and be driven to my house, for, besides my lady, Barbara is there to-day on leave from her attendance, and she will be glad to renew her acquaintance with you."

It was my experience as a young man, and, perchance, other young men may have found the like, that whatsoever apprehensions or embarrassments might be entailed by meeting a comely damsel, and however greatly her displeasure and scorn were to be dreaded, yet the meeting was not forgone, all perils being taken rather than that certain calamity. Therefore I went with my lord to his handsome house in Southampton Square, and found myself kissing my lady's hand before I was resolved on how I should treat Mistress Barbara, or on the more weighty question of how I might look to be treated by her.

I had not to wait long for the test. After a few moments of my lady's amiable and kindly conversation, Barbara entered from the room behind, and with her Lord Carford. He wore a disturbed air, which his affected composure could not wholly conceal; her cheek was flushed, and she seemed vexed; but I did not notice these things so much as the change which had been wrought in her by the last four years. She had become a very beautiful woman, ornamented with a high-bred grace and exquisite haughtiness, tall and slim, carrying herself with a delicate dignity. She gave me her hand to kiss, carelessly enough, and rather as though she acknowledged an old acquaintance than found any pleasure in its renewal. But she was gentle to me, and I detected in her manner a subtle indication that, although she knew all, yet she pitied rather than blamed; was not Simon very young and ignorant, and did not all the world know how easily even honest young men might be beguiled by cunning women? An old friend must not turn her back on account of a folly, distasteful as it might be to her to be reminded of such matters.

My lord, I think, read his daughter very well, and, being determined to afford me an opportunity to make my peace, engaged Lord Carford in conversation, and bade her lead me into the room behind to see the picture that Lely had lately painted of her. She obeyed; and, having brought me to where it hung, listened patiently to my remarks on it, which I tried to shape into compliments that should be pleasing and yet not gross. Then, taking courage, I ventured to assure her that I fell out with Lord Carford in sheer ignorance that he was a friend of her family, and would have borne anything at his hands had I known it. She smiled, answering,

"But you did him no harm," and she glanced at my arm in its sling.

She had not troubled herself to ask how it did, and I, a little nettled at her neglect, said:

"Nay, all ended well. I alone was hurt, and the great lord came off safe."

"Since the great lord was in the right," said she, "we should all rejoice at that. Are you satisfied with your examination of the picture, Mr Dale?"

I was not to be turned aside so easily.

"If you hold me to have been wrong, then I have done what I could to put myself in the right since," said I, not doubting that she knew of my surrender of the commission.

"I don't understand," said she, with a quick glance. "What have you done?"

In wonder that she had not been informed, I cried,

"I have obtained the King's leave to decline his favour."

The colour which had been on her cheeks when she first entered had gone before now, but at my words it returned a little.

"Didn't my lord tell you?" I asked.

"I haven't seen him alone this week past," she answered.

But she had seen Carford alone, and that in the last hour past. It was strange that he, who had known my intention and commended it so highly, should not have touched on it. I looked in her eyes; I think she followed my thoughts, for she glanced aside, and said in visible embarrassment,

"Shall we return?"

"You haven't spoken on the matter with my Lord Carford, then?" I asked.

She hesitated a moment, then answered as though she did not love the truth but must tell it,

"Yes; but he said nothing of this. Tell me of it."

So I told her in simple and few words what I had done.

"Lord Carford said nothing of it," she said, when I ended. Then she added, "But although you will not accept the favour, you have rendered thanks for it?"

"I couldn't find my tongue when I was with the King," I answered with a shamefaced laugh.

"I didn't mean to the King," said Barbara.

It was my turn to colour now; I had not been long enough in town to lose the trick.

"I have seen her," I murmured.

Barbara suddenly made me a curtsey, saying bitterly,

"I wish you joy, sir, of your acquaintance."

When a man is alone with a beautiful lady, he is apt not to love an intruder; yet on my soul I was glad to see Carford in the doorway. He came towards us, but before he could speak Barbara cried to him,

"My lord, Mr Dale tells me news that will interest you."

"Indeed, madame, and what?"

"Why, that he has begged the King's leave to resign his commission. Doesn't it surprise you?"

He looked at her, at me, and again at her. He was caught, for I knew that he had been fully acquainted with my purpose. He gathered himself together to answer her.

"Nay, I knew," he said, "and had ventured to applaud Mr Dale's resolution. But it did not come into my mind to speak of it."

"Strange," said she, "when we were deploring that Mr Dale should obtain his commission by such means!"

She rested her eyes on him steadily, while her lips were set in a scornful smile. A pause followed her words.

"I daresay I should have mentioned it, had we not passed to another topic," said he at last and sullenly enough. Then, attempting a change in tone, he added, "Won't you rejoin us?"

"I am very well here," she said.

He waited a moment, then bowed, and left us. He was frowning heavily, and, as I judged, would have greeted another quarrel with me very gladly, had I been minded to give him an opportunity; but thinking it fair that I should be cured from the first encounter before I faced a second, I held my peace till he was gone; then I said to Barbara,

"I wonder he didn't tell you."

Alas for my presumption! The anger that had been diverted on to Carford's head swept back to mine.

"Indeed, why should he?" she cried. "All the world can't be always thinking of you and your affairs, Mr Dale."

"Yet you were vexed because he hadn't."

"I vexed! Not I!" said Barbara haughtily.

I could not make that out; she had seemed angry with him. But because I spoke of her anger, she was angry now with me. Indeed I began to think that little Charles, the King, and I had been right in that opinion in which the King found us so much of a mind. Suddenly Barbara spoke.

"Tell me what she is like, this friend of yours," she said. "I have never seen her."

It leapt to my lips to cry, "Ay, you have seen her!" but I did not give utterance to the words. Barbara had seen her in the park at Hatchstead, seen her more than once, and more than once found sore offence in what she saw. There is wisdom in silence; I was learning that safety might lie in deceit. The anger under which I had suffered would be doubled if she knew that Cydaria was Nell and Nell Cydaria. Why should she know? Why should my own mouth betray me and add my bygone sins to the offences of to-day? My lord had not told her that Nell was Cydaria. Should I speak where my lord was silent? Neither would I tell her of Cydaria.

"You haven't seen her?" I asked.

"No; and I would learn what she is like."

It was a strange thing to command me, yet Barbara's desire joined with my own thoughts to urge me to it. I began tamely enough, with a stiff list of features and catalogue of colours. But as I talked recollection warmed my voice; and when Barbara's lips curled scornfully, as though she would say, "What is there in this to make men fools? There is nothing in all this," I grew more vehement and painted the picture with all my skill. What malice began, my ardour perfected, until, engrossed in my fancy,

Anthony Hope

I came near to forgetting that I had a listener, and ended with a start as I found Barbara's eyes fixed on mine, while she stood motionless before me. My exultation vanished, and confusion drove away my passion.

"You bade me describe her," said I lamely. "I do not know whether others see as I do, but such is she to my eyes."

A silence followed. Barbara's face was not flushed now, but rather seemed paler than it was wont to be. I could not tell how it was, but I knew that I had wounded her. Is not beauty jealous, and who but a clod will lavish praise on one fair face while another is before him? I should have done better to play the hypocrite and swear that my folly, not Nell's features, was to blame. But now I was stubborn and would recall not a word of all my raptures. Yet I was glad that I had not told her who Cydaria was.

The silence was short. In an instant Barbara gave a little laugh, saying,

"Small wonder you were caught, poor Simon! Yes, the creature must be handsome enough. Shall we return to my mother?"

On that day she spoke no more with me.

CHAPTER VII

WHAT CAME OF HONESTY

I should sin against the truth and thereby rob this my story of its solitary virtue were I to pretend that my troubles and perplexities, severe as they seemed, outweighed the pleasure and new excitement of my life. Ambition was in my head, youth in my veins, my eyes looked out on a gay world with a regard none too austere. Against these things even love's might can wage but an equal battle. For the moment, I must confess, my going to Court, with the prospect it opened and the chances it held, dominated my mind, and Jonah Wall, my servant, was kept busy in preparing me for the great event. I had made a discovery concerning this fellow which afforded me much amusement: coming on him suddenly, I found him deeply engaged on a Puritan Psalm-book, sighing and casting up his eyes to heaven in a ludicrous excess of glum-faced piety. I pressed him hard and merrily, when it appeared that he was as thorough a Ranter as my friend Phineas himself, and held the Court and all in it to be utterly given over to Satan, an opinion not without some warrant, had he observed any moderation in advancing it. Not wishing to harm him, I kept my knowledge to myself, but found a malicious sport in setting him to supply me with all the varieties of raiment, perfumes, and other gauds—that last was his word, not mine—which he abhorred, but which Mr Simon Dale's new-born desire for fashion made imperative, however little Mr Simon Dale's purse could properly afford the expense of them. The truth is that Mistress Barbara's behaviour spurred me on. I had no mind to be set down a rustic; I could stomach disapproval and endure severity; pitied for a misguided be-fooled clod I would not be; and the best way to avoid such a fate seemed to lie in showing myself as reckless a gallant and as fine a roisterer as any at Whitehall. So I dipped freely and deep into my purse, till Jonah groaned as woefully for my extravagance as for my frivolity. All day he was in great fear lest I should take him with me to Court to the extreme peril of his soul; but prudence at last stepped in and bade me spare myself the cost of a rich livery by leaving him behind.

Now Heaven forbid that I should imitate my servant's sour folly (for, if a man must be a fool, I would have him a cheerful fool) or find anything to blame in the pomp and seemly splendour of a Royal Court; yet the profusion that met my eyes amazed me. It was the King's whim that on this night himself, his friends, and principal gentlemen should, for no reason whatsoever except the quicker disbursing of their money, assume Persian attire, and they were one and all decked out in richest Oriental garments, in many cases lavishly embroidered with precious stones. The Duke of Buckingham seemed all ablaze, and the other courtiers and wits were little less magnificent, foremost among them being the young Duke of Monmouth, whom I now saw for the first time and thought as handsome a youth as I had set eyes on. The ladies did not enjoy the licence offered by this new fashion, but they contrived to hold their own in the French mode, and I, who had heard much of the poverty of the nation, the necessities of the fleet, and the straits in which the King found himself for money, was left gaping in sheer wonder whence came all the wealth that was displayed before my eyes. My own poor preparations lost all their charm, and I had not been above half an hour in the place before I was seeking a quiet corner in which to hide the poverty of my coat and the plainness of my cloak. But the desire for privacy thus bred in me was not to find satisfaction. Darrell, whom I had not met all day, now pounced on me and carried me off, declaring that he was charged to present me to the Duke of York. Trembling between fear and exultation, I walked with him across the floor, threading my way through the dazzling throng that covered the space in front of His Majesty's dais. But before we came to the Duke, a gentleman caught my companion by the arm and asked him how he did in a hearty, cheerful, and rather loud voice. Darrell's answer was to pull me forward and present me, saying that Sir Thomas Clifford desired my acquaintance, and adding much that erred through kindness of my parts and disposition.

"Nay, if he's your friend, it's enough for me, Darrell," answered Clifford, and putting his mouth to Darrell's ear he whispered. Darrell shook his head, and I thought that the Treasurer seemed disappointed. However, he bade me farewell with cordiality.

"What did he ask you?" said I, when we started on our way again.

"Only whether you shared my superstition," answered Darrell with a laugh.

"They're all mighty anxious about my religion," thought I. "It would do no harm if they bestowed more attention on their own."

Suddenly turning a corner, we came on a group in a recess hung on three sides with curtains and furnished with low couches in the manner of an Oriental divan. The Duke of York, who seemed to me a handsome courtly prince, was sitting, and by him Lord Arlington. Opposite to them stood a gentleman to whom the Duke, when I had made my bow, presented me, bidding me know Mr Hudleston, the Queen's Chaplain. I was familiar with his name, having often, heard of the Romish priest who befriended the King in his flight from Worcester. I was examining his features with the interest that an unknown face belonging to a well-known name has for us, when the Duke addressed me with a suave and lofty graciousness, his manner being in a marked degree more ceremonious than the King's.

"My Lord Arlington," said he, "has commended you, sir, as a young gentleman of most loyal sentiments. My brother and we who love him have great need of the services of all such."

I stammered out an assurance of devotion. Arlington rose and took me by the arm, whispering that I had no need to be embarrassed. But Mr Hudleston turned a keen and searching glance on me, as though he would read my thoughts.

"I'm sure," said Arlington, "that Mr Dale is most solicitous to serve His Majesty in all things."

I bowed, saying to the Duke,

"Indeed I am, sir. I ask nothing but an opportunity."

"In all things?" asked Hudleston abruptly. "In all things, sir?" He fixed his keen eyes on my face.

Arlington pressed my arm and smiled pleasantly; he knew that kindness binds more sheaves than severity.

"Come, Mr Dale says in all things," he observed. "Do we need more, sir?"

But the Duke was rather of the priest's temper than of the Minister's.

"Why, my lord," he answered, "I have never known Mr Hudleston ask a question without a reason for it."

"By serving the King in all things, some mean in all things in which they may be pleased to serve the King," said Hudleston gravely. "Is Mr Dale one of these? Is it the King's pleasure or his own that sets the limit to his duty and his services?"

They were all looking at me now, and it seemed as though we had passed from courtly phrases, such as fall readily but with little import from a man's lips, and had come to a graver matter. They were asking some pledge of me, or their looks belied them. Why or to what end they desired it, I could not tell; but Darrell, who stood behind the priest, nodded his head to me with an anxious frown.

"I will obey the King in all things," I began.

"Well said, well said," murmured Arlington.

"Saving," I proceeded, thinking it my duty to make this addition, and not conceiving that there could be harm in it, "the liberties of the Kingdom and the safety of the Reformed Religion."

I felt Arlington's hand drawn half-away, but in an instant

it was back, and he smiled no less pleasantly than before. But the Duke, less able or less careful to conceal his mood, frowned heavily, while Hudleston cried impatiently,

"Reservations! Kings are not served with reservations, sir."

He made me angry. Had the Duke said what he did, I would have taken it with a dutiful bow and a silent tongue. But who was this priest to rate me in such a style? My temper banished my prudence, and, bending my head towards him, I answered:

"Yet the Crown itself is worn with these reservations, sir, and the King himself allows them."

For a moment nobody spoke. Then Arlington said,

"I fear, sir, Mr Dale is as yet less a courtier than an honest gentleman."

The Duke rose to his feet.

"I have found no fault with Mr Dale," said he haughtily and coldly, and, taking no more heed of me, he walked away, while Hudleston, having bestowed on me an angry glance, followed him.

"Mr Dale, Mr Dale!" whispered Arlington, and with no more than that, although still with a smile, he slipped his arm out of mine and left me, beckoning Darrell to go with him. Darrell obeyed with a shrug of despair. I was alone—and, as it seemed, ruined. Alas, why must I blurt out my old lessons as though I had been standing again at my father's knee and not in the presence of the Duke of

York? Yes, my race was run before it was begun. The Court was not the place for me. In great bitterness I flung myself down on the cushions and sat there, out of heart and very dismal. A moment passed; then the curtain behind me was drawn aside, and an amused laugh sounded in my ear as I turned. A young man leapt over the couch and threw himself down beside me, laughing heartily and crying,

"Well done, well done! I'd have given a thousand crowns to see their faces!"

I sprang to my feet in amazement and confusion, bowing low, for the young man by me was the Duke of Monmouth.

"Sit, man," said he, pulling me down again. "I was behind the curtain, and heard it all. Thank God, I held my laughter in till they were gone. The liberties of the Kingdom and the safety of the Reformed Religion! Here's a story for the King!" He lay back, seeming to enjoy the jest most hugely.

"For the love of heaven, sir," I cried, "don't tell the King! I'm already ruined."

"Why, so you are, with my good uncle," said he. "You're new to Court, Mr Dale?"

"Most sadly new," I answered in a rueful tone, which set him laughing again.

"You hadn't heard the scandalous stories that accuse the Duke of loving the Reformed Religion no better than the liberties of the Kingdom?"

Anthony Hope

"Indeed, no, sir."

"And my Lord Arlington? I know him! He held your arm, to the last, and he smiled to the last?"

"Indeed, sir, my lord was most gentle to me."

"Aye, I know his way. Mr Dale, for this entertainment let me call you friend. Come then, we'll go to the King with it." And, rising, he seized me by the arm and began to drag me off.

"Indeed your Grace must pardon me—" I began.

"But indeed I will not," he persisted. Then he suddenly grew grave as he said, "I am for the liberties of the Kingdom and the safety of the Reformed Religion. Aren't we friends, then?"

"Your Grace does me infinite honour."

"And am I no good friend? Is there no value in the friendship of the King's son—the King's eldest son?" He drew himself up with a grace and a dignity which became him wonderfully. Often in these later days I see him as he was then, and think of him with tenderness. Say what you will, he made many love him even to death, who would not have lifted a finger for his father or the Duke of York.

Yet in an instant—such slaves are we of our moods—I was more than half in a rage with him. For as we went we encountered Mistress Barbara on Lord Carford's arm. The quarrel between them seemed past and they were talking merrily together. On the sight of her the Duke left me and ran forward. By an adroit movement he thrust Carford aside and began to ply the lady with most extravagant and high-flown compliments, displaying an excess of devotion which witnessed more admiration than respect. She had treated me as a boy, but she did not tell him that he was a boy, although he was younger than I; she listened with heightened colour and sparkling eyes. I glanced at Carford and found, to my surprise, no signs of annoyance at his unceremonious deposition. He was watching the pair with a shrewd smile and seemed to mark with pleasure the girl's pride and the young Duke's evident passion. Yet I, who heard something of what passed, had much ado not to step in and bid her pay no heed to homage that was empty if not dishonouring.

Suddenly the Duke turned round and called to me.

"Mr Dale," he cried, "there needed but one thing to bind us closer, and here it is! For you are, I learn, the friend of Mistress Quinton, and I am the humblest of her slaves, who serve all her friends for her sake."

"Why, what would your Grace do for my sake?" asked Barbara.

"What wouldn't I?" he cried, as if transported. Then he added rather low, "Though I fear you're too cruel to do anything for mine."

"I am listening to the most ridiculous speeches in the world for your Grace's sake," said Barbara with a pretty curtsey and a coquettish smile.

"Is love ridiculous?" he asked. "Is passion a thing to smile at? Cruel Mistress Barbara!"

"Won't your Grace set it in verse?" said she.

"Your grace writes it in verse on my heart," said he.

Then Barbara looked across at me, it might be accidentally, yet it did not appear so, and she laughed merrily. It needed no skill to measure the meaning of her laugh, and I did not blame her for it. She had waited for years to avenge the kiss that I gave Cydaria in the Manor Park at Hatchstead; but was it not well avenged when I stood humbly, in deferential silence, at the back while his Grace the Duke sued for her favour, and half the Court looked on? I will not set myself down a churl where nature has not made me one; I said in my heart, and I tried to say to her with my eyes, "Laugh, sweet mistress, laugh!" For I love a girl who will laugh at you when the game runs in her favour.

The Duke fell to his protestations again, and Carford still listened with an acquiescence that seemed strange in a suitor for the lady's hand. But now Barbara's modesty took alarm; the signal of confusion flew in her cheeks, and she looked round, distressed to see how many watched them. Monmouth cared not a jot. I made bold to slip across to Carford, and said to him in a low tone,

"My lord, his Grace makes Mistress Barbara too much marked. Can't you contrive to interrupt him?"

He stared at me with a smile of wonder. But something in my look banished his smile and set a frown in its place.

"Must I have more lessons in manners from you, sir?" he asked. "And do you include a discourse on the interrupting of princes?"

"Princes?" said I.

"The Duke of Monmouth is—"

"The King's son, my lord," I interposed, and, carrying my hat in my hand, I walked up to Barbara and the Duke. She looked at me as I came, but not now mockingly; there was rather an appeal in her eyes.

"Your Grace will not let me lose my audience with the King?" said I.

He started, looked at me, frowned, looked at Barbara, frowned deeper still. I remained quiet, in an attitude of great deference. Puzzled to know whether I had spoken in sheer simplicity and ignorance, or with a meaning which seemed too bold to believe in, he broke into a doubtful laugh. In an instant Barbara drew away with a curtsey. He did not pursue her, but caught my arm, and looked hard and straight in my face. I am happily somewhat wooden of feature, and a man could not make me colour now, although a woman could. He took nothing by his examination.

"You interrupted me," he said.

"Alas, your Grace knows how poor a courtier I am, and how ignorant—"

"Ignorant!" he cried; "yes, you're mighty ignorant, no doubt; but I begin to think you know a pretty face when you see it, Master Simon Dale. Well, I'll not quarrel. Isn't she the most admirable creature alive?"

"I had supposed Lord Carford thought so, sir."

"Oh! And yet Lord Carford did not hurry me off to find the King! But you? What say you to the question?"

"I'm so dazzled, sir, by all the beautiful ladies of His Majesty's Court that I can hardly perceive individual charms."

He laughed again, and pinched my arm, saying,

"We all love what we have not. The Duke of York is in love with truth, the King with chastity, Buckingham with modesty of demeanour, Rochester with seemliness, Arlington with sincerity, and I, Simon—I do fairly worship discretion!"

"Indeed I fear I can boast of little, sir."

"You shall boast of none, and thereby show the more, Simon. Come, there's the King." And he darted on, in equal good humour, as it seemed, with himself and me. Moreover, he lost no time on his errand; for when I reached his side (since they who made way for him afforded me no such civility) he had not only reached the King's chair, but was half-way through his story of my answer to the Duke of York; all chance of stopping him was gone.

"Now I'm damned indeed," thought I; but I set my teeth, and listened with unmoved face.

At this moment the King was alone, save for ourselves and a little long-eared dog which lay on his lap and was incessantly caressed with his hand. He heard his son's story with a face as impassive as I strove to render mine. At the end he looked up at me, asking,

"What are these liberties which are so dear to you, sir?"

My tongue had got me into trouble enough for one day, so

I set its music to a softer tune.

"Those which I see preserved and honoured by your Majesty," said I, bowing.

Monmouth laughed, and clapped me on the back; but the King proceeded gravely:

"And this Reformed Religion that you set above my orders?"

"The Faith, Sir, of which you are Defender."

"Come, Mr Dale," said he, rather surly, "if you had spoken to my brother as skilfully as you fence with me, he would not have been angry."

I do not know what came over me. I said it in all honest simplicity, meaning only to excuse myself for the disrespect I had shown to the Duke; but I phrased the sentence most vilely, for I said:

"When His Royal Highness questioned me, Sir, I had to speak the truth."

Monmouth burst into a roar, and a moment later the King followed with a more subdued but not less thorough merriment. When his mirth subsided he said,

"True, Mr Dale. I am a King, and no man is bound to speak truth to me. Nor, by heaven—and there's a compensation—I to any man!"

"Nor woman," said Monmouth, looking at the ceiling in apparent absence of mind.

"Nor even boy," added the King, with an amused glance at his son. "Well, Mr Dale, can you serve me and this conscience of yours also?"

"Indeed I cannot doubt it, Sir," said I.

"A man's king should be his conscience," said the King.

"And what should be conscience to the King, Sir?" asked Monmouth.

"Why, James, a recognition of what evil things he may bring into the world, if he doesn't mind his ways."

Monmouth saw the hit, and took it with pretty grace, bending and kissing the King's hand.

"It is difficult, Mr Dale, to serve two masters," said the King, turning again to me.

"Your Majesty is my only master," I began; but the King interrupted me, going on with some amusement:

"Yet I should like to have seen my brother."

"Let him serve me, Sir," cried Monmouth. "For I am firm in my love of these liberties, aye, and of the Reformed Religion."

"I know, James, I know," nodded the King. "It is grievous and strange, however, that you should speak as though my brother were not." He smiled very maliciously at the young Duke, who flushed red. The King suddenly laughed, and fell to fondling the little dog again.

"Then, Sir," said Monmouth, "Mr Dale may come with

me to Dover?"

My heart leapt, for all the talk now was of Dover, of the gaiety that would be there, and the corresponding dulness in London, when the King and the Duke were gone to meet Madame d'Orleans. I longed to go, and the little hope I had cherished that Darrell's good offices with the Secretary of State would serve me to that end had vanished. Now I was full of joy, although I watched the King's face anxiously.

For some reason the suggestion seemed to occasion him amusement; yet, although for the most part he laughed openly without respect of matter or person, he now bent over his little dog, as though he sought to hide the smile, and when he looked up again it hung about his lips like the mere ghost of mirth.

"Why not?" said he. "To Dover, by all means. Mr Dale can serve you, and me, and his principles, as well at Dover as in London."

I bent on one knee and kissed his hand for the favour. When I sought to do the like to Monmouth he was very ready, and received my homage most regally. As I rose, the King was smiling at the pair of us in a whimsical melancholy way.

"Be off with you, boys," said he, as though we were a pair of lads from the grammar school. "Ye are both fools; and James there is but indifferently honest. But every hour's a chance, and every wench an angel to you. Do what you will, and God forgive your sins." And he lay back in his great chair with a good-humoured, lazy, weary smile, as he idly patted the little dog. In spite of all that all men knew of him, I felt my heart warm to him, and I knelt on

Anthony Hope

my knee again, saying:

"God save your Majesty."

"God is omnipotent," said the King gravely. "I thank you, Mr Dale."

Thus dismissed, we walked off together, and I was awaiting the Duke's pleasure to relieve him also of my company, when he turned to me with a smile, his white teeth gleaming:

"The Queen sends a maid of honour to wait on Madame," said he.

"Indeed, sir; it is very fitting."

"And the Duchess sends one also. If you could choose from among the Duchess's—for I swear no man in his senses would choose any of Her Majesty's—whom would you choose, Mr. Dale?"

"It is not for me to say, your Grace," I answered.

"Well," said he, regarding me drolly, "I would choose Mistress Barbara Quinton." And with a last laugh he ran off in hot pursuit of a lady who passed at that moment and cast a very kindly glance at him.

Left alone, but in a good humour that the Duke's last jest could not embitter, I stood watching the scene. The play had begun now on a stage at the end of the hall, but nobody seemed to heed it. They walked to and fro, talking always, ogling, quarrelling, love-making, and intriguing. I caught sight here of great ladies, there of beauties whose faces were their fortune—or their ruin, which you will.

Buckingham went by, fine as a galley in full sail. The Duke of York passed with Mr Hudleston; my salute went unacknowledged. Clifford came soon after; he bowed slightly when I bowed to him, but his heartiness was gone. A moment later Darrell was by my side; his ill-humour was over, but he lifted his hands in comical despair.

"Simon, Simon, you're hard to help," said he. "Alas, I must go to Dover without you, my friend! Couldn't you restrain your tongue?"

"My tongue has done me no great harm," said I, "and you needn't go to Dover alone."

"What?" he cried, amazed.

"Unless the Duke of Monmouth and my Lord Arlington travel apart."

"The Duke of Monmouth? What have you to do with him?"

"I am to enter his service," I answered proudly; "and, moreover, I'm to go with him to Dover to meet Madame d'Orleans."

"Why, why? How comes this? How were you brought to his notice?"

I looked at him, wondering at his eagerness. Then I took him by the arm, and I said laughingly:

"Come, I am teachable, and I have learnt my lesson."

"What lesson do you mean?"

"To restrain my tongue," said I. "Let those who are curious as to the Duke of Monmouth's reasons for his favour to me, ask the Duke."

He laughed, but I caught vexation in his laugh.

"True, you're teachable, Simon," said he.

CHAPTER VIII

MADNESS, MAGIC, AND MOONSHINE

When the curtain had fallen on the little-heeded play and the gay crowd began to disperse, I, perceiving that no more was to be seen or learnt, went home to my lodging alone. After our conversation Darrell had left me abruptly, and I saw him no more. But my own thoughts gave me occupation enough; for even to a dull mind, and one unversed in Court intrigues, it seemed plain that more hung on this expedition to Dover than the meeting of the King's sister with her brother. So far all men were of the same opinion; beyond, their variance began. I had not thought to trouble my head about it, but, not having learnt yet that a small man lives most comfortably with the great by opening his eyes and ears only when bidden and keeping them tight locked for the rest, I was inspired with eagerness to know the full meaning of the scene in which I was now to play a part, however humble. Of one thing at least I was glad—here I touched on a matter more suitable to my condition—and this was that since Barbara Quinton was to go to Dover, I was to go also. But, alas, neither here did perplexity lag far behind! It is easy to know that you are glad to be with a lady; your very blood tells you; but to say why is often difficult. I told myself that my sole cause for pleasure lay in the services I might be able to render to my old friend's daughter; she would want me to run her errands and do her bidding; an attentive cavalier, however lowly, seldom comes amiss; these pleas I muttered to myself, but swelling pride refused them, and for once reason came as pride's ally, urging that in such company as would assemble at Dover a girl might well need protection, no less than compliments. It was true; my new master's bearing to her shewed how true. And Carford was not, it seemed, a jealous lover. I was no lover—my life was vowed to another most unhappy love—but I was a gentleman, and (sweet thought!) the hour might come when the face which had looked so mockingly at me to-night should turn again in appeal to the wit and arm of Simon Dale. I grew taller as I thought of that, and, coming just then to my own door, rapped with my cane as loudly and defiantly as though I had been the Duke of Monmouth himself, and not a gentleman in his suite.

Loud as my rapping was, it brought no immediate answer. Again I knocked; then feet came shuffling along the passage. I had aroused my sleepy wretch; doubtless he would come groaning (for Jonah might not curse save in the way of religion), and rubbing his eyes, to let me in. The door opened and Jonah appeared; his eyes were not dull with sleep but seemed to blaze with some strong excitement; he had not been to his bed, for his dress was not disordered, and a light burnt bright in my parlour. To crown all, from the same parlour came the sound of a psalm most shrilly and villainously chanted through the nose in a voice familiar to my ears. I, unlike my servant, had not bound myself against an oath where the case called, and with a round one that sent Jonah's eyes in agony up to the ceiling I pushed by him and ran into the parlour. A sonorous "Amen" came pat with my entrance; Phineas Tate stood before me, lean and pale, but calm and placid.

"What in the devil's name brings you here?" I cried.

"The service of God," he answered solemnly.

"What, does it forbid sleep at nights?"

"Have you been sleeping, young man?" he asked, pertinently enough, as I must allow.

"I have been paying my respects to His Majesty," said I.

"God forgive him and you," was the retort.

"Perhaps, sir, perhaps not," I replied, for I was growing angry. "But I have asked your intercession no more than has the King. If Jonah brought you here, it was without my leave; I beg you to take your departure.—Jonah, hold the door there for Mr Tate."

The man raised his hand impressively.

"Hear my message first," he said. "I am sent unto you, that you may turn from sin. For the Lord has appointed you to be his instrument. Even now the plot is laid, even now men conspire to bring this kingdom again into the bondage of Rome. Have you no ears, have you no eyes, are you blind and deaf? Turn to me, and I will make you see and hear. For it is given to me to show you the way."

I was utterly weary of the fellow, and, in despair of getting quit of him, flung myself into a chair. But his next words caught my attention.

"The man who lives here with you—what of him? Is he

not an enemy of God?"

"Mr Darrell is of the Romish faith," said I, smiling in spite of myself, for a kinder soul than Darrell I had never met.

Phineas came close to me, leaning over me with an admonishing forefinger and a mysterious air.

"What did he want with you?" he asked. "Yet cleave to him. Be where he is, go where he goes."

"If it comforts you, I am going where he goes," said I, yawning. "For we are both going to Dover when the King goes."

"It is God's finger and God's will!" cried Phineas, catching me by the shoulder.

"Enough!" I shouted, leaping up. "Keep your hands off me, man, if you can't keep your tongue. What is it to you that we go to Dover?"

"Aye, what?" came suddenly in Darrell's voice. He stood in the doorway with a fierce and angry frown on his face. A moment later he was across the room and laid his hand on Phineas. "Do you want another cropping of your ears?" he asked.

"Do your will on me," cried the fanatic. And sweeping away his lanky hair he showed his ears; to my horror they had been cropped level across their tops by the shears. "Do your will," he shrieked, "I am ready. But your hour comes also, yea, your cup shall soon be full."

Darrell spoke to him in low stern tones.

"It may be more than ears, if you will not bridle your tongue. It's not for you to question why the King comes or goes."

I saw Jonah's face at the door, pale with fright as he looked at the two men. The interest of the scene grew on me; the talk of Dover seemed to pursue me strangely.

"But this young man," pursued Phineas, utterly unmoved by Darrell's threat, "is not of you; he shall be snatched from the burning, and by his hand the Lord will work a great deliverance."

Darrell turned to me and said stiffly:

"This room is yours, sir, not mine. Do you suffer the presence of this mischievous knave?"

"I suffer what I can't help," I answered. "Mr Tate doesn't ask my pleasure in his coming and going any more than the King asks Mr Tate's in his."

"It would do you no good, sir, to have it known that he was here," Darrell reminded me with a significant nod of his head.

Darrell had been a good friend to me and had won my regard, but, from an infirmity of temper that I have touched on before, his present tone set me against him. I take reproof badly, and age has hardly tamed me to it.

"No good with whom?" I asked, smiling. "The Duke of York? My Lord Arlington? Or do you mean the Duke of Monmouth? It is he whom I have to please now."

"None of them love Ranters," answered Darrell, keeping

his face stiff and inscrutable.

"But one of them may prefer a Ranter to a Papist," laughed I.

The thrust told, Darrell grew red. To myself I seemed to have hit suddenly on the key of a mystery. Was I then a pawn in the great game of the Churches, and Darrell another, and (to speak it with all due respect), these grand dukes little better? Had Phineas Tate also his place on the board where souls made the stakes? In such a game none is too low for value, none too high for use. Surely my finger was on the spring! At least I had confounded Darrell; his enemy, taking my help readily enough, glared on him in most unchristian exultation, and then, turning to me, cried in a species of fierce ecstasy,

"Think not that because you are unworthy you shall not serve God. The work sanctifies the instrument, yea, it makes clean that which is foul. Verily, at His hour, God may work through a woman of sin." And he fixed his eyes intently on me.

I read a special meaning in his words; my thoughts flew readily to the Cock and Pie in Drury Lane.

"Yea, through a woman of sin," he repeated slowly and solemnly; then he faced round, swift as the wind, on Darrell, and, minding my friend's sullen scowl not a whit, cried to him, "Repent, repent, vengeance is near!" and so at last was out of the room before either of us could hinder him, had we wished, or could question him further. I heard the house-door shut behind him, and I rose, looking at Darrell with an easy smile.

"Madness and moonshine, good friend," said I. "Don't let

it disturb you. If Jonah admits the fellow again he shall answer for it."

"Indeed, Mr Dale, when I prayed you to share my lodging, I did not foresee the nature of your company."

"Fate more than choice makes a man's company," said I. "Now it's you, now Phineas, now my lord the Secretary, and now his Grace the Duke. Indeed, seeing how destiny —or, if you will, chance—rules, a man may well be thought a fool who makes a plan or chooses a companion. For my own part, I am fate's child and fate shall guide me."

He was still stiff and cold with me, but my friendly air and my evident determination to have no quarrel won him to civility if to no warmer demonstration of regard.

"Fate's child?" he asked with a little scorn, but seating himself and smoothing his brow. "You're fate's child? Isn't that an arrogant speech, Simon?"

"If it weren't true, most arrogant," I answered. "Come, I'll tell you; it's too soon for bed and too late to go abroad. Jonah, bring us some wine, and if it be good, you shall be forgiven for admitting Master Tate."

Jonah went off and presently returned with a bottle, which we drank, while I, with the candour I had promised, told my friend of Betty Nasroth and her prophecy. He heard me with an attention which belied the contempt he asserted; I have noticed that men pay heed to these things however much they laugh at them. At the end, growing excited not only with the wine but with the fumes of life which had been mounting into my young brain all the day, I leapt up, crying aloud:

Anthony Hope

"And isn't it true? Shan't I know what he hides? Shan't I drink of his cup? For isn't it true? Don't I already, to my infinite misery, love where he loves?" For the picture of Nell had come suddenly across me in renewed strength and sweetness; when I had spoken I dropped again into my chair and laid my head down on my arms.

Silence followed; Darrell had no words of consolation for my woes and left my love-lorn cry unheeded; presently then (for neglected sorrows do not thrive) I looked furtively at him between the fingers of my hand. He sat moody, thoughtful, and frowning. I raised my head and met his eyes. He leant across the table, saying in a sneering tone, "A fine witch, on my life! You should know what he hides?"

"Aye."

"And drink of his cup?"

"Aye, so she said."

He sat sunk in troubled thought, but I, being all this night torn to and fro by changing and warring moods, sprang up again and cried in boisterous scorn, "What, you believe these fables? Does God reveal hidden things to old crones? I thought you at Court were not the fools of such fancies! Aren't they fitter for rustic churls, Mr Darrell? God save us, do we live in the days of King James?"

He answered me shortly and sternly, as though I had spoken of things not to be named lightly.

"It is devil's work, all of it."

"Then the devil is busier than he seems, even after a night

at Court," I said. "But be it whose work it will, I'll do it. I'll find what he hides. I'll drink of his cup. Come, you're glum! Drink, friend Darrell! Darrell, what's in his cup, what does he hide? Darrell, what does the King hide?"

I had caught him by the shoulder and was staring in his face. I was all aglow, and my eyes, no doubt, shone bright with excitement and the exhilaration of the wine. The look of me, or the hour of the night, or the working of his own superstition, got hold of him, for he sprang up, crying madly:

"My God, do you know?" and glared into my face as though I had been the very devil of whom I spoke.

We stood thus for a full minute. But I grew cool before my companion, wonder working the change in me sooner than confusion could in him. For my random ravings had most marvellously struck on something more than my sober speculations could discern. The man before me was mad—or he had a secret. And friend Darrell was no madman.

"Do I know?" I asked. "Do I know what? What could I, Simon Dale, know? What in Heaven's name is there to know?" And I smiled cunningly, as though I sought to hide knowledge by a parade of ignorance.

"Nothing, nothing," he muttered uneasily. "The wine's got into my head."

"Yet you've drunk but two glasses; I had the rest," said I.

"That damned Ranter has upset me," he growled. "That, and the talk of your cursed witch."

"Can Ranters and witches make secrets where there are none?" said I with a laugh.

"They can make fools think there are secrets where there are none," said he rudely.

"And other fools ask if they're known," I retorted, but with a laugh; and I added, "I'm not for a quarrel, secret or no secret, so if that's your purpose in sitting the night through, to bed with you, my friend."

Whether from prudence, or whether my good humour rebuked his temper, he grew more gentle; he looked at me kindly enough and sighed, as he said:

"I was to be your guide in London, Simon; but you take your own path."

"The path you shewed me was closed in my face," said I, "and I took the first that was opened to me."

"By the Duke of Monmouth?"

"Yes—or by another, if it had chanced to be another."

"But why take any, Simon?" he urged persuasively. "Why not live in peace and leave these great folk alone?"

"With all my heart," I cried. "Is it a bargain? Whither shall we fly from the turmoil?"

"We!" he exclaimed with a start.

"Aren't you sick of the same disease? Isn't the same medicine best for you? Come, shall we both go to-morrow to Hatchstead—a pretty village, Mr Darrell—and let the great folk go alone to Dover?"

"You know I cannot. I serve my Lord Arlington."

"And I the Duke of Monmouth."

"But my Lord is the King's servant."

"And his Grace the King's son."

"Oh, if you're obstinate—" he began, frowning.

"As fate, as prophecy, as witch, as Ranter, as devil, or as yourself!" I said, laughing and throwing myself into a chair as he rose and moved towards the door.

"No good will come of it to you," he said, passing me on his way.

"What loyal servant looks to make a profit of his service?" I asked, smiling.

"I wish you could be warned."

"I'm warned, but not turned, Darrell. Come, we part friends?"

"Why, yes, we are friends," he answered, but with a touch of hesitation.

"Saving our duty to the King?"

"If need should come for that reservation, yes," said he gravely.

"And saving," said I, "the liberties of the Kingdom and

the safety of the Reformed Religion—if need should come for these reservations, Mr Darrell," and I laughed to see the frown gather again on his brow. But he made no reply, being unable to trust his self-control or answer my light banter in its own kind. He left me with no more than a shake of his head and a wave of his hand; and although we parted thus in amity and with no feelings save of kindness for one another, I knew that henceforth there must be a difference in our relations; the days of confidence were gone.

The recognition of my loss weighed little with me. The diffidence born of inexperience and of strangeness to London and the Court was wearing away; the desire for another's arm to lean on and another's eyes to see with gave way before a young man's pride in his own arm's strength and the keenness of his own vision. There was sport afoot; aye, for me in those days all things were sport, even the high disputes of Churches or of Kingdoms. We look at the world through our own glasses; little as it recks of us, it is to us material and opportunity; there in the dead of night I wove a dream wherein the part of hero was played by Simon Dale, with Kings and Dukes to bow him on and off the stage and Christendom to make an audience. These dream-doings are brave things: I pity the man who performs none of them; for in them you may achieve without labour, enjoy without expense, triumph without cruelty, aye, and sin mightily and grandly with never a reckoning for it. Yet do not be a mean villain even in your dreaming, for that sticks to you when you awake.

I had supposed myself alone to be out of bed and Jonah Wall to have slunk off in fear of my anger. But now my meditations were interrupted by his entrance. He crept up to me in an uneasy fashion, but seemed to take courage when I did not break into abuse, but asked him mildly why he had not sought rest and what he wanted with me. His first answer was to implore me to protect him from Mr Darrell's wrath; through Phineas Tate, he told me timidly, he had found grace, and he could deny him nothing; yet, if I bade him, he would not admit him again.

"Let him come," said I carelessly. "Besides, we shall not be long here. For you and I are going on a journey, Jonah."

"A journey, sir?"

"Ay, I go with the Duke of Monmouth, and you go with me, to Dover when the King goes."

Now, either Dover was on everybody's brain, or was very sadly on my brain, for I swear even this fellow's eye seemed to brighten as I named the place.

"To Dover, sir?"

"No less. You shall see all the gaiety there is to be seen, Jonah."

The flush of interest had died away; he was dolefully tranquil and submissive again.

"Well, what do you want with me?" I asked, for I did not wish him to suspect that I detected any change in his manner.

"A lady came here to-day, sir, in a very fine coach with Flemish horses, and asked for you. Hearing you were from home, she called to me and bade me take a message for you. I prayed her to write it, but she laughed, and said she spoke more easily than she wrote; and she bade me say that she wished to see you."

"What sort of lady was she, Jonah?"

"She sat all the while in the coach, sir, but she seemed not tall; she was very merry, sir." Jonah sighed deeply; with him merriment stood high among the vices of our nature.

"She didn't say for what purpose she wanted me?" I asked as carelessly as I could.

"No, sir. She said you would know the purpose, and that she would look for you at noon to-morrow."

"But where, Jonah?"

"At a house called Burford House, sir, in Chelsea."

"She gave you no name?"

"I asked her name, and she gave me one."

"What was it?"

"It was a strange heathenish name, and she laughed as she gave it; indeed she laughed all the time."

"There's no sin in laughter," said I dryly. "You may leave me, I need no help in undressing."

"But the name—"

"By Heaven, man, I know the name! Be off with you!"

He shuffled off, his whole manner expressing reprobation, whether most of my oath, or of the heathenish name, or of the lady who gave it, I know not.

Well, if he were so horror-stricken at these things, what would he say at learning with whom he had talked? Perhaps he would have preached to her, as had Phineas Tate, his master in religion. For, beyond doubt, that heathenish name was Cydaria, and that fine coach with Flemish horses—I left the question of that coach unanswered.

The moment the door was shut behind my servant I sprang to my feet, crying in a low but very vehement voice, "Never!" I would not go. Had she not wounded me enough? Must I tear away the bandage from the gash? She had tortured me, and asked me now, with a laugh, to be so good as stretch myself on the rack again. I would not go. That laugh was cruel insolence. I knew that laugh. Ah, why so I did—I knew it well—how it rose and rippled and fell, losing itself in echoes scarcely audible, but rich with enticing mirth. Surely she was cunningly fashioned for the undoing of men; yes, and of herself, poor soul. What were her coaches, and the Flemish horses, and the house called Burford House in Chelsea? A wave of memory swept over me, and I saw her simple—well then, more simple!—though always merry, in the sweet-smelling fields at home, playing with my boy's heart as with a toy that she knew little of, but yet by instinct handled deftly. It pleased her mightily, that toy, and she seemed to wonder when she found that it felt. She did not feel; joy was hers, nothing deeper. Yet could she not, might she not, would she not? I knew what she was; who knew what she might be? The picture of her rose again before my eyes, inviting a desperate venture, spurring me on to an enterprise in which the effort seemed absurdity, and success would have been in the eyes of the world calamity. Yet an exaltation of spirit was on me, and I wove another dream that drove the first away; now I did not go to Dover to play my part in great affairs and jostle for higher place in a world where in God's eyes all places are equal and all low, but away back to the country I had loved, and not alone. She should be with me, love should dress penitence in glowing robes, and purity be decked more gloriously than all the pomps of sin. Could it be? If it could, it seemed a prize for which all else might be willingly forgone—an achievement rare and great, though the page of no history recorded it.

Phineas Tate had preached to her, and gone away, empty and scorned. I would preach too, in different tones and with a different gospel. Yet my words should have a sweetness his had not, my gospel a power that should draw where his repelled. For my love, shaken not yet shattered, wounded not dead, springing again to full life and force, should breathe its vital energy into her soul and impart of its endless abundance till her heart was full. Entranced by this golden vision, I rose and looked from the window at the dawning day, praying that mine might be the task, the achievement, the reward.

Bright dawned that day as I, with brighter brightness in my heart, climbed the stairs that led to my bedroom. But as I reached the door of it, I paused. There came a sound from the little closet beyond, where Jonah stretched his weary legs, and, as I hoped, had forgotten in harmless sleep the soul that he himself tormented worse than would the hell he feared. No, he did not rest. From his closet came low, fervent, earnest prayers. Listening a minute, half in scorn, half in pity, and in no unkindness, I heard him.

"Praise be to God," he said, "Who maketh the crooked places straight, and openeth a path through the wilderness, and setteth in the hand of His servant a sword wherewith to smite the ungodly even in high places."

What crooked places were made straight, what path opened, what sword set in Jonah's hand? Of the ungodly in high places there was no lack in the days of King Charles. But was Jonah Wall to smite them? I opened my door with a laugh. We were all mad that night, and my madness lasted till the morning. Yes, till the morning grew full my second dream was with me.

CHAPTER IX

OF GEMS AND PEBBLES

How I sought her, how I found her, that fine house of hers with the lawn round it and the river by it, the stare of her lackeys, the pomp of her living, the great lord who was bowed out as I went in, the maid who bridled and glanced and laughed—they are all there in my memory, but blurred, confused, beyond clear recall. Yet all that she was, looked, said, aye, or left the clearer for being unsaid, is graven on my memory in lines that no years obliterate and no change of mind makes hard to read. She wore the great diamond necklace whose purchase was a fresh text with the serious, and a new jest for the wits; on her neck it gleamed and flashed as brilliantly and variously as the dazzling turns in her talk and the unending chase of fleeting moods across her face. Yet I started from my lodging, sworn to win her, and came home sworn to have done with her. Let me tell it; I told it to myself a thousand times in the days that followed. But even now, and for all the times that the scene has played itself again before my unwilling eyes, I can scarcely tell whence and how at the last, the change came. I think that the pomp itself, the lord and the lackeys, the fine house, and all her state struck as it were cold at my heart, dooming to failure the mad appeal which they could not smother. But there was more;

for all these might have been, and yet not reached or infected her soul. But when I spoke to her in words that had for me a sweetness so potent as to win me from all hesitation and make as nothing the whole world beside, she did not understand. I saw that she tried to understand; when she failed, I had failed also. The flower was dead; what use then to cherish or to water it? I had not thought it was dead, but had prayed that, faded and choked though it were, yet it might find life in the sunshine of my love and the water of her tears. But she did not weep, unless in a passing petulance because I asked what she could not give; and the clouds swept dark over my love's bright face.

And now, alas, I am so wise that I cannot weep! I must rather smile to have asked, than lament that my asking was in vain. I must wonder at her patience in refusing kindly, and be no more amazed that she refused at last. Yet this sad wisdom that sits well on age I do not love in youth. I was a fool; but if to hold that good shall win and a true love prevail be folly, let my sons be fools after me until their sons in turn catch up from them the torch of that folly which illuminates the world.

You would have said that she had not looked to see me, for she started as though in surprise when I stood before her, saying, "You sent for me."

"I sent for you?" she cried, still as if puzzled; then, "Ah, I remember. A whim seized me as I passed your lodging. Yet you deserved no such favour, for you treated me very rudely—why, yes, with great unkindness—last time we met. But I wouldn't have you think me resentful. Old friends must forgive one another, mustn't they? Besides, you meant no hurt, you were vexed, perhaps you were even surprised. Were you surprised? No, you weren't surprised. But were you grieved, Simon?"

I had been gazing dully at her, now I spoke heavily and dully.

"You wear gems there on your neck," said I, pointing at the necklace.

"Isn't the neck worthy?" she murmured quickly yet softly, pulling her dress away to let me see the better, and raising her eyes to mine.

"Yes, very worthy. But wouldn't you be grieved to find them pebbles?"

"By my faith, yes!" she laughed, "for I paid the price of gems for them."

"I also paid the price of a gem," said I, "and thought I had it."

"And it proved a pebble?" said she, leaning over me; for I had seated myself in a chair, being in no mood for ceremony.

"Yes, a pebble; a very pebble, a common pebble."

"A common pebble!" she echoed. "Oh, Simon, cruel Simon! But a pretty bright pebble? It looked like a gem, Simon?"

"God forgive you, yes. In Heaven's name—then—long ago, when you came to Hatchstead—what then? Weren't you then—"

"No gem," said she. "Even then a pebble." Her voice sank

a little, as though for a single moment some unfamiliar shame came on her. "A common pebble," she added, echoing my words.

"Then God forgive you," said I again, and I leant my head on my hand.

"And you, good Simon, do you forgive me?"

I was silent. She moved away petulantly, crying,

"You're all so ready to call on God to forgive! Is forgiveness God's only? Will none of you forgive for yourselves? Or are you so righteous that you can't do what God must?"

I sprang up and came to her.

"Forgive?" I cried in a low voice. "Ay, I'll forgive. Don't talk of forgiveness to me. I came to love."

"To love? Now?" Her eyes grew wide in wonder, amusement, and delight.

"Yes," said I.

"You loved the gem; you'd love the pebble? Simon, Simon, where is Madame your mother, where my good friend the Vicar? Ah, where's your virtue, Simon?"

"Where yours shall be," I cried, seizing and covering her hands in mine. "Where yours, there mine, and both in love that makes delight and virtue one." I caught a hand to my lips and kissed it many times. "No sin comes but by desire," said I, pleading, "and if the desire is no sin, there is no sin. Come with me! I will fulfil all your desire and

Anthony Hope

make your sin dead."

She shrank back amazed; this was strange talk to her; yet she left her hand in mine.

"Come with you? But whither, whither? We are no more in the fields at Hatchstead."

"We could be again," I cried. "Alone in the fields at Hatchstead."

Even now she hardly understood what I would have, or, understanding, could not believe that she understood rightly.

"You mean—leave—leave London and go with you? With you alone?"

"Yes—alone with your husband."

She pulled her hand away with a jerk, crying, "You're mad!"

"May be. Let me be mad, and be mad yourself also, sweetheart. If both of us are mad, what hurt?"

"What, I—I go—I leave the town—I leave the Court? And you?—You're here to seek your fortune!"

"Mayn't I dream that I've found it?" And again I caught her hand.

After a moment she drew nearer to me; I felt her fingers press mine in tenderness.

"Poor Simon!" said she with a little laugh. "Indeed he

remembers Cydaria well. But Cydaria, such as she was, even Cydaria is gone. And now I am not she." Then she laughed again, crying, "What folly!"

"A moment ago you didn't call it folly."

"Then I was doubly a fool," she answered with the first touch of bitterness. "For folly it is, deep and black. I am not—nay, was I ever?—one to ramble in green fields all day and go home to a cottage."

"Never," said I. "Nor will be, save for the love of a man you love. Save for that, what woman has been? But for that, how many!"

"Why, very few," said she with a gentle little laugh. "And of that few—I am not one. Nay, nor do I—am I cruel?—nor do I love you, Simon."

"You swear it?"

"But a little—as a friend, an old friend."

"And a dear one?"

"One dear for a certain pleasant folly that he has."

"You'll come?"

"No."

"Why not? But in a day neither you nor I would ask why."

"I don't ask now. There's a regiment of reasons." Her laugh burst out again; yet her eyes seemed tender.

"Give me one."

"I have given one. I don't love you."

"I won't take it."

"I am what I am."

"You should be what I would make you."

"You're to live at the Court. To serve the Duke of Monmouth, isn't it?"

"What do I care for that? Are there no others?"

"Let go my hand—No, let it go. See now, I'll show you. There's a ring on it."

"I see the ring."

"A rich one."

"Very rich."

"Simon, do you guess who set it there?"

"He is your King only while you make him such."

"Nay," she cried with sudden passion, "I am set on my course." Then came defiance. "I wouldn't change it. Didn't I tell you once that I might have power with the King?"

"Power? What's that to you? What's it to any of us beside love?"

"Oh, I don't know anything about your love," she cried

fretfully, "but I know what I love—the stir, and the frowns of great ladies, and the courting of great lords. Ah, but why do I talk? Do we reason with a madman?"

"If we are touched ever so little with his disease."

She turned to me with sparkling eyes; she spoke very softly.

"Ah, Simon, you too have a tongue! Can you also lure women? I think you could. But keep it, Simon, keep it for your wife. There's many a maid would gladly take the title, for you're a fine figure, and I think that you know the way to a woman's heart."

Standing above me (for I had sunk back in my chair) she caressed my cheek gently with her hand. I was checked, but not beaten. My madness, as she called it (as must not I also call it?), was still in me, hot and surging. Hope was yet alive, for she had shown me tenderness, and once it had seemed as though a passing shadow of remorse had shot across her brightness. Putting out my hands, I took both of hers again, and so looked up in her face, dumbly beseeching her; a smile quivered on her lips as she shook her head at me.

"Heaven keeps you for better things," she said.

"I'd be the judge of them myself," I cried, and I sought to carry her hands to my lips.

"Let me go," she said; "Simon, you must let me go. Nay, you must. So! Sit there, and I'll sit opposite to you."

She did as she said, seating herself over against me, although quite close. She looked me in the face. Presently she gave a little sigh.

"Won't you leave me now?" she asked with a plaintive smile.

I shook my head, but made no other answer.

"I'm sorry," she went on softly, "that I came to Hatchstead; I'm sorry that I brought you to London, that I met you in the Lane, that I brought you here to-day. I didn't guess your folly. I've lived with players, and with courtiers, and with—with one other; so I didn't dream of such folly as yours. Yes, I'm sorry."

"You can give me joy infinitely greater than any sorrow I've had by you," said I in a low voice.

On this she sat silent for a full minute, seeming to study my face. Then she looked to right and left, as though she would fain have escaped. She laughed a little, but grew grave again, saying, "I don't know why I laughed," and sighing heavily. I watched every motion and change in her, waiting for her to speak again. At last she spoke.

"You won't be angry with me, Simon?" she asked coaxingly.

"Why, no," I answered, wondering.

"Nor run quite mad, nor talk of death, nor any horrors?"

"I'll hear all you say calmly," I answered.

She sat looking at me in a whimsical distress, seeming to deprecate wrath and to pray my pardon yet still to hint amusement deep-hidden in her mind. Then she drew herself up, and a strange and most pitiful pride appeared on her face. I did not know the meaning of it. She leant forward towards me, blushing a little, and whispered my name.

"I'm waiting to hear you," said I; my voice came hard, stern, and cold.

"You'll be cruel to me, I know you will," she cried petulantly.

"On my life, no," said I. "What is it you want to say?"

She was like a child who shows you some loved forbidden toy that she should not have, but prizes above all her trifles; there was that sly joy, that ashamed exultation in her face.

"I have promises," she whispered, clasping her hands and nodding her head at me. "Ah, they make songs on me, and laugh at me, and Castlemaine looks at me as though I were the street-dirt under her feet. But they shall see! Ay, they shall see that I can match them!" She sprang to her feet in reckless merriment, crying, "Shall I make a pretty countess, Simon?" She came near to me and whispered with a mysterious air, "Simon, Simon!"

I looked up at her sparkling eyes.

"Simon, what's he whom you serve, whom you're proud to serve? Who is he, I say?" She broke into a laugh of triumph.

But I, hearing her laugh, and finding my heart filled with a sudden terror, spread my hands over my eyes and fell back heavily in my chair, like a sick man or a drunken.

For now, indeed, I saw that my gem was but a pebble. And the echo of her laugh rang in my ears.

"So I can't come, Simon," I heard her say. "You see that I can't come. No, no, I can't come"; and again she laughed.

I sat where I was, hearing nothing but the echo of her laugh, unable to think save of the truth that was driven so cruelly into my mind. The first realising of things that cannot be undone brings to a young man a fierce impotent resentment; that was in my heart, and with it a sudden revulsion from what I had desired, as intemperate as the desire, as cruel, it may be, as the thing which gave it birth. Nell's laughter died away, and she was silent. Presently I felt a hand rest on my hands as though seeking to convey sympathy in a grief but half-understood. I shrank away, moving my hands till hers no longer touched them. There are little acts, small matters often, on which remorse attends while life lasts. Even now my heart is sore that I shrank away from her; she was different now in nothing from what I had known of her; but I who had desired passionately now shunned her; the thing had come home to me, plain, close, in an odious intimacy. Yet I wish I had not shrunk away; before I could think I had done it; and I found no words; better perhaps that I attempted none.

I looked up; she was holding out the hand before her; there was a puzzled smile on her lips.

"Does it burn, does it prick, does it soil, Simon?" she asked. "See, touch it, touch it. It is as it was, isn't it?" She put it close by my hand, waiting for me to take it, but I did not take it. "As it was when you kissed it," said she; but still I did not take it.

I rose to my feet slowly and heavily, like a tired man

whose legs are reluctant to resume their load. She stood quite still, regarding me now with alarmed and wondering eyes.

"It's nothing," I stammered. "Indeed it's nothing; only I hadn't thought of it."

Scarcely knowing what I did, I began to move towards the door. An unreasoned instinct impelled me to get away from her. Yet my gaze was drawn to her face; I saw her lips pouting and her cheek flushed, the brightness of her eyes grew clouded. She loved me enough to be hurt by me, if no more. A pity seized me; turning, I fell on my knee, and, seizing the hand whose touch I had refused, I kissed it.

"Ah, you kiss my hand now!" she cried, breaking into smiles again.

"I kiss Cydaria's hand," said I. "For in truth I'm sorry for my Cydaria."

"She was no other than I am," she whispered, and now with a touch of shame; for she saw that I felt shame for her.

"Not what is hurts us, but what we know," said I. "Good-bye, Cydaria," and again I kissed her hand. She drew it away from me and tossed her head, crying angrily:

"I wish I hadn't told you."

"In God's name don't wish that," said I, and drew her gaze on me again in surprise. I moved on my way, the only way my feet could tread. But she darted after me, and laid her hand on my arm. I looked at her in amazed questioning.

"You'll come again, Simon, when—?" The smile would not be denied though it came timidly, afraid for its welcome and distrustful of its right. "When you're better, Simon?"

I longed—with all my heart I longed—to be kind to her. How could the thing be to her what it was to me? She could not understand why I was aghast; extravagant despair, all in the style of a vanquished rival, would have been easy for her to meet, to ridicule, to comfort. I knew all this, but I could not find the means to affect it or to cover my own distress.

"You'll come again then?" she insisted pleadingly.

"No," said I, bluntly, and cruelly with unwilling cruelty.

At that a sudden gust of passion seized her and she turned on me, denouncing me fiercely, in terms she took no care to measure, for a prudish virtue that for good or evil was not mine, and for a narrowness of which my reason was not guilty. I stood defenceless in the storm, crying at the end no more than, "I don't think thus of you."

"You treat me as though you thought thus," she cried. Yet her manner softened and she came across to me, seeming now as if she might fall to weeping. But at the instant the door opened and the saucy maid who had ushered me in entered, running hastily to her mistress, in whose ears she whispered, nodding and glancing the while at me.

"The King!" cried Nell, and, turning to me, she added hastily: "He'd best not find you here."

"I ask no better than to be gone," said I.

"I know, I know," she cried. "We're not disturbed! The King's coming interrupts nothing, for all's finished. Go then, go, out of my sight." Her anger seemed to rise again, while the serving-girl stared back astonished as she passed out. But if she went to stay the King's coming, she was too late. For he was in the doorway the instant she had passed through; he had heard Nell's last speech, and now he showed himself, asking easily,

"Who's the gentleman of whose society you are so ready to be relieved?"

I turned, bowing low. The King arched his brows. It may well be that he had had enough of me already, and that he was not well pleased to stumble on me again and in this place. But he said nothing, merely turning his eyes to Nell in question.

"You know him, Sir," said she, throwing herself into a chair.

"Yes, I know him," said the King. "But, if I may ask without presumption, what brings him here?"

Nell looked at the pair of us, the King and Simon Dale, and answered coolly,

"My invitation."

"The answer is all sufficient," bowed the King. "I'm before my time then, for I received a like honour."

"No, he's after his," said she. "But as you heard, Sir, I was urging him to go."

"Not on my account, I pray," said the King politely.

"No, on his. He's not easy here."

"Yet he outstayed his time!"

"We had a matter of business together, Sir. He came to ask something of me, but matters did not prove to be as he thought."

"Indeed you must tell me more, or should have told me less. I'm of a mighty curious disposition. Won't Mr Dale sit?" And the King seated himself.

"I will beg your Majesty's permission to depart," said I.

"All requests here, sir, lie with this lady to grant or to refuse. In this house I am a servant,—nay, a slave."

Nell rose and coming to the side of the King's chair stood there.

"Had things been other than they are, Mr Dale would have asked me to be his wife," said she.

A silence followed. Then the King remarked,

"Had things been other than they are, Mr Dale would have done well."

"And had they been other than they are, I might well have answered yes," said Nell.

"Why yes, very well," said the King. "For Mr Dale is, I'm very sure, a gentleman of spirit and honour, although he seems, if I may say so, just now rather taciturn."

"But as matters are, Mr Dale would have no more of me."

"It's not for me," said the King, "to quarrel with his resolve, although I'm free to marvel at it."

"And asks no more of me than leave to depart."

"Do you find it hard, madame, to grant him that much?"

She looked in the King's face and laughed in amusement, but whether at him or me or herself I cannot tell.

"Why, yes, mighty hard," said she. "It's strange how hard."

"By my faith," said the King, "I begin to be glad that Mr Dale asked no more. For if it be hard to grant him this little thing, it might have been easy to grant him more. Come, is it granted to him?"

"Let him ask for it again," said she, and leaving the King she came and stood before me, raising her eyes to mine. "Would you leave me, Simon?" she cried.

"Yes, I would leave you, madame," said I.

"To go whither?"

"I don't know."

"Yet the question isn't hard," interposed the King. "And the answer is—elsewhere."

"Elsewhere!" cried Nell. "But what does that mean, Sir?"

"Nay, I don't know her name," said the King. "Nor, may

be, does Mr Dale yet. But he'll learn, and so, I hope, shall I, if I can be of service to him."

"I'm in no haste to learn it," cried Nell.

"Why no," laughed the King.

She turned to me again, holding out her hand as though she challenged me to refuse it.

"Good-bye, Simon," said she, and she broke into a strange little laugh that seemed devoid of mirth, and to express a railing mockery of herself and what she did.

I saw the King watching us with attentive eyes and brows bent in a frown.

"Good-bye," said I. Looking into her eyes, I let my gaze dwell long on her; it dwelt longer than I meant, reluctant to take last leave of old friends. Then I kissed her hand and bowed very low to the King, who replied with a good-natured nod; then turning I passed out of the room.

I take it that the change from youth to manhood, and again from full manhood to decline, comes upon us gradually, never ceasing but never swift, as mind and body alike are insensibly transformed beneath the assault of multitudinous unperceived forces of matter and of circumstances; it is the result we know; that, not the process, is the reality for us. We awake to find done what our sleepy brains missed in the doing, and after months or years perceive ourselves in a second older by all that period. We are jogged by the elbow, roused ruthlessly and curtly bidden to look and see how we are changed, and wonder, weep, or smile as may seem best to us in face of the metamorphosis. A moment of such awakening came to me now; I seemed a man different from him who had, no great number of minutes before, hastened to the house, inspired by an insane hope, and aflame with a passion that defied reason and summed up life in longing. The lackeys were there still, the maid's smile altered only by a fuller and more roguish insinuation. On me the change had passed, and I looked open-eyed on what I had been. Then came a smile, close neighbour to a groan, and the scorn of my old self which is the sad delirium wrought by moving time; but the lackey held the door for me and I passed out.

A noise sounded from above as the casement of the window was thrown open. She looked out; her anger was gone, her emotion also seemed gone. She stood there smiling, very kindly but with mockery. She held in either hand a flower. One she smelt and held her face long to it, as though its sweetness kept her senses willing prisoners; turning to the other, she smelt it for a short instant and then drew away, her face, that told every mood with unfailing aptness, twisted into disappointment or disgust. She leant out looking down on me; now behind her shoulder I saw the King's black face, half-hidden by the hangings of the window. She glanced at the first flower, then at the second, held up both her hands for a moment, turned for an instant with a coquettish smile towards the swarthy face behind, then handed the first flower with a laugh into a hand that was stretched out for it, and flung the second down to me. As it floated through the air, the wind disengaged its loose petals and they drifted away, some reaching ground, some caught by gusts and carried away, circling, towards the house-tops. The stalk fell by me, almost naked, stripped of its bloom. For the second flower was faded, and had no sweetness nor life left in it. Again her laugh sounded above me, and the casement closed.

Anthony Hope

I bent and picked up the stalk. Was it her own mood she told me in the allegory? Or was it the mood she knew to be in me? There had been an echo of sorrow in the laugh, of pity, kindness, and regret: and the laugh that she uttered in giving the fresh bloom to the King had seemed pure derision. It was my love, not hers, that found its symbol in the dying flower and the stalk robbed of its glory. She had said well, it was as she said; I picked up what she flung and went on my way, hugging my dead.

In this manner then, as I, Simon the old, have shewn, was I, Simon the young, brought back to my senses. It is all very long ago.

CHAPTER X

JE VIENS, TU VIENS, IL VIENT

It pleased his Grace the Duke of Monmouth so to do all things that men should heed his doing of them. Even in those days, and notwithstanding certain transactions hereinbefore related, I was not altogether a fool, and I had not been long about him before I detected this propensity and, as I thought, the intention underlying it. To set it down boldly and plainly, the more the Duke of Monmouth was in the eye of the nation, the better the nation accustomed itself to regard him as the king's son; the more it fell into the habit of counting him the king's son, the less astonished and unwilling would it be if fate should place him on the king's seat. Where birth is beyond reproach, dignity may be above display; a defect in the first demands an ample exhibition of the second. It was a small matter, this journey to Dover, yet, that he might not go in the train of his father and the Duke of York, but make men talk of his own going, he chose to start beforehand and alone; lest even thus he should not win his meed of notice, he set all the inns and all the hamlets on the road a-gossiping, by accomplishing the journey from London to Canterbury, in his coach-and-six, between sunrise and sunset of a single day. To this end it was needful that the coach should be light; Lord Carford, now

Anthony Hope

his Grace's inseparable companion, alone sat with him, while the rest of us rode on horseback, and the Post supplied us with relays where we were in want of them. Thus we went down gallantly and in very high style, with his Grace much delighted at being told that never had king or subject made such pace in his travelling since the memory of man began. Here was reward enough for all the jolting, the flogging of horses, and the pain of yokels pressed unwillingly into pushing the coach with their shoulders through miry places.

As I rode, I had many things to think of. My woe I held at arm's length. Of what remained, the intimacy between his Grace and my Lord Carford, who were there in the coach together, occupied my mind most constantly. For by now I had moved about in the world a little, and had learnt that many counted Carford no better than a secret Papist, that he was held in private favour, but not honoured in public, by the Duke of York, and that communications passed freely between him and Arlington by the hand of the secretary's good servant and my good friend Mr Darrell. Therefore I wondered greatly at my lord's friendship with Monmouth, and at his showing an attachment to the Duke which, as I had seen at Whitehall, appeared to keep in check even the natural jealousy and resentment of a lover. But at Court a man went wrong if he held a thing unlikely because there was dishonour in it. There men were not ashamed to be spies themselves, nor to use their wives in the same office. There to see no evil was to shut your eyes. I determined to keep mine open in the interests of my new patron, of an older friend, and perhaps of myself also, for Carford's present civility scarcely masked his dislike.

We reached Canterbury while the light of the long summer evening still served, and clattered up the street in muddy bravery. The town was out to see his Grace, and his Grace was delighted to be seen by the town. If, of their courtesy, they chose to treat him as a Prince, he could scarcely refuse their homage, and if he accepted it, it was better to accept like one to the manner born than awkwardly; yet I wondered whether my lord made a note in his aspiring brain of all that passed, and how soon the Duke of York would know that a Prince of Wales, coming to Canterbury, could have received no greater honour. Nay, and they hailed him as the champion of the Church, with hits at the Romish faith, which my lord heard with eyes downcast to the ground and a rigid smile carved on his face. It was all a forecast of what was one day to be; perhaps to the hero of it a suggestion of what some day might be. At least he was radiant over it, and carried Carford off with him into his apartment in the merriest mood. He did not invite me to join his party, and I was well content to be left to wander for an hour in the quiet close of the great cathedral. For let me say that a young man who has been lately crossed in love is in a better mood for most unworldly meditation, than he is likely to be before or after. And if he would not be taken too strictly at his word in all he says to himself then, why, who would, pray, and when?

It was not my fault, but must be imputed to our nature, that in time my stomach cried out angrily at my heart, and I returned to the inn, seeking supper. His Grace was closeted with my lord, and I turned into the public room, desiring no other company than what should lie on my plate. But my host immediately made me aware that I must share my meal and the table with a traveller who had recently arrived and ordered a repast. This gentleman, concerning whom the host seemed in some perplexity, had been informed that the Duke of Monmouth was in the house, but had shown neither excitement at the news nor

Anthony Hope

surprise, nor, to the host's great scandal, the least desire for a sight of his Grace. His men-servants, of whom he had two, seemed tongue-tied, so that the host doubted if they had more than a few phrases of English, and set the whole party down for Frenchmen.

"Hasn't the gentleman given his name?" I asked.

"No. He didn't offer it, and since he flung down money enough for his entertainment I had no cause to ask it."

"None," I remarked, "unless a man may be allowed more curiosity than a beast. Stir yourself about supper," and walking in, I saluted, with all the courtesy at my command, a young gentleman of elegant appearance (so far as I could judge of him in traveller's garb) who sat at the table. His greetings equalled mine in politeness, and we fell into talk on different matters, he using the English language, which he spoke with remarkable fluency, although evidently as a foreigner. His manner was easy and assured, and I took it for no more than an accident that his pistol lay ready to his hand, beside a small case or pocket-book of leather on the table. He asked me my business, and I told him simply that I was going in the Duke's train to Dover.

"Ah, to meet Madame the Duchess of Orleans?" said he. "I heard of her coming before I left France. Her visit, sir, will give great pleasure to the King her brother."

"More, if report speaks true, than to the Prince her husband," said I with a laugh. For the talk at Court was that the Duke of Orleans hated to let his wife out of his sight, while she for her part hated to be in it. Both had their reasons, I do not doubt.

"Perhaps," he answered with a shrug. "But it's hard to know the truth in these matters. I am myself acquainted with many gentlemen at the French Court, and they have much to say, but I believe little of it."

Though I might commend his prudence, I was not encouraged to pursue the topic, and, seeking a change of conversation, I paid him a compliment on his mastery of English, hazarding a suggestion that he must have passed some time in this country.

"Yes," he replied, "I was in London for a year or more a little while ago."

"Your English puts my French to the blush," I laughed, "else hospitality would bid me use your language."

"You speak French?" he asked. "I confess it is easier to me."

"Only a little, and that learnt from merchants, not at Court." For traders of all nations had come from time to time to my uncle's house at Norwich.

"But I believe you speak very well," he insisted politely. "Pray let me judge of your skill for myself."

I was about to oblige him, when a loud dispute arose outside, French ejaculations mingling with English oaths. Then came a scuffle. With a hurried apology, the gentleman sprang to his feet and rushed out. I went on with my supper, supposing that his servants had fallen into some altercation with the landlord and that the parties could not make one another understand. My conjecture was confirmed when the traveller returned, declaring that the quarrel arose over the capacity of a measure of wine and had been soon arranged. But then, with a little cry of vexation, he caught up the pocket-book from the table and darted a quick glance of suspicion at me. I was more amazed than angry, and my smile caused him confusion, for he saw that I had detected his fear. Thinking him punished enough for his rudeness (although it might find some excuse in the indifferent honesty of many who frequented the roads in the guise of travellers) I relieved him by resuming our conversation, saying with a smile,

"In truth my French is a school-boy's French. I can tell the parts of the verb *J'aime, tu aimes, il aime;* it goes so far, sir, and no farther."

"Not far in speech, though often far enough in act," he laughed.

"Truly," said I with a sigh.

"Yet I swear you do yourself injustice. Is there no more?"

"A little more of the same sort, sir." And, casting about for another phrase with which to humour him, I took the first that came to my tongue; leaning my arms on the table (for I had finished eating), I said with a smile, "Well, what say you to this? This is something to know, isn't it? *Je viens, tu viens, il vient.*"

As I live, he sprang to his feet with a cry of alarm! His hand darted to his breast where he had stowed the pocket-book; he tore it out and examined the fastening with furious haste and anxiety. I sat struck still with wonder; the man seemed mad. He looked at me now, and his glance was full of deepest suspicion. He opened his mouth to speak, but words seemed to fail him; he held out the leathern case towards me. Strange as was the question that his gesture put I could not doubt it.

"I haven't touched the book," said I. "Indeed, sir, only your visible agitation can gain you pardon for the suggestion."

"Then how—how?" he muttered.

"You pass my understanding, sir," said I in petulant amusement. "I say in jest 'I come, thou comest, he comes,' and the words act on you like abracadabra and the blackest of magic. You don't, I presume, carry a hornbook of French in your case; and if you do, I haven't robbed you of it."

He was turning the little case over and over in his hands, again examining the clasps of it. His next freak was to snatch his pistol and look to the priming. I burst out laughing, for his antics seemed absurd. My laughter cooled him, and he made a great effort to regain his composure. But I began to rally him.

"Mayn't a man know how to say in French 'He comes' without stealing the knowledge from your book, sir?" I asked. "You do us wrong if you think that so much is known to nobody in England."

He glared at me like a man who hears a jest, but cannot tell whether it conceals earnest or not.

"Open the case, sir," I continued in raillery. "Make sure all is there. Come, you owe me that much."

To my amazement he obeyed me. He opened the case and searched through certain papers which it contained; at the end he sighed as though in relief, yet his suspicious air did not leave him.

"Now perhaps, sir," said I, squaring my elbows, "you'll explain the comedy."

That he could not do. The very impossibility of any explanation showed that I had, in the most unexpected fashion, stumbled on some secret with him even as I had before with Darrell. Was his secret Darrell's or his own, the same or another? What it was I could not tell, but for certain there it was. He had no resource but to carry the matter with a high hand, and to this he betook himself with the readiness of his nation.

"You ask an explanation, sir?" he cried. "There's nothing to explain, and if there were, I give explanations when I please, and not to every fellow who chooses to ask them of me."

"I come, thou comest, he comes,—'tis a very mysterious phrase," said I. "I can't tell what it means. And if you won't tell me, sir, I must ask others."

"You'll be wiser to ask nobody," he said menacingly.

"Nay, I shall be no wiser if I ask nobody," I retorted with a smile.

"Yet you'll tell nobody of what has passed," said he, advancing towards me with the plain intention of imposing his will on me by fear, since persuasion failed. I rose to my feet and answered, mimicking his insolent words,

"I give promises, sir, when I please, and not to every fellow who chooses to ask them of me."

"You shall give me your promise before you leave this room," he cried.

His voice had been rising in passion and was now loud and fierce. Whether the sound of it had reached the room above, or whether the Duke and Carford had grown weary of one another, I do not know, but as the French gentleman uttered this last threat Carford opened the door, stood aside to let his Grace enter, and followed himself. As they came in, we were in a most hostile attitude; for the Frenchman's pistol was in his hand, and my hand had flown to the hilt of my sword. The Duke looked at us in astonishment.

"Why, what's this, gentlemen?" he said. "Mr Dale, are you at variance with this gentleman?" But before I had time to answer him, he had stepped forward and seen the Frenchman's face. "Why, here is M. de Fontelles!" he cried in surprise. "I am very pleased to see you, sir, again in England. Carford, here is M. de Fontelles. You were acquainted with him when he was in the suite of the French Ambassador? You carry a message, sir?"

I listened keenly to all that the Duke's words told me. M. de Fontelles bowed low, but his confusion was in no way abated, and he made no answer to his Grace's question. The Duke turned to me, saying with some haughtiness,

"This gentleman is a friend of mine, Mr Dale. Pray why was your hand on your sword?"

"Because the gentleman's pistol was in his hand, sir."

"You appear always to be very ready for a quarrel, Mr Dale," said the Duke, with a glance at Carford. "Pray, what's the dispute?"

"I'll tell your Grace the whole matter," said I readily enough, for I had nothing to blame myself with.

"No, I won't have it told," cried M. de Fontelles.

"It's my pleasure to hear it," said the Duke coldly.

"Well, sir, it was thus," said I, with a candid air. "I protested to this gentleman that my French was sadly to seek; he was polite enough to assure me that I spoke it well. Upon this I owned to some small knowledge, and for an example I said to him, '*J'aime, tu aimes, il aime.*' He received the remark, sir, with the utmost amiability."

"He could do no less," said the Duke with a smile.

"But he would have it that this didn't exhaust my treasure of learning. Therefore, after leaving me for a moment to set straight a difference that had arisen between his servants and our host, he returned, put away a leathern case that he had left on the table (concerning which indeed he seemed more uneasy than would be counted courteous here in England, seeing that I had been all the while alone in the room with it), and allowed me to resume my exhibition of French-speaking. To humour him and to pass away the hour during which I was deprived of the pleasure of attending your Grace—"

"Yes, yes, Mr Dale. Don't delay in order to compliment me," said the Duke, smiling still.

"I leant across the table, sir, and I made him a speech that sent him, to all seeming, half-way out of his senses; for he sprang up, seized his case, looked at the fastenings, saw to the priming of his pistol, and finally presumed to exact from me a promise that I would consult nobody as to the perplexity into which this strange behaviour of his had flung me. To that I demurred, and hence the quarrel with which I regret most humbly that your Grace should have been troubled."

"I'm obliged to you, Mr Dale. But what was this wonder-working phrase?"

"Why, sir, just the first that came into my head. I said to the gentleman—to M. de Fontelles, as I understand him to be called—I said to him softly and gently—*Je viens, tu viens*—"

The Duke seized me by the arm, with a sudden air of excitement. Carford stepped forward and stood beside him.

"*Je viens, tu viens*.... Yes! And any more?" cried the Duke.

"Yes, your Grace," I answered, again amazed. "I completed what grammarians call the Singular Number by adding '*Il vient;*' whereupon—but I have told you."

"*Il vient?*" cried the Duke and Carford all in a breath.

"*Il vient,*" I repeated, thinking now that all the three had run mad. Carford screened his mouth with his hand and whispered in the Duke's ear. The Duke nodded and made some answer. Both seemed infinitely stirred and interested. M. de Fontelles had stood in sullen silence by the table while I told the story of our quarrel; now his eyes were fixed intently on the Duke's face.

"But why," said I, "that simple phrase worked such strange agitation in the gentleman, your Grace's wisdom

Anthony Hope

may discover. I am at a loss."

Still Carford whispered, and presently the Duke said,

"Come, gentlemen, you've fallen into a foolish quarrel where no quarrel need have come. Pray be friends again."

M. de Fontelles drew himself up stiffly.

"I asked a promise of that gentleman, and he refused it me," he said.

"And I asked an explanation of that gentleman, and he refused it me," said I, just as stiffly.

"Well, then, Mr Dale shall give his promise to me. Will that be agreeable to you, Mr Dale?"

"I'm at your Grace's commands, in all things," I answered, bowing.

"And you'll tell nobody of M. de Fontelles' agitation?"

"If your Grace pleases. To say the truth, I don't care a fig for his fierceness. But the explanation, sir?"

"Why, to make all level," answered the Duke, smiling and fixing his gaze upon the Frenchman, "M. de Fontelles will give his explanation to me."

"I cry agreed, your Grace!" said I. "Come, let him give it."

"To me, Mr Dale, not to you," smiled the Duke.

"What, am I not to hear why he was so fierce with me?"

"You don't care a fig for his fierceness, Mr Dale," he reminded me, laughing.

I saw that I was caught, and had the sense to show no annoyance, although I must confess to a very lively curiosity.

"Your Grace wishes to be alone with M. de Fontelles?" I asked readily and deferentially.

"For a little while, if you'll give us leave," he answered, but he added to Carford, "No, you needn't move, Carford."

So I made my bow and left them, not well pleased, for my brain was on the rack to discover what might be the secret which hung on that mysterious phrase, and which I had so nearly surprised from M. de Fontelles.

"The gist of it," said I to myself, as I turned to the kitchen, "lies, if I am not mistaken, in the third member. For when I had said *Je viens, tu viens*, the Duke interrupted me, crying, 'Any more?'"

I had made for the kitchen since there was no other room open to me, and I found it tenanted by the French servants of M. de Fontelles. Although peace had been made between them and the host, they sat in deep dejection; the reason was plain to see in two empty glasses and an empty bottle that stood on a table between them. Kindliness, aided, it may be, by another motive, made me resolve to cure their despondency.

"Gentlemen," said I in French, going up to them, "you do not drink!"

They rose, bowing, but I took a third chair between them and motioned them to be seated.

"We have not the wherewithal, sir," said one with a wistful smile.

"The thing is mended as soon as told," I cried, and, calling the host, I bade him bring three bottles. "A man is more at home with his own bottle," said I.

With the wine came new gaiety, and with gaiety a flow of speech. M. de Fontelles would have admired the fluency with which I discoursed with his servants, they telling me of travelling in their country, I describing the incidents of the road in England.

"There are rogues enough on the way in both countries, I'll warrant," I laughed. "But perhaps you carry nothing of great value and laugh at robbers?"

"Our spoil would make a robber a poor meal, sir; but our master is in a different plight."

"Ah! He carries treasure?"

"Not in money, sir," answered one. The other nudged him, as though to bid him hold his tongue.

"Come, fill your glasses," I cried, and they obeyed very readily.

"Well, men have met their death between here and London often enough before now," I pursued meditatively, twisting my glass of wine in my fingers. "But with you for his guard, M. de Fontelles should be safe enough."

"We're charged to guard him with our lives, and not leave him till he comes to the Ambassador's house."

"But these rogues hunt sometimes in threes and fours," said I. "You might well lose one of your number."

"We're cheap, sir," laughed one. "The King of France has many of us."

"But if your master were the one?"

"Even then provision is made."

"What? Could you carry his message—for if his treasure isn't money, I must set it down as tidings—to the Ambassador."

They looked at one another rather doubtfully. But I was not behindhand in filling their glasses.

"Still we should go on, even without *Monsieur*," said one.

"But to what end?" I cried in feigned derision.

"Why, we too have a message."

"Indeed. Can you carry the King's message?"

"None better, sir," said the shorter of the pair, with a shrewd twinkle in his eye. "For we don't understand it."

"Is it difficult then?"

"Nay, it's so simple as to see without meaning."

"What, so simple—but your bottle is empty! Come, another?"

"Indeed no, *Monsieur*."

"A last bottle between us! I'll not be denied." And I called for a fourth.

When we were well started on the drinking of it, I asked carelessly,

"And what's your message?"

But neither the wine nor the negligence of my question had quite lulled their caution to sleep. They shook their heads, and laughed, saying,

"We're forbidden to tell that."

"Yet, if it be so simple as to have no meaning, what harm in telling it?"

"But orders are orders, and we're soldiers," answered the shrewd short fellow.

The idea had been working in my brain, growing stronger and stronger till it reached conviction. I determined now to put it to the proof.

"Tut," said I. "You make a pretty secret of it, and I don't blame you. But I can guess your riddle. Listen. If anything befell M. de Fontelles, which God forbid—"

"Amen, amen," they murmured with a chuckle.

"You two, or if fate left but one, that one, would ride on at his best speed to London, and there seek out the Ambassador of the Most Christian King. Isn't it so?"

"So much, sir, you might guess from what we've said."

"Ay, ay, I claim no powers of divination. Yet I'll guess a little more. On being admitted to the presence of the Ambassador, he would relate the sad fate of his master, and would then deliver his message, and that message would be—" I drew my chair forward between them and laid a finger on the arm of each. "That message," said I, "would be just like this—and indeed it's very simple, and seems devoid of all rational meaning: *Je viens*." They started. "*Tu viens*." They gaped. "*Il vient*," I cried triumphantly, and their chairs shot back as they sprang to their feet, astonishment vivid on their faces. For me, I sat there laughing in sheer delight at the excellence of my aim and the shrewdness of my penetration.

What they would have said, I do not know. The door was flung open and M. de Fontelles appeared. He bowed coldly to me and vented on his servants the anger from which he was not yet free, calling them drunken knaves and bidding them see to their horses and lie down in the stable, for he must be on his way by daybreak. With covert glances at me which implored silence and received the answer of a reassuring nod, they slunk away. I bowed to M. de Fontelles with a merry smile; I could not conceal my amusement and did not care how it might puzzle him. I strode out of the kitchen and made my way up the stairs. I had to pass the Duke's apartment. The light still burned there, and he and Carford were sitting at the table. I put my head in.

"If your Grace has no need of me, I'll seek my bed," said I, mustering a yawn.

"No need at all," he answered. "Good-night to you, Simon." But then he added, "You'll keep your promise to me?"

"Your Grace may depend on me."

"Though in truth I may tell you that the whole affair is nothing; it's no more than a matter of gallantry, eh, Carford?"

"No more," said my Lord Carford.

"But such matters are best not talked of."

I bowed as he dismissed me, and pursued my way to my room. A matter of gallantry might, it seemed, be of moment to the messengers of the King of France. I did not know what to make of the mystery, but I knew there was a mystery.

"And it turns," said I to myself, "on those little words '*Il vient*.' Who is he? Where comes he? And to what end? Perhaps I shall learn these things at Dover."

There is this to be said. A man's heart aches less when his head is full. On that night I did not sigh above half my usual measure.

CHAPTER XI

THE GENTLEMAN FROM CALAIS

Good fortune and bad had combined to make me somewhat more of a figure in the eyes of the Court than was warranted by my abilities or my station. The friend of Mistress Gwyn and the favourite of the Duke of Monmouth (for this latter title his Grace's signal kindness soon extorted from the amused and the envious) was a man whom great folk recognised, and to whom small folk paid civility. Lord Carford had become again all smiles and courtesy; Darrell, who arrived in the Secretary's train, compensated in cordiality for what he lacked in confidence; my Lord Arlington himself presented me in most flattering terms to the French King's envoy, M. Colbert de Croissy, who, in his turn, greeted me with a warmth and regarded me with a curiosity that produced equal gratification and bewilderment in my mind. Finally, the Duke of Monmouth insisted on having me with him in the Castle, though the greater part of the gentlemen attached to the Royal and noble persons were sent to lodge in the town for want of accommodation within the walls. My private distress, from which I recovered but slowly, or, to speak more properly, suppressed with difficulty, served to prevent me from becoming puffed up with the conceit which this success might well have inspired.

The first part of Betty Nasroth's prophecy now stood fulfilled, ay, as I trusted, utterly finished and accomplished; the rest tarried. I had guessed that there was a secret, what it was remained unknown to me and, as I soon suspected, to people more important. The interval before the arrival of the Duchess of Orleans was occupied in many councils and conferences; at most of them the Duke of Monmouth was present, and he told me no more than all the Court conjectured when he said that Madame d'Orleans came with a project for a new French Alliance and a fresh war with the Dutch. But there were conferences at which he was not present, nor the Duke of Buckingham, but only the King, his brother (so soon as his Royal Highness joined us from London), the French Envoy, and Clifford and Arlington. Of what passed at these my master knew nothing, though he feigned knowledge; he would be restless when I, having used my eyes, told him that the King had been with M. Colbert de Croissy for two hours, and that the Duke of York had walked on the wall above an hour in earnest conversation with the Treasurer. He felt himself ignored, and poured out his indignation unreservedly to Carford. Carford would frown and throw his eyes towards me, as though to ask if I were to hear these things, but the Duke refused his suggestion. Nay, once he said in jest:

"What I say is as safe with him as with you, my lord, or safer."

I wondered to see Carford indignant.

"Why do you say safer, sir?" he asked haughtily, while the colour on his cheeks was heightened. "Is any man's honour more to be trusted than mine?"

"Ah, man, I meant nothing against your honour; but Simon here has a discretion that heaven does not give to everyone."

Now, when I see a man so sensitive to suspicion as to find it in every careless word, I am set thinking whether he may not have some cause to fear suspicion. Honesty expects no accusation. Carford's readiness to repel a charge not brought caught my notice, and made me ponder more on certain other conferences to which also his Grace my patron was a stranger. More than once had I found Arlington and Carford together, with M. Colbert in their company, and on the last occasion of such an encounter Carford had requested me not to mention his whereabouts to the Duke, advancing the trivial pretext that he should have been engaged on his Grace's business. His Grace was not our schoolmaster. But I was deceived, most amiably deceived, and held my tongue as he prayed. Yet I watched him close, and soon, had a man told me that the Duke of York thought it well to maintain a friend of his own in his nephew's confidence, I would have hazarded that friend's name without fear of mistake.

So far the affair was little to me, but when Mistress Barbara came from London the day before Madame was to arrive, hardly an hour passed before I perceived that she also, although she knew it not, had her part to play. I cannot tell what reward they offered Carford for successful service; if a man who sells himself at a high price be in any way less a villain than he who takes a penny, I trust that the price was high; for in pursuance of the effort to obtain Monmouth's confidence and an ascendency over him, Carford made use of the lady whom he had courted, and, as I believed, still courted, for his own wife. He threw her in Monmouth's way by tricks too subtle for her to detect, but plain to an attentive observer.

I knew from her father that lately he had again begged her hand, and that she had listened with more show of favour. Yet he was the Duke's very humble servant in all the plans which that headstrong young man now laid against the lady's peace and honour. Is there need to state the scheme more plainly? In those days a man might rise high and learn great secrets, if he knew when to shut his eyes and how to knock loud before he entered the room.

I should have warned her. It is true; but the mischief lay in the fact that by no means could I induce her to exchange a word with me. She was harder by far to me than she had shewn herself in London. Perhaps she had heard how I had gone to Chelsea; but whether for good reason or bad, my crime now seemed beyond pardon. Stay; perhaps my condition was below her notice; or sin and condition so worked together that she would have nothing of me, and I could do nothing but look on with outward calm and hidden sourness while the Duke plied her with flatteries that soon grew to passionate avowals, and Carford paid deferential suit when his superior was not in the way. She triumphed in her success as girls will, blind to its perils as girls are; and Monmouth made no secret of his hopes of success, as he sat between Carford's stolid face and my downcast eyes.

"She's the loveliest creature in the world," he would cry. "Come, drink a toast to her!" I drank silently, while Carford led him on to unrestrained boasts and artfully fanned his passion.

At last—it was the evening of the day before Madame was to come—I met her where she could not avoid me, by the Constable's Tower, and alone. I took my courage in my hands and faced her, warning her of her peril in what delicate words I could find. Alas, I made nothing of it. A scornful jest at me and my righteousness (of which, said she, all London had been talking a little while back) was the first shot from her battery. The mention of the Duke's name brought a blush and a mischievous smile, as she answered:

"Shouldn't I make a fine Duchess, Mr Dale?"

"Ay, if he made you one," said I with gloomy bluntness.

"You insult me, sir," she cried, and the flush on her face deepened.

"Then I do in few words what his Grace does in many," I retorted.

I went about it like a dolt, I do not doubt. For she flew out at me, demanding in what esteem I held her, and in what her birth fell short of Anne Hyde's—"who is now Duchess of York, and in whose service I have the honour to be."

"Is that your pattern?" I asked. "Will the King interpose for you as he did for the daughter of Lord Clarendon?"

She tossed her head, answering:

"Perhaps so much interference will not be needed."

"And does my Lord Carford share these plans of yours?" I asked with a sneer.

The question touched her; she flushed again, but gave way not an inch.

"Lord Carford has done me much honour, as you know," said she, "but he wouldn't stand in my way here."

"Indeed he doesn't!" I cried. "Nor in his Grace's!"

"Have you done, sir?" says she most scornfully.

"I have done, madame," said I, and on she swept.

"Yet you shall come to no harm," I added to myself as I watched her proud free steps carry her away. She also, it seemed, had her dream; I hoped that no more than hurt pride and a heart for the moment sore would come of it. Yet if the flatteries of princes pleased, she was to be better pleased soon, and the Duke of Monmouth seem scarcely higher to her than Simon Dale.

Then came Madame in the morning from Dunkirk, escorted by the Vice-Admiral, and met above a mile from the coast by the King in his barge; the Duke of York, Prince Rupert, and my Duke (on whom, I attended) accompanying His Majesty. Madame seemed scarcely as beautiful as I had heard, although of a very high air and most admirable carriage and address; and my eyes, prone, I must confess, to seek the fairest face, wandered from hers to a lady who stood near, gifted with a delicate and alluring, yet childish, beauty, who gazed on the gay scene with innocent interest and a fresh enjoyment. Madame, having embraced her kinsmen, presented the lady to His Majesty by the name of Mademoiselle Louise Renee de Perrencourt de Querouaille (the name was much shortened by our common folk in later days), and the King kissed her hand, saying that he was rejoiced to see her—as indeed he seemed to be, if a man might judge by the time he spent in looking at her, and the carelessness with which he greeted the others in attendance on Madame.

"And these are all who come with you, sister?" he asked.

She answered him clearly, almost loudly:

"Except a gentleman who is to join me from Calais to-morrow, with messages from the King."

I heard no more, being forced to move away and leave the royal group alone. I had closely examined all who came. For in the presence of Madame I read *Je viens*, in our King's, *Tu viens*; but I saw none whose coming would make the tidings *Il vient* worthy of a special messenger to London. But there was a gentleman to arrive from Calais. I had enough curiosity to ask M. le Comte d'Albon, who (with his wife) accompanied Madame and stood by me on deck as we returned to land, who this gentleman might be.

"He is called M. de Perrencourt," the Count replied, "and is related remotely to the lady whom you saw with Madame."

I was disappointed, or rather checked. Was M. de Perrencourt so important that they wrote *Il vient* about him and sent the tidings to London?

After some time, when we were already coming near to shore, I observed Madame leave the King and go walking to and fro on the deck in company with Monmouth. He was very merry and she was very gracious; I amused myself with watching so handsome and well-matched a pair. I did not wonder that my Duke was in a mighty good temper, for, even had she been no Princess, her company was such as would please a man's pride and content his fancy. So I leant against the mast, thinking it a pity that they troubled their pretty heads with Dutch wars and the like tiresome matters, and were not content to ornament the world, leaving its rule to others. But presently I saw the Duke point towards me, and Madame's glance follow

Anthony Hope

his finger; he talked to her again and both laughed. Then, just as we came by the landing-stage, she laid her hand on his arm, as though in command. He laughed again, shrugging his shoulders, then raised his hand and beckoned to me. Now I, while watching, had been most diligent in seeming not to watch, and it needed a second and unmistakable signal from his Grace before I hastened up, hat in hand. Madame was laughing, and, as I came, I heard her say, "Yes, but I will speak to him." The Duke, with another shrug, bade me come near, and in due form presented me. She gave me her hand to kiss, saying with a smile that showed her white teeth,

"Sir, I asked to be shown the most honest man in Dover, and my cousin Monmouth has brought you to me."

I perceived that Monmouth, seeking how to entertain her, had not scrupled to press me into his service. This I could not resent, and since I saw that she was not too dull to be answered in the spirit of her address, I made her a low bow and said:

"His Grace, Madame, conceived you to mean in Dover Castle. The townsmen, I believe, are very honest."

"And you, though the most honest in the Castle, are not very honest?"

"I take what I find, Madame," I answered.

"So M. Colbert tells me," she said with a swift glance at me. "Yet it's not always worth taking."

"I keep it, in case it should become so," I answered, for I guessed that Colbert had told her of my encounter with M. de Fontelles; if that were so, she might have a curiosity to see me without the added inducement of Monmouth's malicious stories.

"Not if it be a secret? No man keeps that," she cried.

"He may, if he be not in love, Madame."

"But are you that monster, Mr Dale?" said she. "Shame on the ladies of my native land! Yet I'm glad! For, if you're not in love, you'll be more ready to serve me, perhaps."

"Mr Dale, Madame, is not incapable of falling in love," said Monmouth with a bow. "Don't try his virtue too much."

"He shall fall in love then with Louise," she cried.

Monmouth made a grimace, and the Duchess suddenly fell to laughing, as she glanced over her shoulder towards the King, who was busily engaged in conversation with Mlle. de Querouaille.

"Indeed, no!" I exclaimed with a fervour that I had not intended. No more of that part of Betty Nasroth's prophecy for me, and the King's attentions were already particular. "But if I can serve your Royal Highness, I am body and soul at your service."

"Body and soul?" said she. "Ah, you mean saving—what is it? Haven't you reservations?"

"His Grace has spared me nothing," said I, with a reproachful glance at Monmouth.

"The more told of you the better you're liked, Simon," said he kindly. "See, Madame, we're at the landing, and there's a crowd of loyal folk to greet you."

"I know the loyalty of the English well," said she in a low voice and with a curling lip. "They have their reservations like Mr Dale. Ah, you're speaking, Mr Dale?"

"To myself, Madame," I answered, bowing profoundly. She laughed, shaking her head at me, and passed on. I was glad she did not press me, for what I had said was, "Thank God," and I might likely enough have told a lie if she had put me to the question.

That night the King entertained his sister at a great banquet in the hall of the Castle, where there was much drinking of toasts, and much talk of the love that the King of France had for the King of England, and our King for the other King, and we for the French (whereas we hated them) and they for us (although they wasted no kindness on us); but at least every man got as much wine as he wanted, and many of them more than they had fair occasion for; and among these last I must count the Duke of Monmouth. For after the rest had risen from table he sat there still, calling Carford to join him, and even bidding me sit down by his side. Carford seemed in no haste to get him away, although very anxious to relieve me of my post behind his chair, but at last, by dint of upbraiding them both, I prevailed on Carford to offer his arm and the Duke to accept it, while I supported him on the other side. Thus we set out for his Grace's quarters, making a spectacle sad enough to a moralist, but too ordinary at Court for any remark to be excited by it. Carford insisted that he could take the Duke alone; I would not budge. My lord grew offensive, hinting of busybodies who came between the Duke and his friends. Pushed hard, I asked the Duke himself if I should leave him. He bade me stay, swearing that I was an honest fellow and no Papist, as were some he knew. I saw Carford start; his Grace saw nothing save the entrance of his chamber, and that not over-plainly. But we got him in, and into a seat, and the door shut. Then he called for more wine, and Carford at once brought it to him and pledged him once and again, Monmouth drinking deep.

"He's had more than he can carry already," I whispered. Carford turned straight to the Duke, crying, "Mr Dale here says that your Grace is drunk." He made nothing by the move, for the Duke answered good-humouredly,

"Truly I am drunk, but in the legs only, my good Simon. My head is clear, clear as daylight, or the—" He looked round cunningly, and caught each of us by the arm. "We're good Protestants here?" he asked with a would-be shrewd, wine-muddled glance.

"Sound and true, your Grace," said Carford. Then he whispered to me, "Indeed I think he's ill. Pray run for the King's physician, Mr Dale."

"Nay, he'd do well enough if he were alone with me. If you desire the physician's presence, my lord, he's easy to find."

I cared not a jot for Carford's anger, and was determined not to give ground. But we had no more time for quarrelling.

"I am as loyal—as loyal to my father as any man in the kingdom," said the Duke in maudlin confidence. "But you know what's afoot?"

"A new war with the Dutch, I'm told, sir," said I.

Anthony Hope

"A fig for the Dutch! Hush, we must speak low, there may be Papists about. There are some in the Castle, Carford. Hush, hush! Some say my uncle's one, some say the Secretary's one. Gentlemen, I—I say no more. Traitors have said that my father is—"

Carford interrupted him.

"Don't trouble your mind with these slanders, sir," he urged.

"I won't believe it. I'll stand by my father. But if the Duke of York—But I'll say no more." His head fell on his breast. But in a moment he sprang to his feet, crying, "But I'm a Protestant. Yes, and I'm the King's son." He caught Carford by the arm, whispering, "Not a word of it. I'm ready. We know what's afoot. We're loyal to the King; we must save him. But if we can't—if we can't, isn't there one who—who—?"

He lost his tongue for an instant. We stood looking at him, till he spoke again. "One who would be a Protestant King?"

He spoke the last words loud and fiercely; it was the final effort, and he sank back in his chair in a stupor. Carford gave a hasty glance at his face.

"I'll go for the physician," he cried. "His Grace may need blood-letting."

I stepped between him and the door as he advanced.

"His Grace needs nothing," said I, "except the discretion of his friends. We've heard foolish words that we should not have heard to-night, my lord."

"I am sure they're safe with you," he answered.

"And with you?" I retorted quickly.

He drew himself up haughtily.

"Stand aside, sir, and let me pass."

"Where are you going?"

"To fetch the physician. I'll answer none of your questions."

I could not stop him without an open brawl, and that I would not encounter, for it could lead only to my own expulsion. Yet I was sure that he would go straight to Arlington, and that every word the Duke had spoken would be carried to York, and perhaps to the King, before next morning. The King would be informed, if it were thought possible to prejudice him against his son; York, at least, would be warned of the mad scheme which was in the young Duke's head. I drew aside and with a surly bow let Carford pass. He returned my salutation with an equal economy of politeness, and left me alone with Monmouth, who had now sunk into a heavy and uneasy sleep. I roused him and got him to bed, glad to think that his unwary tongue would be silent for a few hours at least. Yet what he had said brought me nearer to the secret and the mystery. There was indeed more afoot than the war with the Dutch. There was, if I mistook not, a matter that touched the religion of the King. Monmouth, whose wits were sharp enough, had gained scent of it; the wits went out as the wine went in, and he blurted out what he suspected, robbing his knowledge of all value by betraying its possession. Our best knowledge lies in what we are not known to know.

Anthony Hope

I repaired, thoughtful and disturbed, to my own small chamber, next the Duke's; but the night was fine and I had no mind for sleep. I turned back again and made my way on to the wall, where it faces towards the sea. The wind was blowing fresh and the sound of the waves filled my ears. No doubt the same sound hid the noise of my feet, for when I came to the wall, I passed unheeded by three persons who stood in a group together. I knew all and made haste to pass by; the man was the King himself, the lady on his right was Mistress Barbara; in the third I recognised Madame's lady, Louise de Querouaille. I proceeded some distance farther till I was at the end of the wall nearest the sea. There I took my stand, looking not at the sea but covertly at the little group. Presently two of them moved away; the third curtseyed low but did not accompany them. When they were gone, she turned and leant on the parapet of the wall with clasped hands. Drawn by some impulse, I moved towards her. She was unconscious of my approach until I came quite near to her; then she turned on me a face stained with tears and pale with agitation and alarm. I stood before her, speechless, and she found no words in which to address me. I was too proud to force my company on her, and made as though to pass with a bow; but her face arrested me.

"What ails you, Mistress Barbara?" I cried impetuously. She smoothed her face to composure as she answered me:

"Nothing, sir." Then she added carelessly, "Unless it be that sometimes the King's conversation is too free for my liking."

"When you want me, I'm here," I said, answering not her words but the frightened look that there was in her eyes.

For an instant I seemed to see in her an impulse to trust me and to lay bare what troubled her. The feeling passed; her face regained its natural hue, and she said petulantly,

"Why, yes, it seems fated that you should always be there, Simon, yet Betty Nasroth said nothing of it."

"It may be well for you that I'm here," I answered hotly; for her scorn stirred me to say what I should have left unsaid.

I do not know how she would have answered, for at the moment we heard a shout from the watchman who stood looking over the sea. He hailed a boat that came prancing over the waves; a light answered his signal. Who came to the Castle? Barbara's eyes and mine sought the ship; we did not know the stranger, but he was expected; for a minute later Darrell ran quickly by us with an eager look on his face; with him was the Count d'Albon, who had come with Madame, and Depuy, the Duke of York's servant. They went by at the top of their speed and in visible excitement. Barbara forgot her anger and haughtyness in fresh girlish interest.

"Who can it be?" she cried, coming so near to me that her sleeve touched mine, and leaning over the wall towards where the ship's black hull was to be seen far below in the moonlight by the jetty.

"Doubtless it's the gentleman whom Madame expects," said I.

Many minutes passed, but through them Barbara and I stood silent side by side. Then the party came back through the gate, which had been opened for them. Depuy walked first, carrying a small trunk; two or three servants followed with more luggage; then came Darrell in company with a short man who walked with a bold and confident air. The rest passed us, and the last pair approached. Now Darrell saw Mistress Barbara and doffed his hat to her. The new-comer did the like and more; he halted immediately opposite to us and looked curiously at her, sparing a curious glance for me. I bowed; she waited unmoved until the gentleman said to Darrell,

"Pray present me."

"This, madame," said Darrell, in whose voice there was a ring of excitement and tremulous agitation, "is M. de Perrencourt, who has the honour of serving Her Royal Highness the Duchess. This lady, sir, is Mistress Barbara Quinton, maid of honour to the Duchess of York, and now in attendance on Madame."

Barbara made a curtsey, M. de Perrencourt bowed. His eyes were fixed on her face; he studied her openly and fearlessly, yet the regard was difficult to resent, it was so calm, assured, and dignified. It seemed beyond challenge, if not beyond reproach. I stood by in silence, angry at a scrutiny so prolonged, but without title to interfere.

"I trust, madame, that we shall be better acquainted," he said at last, and with a lingering look at her face passed on. I turned to her; she was gazing after him with eager eyes. My presence seemed forgotten; I would not remind her of it; I turned away in silence, and hastened after Darrell and his companion. The curve of the wall hid them from my sight, but I quickened my pace; I gained on them, for now I heard their steps ahead; I ran round the next corner, for I was ablaze with curiosity to see more of this man, who came at so strange an hour and yet was expected, who bore himself so loftily, and yet was but a gentleman-in-waiting as I was. Round the next corner I should come in sight of him. Round I went, and I came plump into the arms of my good friend Darrell, who stood there, squarely across the path!

"Whither away, Simon?" said he coldly.

I halted, stood still, looked him in the face. He met my gaze with a calm, self-controlled smile.

"Why," said I, "I'm on my way to bed, Darrell. Let me pass, I beg you."

"A moment later will serve," said he.

"Not a moment," I replied testily, and caught him by the arm. He was stiff as a rock, but I put out my strength and in another instant should have thrown him aside. But he cried in a loud angry voice,

"By the King's orders, no man is to pass this way."

Amazed, I fell back. But over his head, some twenty yards from us, I saw two men embracing one another warmly. Nobody else was near; Darrell's eyes were fixed on me, and his hand detained me in an eager grasp. But I looked hard at the pair there ahead of me; there was a cloud over the moon now, in a second it passed. The next moment the two had turned their backs and were walking off together. Darrell, seeing my fixed gaze, turned also. His face was pale, as if with excitement, but he spoke in cool, level tones.

"It's only M. Colbert greeting M. de Perrencourt," said he.

"Ah, of course!" I cried, turning to him with a smile. "But

where did M. Colbert get that Star?" For the glitter of the decoration had caught my eye, as it sparkled in the moonlight.

There was a pause before Darrell answered. Then he said,

"The King gave him his own Star to-night, in compliment to Madame."

And in truth M. Colbert wore that Star when he walked abroad next morning, and professed much gratitude for it to the King. I have wondered since whether he should not have thanked a humbler man. Had I not seen the Star on the breast of the gentleman who embraced M. de Perrencourt, should I have seen it on the breast of M. Colbert de Croissy? In truth I doubt it.

CHAPTER XII

THE DEFERENCE OF HIS GRACE THE DUKE

Certainly he had some strange ways, this M. de Perrencourt. It was not enough for him to arrive by night, nor to have his meeting with M. Colbert (whose Star Darrell made me observe most particularly next morning) guarded from intruding eyes by the King's own order. He shewed a predilection for darkness and was visible in the daytime only in Madame's apartment, or when she went to visit the King. The other French gentlemen and ladies manifested much curiosity concerning the town and the neighbourhood, and with Madame and the Duke of Monmouth at their head took part in many pleasant excursions. In a day or two the Queen also and the Duchess of York came from London, and the doings grew more gay and merry. But M. de Perrencourt was not to be tempted; no pastimes, no jaunts allured him; he did not put his foot outside the walls of the Castle, and was little seen inside it. I myself did not set eyes on him for two days after my first sight of him; but after that I beheld him fairly often, and the more I saw him the more I wondered. Of a truth his retiring behaviour was dictated by no want of assurance nor by undue modesty; he was not abashed in the presence of the great and bore himself as composedly before the King as in the presence of a lackey. It was plain, too, that he enjoyed Madame's confidence in no common degree, for when affairs of State were discussed and all withdrew saving Madame, her brothers and the Secretary (even the Duke of Monmouth not being admitted), the last we saw as we made our bows and backed out of the doorway would be M. de Perrencourt standing in an easy and unconstrained attitude behind Madame's chair and manifesting no overpowering sense of the signal honour paid to him by the permission to remain. As may be supposed, a theory sprang up to account for the curious regard this gentleman commanded; it was put about (some said that Lord Arlington himself gave his authority for the report) that M. de Perrencourt was legal guardian to his cousin Mlle. de Querouaille, and that the King had discovered special reasons for conciliating the gentleman by every means, and took as much pains to please him as to gain favour with the lady herself. Here was a good reason for M. de Perrencourt's distinguished treatment, and no less for the composure and calm with which M. de Perrencourt accepted it. To my mind, however, the manner of M. de Perrencourt's arrival and the incident of M. Colbert's Star found scarcely a sufficient explanation in this ingenious conjecture; yet the story, thus circulated, was generally accepted and served its office of satisfying curiosity and blunting question well enough.

Again (for my curiosity would not be satisfied, nor the edge of my questioning be turned)—what had the Duke of Monmouth to gain from M. de Perrencourt? Something it seemed, or his conduct was most mysterious. He cared nothing for Mlle. de Querouaille, and I could not suppose that the mere desire to please his father would have weighed with him so strongly as to make him to all appearance the humble servant of this French gentleman. The thing was brought home most forcibly to my mind on the third evening after M. de Perrencourt's arrival. A private conference was held and lasted some hours; outside the closed doors we all paced to and fro, hearing nothing save now and then Madame's clear voice, raised, as it seemed, in exhortation or persuasion. The Duke, who was glad enough to escape the tedium of State affairs but at the same time visibly annoyed at his exclusion, sauntered listlessly up and down, speaking to nobody. Perceiving that he did not desire my company, I withdrew to a distance, and, having seated myself in a retired corner, was soon lost in consideration of my own fortunes past and to come. The hour grew late; the gentlemen and ladies of the Court, having offered and accepted compliments and gallantries till invention and complaisance alike were exhausted, dropped off one by one, in search of supper, wine, or rest. I sat on in my corner. Nothing was to be heard save the occasional voices of the two musketeers on guard on the steps leading from the second storey of the keep to the State apartments. I knew that I must move soon, for at night the gate on the stairs was shut. It was another of the peculiar facts about M. de Perrencourt that he alone of the gentlemen-in-waiting had been lodged within the precincts of the royal quarters, occupying an apartment next to the Duke of York, who had his sister Madame for his neighbour on the other side. The prolonged conference was taking place in the King's cabinet farther along the passage.

Suddenly I heard steps on the stairs, the word of the night was asked, and Monmouth's voice made answer "Saint Denis"; for just now everything was French in compliment to Madame. The steps continued to ascend; the light in the corridor was very dim, but a moment later I perceived Monmouth and Carford. Carford's arm was through his Grace's, and he seemed to be endeavouring to restrain him. Monmouth shook him off with a laugh and an oath.

"I'm not going to listen," he cried. "Why should I listen? Do I want to hear the King praying to the Virgin?"

"Silence, for God's sake, silence, your Grace," implored Carford.

"That's what he does, isn't it? He, and the Queen's Chaplain, and the—"

"Pray, sir!"

"And our good M. de Perrencourt, then?" He burst into a bitter laugh as he mentioned the gentleman's name.

I had heard more than was meant for my ears, and what was enough (if I may use a distinction drawn by my old friend the Vicar) for my understanding. I was in doubt whether to declare my presence or not. Had Monmouth been alone, I would have shown myself directly, but I did not wish Carford to be aware that I had overheard so much. I sat still a moment longer in hesitation; then I uttered a loud yawn, groaned, stretched myself, rose to my feet, and gave a sudden and very obvious start, as I let my eyes fall on the Duke.

"Why, Simon," he cried, "what brings you here?"

"I thought your Grace was in the King's cabinet," I answered.

"But you knew that I left them some hours since."

"Yes, but having lost sight of your Grace, I supposed that you'd returned, and while waiting for you I fell asleep."

My explanation abundantly satisfied the Duke; Carford maintained a wary silence.

"We're after other game than conferences to-night," said Monmouth, laughing again. "Go down to the hall and wait there for me, Simon. My lord and I are going to pay a visit to the ladies of Madame and the Duchess of York."

I saw that he was merry with wine; Carford had been drinking too, but he grew only more glum and malicious with his liquor. Neither their state nor the hour seemed fitted for the visit the Duke spoke of, but I was helpless, and with a bow took my way down the stairs to the hall below, where I sat down on the steps that led up to one of the loop-holes. A great chair, standing by the wall, served to hide me from observation. For a few moments nothing occurred. Then I heard a loud burst of laughter from above. Feet came running down the steps into the hall, and a girl in a white dress darted across the floor. I heard her laugh, and knew that she was Barbara Quinton. An instant later came Monmouth hot on her heels, and imploring her in extravagant words not to be so cruel and heartless as to fly from him. But where was Carford? I could only suppose that my lord had the discretion to stay behind when the Duke of Monmouth desired to speak with the lady whom my lord sought for his wife.

In my humble judgment, a very fine, large, and subtle volume might be composed on the canons of eaves-dropping—when a man may listen, when he may not, and for how long he may, to what end, for what motives, in what causes, and on what provocations. It may be that the Roman Divines, who, as I understand, are greatly adept in the science of casuistry, have accomplished already the task I indicate. I know not; at least I have nowhere encountered the result of their labours. But now I sat still behind the great chair and listened without doubt or hesitation. Yet how long I could have controlled myself I know not, for his Grace made light of scruples that night and set bounds at nought. At first Mistress Barbara was merry with him, fencing and parrying, in confidence that he would use no roughness nor an undue vehemence. But on he went; and presently a note of alarm sounded in her voice as she prayed him to suffer her to depart and return to the Duchess, who must have need of her.

"Nay, I won't let you go, sweet mistress. Rather, I can't let you go."

"Indeed, sir, I must go," she said. "Come, I will call my Lord Carford, to aid me in persuading your Grace."

He laughed at the suggestion that a call for Carford would hinder him.

"He won't come," he said; "and if he came, he would be my ally, not yours."

She answered now haughtily and coldly:

"Sir, Lord Carford is a suitor for my hand. It is in your Grace's knowledge that he is."

"But he thinks a hand none the worse because I've kissed it," retorted Monmouth. "You don't know how amiable a husband you're to have, Mistress Barbara."

I was on my feet now, and, peering round the chair which hid me from them, I could see her standing against the wall, with Monmouth opposite to her. He offered to seize her hand, but she drew it away sharply. With a laugh he stepped nearer to her. A slight sound caught my ear, and, turning my head, I saw Carford on the lowest step of the stairs; he was looking at the pair, and a moment later stepped backwards, till he was almost hidden from my sight, though I could still make out the shape of his figure. A cry of triumph from Monmouth echoed low but intense through the hall; he had caught the elusive hand and was kissing it passionately. Barbara stood still and stiff. The Duke, keeping her hand still in his, said mockingly:

"You pretty fool, would you refuse fortune? Hark, madame, I am a King's son."

I saw no movement in her, but the light was dim. He went on, lowering his voice a little, yet not much.

"And I may be a King; stranger things have come to pass. Wouldn't you like to be a Queen?" He laughed as he put the question; he lacked the care or the cunning to make even a show of honesty.

"Let me go," I heard her whisper in a strained, timid voice.

"Well, for to-night you shall go, sweetheart, but not without a kiss, I swear."

She was frightened now and sought to propitiate him, saying gently and with attempted lightness,

"Your Grace has my hand prisoner. You can work your will on it."

"Your hand! I mean your lips this time," he cried in audacious insolence. He came nearer to her, his arm crept round her waist. I had endured what I could, yes, and as long as I could; for I was persuaded that I could serve her better by leaving her unaided for the moment. But my limit was reached; I stepped out from behind the chair. But in an instant I was back again. Monmouth had paused; in one hand he held Barbara's hand, the other rested on her girdle, but he turned his head and looked at the stairs. Voices had come from there; he had heard them as I had, as Barbara had.

"You can't pass out," had come in a blustering tone from Carford.

"Stand aside, sir," was the answer in a calm, imperative voice.

Carford hesitated for a single instant, then he seemed to shrink away, making himself small and leaving free passage for a man who came down the steps and walked confidently and briskly across the hall towards where the Duke stood with Barbara.

Above us, at the top of the stairs, there were the sound of voices and the tread of feet. The conference was broken up and the parties to it were talking in the passage on their way to regain their own apartments. I paid no heed to them; my eyes were fixed on the intruder who came so boldly and unabashed up to the Duke. I knew him now; he was M. de Perrencourt, Madame's gentleman.

Without wavering or pausing, straight he walked. Monmouth seemed turned to stone; I could see his face set and rigid, although light failed me to catch that look in the eyes by which you may best know a man's mood. Not a sound or a motion came from Carford. Barbara herself was stiff and still, her regard bent on M. de Perrencourt. He stood now directly over against her and Monmouth; it seemed long before he spoke. Indeed, I had looked for

Monmouth's voice first, for an oath of vexation at the interruption, for a curse on the intruder and a haughty order to him to be gone and not interfere with what concerned his betters. No such word, nor any words, issued from the mouth of the Duke. And still M. de Perrencourt was silent. Carford stole covertly from the steps nearer to the group until, gliding across the hall, he was almost at the Frenchman's elbow. Still M. de Perrencourt was silent.

Slowly and reluctantly, as though in deference to an order that he loathed but dared not disobey, Monmouth drew his arm away; he loosed Barbara's hand, she drew back, leaning against the wall; the Duke stood with his arms by his side, looking at the man who interrupted his sport and seemed to have power to control his will. Then, at last, in crisp, curt, ungracious tones, M. de Perrencourt spoke.

"I thank you, Monsieur le Duc," said he. "I was sure that you would perceive your error soon. This is not the lady you supposed, this is Mistress Quinton. I desire to speak with her, pray give me leave."

The King would not have spoken in this style to his pampered son, and the Duke of York himself dared not have done it. But no touch of uneasiness or self-distrust appeared in M. de Perrencourt's smooth cutting speech. Truly he was high in Madame's confidence, and, likely enough, a great man in his own country; but, on my life, I looked to see the hot-tempered Duke strike him across the face. Even I, who had been about to interfere myself, by some odd momentary turn of feeling resented the insolence with which Monmouth was assailed. Would he not resent it much more for himself? No. For an instant I heard his quick breathing, the breathing of a man who fights anger, holding it under with great labour and

Anthony Hope

struggling. Then he spoke; in his voice also there was passion hard held.

"Here, sir, and everywhere," he said, "you have only to command to be obeyed." Slowly he bent his head low, the gesture matching the humility of his words, while it emphasised their unwillingness.

The strange submission won no praise. M. de Perrencourt did not accord the speech so much courtesy as lay in an answer. His silent slight bow was all his acknowledgement; he stood there waiting for his command to be obeyed.

Monmouth turned once towards Barbara, but his eyes came back to M. de Perrencourt. Carford advanced to him and offered his arm. The Duke laid his hand on his friend's shoulder. For a moment they stood still thus, then both bowed low to M. de Perrencourt, who answered with another of his slight inclinations of the head. They turned and walked out of the hall, the Duke seeming almost to stagger and to lean on Carford, as though to steady his steps. As they went they passed within two yards of me, and I saw Monmouth's face pale with rage. With a long indrawing of my breath I drew back into the shadow of my shelter. They passed, the hall was empty save for myself and the two who stood there by the wall.

I had no thought now of justifying my part of eavesdropper. Scruples were drowned in excitement; keen interest bound me to my place with chains of iron. My brain was full of previous suspicion thrice magnified; all that was mysterious in this man came back to me; the message I had surprised at Canterbury ran echoing through my head again and again. Yet I bent myself to the task of listening, resolute to catch every word. Alas, my efforts were in vain! M. de Perrencourt was of different clay from his Grace the Duke. He was indeed speaking now, but so low and warily that no more than a gentle murmur reached my ears. Nor did his gestures aid; they were as far from Monmouth's jovial violence as his tones from the Duke's reckless exclaiming. He was urgent but courteous, most insistent yet most deferential. Monmouth claimed and challenged, M. de Perrencourt seemed to beseech and woo. Yet he asked as though none could refuse, and his prayer presumed a favourable answer. Barbara listened in quiet; I could not tell whether fear alone bound her, or whether the soft courtly voice bred fascination also. I was half-mad that I could not hear, and had much ado not to rush out, unprovoked, and defy the man before whom my master had bowed almost to the ground, beaten and dismayed.

At last she spoke a few hurried imploring words.

"No, no," she panted. "No; pray leave me. No."

M. de Perrencourt answered gently and beseechingly,

"Nay, say 'Not yet,' madame."

They were silent again, he seeming to regard her intently. Suddenly she covered her face with her hands; yet, dropping her hands almost immediately, she set her eyes on his; I saw him shake his head.

"For to-night, then, good-night, fairest lady," said he. He took her hand and kissed it lightly, bowing very low and respectfully, she looking down at him as he stooped. Then he drew away from her, bowing again and repeating again,

Anthony Hope

"For to-night, good-night."

With this he turned towards the stairs, crossing the hall with the same brisk, confident tread that had marked his entry. He left her, but it looked as though she were indulged, not he defeated. At the lowest step he paused, turned, bowed low again. This time she answered with a deep and sweeping curtsey. Then he was gone, and she was leaning by the wall again, her face buried in her hands. I heard her sob, and her broken words reached me:

"What shall I do? Oh, what shall I do?"

At once I stepped out from the hiding-place that had shown me such strange things, and, crossing to her, hat in hand, answered her sad desolate question.

"Why, trust in your friends, Mistress Barbara," said I cheerily. "What else can any lady do?"

"Simon!" she cried eagerly, and as I thought gladly; for her hand flew out to mine. "You, here?"

"And at your service always," said I.

"But have you been here? Where did you come from?"

"Why, from across the hall, behind the chair there," I answered. "I've been there a long while back. His Grace told me to wait in the hall, and in the hall I waited, though the Duke, having other things to think of, forgot both his order and his servant."

"Then you heard?" she asked in a whisper.

"All, I think, that the Duke said. Lord Carford said

nothing. I was about to interrupt his Grace when the task was better performed for me. I think, madame, you owe some thanks to M. de Perrencourt."

"You heard what he said?"

"The last few words only," I answered regretfully.

She looked at me for an instant, and then said with a dreary little smile,

"I'm to be grateful to M. de Perrencourt?"

"I know no other man who could or would have rid you of the Duke so finely. Besides, he appeared to treat you with much courtesy."

"Courtesy, yes!" she cried, but seemed to check herself. She was still in great agitation, and a moment later she covered her face and I heard her sob again.

"Come, take heart," said I. "The Duke's a great man, of course; but no harm shall come to you, Mistress Barbara. Your father bade me have my services in readiness for you, and although I didn't need his order as a spur, I may pray leave to use it as an excuse for thrusting myself on you."

"Indeed I—I'm glad to see you, Simon. But what shall I do? Ah, Heaven, why did I ever come to this place?"

"That can be mended by leaving it, madame."

"But how? How can I leave it?" she asked despairingly.

"The Duchess will grant you leave."

"Without the King's consent?"

"But won't the King consent? Madame will ask for you; she's kind."

"Madame won't ask for me; nobody will ask for me."

"Then if leave be impossible, we must go without leave, if you speak the word."

"Ah, you don't know," she said sadly. Then she caught my hand again and whispered hurriedly and fearfully: "I'm afraid, Simon. I—I fear him. What can I do? How can I resist? They can do what they will with me, what can I do? If I weep, they laugh; if I try to laugh, they take it for consent. What can I do?"

There is nothing that so binds a man to a woman as to feel her hand seeking his in weakness and appeal. I had thought that one day so Barbara's might seek mine and I should exult in it, nay, might even let her perceive my triumph. The thing I had dreamed of was come, but where was my exultation? There was a choking in my throat and I swallowed twice before I contrived to answer:

"What can we do, you mean, Mistress Barbara."

"Alas, alas," she cried, between tears and laughter, "what can we—even we—do, Simon?"

I noticed that she called me Simon, as in the old days before my apostacy and great offence. I was glad of it, for if I was to be of service to her we must be friends. Suddenly she said,

"You know what it means—I can't tell you; you know?"

"Aye, I know," said I, "none better. But the Duke shan't have his way."

"The Duke? If it were only the Duke—Ah!" She stopped, a new alarm in her eyes. She searched my face eagerly. Of deliberate purpose I set it to an immutable stolidity.

"Already he's very docile," said I. "See how M. de Perrencourt turned and twisted him, and sent him off crestfallen."

She laid her hand on my arm.

"If I might tell you," she said, "a thing that few know here; none but the King and his near kindred and one or two more."

"But how came you to know of it?" I interrupted.

"I—I also came to know it," she murmured.

"There are many ways of coming to know a thing," said I. "One is by being told; another, madame, is by finding out. Certainly it was amazing how M. de Perrencourt dealt with his Grace; ay, and with my Lord Carford, who shrank out of his path as though he had been—a King." I let my tones give the last word full effect.

"Simon," she whispered in eagerness mingled with alarm, "Simon, what are you saying? Silence for your life!"

"My life, madame, is rooted too deep for a syllable to tear it up. I said only 'as though he had been a king.' Tell me why M. Colbert wears the King's Star. Was it because somebody saw a gentleman wearing the King's Star embrace and kiss M. de Perrencourt the night that he arrived?"

"It was you?"

"It was I, madame. Tell me on whose account three messengers went to London, carrying the words '*Il vient*.'"

She was hanging to my arm now, full of eagerness.

"And tell me now what M. de Perrencourt said to you. A plague on him, he spoke so low that I couldn't hear!"

A blush swept over her face; her eyes, losing the fire of excitement, dropped in confusion to the ground.

"I can't tell you," she murmured.

"Yet I know," said I. "And if you'll trust me, madame—"

"Ah, Simon, you know I trust you."

"Yet you were angry with me."

"Not angry—I had no right—I mean I had no cause to be angry. I—I was grieved."

"You need be grieved no longer, madame."

"Poor Simon!" said she very gently. I felt the lightest pressure on my hand, the touch of two slim fingers, speaking of sympathy and comradeship.

"By God, I'll bring you safe out of it," I cried.

"But how, how? Simon, I fear that he has—"

"The Duke?"

"No, the—the other—M. de Perrencourt; he has set his heart on—on what he told me."

"A man may set his heart on a thing and yet not win it," said I grimly.

"Yes, a man—yes, Simon, I know; a man may—"

"Ay, and even a—"

"Hush, hush! If you were overheard—your life wouldn't be safe if you were overheard."

"What do I care?"

"But I care!" she cried, and added very hastily, "I'm selfish. I care, because I want your help."

"You shall have it. Against the Duke of Monmouth, and against the—"

"Ah, be careful!"

I would not be careful. My blood was up. My voice was loud and bold as I gave to M. de Perrencourt the name that was his, the name by which the frightened lord and the cowed Duke knew him, the name that gave him entrance to those inmost secret conferences, and yet kept him himself hidden and half a prisoner in the Castle. The secret was no secret to me now.

"Against the Duke of Monmouth," said I sturdily, "and also, if need be, against the King of France."

Barbara caught at my arm in alarm. I laughed, till I saw her finger point warily over my shoulder. With a start I turned and saw a man coming down the steps. In the dim light the bright Star gleamed on his breast. He was M. Colbert de Croissy. He stood on the lowest step, peering at us through the gloom.

"Who speaks of the King of France here?" he said suspiciously.

"I, Simon Dale, gentleman-in-waiting to the Duke of Monmouth, at your Excellency's service," I answered, advancing towards him and making my bow.

"What have you to say of my master?" he demanded.

For a moment I was at a loss; for although my heart was full of things that I should have taken much pleasure in saying concerning His Majesty, they were none of them acceptable to the ears of His Majesty's Envoy. I stood, looking at Colbert, and my eyes fell on the Star that he wore. I knew that I committed an imprudence, but for the life of me I could not withstand the temptation. I made another bow, and, smiling easily, answered M. Colbert.

"I was remarking, sir," said I, "that the compliment paid to you by the King of England in bestowing on you the Star from His Majesty's own breast, could not fail to cause much gratification to the King of France."

He looked me hard in the eyes, but his eyes fell to the ground before mine. I warrant he took nothing by his searching glance, and did well to give up the conflict. Without a word, and with a stiff little bow, he passed on his way to the hall. The moment he was gone, Barbara was by me. Her face was alight with merriment.

"Oh, Simon, Simon!" she whispered reprovingly. "But I love you for it!" And she was gone up the stairs like a flitting moonbeam.

Upon this, having my head full and to spare of many matters, and my heart beating quick with more than one emotion, I thought my bed the best and safest place for me, and repaired to it without delay.

"But I'll have some conversation with M. de Perrencourt to-morrow," said I, as I turned on my pillow and sought to sleep.

CHAPTER XIII

THE MEED OF CURIOSITY

The next morning my exaltation had gone. I woke a prey
to despondency and sickness of soul. Not only did
difficulty loom large, and failure seem inevitable, but a
disgust for all that surrounded me seized on my mind,
displacing the zest of adventure and the excitement of
enterprise. But let me not set my virtue too high. It is
better to be plain. Old maxims of morality, and a standard
of right acknowledged by all but observed by none, have
little power over a young man's hot blood; to be stirred to
indignation, he must see the wrong threaten one he
respects, touch one he loves, or menace his own honour
and pride. I had supported the scandals of this Court, of
which I made a humble part, with shrugs, smiles, and acid
jests; I had felt no dislike for the chief actors, and no
horror at the things they did or attempted; nay, for one of
them, who might seem to sum up in her own person the
worst of all that was to be urged against King and Court, I
had cherished a desperate love that bred even in death an
obstinate and longing memory. Now a change had come
over me; I seemed to see no longer through my own
careless eyes, but with the shamed and terrified vision of
the girl who, cast into this furnace, caught at my hand as
offering her the sole chance to pass unscathed through the

fire. They were using her in their schemes, she was to be sacrificed; first she had been chosen as the lure with which to draw forth Monmouth's ambitions from their lair, and reveal them to the spying eyes of York and his tool Carford; if that plan were changed now, she would be no better for the change. The King would and could refuse this M. de Perrencourt (I laughed bitterly as I muttered his name) nothing, however great; without a thought he would fling the girl to him, if the all-powerful finger were raised to ask for her. Charles would think himself well paid by his brother king's complaisance towards his own inclination. Doubtless there were great bargains of policy a-making here in the Castle, and the nature of them I made shift to guess. What was it to throw in a trifle on either side, barter Barbara Quinton against the French lady, and content two Princes at a price so low as the dishonour of two ladies? That was the game; otherwise, whence came M. de Perrencourt's court and Monmouth's deference? The King saw eye to eye with M. de Perrencourt, and the King's son did not venture to thwart him. What matter that men spoke of other loves which the French King had? The gallants of Paris might think us in England rude and ignorant, but at least we had learnt that a large heart was a prerogative of royalty which even the Parliament dared not question. With a new loathing I loathed it all, for it seemed now to lay aside its trappings of pomp and brilliancy, of jest and wit, and display itself before me in ugly nakedness, all unashamed. In sudden frenzy I sat up in my bed, crying, "Heaven will find a way!" For surely heaven could find one, where the devil found so many! Ah, righteous wert thou, Simon Dale, so soon as unrighteousness hurt thee! But Phineas Tate might have preached until the end of time.

Earlier than usual by an hour Jonah Wall came up from the town where he was lodged, but he found me up and dressed, eager to act, ready for what might chance. I had seen little of the fellow lately, calling on him for necessary services only, and ridding myself of his sombre company as quickly as I could. Yet I looked on him to-day with more consideration; his was a repulsive form of righteousness, grim and gloomy, but it was righteousness, or seemed such to me against the background of iniquity which threw it up in strong relief. I spoke to him kindly, but taking no heed of my advances he came straight up to me and said brusquely: "The woman who came to your lodging in London is here in Dover. She bids you be silent and come quickly. I can lead you."

I started and stared at him. I had set "Finis" to that chapter; was fate minded to overrule me and write more? Strange also that Jonah Wall should play Mercury!

"She here in Dover? For what?" I asked as calmly as I could.

"I don't doubt, for sin," he answered uncompromisingly.

"Yet you can lead me to her house?" said I with a smile.

"I can," said he, in sour disregard of my hinted banter.

"I won't go," I declared.

"The matter concerns you, she said, and might concern another."

It was early, the Court would not be moving for two hours yet. I could go and come, and thereby lose no opportunity. Curiosity led me on, and with it the attraction which still draws us to those we have loved, though the love be gone and more pain than pleasure wait on our visiting. In ten minutes I was following Jonah down the cliff, and plunged thence into a narrow street that ran curling and curving towards the sea. Jonah held on quickly, and without hesitation, until we reached a confined alley, and came to a halt before a mean house.

"She's here," said Jonah, pointing to the door and twisting his face as though he was swallowing something nauseous.

I could not doubt of her presence, for I heard her voice singing gaily from within. My heart beat quick, and I had above half a mind not to enter. But she had seen us, and herself flung the door open wide. She lodged on the ground floor; and, in obedience to her beckoning finger, I entered a small room. Lodging was hard to be had in Dover now, and the apartment served her (as the bed, carelessly covered with a curtain, showed) for sleeping and living. I did not notice what became of Jonah, but sat down, puzzled and awkward, in a crazy chair.

"What brings you here?" I blurted out, fixing my eyes on her, as she stood opposite to me, smiling and swaying to and fro a little, with her hands on her hips.

"Even what brings you. My business," she answered. "If you ask more, the King's invitation. Does that grieve you, Simon?"

"No, madame," said I.

"A little, still a little, Simon? Be consoled! The King invited me, but he hasn't come to see me. There lies my business. Why hasn't he come to see me? I hear certain things, but my eyes, though they are counted good if not large, can't pierce the walls of the Castle yonder, and my

Anthony Hope

poor feet aren't fit to pass its threshold."

"You needn't grieve for that," said I sullenly.

"Yet some things I know. As that a French lady is there. Of what appearance is she, Simon?"

"She is very pretty, so far as I've looked at her."

"Ah, and you've a discriminating glance, haven't you? Will she stay long?"

"They say Madame will be here for ten or fourteen days yet."

"And the French lady goes when Madame goes?"

"I don't know as to that."

"Why, nor I neither." She paused an instant. "You don't love Lord Carford?" Her question came abruptly and unlooked for.

"I don't know your meaning." What concern had Carford with the French lady?

"I think you are in the way to learn it. Love makes men quick, doesn't it? Yes, since you ask (your eyes asked), why, I'll confess that I'm a little sorry that you fall in love again. But that by the way. Simon, neither do I love this French lady."

Had it not been for that morning's mood of mine, she would have won on me again, and all my resolutions gone for naught. But she, not knowing the working of my mind, took no pains to hide or to soften what repelled me in her. I had seen it before, and yet loved; to her it would seem strange that because a man saw, he should not love. I found myself sorry for her, with a new and pitiful grief, but passion did not rise in me. And concerning my pity I held my tongue; she would have only wonder and mockery for it. But I think she was vexed to see me so unmoved; it irks a woman to lose a man, however little she may have prized him when he was her own. Nor do I mean to say that we are different from their sex in that; it is, I take it, nature in woman and man alike.

"At least we're friends, Simon," she said with a laugh. "And at least we're Protestants." She laughed again. I looked up with a questioning glance. "And at least we both hate the French," she continued.

"It's true; I have no love for them. What then? What can we do?"

She looked round cautiously, and, coming a little nearer to me, whispered:

"Late last night I had a visitor, one who doesn't love me greatly. What does that matter? We row now in the same boat. I speak of the Duke of Buckingham."

"He is reconciled to my Lord Arlington by Madame's good offices," said I. For so the story ran in the Castle.

"Why, yes, he's reconciled to Arlington as the dog to the cat when their master is by. Now there's a thing that the Duke suspects; and there's another thing that he knows. He suspects that this treaty touches more than war with the Dutch; though that I hate, for war swallows the King's money like a well."

"Some passes the mouth of the well, if report speaks true," I observed.

"Peace, peace! Simon, the treaty touches more."

"A man need not be Duke nor Minister to suspect that," said I.

"Ah, you suspect? The King's religion?" she whispered.

I nodded; the secret was no surprise to me, though I had not known whether Buckingham were in it.

"And what does the Duke of Buckingham know?" I asked.

"Why, that the King sometimes listens to a woman's counsel," said she, nodding her head and smiling very wisely.

"Prodigious sagacity!" I cried. "You told him that, may be?"

"Indeed, he had learnt it before my day, Master Simon. Therefore, should the King turn Catholic, he will be a better Catholic for the society of a Catholic lady. Now this Madame—how do you name her?"

"Mlle. de Querouaille?"

"Aye. She is a most devout Catholic. Indeed, her devotion to her religion knows no bounds. It's like mine to the King. Don't frown, Simon. Loyalty is a virtue."

"And piety also, by the same rule, and in the same unstinted measure?" I asked bitterly.

"Beyond doubt, sir. But the French King has sent word from Calais—"

"Oh, from Calais! The Duke revealed that to you?" I asked with a smile I could not smother. There was a limit then to the Duke's confidence in his ally; for the Duke had been at Paris and could be no stranger to M. de Perrencourt.

"Yes, he told me all. The King of France has sent word from Calais, where he awaits the signing of the treaty, that the loss of this Madame Querouaille would rob his Court of beauty, and he cannot be so bereft. And Madame, the Duke says, swears she can't be robbed of her fairest Maid of Honour ('tis a good name that, on my life) and left desolate. But Madame has seen one who might make up the loss, and the King of France, having studied the lady's picture, thinks the same. In fine, Simon, our King feels that he can't be a good Catholic without the counsels of Madame Querouaille, and the French King feels that he must by all means convert and save so fair a lady as—is the name on your tongue, nay, is it in your heart, Simon?"

"I know whom you mean," I answered, for her revelation came to no more than what I had scented out for myself. "But what says Buckingham to this?"

"Why, that the King mustn't have his way lest he should thereby be confirmed in his Popish inclinations. The Duke is Protestant, as you are—and as I am, so please you."

"Can he hinder it?"

"Aye, if he can hinder the French King from having his way. And for this purpose his Grace has need of certain things."

"Do you carry a message from him to me?"

"I did but say that I knew a gentleman who might supply his needs. They are four; a heart, a head, a hand, and perhaps a sword."

"All men have them, then."

"The first true, the second long, the third strong, and the fourth ready."

"I fear then that I haven't all of them."

"And for reward—"

"I know. His life, if he can come off with it."

Nell burst out laughing.

"He didn't say that, but it may well reckon up to much that figure," she admitted. "You'll think of it, Simon?"

"Think of it? I! Not I!"

"You won't?"

"Or I mightn't attempt it."

"Ah! You will attempt it?"

"Of a certainty."

"You're very ready. Is it all honesty?"

"Is ever anything all honesty, madame—saving your devotion to the King?"

"And the French lady's to her religion?" laughed Nell. "On my soul, I think the picture that the King of France saw was a fair one. Have you looked on it, Simon?"

"On my life I don't love her."

"On my life you will."

"You seek to stop me by that prophecy?"

"I don't care whom you love," said she. Then her face broke into smiles. "What liars women are!" she cried. "Yes, I do care; not enough to grow wrinkled, but enough to wish I hadn't grown half a lady and could—"

"You stop?"

"Could—could—could slap your face, Simon."

"It would be a light infliction after breaking a man's heart," said I, turning my cheek to her and beckoning with my hand.

"You should have a revenge on my face; not in kind, but in kindness. I can't strike a man who won't hit back." She laughed at me with all her old enticing gaiety.

I had almost sealed the bargain; she was so roguish and so pretty. Had we met first then, it is very likely she would have made the offer, and very certain that I should have taken it. But there had been other days; I sighed.

"I loved you too well once to kiss you now, mistress," said I,

"You're mighty strange at times, Simon," said she, sighing

Anthony Hope

also, and lifting her brows. "Now, I'd as lief kiss a man I had loved as any other."

"Or slap his face?"

"If I'd never cared to kiss, I'd never care for the other either. You rise?"

"Why, yes. I have my commission, haven't I?"

"I give you this one also, and yet you keep it?"

"Is that slight not yet forgiven?"

"All is forgiven and all is forgotten—nearly, Simon."

At this instant—and since man is human, woman persistent, and courtesy imperative, I did not quarrel with the interruption—a sound came from the room above, strange in a house where Nell lived (if she will pardon so much candour), but oddly familiar to me. I held up my hand and listened. Nell's rippling laugh broke in.

"Plague on him!" she cried. "Yes, he's here. Of a truth he's resolute to convert me, and the fool amuses me."

"Phineas Tate!" I exclaimed, amazed; for beyond doubt his was the voice. I could tell his intonation of a penitential psalm among a thousand. I had heard it in no other key.

"You didn't know? Yet that other fool, your servant, is always with him. They've been closeted together for two hours at a time."

"Psalm-singing?"

"Now and again. They're often quiet too."

"He preaches to you?"

"Only a little; when we chance to meet at the door he gives me a curse and promises a blessing; no more."

"It's very little to come to Dover for."

"You would have come farther for less of my company once, sir."

It was true, but it did not solve my wonder at the presence of Phineas Tate. What brought the fellow? Had he too sniffed out something of what was afoot and come to fight for his religion, even as Louise de Querouaille fought for hers, though in a most different fashion?

I had reached the door of the room and was in the passage. Nell came to the threshold and stood there smiling. I had asked no more questions and made no conditions; I knew that Buckingham must not show himself in the matter, and that all was left to me, heart, head, hand, sword, and also that same reward, if I were so lucky as to come by it. I waited for a moment, half expecting that Phineas, hearing my voice, would show himself, but he did not appear. Nell waved her hand to me; I bowed and took my leave, turning my steps back towards the Castle. The Court would be awake, and whether on my own account or for my new commission's sake I must be there.

I had not mounted far before I heard a puffing and blowing behind. The sound proved to come from Jonah Wall, who was toiling after me, laden with a large basket. I had no eagerness for Jonah's society, but rejoiced to see

Anthony Hope

the basket; for my private store of food and wine had run low, and if a man is to find out what he wants to know, it is well for him to have a pasty and a bottle ready for those who can help him.

"What have you there?" I called, waiting for him to overtake me.

He explained that he had been making purchases in the town and I praised his zeal. Then I asked him suddenly:

"And have you visited your friend Mr Tate?"

As I live, the fellow went suddenly pale, and the bottles clinked in his basket from the shaking of his hand. Yet I spoke mildly enough.

"I—I have seen him but once or twice, sir, since I learnt that he was in the town. I thought you did not wish me to see him."

"Nay, you can see him as much as you like, as long as I don't," I answered in a careless tone, but keeping an attentive eye on Jonah. His perturbation seemed strange. If Phineas' business were only the conversion of Mistress Gwyn, what reason had Jonah Wall to go white as Dover cliffs over it?

We came to the Castle and I dismissed him, bidding him stow his load safely in my quarters. Then I repaired to the Duke of Monmouth's apartments, wondering in what mood I should find him after last night's rebuff. Little did he think that I had been a witness of it. I entered his room; he was sitting in his chair, with him was Carford. The Duke's face was as glum and his air as ill-tempered as I could wish. Carford's manner was subdued, calm, and sympathetic. They were talking earnestly as I entered but ceased their conversation at once. I offered my services.

"I have no need of you this morning, Simon," answered the Duke. "I'm engaged with Lord Carford."

I retired. But of a truth that morning every one in the Castle was engaged with someone else. At every turn I came on couples in anxious consultation. The approach of an intruder brought immediate silence, the barest civility delayed him, his departure was received gladly and was signal for renewed consultation. Well, the King sets the mode, and the King, I heard, was closeted with Madame and the Duke of York.

But not with M. de Perrencourt. There was a hundred feet of the wall, with a guard at one end and a guard at the other, and mid-way between them a solitary figure stood looking down on Dover town and thence out to sea. In an instant I recognised him, and a great desire came over me to speak to him. He was the foremost man alive in that day, and I longed to speak with him. To have known the great is to have tasted the true flavour of your times. But how to pass the sentries? Their presence meant that M. de Perrencourt desired privacy. I stepped up to one and offered to pass. He barred the way.

"But I'm in the service of his Grace the Duke of Monmouth," I expostulated.

"If you were in the service of the devil himself you couldn't pass here without the King's order," retorted the fellow.

"Won't his head serve as well as his order?" I asked, slipping a crown into his hand. "Come, I've a message from his Grace for the French gentleman. Yes, it's private. Deuce take it, do fathers always know of their sons' doings?"

"No, nor sons all their father's sometimes," he chuckled. "Along with you quick, and run if you hear me whistle; it will mean my officer is coming."

I was alone in the sacred space with M. de Perrencourt. I assumed an easy air and sauntered along, till I was within a few yards of him. Hearing my step then, he looked round with a start and asked peremptorily,

"What's your desire, sir?"

By an avowal of himself, even by quoting the King's order, he could banish me. But if his cue were conceal-ment and ignorance of the order, why, I might indulge my curiosity.

"Like your own, sir," I replied courteously, "a breath of fresh air and a sight of the sea."

He frowned a little, but I gave him no time to speak.

"That fellow though," I pursued, "gave me to understand that none might pass; yet the King is not here, is he?"

"Then how did you pass, sir?" asked M. de Perrencourt, ignoring my last question.

"Why, with a lie, sir," I answered. "I said I had a message for you from the Duke of Monmouth, and the fool believed me. But we gentlemen in attendance must stand by one another. You'll not betray me? Your word on it?"

A slow smile broke across his face.

"No, I'll not betray you," said he. "You speak French well, sir."

"So M. de Fontelles, whom I met at Canterbury, told me. Do you chance to know him, sir?"

M. de Perrencourt did not start now; I should have been disappointed if he had.

"Very well," he answered. "If you're his friend, you're mine." He held out his hand.

"I take it on false pretences," said I with a laugh, as I shook it. "For we came near to quarrelling, M. de Fontelles and I."

"Ah, on what point?"

"A nothing, sir."

"Nay, but tell me."

"Indeed I will not, if you'll pardon me."

"Sir, I wish to know. I ins—I beg." A stare from me had stopped the "insist" when it was half-way through his lips. On my soul, he flushed! I tell my children sometimes how I made him flush; the thing was not done often. Yet his confusion was but momentary, and suddenly, I know not how, I in my turn became abashed with the cold stare of his eyes, and when he asked me my name, I answered baldly, with never a bow and never a flourish, "Simon Dale."

"I have heard your name," said he gravely. Then he turned round and began looking at the sea again.

Now, had he been wearing his own clothes (if I may so say) this conduct would have been appropriate enough; it would have been a dismissal and I should have passed on my way. But a man should be consistent in his disguises, and from M. de Perrencourt, gentleman-in-waiting, the behaviour was mighty uncivil. Yet my revenge must be indirect.

"Is it true, sir," I asked, coming close to him, "that the King of France is yonder at Calais? So it's said."

"I believe it to be true," answered M. de Perrencourt.

"I wish he had come over," I cried. "I should love to see him, for they say he's a very proper man, although he's somewhat short."

M. de Perrencourt did not turn his head, but again I saw his cheek flush. To speak of his low stature was, I had heard Monmouth say, to commit the most dire offence in King Louis' eyes.

"Now, how tall is the King, sir?" I asked. "Is he tall as you, sir?"

M. de Perrencourt was still silent. To tell the truth, I began to be a little uneasy; there were cells under the Castle, and I had need to be at large for the coming few days.

"For," said I, "they tell such lies concerning princes."

Now he turned towards me, saying,

"There you're right, sir. The King of France, is of middle size, about my own height."

For the life of me I could not resist it. I said nothing with my tongue, but for a moment I allowed my eyes to say, "But then you're short, sir." He understood, and for the third time he flushed.

"I thought as much," said I, and with a bow I began to walk on.

But, as ill-luck would have it, I was not to come clear off from my indiscretion. In a moment I should have been out of sight. But as I started I saw a gentleman pass the guard, who stood at the salute. It was the King; escape was impossible. He walked straight up to me, bowing carelessly in response to M. de Perrencourt's deferential inclination of his person.

"How come you here, Mr Dale?" he asked abruptly. "The guard tells me that he informed you of my orders and that you insisted on passing."

M. de Perrencourt felt that his turn was come; he stood there smiling. I found nothing to say; if I repeated my fiction of a message, the French gentleman, justly enraged, would betray me.

"M. de Perrencourt seemed lonely, sir," I answered at last.

"A little loneliness hurts no man," said the King. He took out his tablets and began to write. When he was done, he gave me the message, adding, "Read it." I read, "Mr Simon Dale will remain under arrest in his own apartment for twenty-four hours, and will not leave it except by the express command of the King." I made a wry face.

"If the Duke of Monmouth wants me—" I began.

"He'll have to do without you, Mr Dale," interrupted the King. "Come, M. de Perrencourt, will you give me your arm?" And off he went on the French gentleman's arm, leaving me most utterly abashed, and cursing the curiosity that had brought me to this trouble.

"So much for the Duke of Buckingham's 'long head,'" said I to myself ruefully, as I made my way towards the Constable's Tower, in which his Grace was lodged, and where I had my small quarters.

Indeed, I might well feel a fool; for the next twenty-four hours, during which I was to be a prisoner, would in all likelihood see the issue in which I was pledged to bear a part. Now I could do nothing. Yet at least I must send speedy word to the town that I was no longer to be looked to for any help, and when I reached my room I called loudly for Jonah Wall. It was but the middle of the day, yet he was not to be seen. I walked to the door and found, not Jonah, but a guard on duty.

"What are you doing here?"

"Seeing that you stay here, sir," he answered, with a grin.

Then the King was very anxious that I should obey his orders, and had lost no time in ensuring my obedience; he was right to take his measures, for, standing where I did, his orders would not have restrained me. I was glad that he had set a guard on me in lieu of asking my parole. For much as I love sin, I hate temptation. Yet where was Jonah Wall, and how could I send my message? I flung myself on the bed in deep despondency. A moment later the door opened, and Robert, Darrell's servant, entered.

"My master begs to know if you will sup with him to-night, sir."

"Thank him kindly," said I; "but if you ask that gentleman outside, Robert, he'll tell you that I must sup at home by the King's desire. I'm under arrest, Robert."

"My master will be grieved to hear it, sir, and the more because he hoped that you would bring some wine with you, for he has none, and he has guests to sup with him."

"Ah, an interested invitation! How did Mr Darrell know that I had wine?"

"Your servant Jonah spoke of it to me, sir, and said that you would be glad to send my master some."

"Jonah is liberal! But I'm glad, and assure Mr Darrell of it. Where is my rascal?"

"I saw him leave the Castle about an hour ago; just after he spoke to me about the wine."

"Curse him! I wanted him. Well, take the wine. There are six bottles that he got to-day."

"There is French wine here, sir, and Spanish. May I take either?"

"Take the French in God's name. I don't want that. I've had enough of France. Stay, though, I believe Mr Darrell likes the Spanish better."

"Yes, sir; but his guests will like the French."

"And who are these guests?"

Robert swelled with pride.

"I thought Jonah would have told you, sir," said he. "The King is to sup with my master."

"Then," said I, "I'm well excused. For no man knows better than the King why I can't come."

The fellow took his bottles and went off grinning. I, being left, fell again to cursing myself for a fool, and in this occupation I passed the hours of the afternoon.

CHAPTER XIV

THE KING'S CUP

At least the Vicar would be pleased! A whimsical joy in the anticipation of his delight shot across my gloomy meditations as the sunset rays threaded their way through the narrow window of the chamber that was my cell. The thought of him stayed with me, amusing my idleness and entertaining my fancy. I could imagine his wise, contented nod, far from surprise as the poles are apart, full of self-approval as an egg of meat. For his vision had been clear, in him faith had never wavered. Of a truth, the prophecy which old Betty Nasroth spoke (foolishness though it were) was, through Fortune's freak, two parts fulfilled. What remained might rest unjustified to my great content; small comfort had I won from so much as had come to pass. I had loved where the King loved, and my youth, though it raised its head again, still reeled under the blow; I knew what the King hid—aye, it might be more than one thing that he hid; my knowledge landed me where I lay now, in close confinement with a gaoler at my door. For my own choice, I would crave the Vicar's pardon, would compound with destiny, and, taking the proportion of fate's gifts already dealt to me in lieu of all, would go in peace to humbler doings, beneath the dignity of dark prophecy, but more fit to give a man quiet days

Anthony Hope

and comfort in his life. Indeed, as my lord Quinton had said long ago, there was strange wine in the King's cup, and I had no desire to drink of it. Yet who would not have been moved by the strange working of events which made the old woman's prophecy seem the true reading of a future beyond guess or reasonable forecast? I jeered and snarled at myself, at Betty, at her prophecy, at the Vicar's credulity. But the notion would not be expelled; two parts stood accomplished, but the third remained. "Glamis thou art, and Cawdor, and shalt be what thou art promised!"—I forget how it runs on, for it is long since I saw the play, though I make bold to think that it is well enough written. Alas, no good came of listening to witches there, if my memory holds the story of the piece rightly.

There is little profit, and less entertainment, in the record of my angry desponding thoughts. Now I lay like a log, again I ranged the cell as a beast his cage. I cared not a stiver for Buckingham's schemes, I paid small heed to Nell's jealousy. It was nought to me who should be the King's next favourite, and although I, with all other honest men, hated a Popish King, the fear of him would not have kept me from my sleep or from my supper. Who eats his dinner the less though a kingdom fall? To take a young man's appetite away, and keep his eyes open o' nights, needs a nearer touch than that. But I had on me a horror of what was being done in this place; they sold a lady's honour there, throwing it in for a make-weight in their bargain. I would have dashed the scales from their hands, but I was helpless. There is the truth: a man need not be ashamed for having had a trifle of honesty about him when he was young. And if my honesty had the backing of something else that I myself knew not yet, why, for honesty's good safety, God send it such backing always! Without some such aid, it is too often brought to terms and sings small in the end.

The evening grew late and darkness had fallen. I turned again to my supper and contrived to eat and to drink a glass or two of wine. Suddenly I remembered Jonah Wall, and sent a curse after the negligent fellow, wherever he might be, determining that next morning he should take his choice between a drubbing and dismissal. Then I stretched myself again on the pallet, resolute to see whether a man could will himself asleep. But I had hardly closed my eyes when I opened them again and started up, leaning on my elbow. There was somebody in conversation with my gaoler. The conference was brief.

"Here's the King's order," I heard, in a haughty, careless tone. "Open the door, fellow, and be quick."

The door was flung open. I sprang to my feet with a bow. The Duke of Buckingham stood before me, surveying my person (in truth, my state was very dishevelled) and my quarters with supercilious amusement. There was one chair, and I set it for him; he sat down, pulling off his lace-trimmed gloves.

"You are the gentleman I wanted?" he asked.

"I have reason to suppose so, your Grace," I answered.

"Good," said he. "The Duke of Monmouth and I have spoken to the King on your behalf."

I bowed grateful acknowledgments.

"You are free," he continued, to my joy. "You'll leave the Castle in two hours," he added, to my consternation. But he appeared to perceive neither effect of his words. "Those are the King's orders," he ended composedly.

"But," I cried, "if I leave the Castle how can I fulfil your Grace's desire?"

"I said those were the King's orders. I have something to add to them. Here, I have written it down, that you may understand and not forget. Your lantern there gives a poor light, but your eyes are young. Read what is written, sir."

I took the paper that he handed me and read:

"In two hours' time be at Canonsgate. The gate will be open. Two serving men will be there with two horses. A lady will be conducted to the gate and delivered into your charge. You will ride with her as speedily as possible to Deal. You will call her your sister, if need arise to speak of her. Go to the hostelry of the Merry Mariners in Deal, and there await a gentleman, who will come in the morning and hand you fifty guineas in gold. Deliver the lady to this gentleman, return immediately to London, and lie in safe hiding till word reaches you from me."

I read and turned to him in amazement.

"Well," he asked, "isn't it plain enough?"

"The lady I can guess," I answered, "but I pray your Grace to tell me who is the gentleman."

"What need is there for you to know? Do you think that more than one will seek you at the Merry Mariners Tavern and pray your acceptance of fifty guineas?"

"But I should like to know who this one is."

"You'll know when you see him."

"With respect to your Grace, this is not enough to tell me."

"You can't be told more, sir."

"Then I won't go."

He frowned and beat his gloves on his thigh impatiently.

"A gentleman, your Grace," said I, "must be trusted, or he cannot serve."

He looked round the little cell and asked significantly,

"Is your state such as to entitle you to make conditions?"

"Only if your Grace has need of services which I can give or refuse," I answered, bowing.

His irritation suddenly vanished, or seemed to vanish. He leant back in his chair and laughed.

"Yet all the time," said he, "you've guessed the gentleman! Isn't it so? Come, Mr Dale, we understand one another. This service, if all goes well, is simple. But if you're interrupted in leaving the Castle, you must use your sword. Well, if you use your sword and don't prove victorious, you may be taken. If you're taken it will be best for us all that you shouldn't know the name of this gentleman, and best for him and for me that I should not have mentioned it."

The little doubt I had harboured was gone. Buckingham and Monmouth were hand in hand. Buckingham's object was political, Monmouth was to find his reward in the prize that I was to rescue from the clutches of M. de

Perrencourt and hand over to him at the hostelry in Deal. If success attended the attempt, I was to disappear; if it failed, my name and I were to be the shield and bear the brunt. The reward was fifty guineas, and perhaps a serviceable gratitude in the minds of two great men, provided I lived to enjoy the fruit of it.

"You'll accept this task?" asked the Duke.

The task was to thwart M. de Perrencourt and gratify the Duke of Monmouth. If I refused it, another might accept and accomplish it; if such a champion failed, M. de Perrencourt would triumph. If I accepted, I should accept in the fixed intention of playing traitor to one of my employers. I might serve Buckingham's turn, I should seek to thwart Monmouth.

"Who pays me fifty guineas?" I asked.

"Faith, I," he answered with a shrug. "Young Monmouth is enough his father's son to have his pockets always empty."

On this excuse I settled my point of casuistry in an instant.

"Then I'll carry the lady away from the Castle," I cried.

He started, leant forward, and looked hard in my face. "What do you mean, what do you know?" he asked plainly enough, although silently. But I had cried out with an appearance of zeal and innocence that baffled his curiosity, and my guileless expression gave his suspicions no food. Perhaps, too, he had no wish to enquire. There was little love between him and Monmouth, for he had been bitterly offended by the honours and precedence assigned to the Duke; only a momentary coincidence of interest bound them together in this scheme. If the part that concerned Buckingham were accomplished, he would not break his heart on account of the lady not being ready for Monmouth at the hostelry of the Merry Mariners.

"I think, then, that we understand one another, Mr Dale?" said he, rising.

"Well enough, your Grace," I answered with a bow, and I rapped on the door. The gaoler opened it.

"Mr Dale is free to go where he will within the Castle. You can return to your quarters," said Buckingham.

The soldier marched off. Buckingham turned to me.

"Good fortune in your enterprise," he said. "And I give you joy on your liberty."

The words were not out of his mouth when a lieutenant and two men appeared, approaching us at a rapid walk, nay, almost at a run. They made directly for us, the Duke and I both watching them. The officer's sword was drawn in his hand, their daggers were fixed in the muzzles of the soldiers' muskets.

"What's happened now?" asked Buckingham in a whisper.

The answer was not long in coming. The lieutenant halted before us, crying,

"In the King's name, I arrest you, sir."

"On my soul, you've a habit of being arrested, sir," said the Duke sharply. "What's the cause this time?"

"I don't know," I answered; and I asked the officer, "On what account, sir?"

"The King's orders," he answered curtly. "You must come with me at once." At a sign from him his men took their stand on either side of me. Verily, my liberty had been short! "I must warn you that we shall stand at nothing if you try to escape," said the officer sternly.

"I'm not a fool, sir," I answered. "Where are you going to take me?"

"Where my orders direct."

"Come, come," interrupted Buckingham impatiently, "not so much mystery. You know me? Well, this gentleman is my friend, and I desire to know where you take him."

"I crave your Grace's pardon, but I must not answer."

"Then I'll follow you and discover," cried the Duke angrily.

"At your Grace's peril," answered the officer firmly. "If you insist, I must leave one of my men to detain you here. Mr Dale must go alone with me."

Wrath and wonder were eloquent on the proud Duke's face. In me this new misadventure bred a species of resignation. I smiled at him, as I said,

"My business with your Grace must wait, it seems."

"Forward, sir," cried the officer, impatiently, and I was marched off at a round pace, Buckingham not attempting to follow, but turning back in the direction of the Duke of

Monmouth's quarters. The confederates must seek a new instrument now; if their purpose were to thwart the King's wishes, they might not find what they wanted again so easily.

I was conducted straight and quickly to the keep, and passed up the steps that led to the corridor in which the King was lodged. They hurried me along, and I had time to notice nothing until I came to a door near the end of the building, on the western side. Here I found Darrell, apparently on guard, for his sword was drawn and a pistol in his left hand.

"Here, sir, is Mr Dale," said my conductor.

"Good," answered Darrell briefly. I saw that his face was very pale, and he accorded me not the least sign of recognition. "Is he armed?" he asked.

"You see I have no weapons, Mr Darrell," said I stiffly.

"Search him," commanded Darrell, ignoring me utterly.

I grew hot and angry. The soldiers obeyed the order. I fixed my eyes on Darrell, but he would not meet my gaze; the point of his sword tapped the floor on which it rested, for his hand was shaking like a leaf.

"There's no weapon on him," announced the officer.

"Very well. Leave him with me, sir, and retire with your men to the foot of the steps. If you hear a whistle, return as quickly as possible."

The officer bowed, turned about, and departed, followed by his men. Darrell and I stood facing one another for

Anthony Hope

a moment.

"In hell's name, what's the meaning of this, Darrell?" I cried. "Has Madame brought the Bastille over with her, and are you made Governor?"

He answered not a word. Keeping his sword still in readiness, he knocked with the muzzle of his pistol on the door by him. After a moment it was opened, and a head looked out. The face was Sir Thomas Clifford's; the door was flung wide, a gesture from Darrell bade me enter. I stepped in, he followed, and the door was instantly shut close behind us.

I shall not readily forget the view disclosed to me by the flaring oil lamps hung in sconces to the ancient smoky walls. I was in a narrow room, low and not large, scantly furnished with faded richness, and hung to half its height with mouldering tapestries. The floor was bare, and uneven from time and use. In the middle of the room was a long table of polished oak wood; in the centre of it sat the King, on his left was the Duchess of Orleans, and beyond her the Duke of York; on the King's right at the end of the table was an empty chair; Clifford moved towards it now and took his seat; next to him was Arlington, then Colbert de Croissy, the Special Envoy of the French King. Next to our King was another empty chair, an arm-chair, like the King's; empty it was, but M. de Perrencourt leant easily over the back of it, with his eyes fixed on me. On the table were materials for writing, and a large sheet of paper faced the King—or M. de Perrencourt; it seemed just between them. There was nothing else on the table except a bottle of wine and two cups; one was full to the brim, while the liquor in the other fell short of the top of the glass by a quarter of an inch. All present were silent; save M. de Perrencourt, all seemed disturbed; the King's swarthy face appeared rather pale than swarthy, and his hand rapped nervously on the table. All this I saw, while Darrell stood rigidly by me, sword in hand.

Madame was the first to speak; her delicate subtle face lit up with recognition.

"Why, I have spoken with this gentleman," she said in a low voice.

"And I also," said M. de Perrencourt under his breath.

I think he hardly knew that he spoke, for the words seemed the merest unconscious outcome of his thoughts.

The King raised his hand, as though to impose silence. Madame bowed in apologetic submission, M. de Perrencourt took no heed of the gesture, although he did not speak again. A moment later he laid his hand on Colbert's shoulder and whispered to him. I thought I heard just a word—it was "Fontelles." Colbert looked up and nodded. M. de Perrencourt folded his arms on the back of the chair, and his face resumed its impassivity.

Another moment elapsed before the King spoke. His voice was calm, but there seemed still to echo in it a trace of some violent emotion newly passed; a slight smile curved his lips, but there was more malice than mirth in it.

"Mr Dale," said he, "the gentleman who stands by you once beguiled an idle minute for me by telling me of a certain strange prophecy made concerning you which he had, he said, from your own lips, and in which my name—or at least some King's name—and yours were quaintly coupled. You know what I refer to?"

I bowed low, wondering what in Heaven's name he would be at. It was, no doubt, high folly to love Mistress Gwyn, but scarcely high treason. Besides, had not I repented and forsworn her? Ah, but the second member of the prophecy? I glanced eagerly at M. de Perrencourt, eagerly at the paper before the King. There were lines on the paper, but I could not read them, and M. de Perrencourt's face was fully as baffling.

"If I remember rightly," pursued the King, after listening to a whispered sentence from his sister, "the prediction foretold that you should drink of my cup. Is it not so?"

"It was so, Sir, although what your Majesty quotes was the end, not the beginning of it."

For an instant a smile glimmered on the King's face; it was gone and he proceeded gravely.

"I am concerned only with that part of it. I love prophecies and I love to see them fulfilled. You see that cup there, the one that is not quite full. That cup of wine was poured out for me, the other for my friend M. de Perrencourt. I pray you, drink of my cup and let the prophecy stand fulfilled."

In honest truth I began to think that the King had drunk other cups before and left them not so full. Yet he looked sober enough, and the rest were grave and mute. What masquerade was this, to bring me under guard and threat of death to drink a cup of wine? I would have drunk a dozen of my free will, for the asking.

"Your Majesty desires me to drink that cup of wine?" I asked.

"If you please, sir; the cup that was poured out for me."

"With all my heart," I cried, and, remembering my manners, I added, "and with most dutiful thanks to Your Majesty for this signal honour."

A stir, hardly to be seen, yet certain, ran round the table. Madame stretched out a hand towards the cup as though with a sudden impulse to seize it; the King caught her hand and held it prisoner. M. de Perrencourt suddenly dragged his chair back and, passing in front of it, stood close over the table. Colbert looked up at him, but his eyes were fixed on me, and the Envoy went unnoticed.

"Then come and take it," said the King.

I advanced after a low bow. Darrell, to my fresh wonder, kept pace with me, and when I reached the table was still at my side. Before I could move his sword might be through me or the ball from his pistol in my brains. The strange scene began to intoxicate me, its stirring suggestion mounting to my head like fumes of wine. I seized the cup and held it high in my hand. I looked down in the King's face, and thence to Madame's; to her I bowed low and cried:

"By His Majesty's permission I will drain this cup to the honour of the fairest and most illustrious Princess, Madame the Duchess of Orleans."

The Duchess half-rose from her seat, crying in a loud whisper, "Not to me, no, no! I can't have him drink it to me."

The King still held her hand.

"Drink it to me, Mr Dale," said he.

I bowed to him and put the cup to my lips. I was in the act to drink, when M. de Perrencourt spoke.

"A moment, sir," he said calmly. "Have I the King's permission to tell Mr Dale a secret concerning this wine?"

The Duke of York looked up with a frown, the King turned to M. de Perrencourt as if in doubt, the Frenchman met his glance and nodded.

"M. de Perrencourt is our guest," said the King. "He must do as he will."

M. de Perrencourt, having thus obtained permission (when was his will denied him?), leant one hand on the table and, bending across towards me, said in slow, calm, yet impressive tones:

"The King, sir, was wearied with business and parched with talking; of his goodness he detected in me the same condition. So he bade my good friend and his good subject Mr Darrell furnish him with a bottle of wine, and Mr Darrell brought a bottle, saying that the King's cellar was shut and the cellarman in bed, but praying the King to honour him by drinking his wine, which was good French wine, such as the King loved and such as he hoped to put before His Majesty at supper presently. Then His Majesty asked whence it came, and Mr Darrell answered that he was indebted for it to his good friend Mr Simon Dale, who would be honoured by the King's drinking it."

"Why, it's my own wine then!" I cried, smiling now.

"He spoke the truth, did he?" pursued M. de Perrencourt

composedly. "It is your wine, sent by you to Mr Darrell?"

"Even so, sir," I answered. "Mr. Darrell's wine was out, and I sent him some bottles of wine by his servant."

"You knew for what he needed it?"

I had forgotten for the moment what Robert said, and hesitated in my answer. M. de Perrencourt looked intently at me.

"I think," said I, "that Robert told me Mr Darrell expected the King to sup with him."

"He told you that?" he asked sharply.

"Yes, I remember that," said I, now thoroughly bewildered by the history and the catechism which seemed necessary to an act so simple as drinking a glass of my own wine.

M. de Perrencourt said nothing more, but his eyes were still set on my face with a puzzled searching expression. His glance confused me, and I looked round the table. Often at such moments the merest trifles catch our attention, and now for the first time I observed that a little of the wine had been spilt on the polished oak of the table; where it had fallen the bright surface seemed rusted to dull brown. I noticed the change, and wondered for an idle second how it came that wine turned a polished table dull. The thing was driven from my head the next moment by a brief and harsh order from the King.

"Drink, sir, drink."

Strained with excitement, I started at the order, and

slopped some of the wine from the cup on my hand. I felt a strange burning where it fell; but again the King cried, "Drink, sir."

I hesitated no more. Recalling my wandering wits and determining to play my part in the comedy, whatever it might mean, I bowed, cried "God save your Majesty," and raised the cup to my lips. As it touched them, I saw Madame hide her eyes with her hand and M. de Perrencourt lean farther across the table, while a short quick gasp of breath came from where Darrell stood by my side.

I knew how to take off a bumper of wine. No sippings and swallowings for me! I laid my tongue well down in the bottom of my mouth that the liquor might have fair passage to my gullet, and threw my head back as you see a hen do (in thanks to heaven, they say, though she drinks only water). Then I tilted the cup, and my mouth was full of the wine. I was conscious of a taste in it, a strange acrid taste. Why, it was poor wine, turned sour; it should go back to-morrow; that fool Jonah was a fool in all things; and I stood disgraced for offering this acrid stuff to a friend. And he gave it to the King! It was the cruellest chance. Why—

Suddenly, when I had gulped down but one good mouthful, I saw M. de Perrencourt lean right across the table. Yet I saw him dimly, for my eyes seemed to grow glazed and the room to spin round me, the figures at the table taking strange shapes and weird dim faces, and a singing sounding in my ears, as though the sea roared there and not on Dover beach. There was a woman's cry, and a man's arm shot out at me. I felt a sharp blow on my wrist, the cup was dashed from my hand on to the stone floor, breaking into ten thousand pieces, while the wine made a puddle at my feet. I stood there for an instant, struck motionless, glaring into the face that was opposite to mine. It was M. de Perrencourt's, no longer calm, but pale and twitching. This was the last thing I saw clearly. The King and his companions were fused in a shifting mass of trunks and faces, the walls raced round, the singing of the sea roared and fretted in my ears. I caught my hand to my brow and staggered; I could not stand, I heard a clatter as though of a sword falling to the floor, arms were stretched out to receive me and I sank into them, hearing a murmur close by me, "Simon, Simon!"

Yet one thing more I heard, before my senses left me—a loud, proud, imperious voice, the voice that speaks to be obeyed, whose assertion brooks no contradiction. It rang in my ears where nothing else could reach them, and even then I knew whence it came. The voice was the voice of M. de Perrencourt, and it seemed that he spoke to the King of England.

"Brother," he cried, "by my faith in God, this gentleman is innocent, and his life is on our heads, if he lose it."

I heard no more. Stupor veiled me round in an impenetrable mist. The figures vanished, the tumultuous singing ceased. A great silence encompassed me, and all was gone.

CHAPTER XV

M. DE PERRENCOURT WHISPERS

Slowly the room and the scene came back to me, disengaging themselves from the darkness which had settled on my eyes, regaining distinctness and their proper form. I was sitting in a chair, and there were wet bandages about my head. Those present before were there still, save M. de Perrencourt, whose place at the table was vacant; the large sheet of paper and the materials for writing had vanished. There was a fresh group at the end, next to Arlington; here now sat the Dukes of Monmouth and Buckingham, carrying on a low conversation with the Secretary. The King lay back in his chair, frowning and regarding with severe gaze a man who stood opposite to him, almost where I had been when I drank of the King's cup. There stood Darrell and the lieutenant of the Guards who had arrested me, and between them, with clothes torn and muddy, face scratched and stained with blood, with panting breath and gleaming eyes, firmly held by either arm, was Phineas Tate the Ranter. They had sent and caught him then, while I lay unconscious. But what led them to suspect him?

There was the voice of a man speaking from the other side of this party of three. I could not see him, for their bodies came between, but I recognised the tones of Robert, Darrell's servant. It was he, then, who had put them on Jonah's track, and, in following that, they must have come on Phineas.

"We found the two together," he was saying, "this man and Mr Dale's servant who had brought the wine from the town. Both were armed with pistols and daggers, and seemed ready to meet an attack. In the alley in front of the house that I have named—"

"Yes, yes, enough of the house," interrupted the King impatiently.

"In the alley there were two horses ready. We attacked the men at once, the lieutenant and I making for this one here, the two with us striving to secure Jonah Wall. This man struggled desperately, but seemed ignorant of how to handle his weapons. Yet he gave us trouble enough, and we had to use him roughly. At last we had him, but then we found that Jonah, who fought like a wild cat, had wounded both the soldiers with his knife, and, although himself wounded, had escaped by the stairs. Leaving this man with the lieutenant, I rushed down after him, but one of the horses was gone, and I heard no sound of hoofs. He had got a start of us, and is well out of Dover by now."

I was straining all my attention to listen, yet my eyes fixed themselves on Phineas, whose head was thrown back defiantly. Suddenly a voice came from behind my chair.

"That man must be pursued," said M. de Perrencourt. "Who knows that there may not be accomplices in this devilish plot? This man has planned to poison the King; the servant was his confederate. I say, may there not have

Anthony Hope

been others in the wicked scheme?"

"True, true," said the King uneasily. "We must lay this Jonah Wall by the heels. What's known of him?"

Thinking the appeal was made to me, I strove to rise. M. de Perrencourt's arm reached over the back of my chair and kept me down. I heard Darrell take up the story and tell what he knew—and it was as much as I knew—of Jonah Wall, and what he knew of Phineas Tate also.

"It is a devilish plot," said the King, who was still greatly shaken and perturbed.

Then Phineas spoke loudly, boldly, and with a voice full of the rapturous fanaticism which drowned conscience and usurped in him religion's place.

"Here," he cried, "are the plots, here are the devilish plots! What do you here? Aye, what do you plot here? Is this man's life more than God's Truth? Is God's Word to be lost that the sins and debauchery of this man may continue?"

His long lean forefinger pointed at the King. A mute consternation fell for an instant on them all, and none interrupted him. They had no answer ready for his question; men do not count on such questions being asked at Court, the manners are too good there.

"Here are the plots! I count myself blessed to die in the effort to thwart them! I have failed, but others shall not fail! God's Judgment is sure. What do you here, Charles Stuart?"

M. de Perrencourt walked suddenly and briskly round to

where the King sat and whispered in his ear. The King nodded, and said,

"I think this fellow is mad, but it's a dangerous madness."

Phineas did not heed him, but cried aloud,

"And you here—are you all with him? Are you all apostates from God? Are you all given over to the superstitions of Rome? Are you all here to barter God's word and—"

The King sprang to his feet.

"I won't listen," he cried. "Stop his cursed mouth. I won't listen." He looked round with fear and alarm in his eyes. I perceived his gaze turned towards his son and Buckingham. Following it, I saw their faces alight with eagerness, excitement, and curiosity. Arlington looked down at the table; Clifford leant his head on his hand. At the other end the Duke of York had sprung up like his brother, and was glaring angrily at the bold prisoner. Darrell did not wait to be bidden twice, but whipped a silk handkerchief from his pocket.

"Here and now the deed is being done!" cried Phineas. "Here and now—" He could say no more; in spite of his desperate struggles, he was gagged and stood silent, his eyes still burning with the message which his lips were not suffered to utter. The King sank back in his seat, and cast a furtive glance round the table. Then he sighed, as though in relief, and wiped his brow. Monmouth's voice came clear, careless, confident.

"What's this madness?" he asked. "Who here is bartering God's Word? And for what, pray?"

No answer was given to him; he glanced in insolent amusement at Arlington and Clifford, then in insolent defiance at the Duke of York.

"Is not the religion of the country safe with the King?" he asked, bowing to his father.

"So safe, James, that it does not need you to champion it," said the King dryly; yet his voice trembled a little. Phineas raised that lean forefinger at him again, and pointed. "Tie the fellow's arms to his side," the King commanded in hasty irritation; he sighed again when the finger could no longer point at him, and his eyes again furtively sought Monmouth's face. The young Duke leant back with a scornful smile, and the consciousness of the King's regard did not lead him to school his face to any more seemly expression. My wits had come back now, although my head ached fiercely and my body was full of acute pain; but I watched all that passed, and I knew that, come what might, they would not let Phineas speak. Yet Phineas could know nothing. Nay, but the shafts of madness, often wide, may once hit the mark. The paper that had lain between the King and M. de Perrencourt was hidden.

Again the French gentleman bent and whispered in the King's ear. He spoke long this time, and all kept silence while he spoke—Phineas because he must, the lieutenant with surprised eyes, the rest in that seeming indifference which, as I knew, masked their real deference. At last the King looked up, nodded, and smiled. His air grew calmer and more assured, and the trembling was gone from his voice as he spoke.

"Come, gentlemen," said he, "while we talk this ruffian who has escaped us makes good pace from Dover. Let the

Duke of Monmouth and the Duke of Buckingham each take a dozen men and scour the country for him. I shall be greatly in the debt of either who brings him to me."

The two Dukes started. The service which the King demanded of them entailed an absence of several hours from the Castle. It might be that they, or one of them, would learn something from Jonah Wall; but it was far more likely that they would not find him, or that he would not suffer himself to be taken alive. Why were they sent, and not a couple of the officers on duty? But if the King's object were to secure their absence, the scheme was well laid. I thought now that I could guess what M. de Perrencourt had said in that whispered conference. Buckingham had the discretion to recognise when the game went against him. He rose at once with a bow, declaring that he hastened to obey the King's command, and would bring the fellow in, dead or alive. Monmouth had less self-control. He rose indeed, but reluctantly and with a sullen frown on his handsome face.

"It's poor work looking for a single man over the countryside," he grumbled.

"Your devotion to me will inspire and guide you, James," observed the King. A chance of mocking another made him himself again as no other cure could. "Come, lose no time." Then the King added: "Take this fellow away, and lock him up. Mr Darrell, see that you guard him well, and let nobody come near him."

M. de Perrencourt whispered.

"Above all, let him speak to nobody. He must tell what he knows only at the right time," added the King.

Anthony Hope

"When will that be?" asked Monmouth audibly, yet so low that the King could feign not to hear and smiled pleasantly at his son. But still the Duke lingered, although Buckingham was gone and Phineas Tate had been led out between his custodians. His eyes sought mine, and I read an appeal in them. That he desired to take me with him in pursuit of Jonah Wall, I did not think; but he desired above all things to get me out of that room, to have speech with me, to know that I was free to work out the scheme which Buckingham had disclosed to me. Nay, it was not unlikely that his search for Jonah Wall would lead him to the hostelry of the Merry Mariners at Deal. And for my plan too, which differed so little yet so much from his, for that also I must be free. I rose to my feet, delighted to find that I could stand well and that my pains grew no more severe with movement.

"I am at your Grace's orders," said I. "May I ride with you, sir?"

The King looked at me doubtfully.

"I should be glad of your company," said the Duke, "if your health allows."

"Most fully, sir," I answered, and turning to the King I begged his leave to depart. And that leave I should, as I think, have obtained, but for the fact that once again M. de Perrencourt whispered to the King. The King rose from his seat, took M. de Perrencourt's arm and walked with him to where his Grace stood. I watched them, till a little stifled laugh caught my attention. Madame's face was merry, and hers the laugh. She saw my look on her and laughed again, raising her finger to her lips in a swift stealthy motion. She glanced round apprehensively, but her action had passed unnoticed; the Duke of York seemed sunk in a dull apathy, Clifford and Arlington were busy in conversation. What did she mean? Did she confess that I held their secret and impose silence on me by a more than royal command, by the behest of bright eyes and red lips which dared me to betray their confidence? On the moment's impulse I bowed assent; Madame nodded merrily and waved a kiss with her dainty hand; no word passed, but I felt that I, being a gentleman, could tell no man alive what I suspected, aye, what I knew, concerning M. de Perrencourt. Thus lightly are pledges given when ladies ask them.

The Duke of Monmouth started back with a sudden angry motion. The King smiled at him; M. de Perrencourt laid a hand, decked with rich rings, on his lace cuff. Madame rose, laughing still, and joined the three. I cannot tell what passed—alas, that the matters of highest interest are always elusive!—but a moment later Monmouth fell back with as sour a look as I have ever seen on a man's face, bowed slightly and not over-courteously, faced round and strode through the doorway, opening the door for himself. I heard Madame's gay laugh, again the King spoke, Madame cried, "Fie," and hid her face with her hand. M. de Perrencourt advanced towards me; the King caught his arm. "Pooh, he knows already," muttered Perrencourt, half under his breath, but he gave way, and the King came to me first.

"Sir," said he, "the Duke of Monmouth has had the dutiful kindness to release his claim on your present services, and to set you free to serve me."

I bowed very low, answering,

"His Grace is bountiful of kindness to me, and has given the greatest proof of it in enabling me to serve

Your Majesty."

"My pleasure is," pursued the King, "that you attach yourself to my friend M. de Perrencourt here, and accompany him and hold yourself at his disposal until further commands from me reach you."

M. de Perrencourt stepped forward and addressed me.

"In two hours' time, sir," said he, "I beg you to be ready to accompany me. A ship lies yonder at the pier, waiting to carry His Excellency M. Colbert de Croissy and myself to Calais to-night on business of moment. Since the King gives you to me, I pray your company."

"Till then, Mr Dale, adieu," said the King. "Not a word of what has passed here to-night to any man—or any woman. Be in readiness. You know enough, I think, to tell you that you receive a great honour in M. de Perrencourt's request. Your discretion will show your worthiness. Kiss Madame's hand and leave us."

They both smiled at me, and I stood half-bewildered. "Go," said M. de Perrencourt with a laugh, clapping me on the shoulder. The two turned away. Madame held out her hand towards me; I bent and kissed it.

"Mr Dale," said she, "you have all the virtues."

"Alas, Madame, I fear you don't mean to commend me."

"Yes, for a rarity, at least. But you have one vice."

"It shall be mended, if your Royal Highness will tell its name."

"Nay, I shall increase it by naming it. But here it is; your eyes are too wide open, Mr Dale."

"My mother, Madame, used to accuse me of a trick of keeping them half-shut."

"Your mother had not seen you at Court, sir."

"True, Madame, nor had my eyes beheld your Royal Highness."

She laughed, pleased with a compliment which was well in the mode then, though my sons may ridicule it; but as she turned away she added,

"I shall not be with you to-night, and M. de Perrencourt hates a staring eye."

I was warned and I was grateful. But there I stopped. Since Heaven had given me my eyes, nothing on earth could prevent them opening when matter worth the looking was presented. And perhaps they might be open, and yet seem shut to M. de Perrencourt. With a final salute to the exalted company I went out; as I went they resumed their places at the table, M. de Perrencourt saying, "Come, let us finish. I must be away before dawn."

I returned to my quarters in no small turmoil; yet my head, though it still ached sorely from the effect of tasting that draught so fortunately dashed from my hand, was clear enough, and I could put together all the pieces of the puzzle save one. But that one chanced to be of some moment to me, for it was myself. The business with the King which had brought M. de Perrencourt so stealthily to Dover was finished, or was even now being

Anthony Hope

accomplished; his presence and authority had reinforced Madame's persuasions, and the treaty was made. But in these high affairs I had no place. If I would find my work I must look elsewhere, to the struggle that had arisen between M. de Perrencourt and his Grace the Duke of Monmouth, in which the stakes were not wars or religions, and the quarrel of simpler nature. In that fight Louis (for I did not trouble to maintain his disguise in my thoughts) had won, as he was certain to win if he put forth his strength. My heart was sore for Mistress Barbara. I knew that she was to be the spoil of the French King's victory, and that the loss to the beauty of his Court caused by the departure of Mlle. de Querouaille was to find compensation. But, still, where was my part? I saw only one thing: that Louis had taken a liking for me, and might well choose me as his instrument, if an instrument were needed. But for what and where it was needed I could not conceive; since all France was under his feet, and a thousand men would spring up to do his bidding at a word—aye, let the bidding be what it might, and the task as disgraceful as you will. What were the qualities in me or in my condition that dictated his choice baffled conjecture.

Suddenly came a low knock on the door. I opened it and a man slipped in quickly and covertly. To my amazement, I saw Carford. He had kept much out of sight lately; I supposed that he had discovered all he wanted from Monmouth's ready confidence, and had carried his ill-won gains to his paymaster. But supposing that he would keep up the comedy I said stiffly,

"You come to me from the Duke of Monmouth, my lord?"

He was in no mood for pretence to-night. He was in a state of great excitement, and, brushing aside all reserve, made at once for the point.

"I am come," said he, "to speak a word with you. In an hour you're to sail for France?"

"Yes," said I. "Those are the King's orders."

"But in an hour you could be so far from here that he with whom you go could not wait for your return."

"Well, my lord?"

"To be brief, what's your price to fly and not to sail?"

We were standing, facing one another. I answered him slowly, trying to catch his purpose.

"Why are you willing to pay me a price?" said I. "For it's you who pays?"

"Yes, I pay. Come, man, you know why you go and who goes with you?"

"M. de Perrencourt and M. Colbert go," said I. "Why I go, I don't know."

"Nor who else goes?" he asked, looking in my eyes. I paused for a moment and then answered,

"Yes, she goes."

"And you know for what purpose?"

"I can guess the purpose."

"Well, I want to go in your place. I have done with that

fool Monmouth, and the French King would suit me well for a master."

"Then ask him to take you also."

"He will not; he'll rather take you."

"Then I'll go," said I.

He drew a step nearer to me. I watched him closely, for, on my life, I did not know in what mood he was, and his honour was ill to lean on as a waving reed.

"What will you gain by going?" he asked. "And if you fly he will take me. Somebody he must take."

"Is not M. Colbert enough?"

He looked at me suspiciously, as though he thought that I assumed ignorance.

"You know very well that Colbert wouldn't serve his purpose."

"By my faith," I cried, "I don't know what his purpose is."

"You swear it?" he asked in distrust and amazement.

"Most willingly," I answered. "It is simple truth."

He gazed at me still as though but half-convinced.

"Then what's your purpose in going?" he asked.

"I obey my orders. Yet I have a purpose, and one I had rather trust with myself than with you, my lord."

"Pray, sir, what is it?"

"To serve and guard the lady who goes also."

After a moment of seeming surprise, he broke into a sneering laugh.

"You go to guard her?" he said.

"Her and her honour," I answered steadily. "And I do not desire to resign that task into your hands, my lord."

"What will you do? How will you serve her?" he asked.

A sudden suspicion of him seized me. His manner had changed to a forced urbanity; when he was civil he was treacherous.

"That's my secret, my lord," I answered. "I have preparations to make. I pray you, give me leave." I opened the door and held it for him.

His rage mastered him; he grew red and the veins swelled on his forehead.

"By heaven, you shan't go," he cried, and clapped his hand to his sword.

"Who says that Mr Dale shall not go?"

A man stood in the doorway, plainly attired, wearing boots, and a cloak that half-hid his face. Yet I knew him, and Carford knew him. Carford shrank back, I bowed, and we both bared our heads. M. de Perrencourt advanced into the room, fixing his eyes on Carford.

"My lord," he said, "when I decline a gentleman's services I am not to be forced into accepting them, and when I say a gentleman shall go with me he goes. Have you a quarrel with me on that account?"

Carford found no words in which to answer him, but his eyes told that he would have given the world to draw his sword against M. de Perrencourt, or, indeed, against the pair of us. A gesture of the newcomer's arm motioned him to the door. But he had one sentence more to hear before he was suffered to slink away.

"Kings, my lord," said M. de Perrencourt, "may be compelled to set spies about the persons of others. They do not need them about their own."

Carford turned suddenly white, and his teeth set. I thought that he would fly at the man who rebuked him so scornfully; but such an outbreak meant death; he controlled himself. He passed out, and Louis, with a careless laugh, seated himself on my bed. I stood respectfully opposite to him.

"Make your preparations," said he. "In half an hour's time we depart."

I obeyed him, setting about the task of filling my saddlebags with my few possessions. He watched me in silence for awhile. At last he spoke.

"I have chosen you to go with me," he said, "because although you know a thing, you don't speak of it, and although you see a thing, you can appear blind."

I remembered that Madame thought my blindness deficient, but I received the compliment in silence.

"These great qualities," he pursued, "make a man's fortune. You shall come with me to Paris."

"To Paris, sir?"

"Yes. I'll find work for you there, and those who do my work lack neither reward nor honour. Come, sir, am I not as good a King to serve as another?"

"Your Majesty is the greatest Prince in Christendom," said I. For such indeed all the world held him.

"Yet even the greatest Prince in Christendom fears some things," said he, smiling.

"Surely nothing, sir?"

"Why, yes. A woman's tongue, a woman's tears, a woman's rage, a woman's jealousy; I say, Mr Dale, a woman's jealousy."

It was well that my preparations were done, or they had never been done. I was staring at him now with my hands dropped to my side.

"I am married," he pursued. "That is little." And he shrugged his shoulders.

"Little enough at Courts, in all conscience," thought I; perhaps my face betrayed something of the thought, for King Louis smiled.

"But I am more than a husband," he pursued. "I am a lover, Mr Dale."

Not knowing what comment to make on this, I made

none. I had heard the talk about his infatuation, but it was not for me to mention the lady's name. Nor did the King name her. He rose and approached me, looking full in my face.

"You are neither a husband nor a lover?" he asked.

"Neither, sir."

"You know Mistress Quinton?"

"Yes, sir."

He was close to me now, and he whispered to me as he had whispered to the King in the Council Chamber.

"With my favour and such a lady for his wife, a gentleman might climb high."

I heard the words, and I could not repress a start. At last the puzzle was pieced, and my part plain. I knew now the work I was to do, the price of the reward I was to gain. Had he said it a month before, when I was not yet trained to self-control and concealment, King as he was, I would have drawn my sword on him. For good or evil dissimulation is soon learnt. With a great effort I repressed my agitation and hid my disgust. King Louis smiled at me, deeming what he had suggested no insult.

"Your wedding shall take place at Calais," he said; and I (I wonder now to think of it) bowed and smiled.

"Be ready in a quarter of an hour," said he, and left me with a gracious smile.

I stood there where I was for the best part of the time still left to me. I saw why Carford desired the mission on which I went, why Madame bade me practise the closing of my eyes, how my fortune was to come from the hand of King Louis. An English gentleman and his wife would travel back with the King; the King would give his favour to both; and the lady was Barbara Quinton.

I turned at last, and made my final preparation. It was simple; I loaded my pistol and hid it about me, and I buckled on my sword, seeing that it moved easily in the sheath. By fortune's will, I had to redeem the pledge which I had given to my lord; his daughter's honour now knew no safety but in my arm and wits. Alas, how slender the chance was, and how great the odds!

Then a sudden fear came upon me. I had lived of late in a Court where honour seemed dead, and women, no less than men, gave everything for wealth or place. I had seen nothing of her, no word had come from her to me. She had scorned Monmouth, but might she not be won to smile on M. de Perrencourt? I drove the thought from me, but it came again and again, shaming me and yet fastening on me. She went with M. de Perrencourt; did she go willingly?

With that thought beating in my brain, I stepped forth to my adventure.

CHAPTER XVI

M. DE PERRENCOURT WONDERS

As I walked briskly from my quarters down to the sea, M. de Perrencourt's last whisper, "With my favour and such a lady for his wife, a gentleman might climb high," echoed in my ears so loudly and insistently as to smother all thought of what had passed in the Council Chamber, and to make of no moment for me the plots and plans alike of Kings, Catholics, and Ranters. That night I cared little though the King had signed away the liberties of our religion and his realm; I spared no more than a passing wonder for the attempt to which conscience run mad had urged Phineas Tate, and in which he in his turn had involved my simpleton of a servant. Let them all plot and plan; the issue lay in God's hand, above my knowledge and beyond my power. My task was enough, and more than enough, for my weakness; to it I turned, with no fixed design and no lively hope, with a prayer for success only, and a resolve not to be King Louis' catspaw. A month ago I might have marvelled that he offered such a part to any gentleman; the illusions of youth and ignorance were melting fast; now I was left to ask why he had selected one so humble for a place that great men held in those days with open profit and without open shame; aye, and have held since. For although I have lived to call myself a Whig, I do not hold that the devil left England for good and all with the House of Stuart.

We were on the quay now, and the little ship lay ready for us. A very light breeze blew off the land, enough to carry us over if it held, but promising a long passage; the weather was damp and misty. M. Colbert had shrugged his shoulders over the prospect of a fog; his master would hear of no delay, and the King had sent for Thomas Lie, a famous pilot of the Cinque Ports, to go with us till the French coast should be sighted. The two Kings were walking up and down together in eager and engrossed conversation. Looking about, I perceived the figures of two women standing near the edge of the water. I saw Colbert approach them and enter into conversation; soon he came to me, and with the smoothest of smiles bade me charge myself with the care of Mistress Quinton.

"Madame," said he, "has sent a discreet and trustworthy waiting-woman with her, but a lady needs a squire, and we are still hampered by business." With which he went off to join his master, bestowing another significant smile on me.

I lost no time in approaching Barbara. The woman with her was stout and short, having a broad hard face; she stood by her charge square and sturdy as a soldier on guard. Barbara acknowledged my salutation stiffly; she was pale and seemed anxious, but in no great distress or horror. But did she know what was planned for her or the part I was to play? The first words she spoke showed me that she knew nothing, for when I began to feel my way, saying: "The wind is fair for us," she started, crying: "For us? Why, are you coming with us?"

I glanced at the waiting-woman, who stood stolidly by.

"She understands no English," said Barbara, catching my meaning. "You can speak freely. Why are you coming?"

"Nay, but why are you going?"

She answered me with a touch of defiance in her voice.

"The Duchess of York is to return with Madame on a visit to the French Court, and I go to prepare for her coming."

So this was the story by which they were inducing her to trust herself in their hands. Doubtless they might have forced her, but deceit furnished a better way. Yet agitation had mingled with defiance in her voice. In an instant she went on:

"You are coming, in truth are you? Don't jest with me."

"Indeed I'm coming, madame. I hope my company is to your liking?"

"But why, why?"

"M. de Perrencourt has one answer to that question and I another."

Her eyes questioned me, but she did not put her question into words. With a little shiver she said:

"I am glad to be quit of this place."

"You're right in that," I answered gravely.

Her cheek flushed, and her eyes fell to the ground.

"Yes," she murmured.

"But Dover Castle is not the only place where danger lies," said I.

"Madame has sworn—" she began impetuously.

"And M. de Perrencourt?" I interrupted.

"He—he gave his word to his sister," she said in a very low voice. Then she stretched her hand out towards me, whispering, "Simon, Simon!"

I interpreted the appeal, although it was but an inarticulate cry, witnessing to a fear of dangers unknown. The woman had edged a little away, but still kept a careful watch. I paid no heed to her. I must give my warning.

"My services are always at your disposal, Mistress Barbara," said I, "even without the right to them that M. de Perrencourt purposes to give you."

"I don't understand. How can he—Why, you wouldn't enter my service?"

She laughed a little as she made this suggestion, but there was an eagerness in her voice; my heart answered to it, for I saw that she found comfort in the thought of my company.

"M. de Perrencourt," said I, "purposes that I should enter your service, and his also."

"Mine and his?" she murmured, puzzled and alarmed.

I did not know how to tell her; I was ashamed. But the last moments fled, and she must know before we were at sea.

"Yonder where we're going," I said, "the word of M. de Perrencourt is law and his pleasure right."

She took alarm, and her voice trembled.

"He has promised—Madame told me," she stammered. "Ah, Simon, must I go? Yet I should be worse here."

"You must go. What can we do here? I go willingly."

"For what?"

"To serve you, if it be in my power. Will you listen?"

"Quick, quick. Tell me!"

"Of all that he swore, he will observe nothing. Hush, don't cry out. Nothing."

I feared that she would fall, for she reeled where she stood. I dared not support her.

"If he asks a strange thing, agree to it. It's the only way."

"What? What will he ask?"

"He will propose a husband to you."

She tore at the lace wrapping about her throat as though it were choking her; her eyes were fixed on mine. I answered her gaze with a steady regard, and her cheek grew red with a hot blush.

"His motive you may guess," said I. "There is convenience in a husband."

I had put it at last plainly enough, and when I had said it I averted my eyes from hers.

"I won't go," I heard her gasp. "I'll throw myself at the King's feet."

"He'll make a clever jest on you," said I bitterly.

"I'll implore M. de Perrencourt—"

"His answer will be—polite."

For a while there was silence. Then she spoke again in a low whisper; her voice now sounded hard and cold, and she stood rigid.

"Who is the man?" she asked. Then she broke into a sudden passion, and, forgetting caution, seized me by the arm, whispering, "Have you your sword?"

"Aye, it is here."

"Will you use it for me?"

"At your bidding."

"Then use it on the body of the man."

"I'm the man," said I.

"You, Simon!"

Now what a poor thing is this writing, and how small a fragment of truth can it hold! "You, Simon!" The words are nothing, but they came from her lips full-charged with wonder, most incredulous, yet coloured with sudden hope of deliverance. She doubted, yet she caught at the strange chance. Nay, there was more still, but what I could not tell; for her eyes lit up with a sudden sparkle, which shone a brief moment and then was screened by drooping lids.

"That is why I go," said I. "With M. de Perrencourt's favour and such a lady for my wife I might climb high. So whispered M. de Perrencourt himself."

"You!" she murmured again; and again her cheek was red.

"We must not reach Calais, if we can escape by the way. Be near me always on the ship, fortune may give us a chance. And if we come to Calais, be near me, while you can."

"But if we can't escape?"

I was puzzled by her. It must be that she found in my company new hope of escape. Hence came the light in her eyes, and the agitation which seemed to show excitement rather than fear. But I had no answer to her question, "If we can't escape?"

Had I been ready with fifty answers, time would have failed for one. M. Colbert called to me. The King was embracing his guest for the last time; the sails were spread; Thomas Lie was at the helm. I hastened to obey M. Colbert's summons. He pointed to the King; going forward, I knelt and kissed the hand extended to me. Then I rose and stood for a moment, in case it should be the King's pleasure to address me. M. de Perrencourt was by his side.

The King's face wore a smile and the smile broadened as he spoke to me.

"You're a wilful man, Mr Dale," said he, "but fortune is more wilful still. You would not woo her, therefore woman-like she loves you. You were stubborn, but she is resolute to overcome your stubbornness. But don't try her too far. She stands waiting for you open-armed. Isn't it so, my brother?"

"Your Majesty speaks no more than truth," answered M. de Perrencourt.

"Will you accept her embraces?" asked the King.

I bowed very low and raised my head with a cheerful and gay smile.

"Most willingly," I answered.

"And what of reservations, Mr. Dale?"

"May it please your Majesty, they do not hold across the water."

"Good. My brother is more fortunate than I. God be with you, Mr Dale."

At that I smiled again. And the King smiled. My errand was a strange one to earn a benediction.

"Be off with you," he said with an impatient laugh. "A man must pick his words in talking with you." A gesture of his hand dismissed me. I went on board and watched him standing on the quay as Thomas Lie steered us out of harbour and laid us so as to catch the wind. As we moved, the King turned and began to mount the hill.

We moved, but slowly. For an hour we made way. All

this while I was alone on deck, except for the crew and
Thomas Lie. The rest had gone below; I had offered to
follow, but a gesture from M. Colbert sent me back. The
sense of helplessness was on me, overwhelming and
bitter. When the time came for my part I should be sent
for, until then none had need of me. I could guess well
enough what was passing below, and I found no comfort
in the knowledge of it. Up and down I walked quickly, as
a man torn and tormented with thoughts that his steps,
however hasty, cannot outstrip. The crew stared at me, the
pilot himself spared a glance of amused wonder at the
man who strode to and fro so restlessly. Once I paused at
the stern of the ship, where Lie's boat, towed behind us,
cut through the water as a diamond cuts a pane of glass.
For an instant I thought of leaping in and making a bid for
liberty alone. The strange tone in which "You, Simon!"
had struck home to my heart forbade me. But I was sick
with the world, and turned from the boat to gaze over the
sea. There is a power in the quiet water by night; it draws
a man with a promise of peace in the soft lap of
forgetfulness. So strong is the allurement that, though I
count myself sane and of sound mind, I do not love to
look too long on the bosom of deep waters when the night
is full; for the doubt comes then whether to live is sanity
and not rather to die and have an end of the tossing of life
and the unresting dissatisfaction of our state. That night
the impulse came on me mightily, and I fought it, forcing
myself to look, refusing the weakness of flight from the
seductive siren. For I was fenced round with troubles and
of a sore heart: there lay the open country and a heart at
peace.

Suddenly I gave a low exclamation; the water, which had
fled from us as we moved, seeming glad to pass us by and
rush again on its race undisturbed, stood still. From the
swill came quiet, out of the shimmer a mirror

disentangled itself, and lay there on the sea, smooth and bright. But it grew dull in an instant; I heard the sails flap, but saw them no more. A dense white vapour settled on us, the length of my arm bounded my sight, all movement ceased, and we lay on the water, inert and idle. I leant beside the gunwale, feeling the fog moist on my face, seeing in its baffling folds a type of the toils that bound and fettered me. Now voices rose round me, and again fell; the crew questioned, the captain urged; I heard Colbert's voice as he hurried on deck. The sufficient answer was all around us; where the mist was there could be no wind; in grumbling the voices died away.

The rest of what passed seems even now a strange dream that I can hardly follow, whose issue alone I know, which I can recover only dimly and vaguely in my memory. I was there in the stern, leaning over, listening to the soft sound of the sea as Thomas Lie's boat rolled lazily from side to side and the water murmured gently under the gentle stroke. Then came voices again just by my shoulder. I did not move. I knew the tones that spoke, the persuasive commanding tones hard to resist, apt to compel. Slowly I turned myself round; the speakers must be within eight or ten feet of me, but I could not see them. Still they came nearer. Then I heard the sound of a sob, and at it sprang to rigidity, poised on ready feet, with my hand on the hilt of my sword.

"You're weary now," said the smooth strong voice. "We will talk again in the morning. From my heart I grieve to have distressed you. Come, we'll find the gentleman whom you desire to speak with, and I'll trouble you no more. Indeed I count myself fortunate in having asked my good brother for one whose company is agreeable to you. For your sake, your friend shall be mine. Come, I'll take you to him, and then leave you."

Anthony Hope

Barbara's sobs ceased; I did not wonder that his persuasions won her to repose and almost to trust. It seemed that the mist grew a little less thick; I saw their figures. Knowing that at the same moment I must myself be seen, I spoke on the instant.

"I am here, at Mistress Quinton's service."

M. de Perrencourt (to call him still by his chosen name) came forward and groped his way to my arm, whispering in French,

"All is easy. Be gentle with her. Why, she turns to you of her own accord! All will go smoothly."

"You may be sure of it, sir," I said. "Will you leave her with me?"

"Yes," he answered. "I can trust you, can't I?"

"I may be trusted to death," I answered, smiling behind the mist's kind screen.

Barbara was by his side now; with a bow he drew back. I traced him as he went towards where Lie stood, and I heard a murmur of voices as he and the helmsman spoke to one another. Then I heard no more, and lost sight of him in the thick close darkness. I put out my hand and felt for Barbara's; it came straight to mine.

"You—you'll stay with me?" she murmured. "I'm frightened, Simon."

As she spoke, I felt on my cheek the cold breath of the wind. Turning my full face, I felt it more. The breeze was rising, the sails flapped again, Thomas Lie's boat buffeted the waves with a quicker beat. When I looked towards her, I saw her face, framed in mist, pale and wet with tears, beseeching me. There at that moment, born in danger and nursed by her helplessness, there came to me a new feeling, that was yet an old one; now I knew that I would not leave her. Nay, for an instant I was tempted to abandon all effort and drift on to the French shore, looking there to play my own game, despite of her and despite of King Louis himself. But the risk was too desperate.

"No, I won't leave you," I said in low tones that trembled under the fresh burden which they bore.

But yes, the wind rose, the mist began to lift, the water was running lazily from under our keel, the little boat bobbed and danced to a leisurely tune.

"The wind serves," cried Thomas Lie. "We shall make land in two hours if it hold as it blows now."

The plan was in my head. It was such an impulse as coming to a man seems revelation and forbids all questioning of its authority. I held Barbara still by the hand, and drew her to me. There, leaning over the gunwale, we saw Thomas Lie's boat moving after us. His sculls lay ready. I looked in her eyes, and was answered with wonder, perplexity, and dawning intelligence.

"I daren't let him carry you to Calais," I whispered; "we should be helpless there."

"But you—it's you."

"As his tool and his fool," I muttered. Low as I spoke, she heard me, and asked despairingly:

Anthony Hope

"What then, Simon? What can we do?"

"If I go there, will you jump into my arms? The distance isn't far."

"Into the boat! Into your arms in the boat?"

"Yes. I can hold you. There's a chance if we go now—now, before the mist lifts more."

"If we're seen?"

"We're no worse off."

"Yes, I'll jump, Simon."

We were moving now briskly enough, though the wind came in fitful gusts and with no steady blast, and the mist now lifted, now again swathed us in close folds. I gripped Barbara's hand, whispering, "Be ready," and, throwing one leg over the side, followed with the other, and dropped gently into Thomas Lie's boat. It swayed under me, but it was broad in the beam and rode high in the water; no harm happened. Then I stood square in the bows and whispered "Now!" For the beating of my heart I scarcely heard my own voice, but I spoke louder than I knew. At the same instant that Barbara sprang into my arms, there was a rush of feet across the deck, an oath rang loud in French, and another figure appeared on the gunwale, with one leg thrown over. Barbara was in my arms. I felt her trembling body cling to mine, but I disengaged her grasp quickly and roughly—for gentleness asks time, and time had we none—and set her down in the boat. Then I turned to the figure above me. A momentary glance showed me the face of King Louis. I paid no more heed, but drew my knife and flung myself on the rope that bound the boat to the ship.

Then the breeze dropped, and the fog fell thick and enveloping. My knife was on the rope and I severed the strands with desperate strength. One by one I felt them go. As the last went I raised my head. From the ship above me flashed the fire of a pistol, and a ball whistled by my ear. Wild with excitement, I laughed derisively. The last strand was gone, slowly the ship forged ahead; but then the man on the gunwale gathered himself together and sprang across the water between us. He came full on the top of me, and we fell together on the floor of the boat. By the narrowest chance we escaped foundering, but the sturdy boat proved true. I clutched my assailant with all my strength, pinning him arm to arm, breast to breast, shoulder to shoulder. His breath was hot on my face. I gasped "Row, row." From the ship came a sudden alarmed cry: "The boat, the boat!" But already the ship grew dim and indistinct.

"Row, row," I muttered; then I heard the sculls set in their tholes, and with a slow faltering stroke the boat was guided away from the ship, moving nearly at a right angle to it. I put out all my strength. I was by far a bigger man than the King, and I did not spare him. I hugged him with a bear's hug, and his strength was squeezed out of him. Now I was on the top and he below. I twisted his pistol from his hand and flung it overboard. Tumultuous cries came from the blurred mass that was the ship; but the breeze had fallen, the fog was thick, they had no other boat. The King lay still. "Give me the sculls," I whispered. Barbara yielded them; her hands were cold as death when they encountered mine. She scrambled into the stern. I dragged the King back—he was like a log now—till he lay with the middle of his body under the seat on which I sat; his face looked up from between my

Anthony Hope

feet. Then I fell to rowing, choosing no course except that our way should be from the ship, and ready, at any movement of the still form below me, to drop my sculls and set my pistol at his head. Yet till that need came I bent lustily to my work, and when I looked over the sea the ship was not to be seen, but all around hung the white vapour, the friendly accomplice of my enterprise.

That leap of his was a gallant thing. He knew that I was his master in strength, and that I stood where no motive of prudence could reach and no fear restrain me. If I were caught, the grave or a French prison would be my fate; to get clear off, he might suppose that I should count even the most august life in Christendom well taken. Yet he had leapt, and, before heaven, I feared that I had killed him. If it were so, I must set Barbara in safety, and then follow him where he was gone; there would be no place for me among living men, and I had better choose my own end than be hunted to death like a mad dog. These thoughts spun through my brain as my arms drove the blades into the water, on an aimless course through the mist, till the mass of the ship utterly disappeared, and we three were alone on the sea. Then the fear overcame me. I rested on my oars, and leaning over to where Barbara sat in the stern, I shaped with awe-struck lips the question— "Is he dead? My God, is he dead?"

She sat there, herself, as it seemed, half-dead. But at my words she shivered and with an effort mastered her relaxed limbs. Slowly she dropped on her knees by the King and raised his head in her arms. She felt in her bosom and drew out a flask of salts, which she set to his nostrils. I watched his face; the muscles of it contracted into a grimace, then were smoothed again to calmness; he opened his eyes. "Thank God," I muttered to myself; and the peril to him being gone by, I remembered our danger, and taking out my pistol looked to it, and sat dangling it in my hand.

Barbara, still supporting the King's head, looked up at me.

"What will become of us?" she asked.

"At least we shan't be married in Calais," I answered with a grim smile.

"No," she murmured, and bent again over the King.

Now his eyes were wide-opened, and I fixed mine on them. I saw the return of consciousness and intelligence; the quick glance that fell on me, on the oars, on the pistol in my hand, witnessed to it. Then he raised himself on his elbow, Barbara drawing quickly away, and so rested an instant, regarding me still. He drew himself up into a sitting posture, and seemed as though he would rise to his feet. I raised the pistol and pointed it at him.

"No higher, if you please," said I. "It's a matter of danger to walk about in so small a boat, and you came near to upsetting us before."

He turned his head and saw Barbara, then gazed round on the sea. No sail was to be seen, and the fog still screened the boat in impenetrable solitude. The sight brought to his mind a conviction of what his plight was. Yet no dismay nor fear showed in his face. He sat there, regarding me with an earnest curiosity. At last he spoke.

"You were deluding me all the time?" he asked.

"Even so," said I, with an inclination of my head.

"You did not mean to take my offer?"

"Since I am a gentleman, I did not."

"I also am accounted a gentleman, sir."

"Nay, I took you for a prince," said I.

He made me no answer, but, looking round him again, observed:

"The ship must be near. But for this cursed fog she would be in sight."

"It's well for us she isn't," I said.

"Why, sir?" he asked brusquely.

"If she were, there's the pistol for the lady, and this sword here for you and me," said I coolly. For a man may contrive to speak coolly, though his bearing be a lie and his heart beat quick.

"You daren't," he cried in amazement.

"I should be unwilling," I conceded.

For an instant there was silence. Then came Barbara's voice, soft and fearful:

"Simon, the fog lifts."

It was true. The breeze blew and the fog lifted. Louis' eyes sparkled. All three of us, by one impulse, looked round on the sea. The fresh wind struck my cheek, and the enveloping folds curled lazily away. Barbara held up her hand and pointed. Away on the right, dimly visible, just detached from the remaining clouds of mist, was a dark object, sitting high on the water. A ship it was, in all likelihood the king's ship. We should be sighted soon. My eyes met the King's and his were exultant and joyful; he did not yet believe that I would do what I had said, and he thought that the trap closed on us again. For still the mist rose, and in a few moments they on the ship must see us.

"You shall pay for your trick," he said between his teeth.

"It is very likely," said I. "But I think that the debt will be paid to your Majesty's successor."

Still he did not believe. I burst into a laugh of grim amusement. These great folk find it hard to understand how sometimes their greatness is nothing, and the thing is man to man; but now and then fortune takes a whim and teaches them the lesson for her sport.

"But since you are a King," said I, "you shall have your privilege. You shall pass out before the lady. See, the ship is very plain now. Soon we shall be plain to the ship. Come, sir, you go first."

He looked at me, now puzzled and alarmed.

"I am unarmed," he said.

"It is no fight," I answered. Then I turned to Barbara. "Go and sit in the stern," I said, "and cover your face with your hands."

"Simon, Simon," she moaned, but she obeyed me, and threw herself down, burying her face in her hands. I turned to the king.

"How will you die, sir?" said I quietly, and, as I believe, in a civil manner.

A sudden shout rang in my ears. I would not look away from him, lest he should spring on me or fling himself from the boat. But I knew whence the shout came, for it was charged with joy and the relief of unbearable anxiety. The ship was the King's ship and his servants had seen their master. Yet they would not dare to fire without his orders, and with the risk of killing him; therefore I was easy concerning musket shot. But we must not come near enough for a voice to be heard from us, and a pistol to carry to us.

"How will you die?" I asked again. His eyes questioned me. I added, "As God lives I will." And I smiled at him.

CHAPTER XVII

WHAT BEFELL MY LAST GUINEA

There is this in great station, that it imparts to a man a bearing sedate in good times and debonair in evil. A king may be unkinged, as befell him whom in my youth we called the Royal Martyr, but he need not be unmanned. He has tasted of what men count the best, and, having found even in it much bitterness, turns to greet fortune's new caprice smiling or unmoved. Thus it falls out that though princes live no better lives than common men, yet for the most part they die more noble deaths; their sunset paints all their sky, and we remember not how they bore their glorious burden, but with what grace they laid it down. Much is forgiven to him who dies becomingly, and on earth, as in heaven, there is pardon for the parting soul. Are we to reject what we are taught that God receives? I have need enough of forgiveness to espouse the softer argument.

Now King Louis, surnamed the Great, having more matters in his head than the scheme I thought to baffle, and (to say truth) more ladies in his heart than Barbara Quinton, was not minded to die for the one or the other. But had you been there (which Heaven for your sake forbid, I have passed many a pleasanter night), you would

Anthony Hope

have sworn that death or life weighed not a straw in the balance with him, and that he had no thought save of the destiny God had marked for him and the realm that called him master. So lofty and serene he was, when he perceived my resolution and saw my pistol at his head. On my faith, the victory was mine, but he robbed me of my triumph, and he, submitting, seemed to put terms on me who held him at my mercy. It is all a trick, no doubt; they get it in childhood, as (I mean no harm by my comparisons) the beggar's child learns to whine or the thief's to pick. Yet it is pretty. I wish I had it.

"In truth," said he with a smile that had not a trace of wryness, "I have chosen my means ill for this one time, though they say that I choose well. Well, God rules the world."

"By deputy, sir," said I.

"And deputies don't do His will always? Come, Mr Dale, for this hour you hold the post and fill it well. Wear this for my sake"; and he handed across to me a dagger with a handle richly wrought and studded with precious stones.

I bowed low; yet I kept my finger on the trigger.

"Man, I give you my word, though not in words," said he, and I, rebuked, set my weapon back in its place. "Alas, for a sad moment!" he cried. "I must bid farewell to Mistress Barbara. Yet (this he added, turning to her) life is long, madame, and has many changes. I pray you may never need friends, but should you, there is one ready so long as Louis is King of France. Call on him by the token of his ring and count him your humble servant." With this he stripped his finger of a fine brilliant, and, sinking on his knee in the boat, took her hand very delicately, and, having set the ring on her finger, kissed her hand, sighed lightly yet gallantly, and rose with his eyes set on the ship.

"Row me to her," he commanded me, shortly but not uncivilly; and I, who held his life in my hands, sat down obediently and bent to my oars. In faith, I wish I had that air, it's worth a fortune to a man!

Soon we came to the side of the ship. Over it looked the face of Colbert, amazed that I had stolen his King, and the face of Thomas Lie, indignant that I had made free with his boat; by them were two or three of the crew agape with wonder. King Louis paid no respect to their feelings and stayed their exclamations with a gesture of his hand. He turned to me, saying in low tones and with a smile,

"You must make your own terms with my brother, sir. It has been hard fighting between us, and I am in no mood for generosity."

I did not know what to answer him, but I stammered:

"I ask nothing but that your Majesty should remember me as an honest man."

"And a brave gentleman," he added gravely, with a slight inclination of his head. Then he turned to Barbara and took her hand again, bowing low and saying, "Madame, I had meant you much good in my heart, and my state forced me to mean you some evil. I pray you remember the one and forget the other." He kissed her hand again with a fine grace. It was a fair sounding apology for a thing beyond defence. I admired while I smiled.

But Barbara did not smile. She looked up in his face, then

dropped on her knees in the boat and caught his hand, kissing it twice and trying to speak to him. He stood looking down on her; then he said softly, "Yet I have forgiven your friend," and gently drew his hand away. I stood up, baring my head. He faced round on me and said abruptly, "This affair is between you and me, sir."

"I am obedient to a command I did not need," said I.

"Your pardon. Cover your head. I do not value outward signs of respect where the will is wanting. Fare you well."

At a sign from him Colbert stretched out a hand. Not a question, not a word, scarcely now a show of wonder came from any, save honest Lie, whose eyes stood out of his head and whose tongue was still only because it could not speak. The King leapt lightly on the deck of his ship.

"You'll be paid for the boat," I heard him say to Lie. "Make all sail for Calais."

None spoke to him, none questioned him. He saw no need for explanation and accorded no enlightenment. I marvelled that fear or respect for any man could so bind their tongues. The King waved them away; Lie alone hesitated, but Colbert caught him by the arm and drew him off to the helm. The course was given, and the ship forged ahead. The King stood in the stern. Now he raised his hat from his head and bowed low to Mistress Barbara. I turned to see how she took the salutation; but her face was downcast, resting on her hands. I stood and lifted my hat; then I sat down to the oars. I saw King Louis' set courtly smile, and as our ways parted asunder, his to France, where he ruled, mine to England where I prayed nothing but a hiding-place, we sent into one another's eyes a long look as of men who have measured strength, and part each in his own pride, each in respect for the powers of his enemy. In truth it was something to have played a winning hand with the Most Christian King. With regret I watched him go; though I could not serve him in his affairs of love, I would gladly have fought for him in his wars.

We were alone now on the sea; dawn was breaking and the sky cleared till the cliffs were dimly visible behind us. I pulled the boat round, and set her head for home. Barbara sat in the stern, pale and still, exhausted by the efforts and emotion of the night. The great peril and her great salvation left her numb rather than thankful; and in truth, if she looked into the future, her joy must be dashed with sore apprehension. M. de Perrencourt was gone, the Duke of Monmouth remained; till she could reach her father I was her only help, and I dared not show my face in Dover. But these thoughts were for myself, not for her, and seeking to cheer her I leant forward and said,

"Courage, Mistress Barbara." And I added, "At least we shan't be married, you and I, in Calais."

She started a little, flushed a little, and answered gravely,

"We owe Heaven thanks for a great escape, Simon."

It was true, and the knowledge of its truth had nerved us to the attempt so marvellously crowned with success. Great was the escape from such a marriage, made for such purposes as King Louis had planned. Yet some feeling shot through me, and I gave it voice in saying,

"Nay, but we might have escaped after the marriage also."

Barbara made no reply; for it was none to say, "The cliffs

Anthony Hope

grow very plain."

"But that wouldn't have served our turn," I added with a laugh. "You would have come out of the business saddled with a sore encumbrance."

"Shall you go to Dover?" asked Barbara, seeming to pay no heed to all that I had been saying.

"Where God pleases," I answered rather peevishly. "Her head's to the land, and I'll row straight to land. The land is safer than the sea."

"No place is safe?"

"None," I answered. But then, repenting of my surliness, I added, "And none so perilous that you need fear, Mistress Barbara."

"I don't fear while you're with me, Simon," said she. "You won't leave me till we find my father?"

"Surely not," said I. "Is it your pleasure to seek him?"

"As speedily as we can," she murmured. "He's in London. Even the King won't dare to touch me when I'm with him."

"To London, then!" I said. "Can you make out the coast?"

"There's a little bay just ahead where the cliff breaks; and I see Dover Castle away on my left hand."

"We'll make for the bay," said I, "and then seek means to get to London."

Even as I spoke a sudden thought struck me. I laid down my oars and sought my purse. Barbara was not looking at me, but gazed in a dreamy fashion towards where the Castle rose on its cliff. I opened the purse; it held a single guinea; the rest of my store lay with my saddle-bags in the French King's ship; my head had been too full to think of them. There is none of life's small matters that so irks a man as to confess that he has no money for necessary charges, and it is most sore when a lady looks to him for hers. I, who had praised myself for forgetting how to blush, went red as a cock's comb and felt fit to cry with mortification. A guinea would feed us on the road to London if we fared plainly; but Barbara could not go on her feet.

Her eyes must have come back to my sullen downcast face, for in a moment she cried, "What's the matter, Simon?"

Perhaps she carried money. Well then, I must ask for it. I held out my guinea in my hand.

"It's all I have," said I. "King Louis has the rest."

She gave a little cry of dismay. "I hadn't thought of money," she cried.

"I must beg of you."

"Ah, but, Simon, I have none. I gave my purse to the waiting-woman to carry, so that mine also is in the French King's ship."

Here was humiliation! Our fine schemes stood blocked for the want of so vulgar a thing as money; such fate waits often on fine schemes, but surely never more perversely.

Yet, I know not why, I was glad that she had none. I was a guinea the better of her; the amount was not large, but it served to keep me still her Providence, and that, I fear, is what man, in his vanity, loves to be in woman's eyes; he struts and plumes himself in the pride of it. I had a guinea, and Barbara had nothing. I had sooner it were so than that she had a hundred.

But to her came no such subtle consolation. To lack money was a new horror, untried, undreamt of; the thing had come to her all her days in such measure as she needed it, its want had never thwarted her desires or confined her purpose. To lack the price of post-horses seemed to her as strange as to go fasting for want of bread.

"What shall we do?" she cried in a dismay greater than all the perils of the night had summoned to her heart.

We had about us wealth enough; Louis' dagger was in my belt, his ring on her finger. Yet of what value were they, since there was nobody to buy them? To offer such wares in return for a carriage would seem strange and draw suspicion. I doubted whether even in Dover I should find a Jew with whom to pledge my dagger, and to Dover in broad day I dared not go.

I took up my oars and set again to rowing. The shore was but a mile or two away. The sun shone now and the light was full, the little bay seemed to smile at me as I turned my head; but all smiles are short for a man who has but a guinea in his purse.

"What shall we do?" asked Barbara again. "Is there nobody to whom you can go, Simon?"

There seemed nobody. Buckingham I dared not trust, he was in Monmouth's interest; Darrell had called himself my friend, but he was the servant of Lord Arlington, and my lord the Secretary was not a man to trust. My messenger would guide my enemies and my charge be put in danger.

"Is there nobody, Simon?" she implored.

There was one, one who would aid me with merry willingness and, had she means at the moment, with lavish hand. The thought had sprung to my mind as Barbara spoke. If I could come safely and secretly to a certain house in a certain alley in the town of Dover, I could have money for the sake of old acquaintance, and what had once been something more, between her and me. But would Barbara take largesse from that hand? I am a coward with women; ignorance is fear's mother and, on my life, I do not know how they will take this thing or that, with scorn or tears or shame or what, or again with some surprising turn of softness and (if I may make bold to say it) a pliability of mind to which few of us men lay claim and none give honour. But the last mood was not Barbara's, and, as I looked at her, I dared not tell her where lay my only hope of help in Dover. I put my wits to work how I could win the aid for her, and keep the hand a secret. Such deception would sit lightly on my conscience.

"I am thinking," I replied to her, "whether there is anyone, and how I might reach him, if there is."

"Surely there's someone who would serve you and whom you could trust?" she urged.

"Would you trust anyone whom I trust?" I asked.

Anthony Hope

"In truth, yes."

"And would you take the service if I would?"

"Am I so rich that I can choose?" she said piteously.

"I have your promise to it?"

"Yes," she answered with no hesitation, nay, with a readiness that made me ashamed of my stratagem. Yet, as Barbara said, beggars cannot be choosers even in their stratagems, and, if need were, I must hold her to her word.

Now we were at the land and the keel of our boat grated on the shingle. We disembarked under the shadow of the cliffs at the eastern end of the bay; all was solitude, save for a little house standing some way back from the sea, half-way up the cliff, on a level platform cut in the face of the rock. It seemed a fisherman's cottage; thence might come breakfast, and for so much our guinea would hold good. There was a recess in the cliffs, and here I bade Barbara sit and rest herself, sheltered from view on either side, while I went forward to try my luck at the cottage. She seemed reluctant to be left, but obeyed me, standing and watching while I took my way, which I chose cautiously, keeping myself as much within the shadow as might be. I had sooner not have ventured this much exposure, but it is ill to face starvation for safety's sake.

The cottage lay but a hundred yards off, and soon I approached it. It was hard on six o'clock now, and I looked to find the inmates up and stirring. I wondered also whether Monmouth were gone to await Barbara and myself at the Merry Mariners in Deal; alas, we were too near the trysting-place! Or had he heard by now that the bird was flown from his lure and caged by that M. de

Perrencourt who had treated him so cavalierly? I could not tell. Here was the cottage; but I stood still suddenly, amazed and cautious. For there, in the peaceful morning, in the sun's kindly light, there lay across the threshold the body of a man; his eyes, wide-opened, stared at the sky, but seemed to see nothing of what they gazed at; his brown coat was stained to a dark rusty hue on the breast, where a gash in the stuff showed the passage of a sword. His hand clasped a long knife, and his face was known to me. I had seen it daily at my uprising and lying-down. The body was that of Jonah Wall, in the flesh my servant, in spirit the slave of Phineas Tate, whose teaching had brought him to this pass.

The sight bred in me swift horror and enduring caution. The two Dukes had been despatched, sorely against their will, in chase of this man. Was it to their hands that he had yielded up his life and by their doing that he lay like carrion? It might well be that he had sought refuge in this cottage, and having found there death, not comfort, had been flung forth a corpse. I pitied him; although he had been party to a plot which had well nigh caused my own death and taken no account of my honour, yet I was sorry for him. He had been about me; I grieved for him as for the cat on my hearth. Well, now in death he warned me; it was some recompense; I lifted my hat as I stole by him and slunk round to the side of the house. There was a window there, or rather a window-frame, for glass there was none; it stood some six feet from the ground and I crouched beneath it, for I now heard voices in the cottage.

"I wish the rascal hadn't fought," said one voice. "But he flew at me like a tiger, and I had much ado to stop him. I was compelled to run him through."

"Yet he might have served me alive," said another.

"Your Grace is right. For although we hate these foul schemes, the men had the root of the matter in them."

"They were no Papists, at least," said the second voice.

"But the King will be pleased."

"Oh, a curse on the King, although he's what he is to me! Haven't you heard? When I returned to the Castle from my search on the other side of the town, seeking you or Buckingham—by the way, where is he?"

"Back in his bed, I warrant, sir."

"The lazy dog! Well then, they told me she was gone with Louis. I rode on to tell you, for, said I, the King may hunt his conspirators himself now. But who went with them?"

"Your Grace will wonder if I say Simon Dale was the man?"

"The scoundrel! It was he! He has deluded us most handsomely. He was in Louis' pay, and Louis has a use for him! I'll slit the knave's throat if I get at him."

"I pray your Grace's leave to be the first man at him."

"In truth I'm much obliged to you, my Lord Carford," said I to myself under the window.

"There's no use in going to Deal," cried Monmouth. "Oh, I wish I had the fellow here! She's gone, Carford; God's curse on it, she's gone! The prettiest wench at Court! Louis has captured her. 'Fore heaven, if only I were a King!"

"Heaven has its own times, sir," said Carford insidiously. But the Duke, suffering from disappointed desire, was not to be led to affairs of State.

"She's gone," he exclaimed again. "By God, sooner than lose her, I'd have married her."

This speech made me start. She was near him; what if she had been as near him as I, and had heard those words? A pang shot through me, and, of its own accord, my hand moved to my sword-hilt.

"She is beneath your Grace's station. The spouse of your Grace may one day be—" Carford interrupted himself with a laugh, and added, "What God wills."

"So may Anne Hyde," exclaimed the Duke. "But I forget. You yourself had marked her."

"I am your Grace's humble servant always," answered Carford smoothly.

Monmouth laughed. Carford had his pay, no doubt, and I trust it was large; for he heard quietly a laugh that called him what King Louis had graciously proposed to make of me. I am glad when men who live by dirty ways are made to eat dirt.

"And my father," said the Duke, "is happy. She is gone, Querouaille stays; why, he's so enamoured that he has charged Nell to return to London to-day, or at the latest by to-morrow, lest the French lady's virtue should be offended."

At this both laughed, Monmouth at his father, Carford at his King.

Anthony Hope

"What's that?" cried the Duke an instant later.

Now what disturbed him was no other than a most imprudent exclamation wrung from me by what I heard; it must have reached them faintly, yet it was enough. I heard their swords rattle and their spurs jingle as they sprang to their feet. I slipped hastily behind the cottage. But by good luck at this instant came other steps. As the Duke and Carford ran to the door, the owner of the cottage (as I judged him to be) walked up, and Carford cried:

"Ah, the fisherman! Come, sir, we'll make him show us the nearest way. Have you fed the horses, fellow?"

"They have been fed, my lord, and are ready," was the answer.

I did not hear more speech, but only (to my relief) the tramp of feet as the three went off together. I stole cautiously out and watched them heading for the top of the cliff. Jonah Wall lay still where he was, and when the retreating party were out of sight I did not hesitate to search his body for money. I had supplied his purse, but now his purse was emptier than mine. Then I stepped into the cottage, seeking not money but food. Fortune was kinder here and rewarded me with a pasty, half-eaten, and a jug of ale. By the side of these lay, left by the Duke in his wonted profusion, a guinea. The Devil has whimsical ways; I protest that the temptation I suffered here was among the strongest of my life! I could repay the fellow some day; two guineas would be by far more than twice as much as one. Yet I left the pleasant golden thing there, carrying off only the pasty and the ale; as for the jug—a man must not stand on nice scruples, and Monmouth's guinea would more than pay for all.

I made my way quickly back to Barbara with the poor spoils of my expedition. I rounded the bluff of cliff that protected her hiding-place. Again I stood amazed, asking if fortune had more tricks in her bag for me. The recess was empty. But a moment later I was reassured; a voice called to me, and I saw her some thirty yards away, down on the sea-beach. I set down pasty and jug and turned to watch. Then I perceived what went on; white feet were visible in the shallow water, twinkling in and out as the tide rolled up and back.

"I had best employ myself in making breakfast ready," said I, turning my back. But she called out to me again, saying how delightful was the cool water. So I looked, and saw her gay and merry. Her hat was in her hand now, and her hair blew free in the breeze. She had given herself up to the joy of the moment. I rejoiced in a feeling which I could not share; the rebound from the strain of the night left me sad and apprehensive. I sat down and rested my head on my hands, waiting till she came back. When she came, she would not take the food I offered her, but stood a moment, looking at me with puzzled eyes, before she seated herself near.

"You're sad," she said, almost as though in accusation.

"Could I be otherwise, Mistress Barbara?" I asked. "We're in some danger, and, what's worse, we've hardly a penny."

"But we've escaped the greatest peril," she reminded me.

"True, for the moment."

"We—you won't be married to-night," she laughed, with rising colour, and turning away as though a tuft of rank grass by her had caught her attention and for some hidden reason much deserved it.

"By God's help we've come out of that snare," said I gravely.

She said nothing for a moment or two; then she turned to me again, asking,

"If your friend furnishes money, can we reach London in two days?"

"I'm sorry," I answered, "but the journey will need nearer three, unless we travel at the King's pace or the Duke of Monmouth's."

"You needn't come all the way with me. Set me safe on the road, and go where your business calls you."

"For what crime is this punishment?" I asked with a smile.

"No, I'm serious. I'm not seeking a compliment from you. I see that you're sad. You have been very kind to me, Simon. You risked life and liberty to save me."

"Well, who could do less? Besides, I had given my promise to my lord your father."

She made no reply, and I, desiring to warn her against every danger, related what had passed at the cottage, omitting only Monmouth's loudmouthed threats against myself. At last, moved by some impulse of curiosity rather than anything higher, I repeated how the Duke had said that, sooner than lose her altogether, he would have married her, and how my Lord Carford had been still his humble servant in this project as in any other. She flushed again as she heard me, and plucked her tuft of grass.

"Indeed," I ended, "I believe his Grace spoke no more than the truth; I've never seen a man more in love."

"And you know well what it is to be in love, don't you?"

"Very well," I answered calmly, although I thought that the taunt might have been spared. "Therefore it may well be that some day I shall kiss the hand of her Grace the Duchess."

"You think I desire it?" she asked.

"I think most ladies would."

"I don't desire it." She sprang up and stamped her foot on the ground, crying again, "Simon, I do not desire it. I wouldn't be his wife. You smile! You don't believe me?"

"No offer is refused until it's made," said I, and, with a bow that asked permission, I took a draught of the ale.

She looked at me in great anger, her cheek suffused with underlying red and her dark eyes sparkling.

"I wish you hadn't saved me," she said in a fury.

"That we had gone forward to Calais?" I asked maliciously.

"Sir, you're insolent." She flung the reproof at me like a stone from a catapult. But then she repeated, "I wouldn't be his wife."

"Well, then, you wouldn't," said I, setting down the jug and rising. "How shall we pass the day? For we mustn't go to Dover till nightfall."

"I must be all day here with you?" she cried in visible consternation.

"You must be all day here, but you needn't be with me. I'll go down to the beach; I shall be within hail if need arises, and you can rest here alone."

"Thank you, Simon," she answered with a most sudden and wonderful meekness.

Without more, I took my way to the seashore and lay down on the sun-warmed shingle. Being very weary and without sleep now for six-and-thirty hours, I soon closed my eyes, keeping the pistol ready by my side. I slept peacefully and without a dream; the sun was high in heaven when, with a yawn and a stretching of my limbs, I awoke. I heard, as I opened my eyes, a little rustling as of somebody moving; my hand flew to the butt of my pistol. But when I turned round I saw Barbara only. She was sitting a little way behind me, looking out over the sea. Feeling my gaze she looked round.

"I grew afraid, left all alone," she said in a timid voice.

"Alas, I snored when I should have been on guard!" I exclaimed.

"You didn't snore," she cried. "I—I mean not in the last few moments. I had only just come near you. I'm afraid I spoke unkindly to you."

"I hadn't given a thought to it," I hastened to assure her.

"You were indifferent to what I said?" she cried.

I rose to my feet and made her a bow of mock ceremony.

My rest had put me in heart again, and I was in a mood to be merry.

"Nay, madame," said I, "you know that I am your devoted servant, and that all I have in the world is held at your disposal."

She looked sideways at me, then at the sea again.

"By heaven, it's true!" I cried. "All I have is yours. See!" I took out my precious guinea, and bending on my knee with uncovered head presented it to Mistress Barbara.

She turned her eyes down to it and sat regarding it for a moment.

"It's all I have, but it's yours," said I most humbly.

"Mine?"

"Most heartily."

She lifted it from my palm with finger and thumb very daintily, and, before I knew what she was doing, or could have moved to hinder her if I had the mind, she raised her arm over her head and with all her strength flung the guinea into the sparkling waves.

"Heaven help us!" I cried.

"It was mine. That's what I chose to do with it," said Barbara.

CHAPTER XVIII

SOME MIGHTY SILLY BUSINESS

"In truth, madame," said I, "it's the wont of your sex. As soon as a woman knows a thing to be hers entirely, she'll fling it away." With this scrap of love's lore and youth's philosophy I turned my back on my companion, and having walked to where the battered pasty lay beside the empty jug sat down in high dudgeon. Barbara's eyes were set on the spot where the guinea had been swallowed by the waves, and she took no heed of my remark nor of my going.

Say that my pleasantry was misplaced, say that she was weary and strained beyond her power, say what you will in excuse, I allow it all. Yet it was not reason to fling my last guinea into the sea. A flash of petulance is well enough and may become beauty as summer lightning decks the sky, but fury is for termagants, and nought but fury could fling my last guinea to the waves. The offence, if offence there were, was too small for so monstrous an outburst. Well, if she would quarrel, I was ready; I had no patience with such tricks; they weary a man of sense; women serve their turn ill by using them. Also I had done her some small service. I would die sooner than call it to her mind, but it would have been a grace in her to remember it.

The afternoon came, grew to its height, and waned as I lay, back to sea and face to cliff, thinking now of all that had passed, now of what was before me, sparing a moment's fitful sorrow for the poor wretch who lay dead there by the cottage door, but returning always in resentful mood to my lost guinea and Barbara's sore lack of courtesy. If she needed me, I was ready; but heaven forbid that I should face fresh rebuffs by seeking her! I would do my duty to her and redeem my pledge. More could not now be looked for, nay, by no possibility could be welcome; to keep away from her was to please her best. It was well, for in that her mind jumped with mine. In two hours now we could set out for Dover.

"Simon, I'm hungry."

The voice came from behind my shoulder, a yard or two away, a voice very meek and piteous, eloquent of an exhaustion and a weakness so great that, had they been real, she must have fallen by me, not stood upright on her feet. Against such stratagems I would be iron. I paid no heed, but lay like a log.

"Simon, I'm very thirsty too."

Slowly I gathered myself up and, standing, bowed.

"There's a fragment of the pasty," said I; "but the jug is empty."

I did not look in her face and I knew she did not look in mine.

"I can't eat without drinking," she murmured.

"I have nothing with which to buy liquor, and there's nowhere to buy it."

"But water, Simon? Ah, but I mustn't trouble you."

"I'll go to the cottage and seek some."

"But that's dangerous."

"You shall come to no hurt."

"But you?"

"Indeed I need a draught for myself. I should have gone after one in any case."

There was a pause, then Barbara said:

"I don't want it. My thirst has passed away."

"Will you take the pasty?"

"No, my hunger is gone too."

I bowed again. We stood in silence for a moment.

"I'll walk a little," said Barbara.

"At your pleasure," said I. "But pray don't go far, there may be danger."

She turned away and retraced her steps to the beach. The instant she was gone, I sprang up, seized the jug, and ran at the best of my speed to the cottage. Jonah Wall lay still across the entrance, no living creature was in sight; I darted in and looked round for water; a pitcher stood on the table, and I filled the jug hastily. Then, with a smile of sour triumph, I hurried back the way I had come. She should have no cause to complain of me. I had been wronged, and was minded to hug my grievance and keep the merit of the difference all on my side. That motive too commonly underlies a seeming patience of wrong. I would not for the world enrich her with a just quarrel, therefore I brought her water, ay, although she feigned not to desire it. There it was for her, let her take it if she would, or leave it if she would; and I set the jug down by the pasty. She should not say that I had refused to fetch her what she asked, although she had, for her own good reasons, flung my guinea into the sea. She would come soon, then would be my hour. Yet I would spare her; a gentleman should show no exultation; silence would serve to point the moral.

But where was she? To say truth, I was impatient for the play to begin and anticipation grew flat with waiting. I looked down to the shore but could not see her. I rose and walked forward till the beach lay open before me. Where was Barbara?

A sudden fear ran through me. Had any madness seized the girl, some uncontrolled whim made her fly from me? She could not be so foolish. But where was she? On the moment of the question a cry of surprise rang from my lips. There, ahead of me, not on the shore, but on the sea, was Barbara. The boat was twelve or fifteen yards from the beach, Barbara's face was towards me, and she was rowing out to sea. Forgetting pasty and jug, I bounded down. What new folly was this? To show herself in the boat was to court capture. And why did she row out to sea? In an instant I was on the margin of the water. I called out to her, she took no heed; the boat was heavy, but putting her strength into the strokes she drove it along.

Anthony Hope

Again I called, and called unheeded. Was this my triumph? I saw a smile on her face. Not she, but I, afforded the sport then. I would not stand there, mocked for a fool by her eyes and her smile.

"Come back," I cried.

The boat moved on. I was in the water to my knees. "Come back," I cried. I heard a laugh from the boat, a high nervous laugh; but the boat moved on. With an oath I cast my sword from me, throwing it behind me on the beach, and plunged into the water. Soon I was up to the neck, and I took to swimming. Straight out to sea went the boat, not fast, but relentlessly. In grim anger I swam with all my strength. I could not gain on her. She had ceased now even to look where my head bobbed among the waves; her face was lifted towards the sky. By heaven, did she in very truth mean to leave me? I called once more. Now she answered.

"Go back," she said. "I'm going alone."

"By heaven, you aren't," I muttered with a gasp, and set myself to a faster stroke. Bad to deal with are women! Must she fly from me and risk all because I had not smiled and grinned and run for what she needed, like a well-trained monkey? Well, I would catch her and bring her back.

But catch her I could not. A poor oarsman may beat a fair swimmer, and she had the start of me. Steadily out to sea she rowed, and I toiled behind. If her mood lasted—and hurt pride lasts long in disdainful ladies who are more wont to deal strokes than to bear them—my choice was plain. I must drown there like a rat, or turn back a beaten cur. Alas for my triumph! If to have thought on it were sin, I was now chastened. But Barbara rowed on. In very truth she meant to leave me, punishing herself if by that she might sting me. What man would have shown that folly—or that flower of pride?

Yet was I beaten? I do not love to be beaten, above all when the game has seemed in my hands. I had a card to play, and, between my pants, smiled grimly as it came into my mind. I glanced over my shoulder; I was hard on half-a-mile from shore. Women are compassionate; quick on pride's heels there comes remorse. I looked at the boat; the interval that parted me from it had not narrowed by an inch, and its head was straight for the coast of France. I raised my voice, crying:

"Stop, stop!"

No answer came. The boat moved on. The slim figure bent and rose again, the blades moved through the water. Well then, the card should be played, the trick of a wily gamester, but my only resource.

"Help, help!" I cried; and letting my legs fall and raising my hands over my head, I inhaled a full breath and sank like a stone, far out of sight beneath the water. Here I abode as long as I could; then, after swimming some yards under the surface, I rose and put my head out again, gasping hard and clearing my matted hair from before my eyes. I could scarcely stifle a cry. The boat's head was turned now, and Barbara was rowing with furious speed towards where I had sunk, her head turned over her shoulder and her eyes fixed on the spot. She passed by where I was, but did not see me. She reached the spot and dropped her oars.

"Help, help!" I cried a second time, and stayed long

Anthony Hope

enough to let her see my head before I dived below. But my stay was shorter now. Up again, I looked for her. She was all but over me as she went by; she panted, she sobbed, and the oars only just touched water. I swam five strokes and caught at the gunwale of the boat. A loud cry broke from her. The oars fell from her hand. The boat was broad and steady. I flung my leg over and climbed in, panting hard. In truth I was out of breath. Barbara cried, "You're safe!" and hid her face in her hands.

We were mad both of us, beyond a doubt, she sobbing there on the thwart, I panting and dripping in the bows. Yet for a touch of such sweet madness now, when all young nature was strung to a delicious contest, and the blood spun through the veins full of life! Our boat lay motionless on the sea, and the setting sun caught the undergrowth of red-brown hair that shot through Barbara's dark locks. My own state was, I must confess, less fair to look on.

I controlled my voice to a cold steadiness, as I wrung the water from my clothes.

"This is a mighty silly business, Mistress Barbara," said I.

I had angled for a new outburst of fury, my catch was not what I looked for. Her hands were stretched out towards me, and her face, pale and tearful, pleaded with me.

"Simon, Simon, you were drowning! Through my—my folly! Oh, will you ever forgive me? If—if you had come to hurt, I wouldn't have lived."

"Yet you were running away from me."

"I didn't dream that you'd follow. Indeed I didn't think that you'd risk death." Then her eyes seemed to fall on my dripping clothes. In an instant she snatched up the cloak that lay by her, and held it towards me, crying "Wrap yourself in it."

"Nay, keep your cloak," said I, "I shall be warm enough with rowing. I pray you, madame, tell me the meaning of this freak of yours."

"Nothing, nothing. I—Oh, forgive me, Simon. Ah, how I shuddered when I looked round on the water and couldn't see you! I vowed to God that if you were saved—." She stopped abruptly.

"My death would have been on your conscience?" I asked.

"Till my own death," she said.

"Then indeed," said I, "I'm very glad that I wasn't drowned."

"It's enough that you were in peril of it," she murmured woefully.

"I pray heaven," said I cheerfully, "that I may never be in greater. Come, Mistress Barbara, sport for sport, trick for trick, feint for feint. I think your intention of leaving me was pretty much as real as this peril of drowning from which I have escaped."

Her hands, which still implored me, fell to her side. An expression of wonder spread over her face.

"In truth, I meant to leave you," she said.

"And why, madame?"

"Because I burdened you."

"But you had consented to accept my aid."

"While you seemed to give it willingly. But I had angered you in the matter of that—"

"Ay, of that guinea. Well, it was my last."

"Yes, of the guinea. Although I was foolish, yet I could not endure your—" Again she hesitated.

"Pray let me hear?" said I.

"I would not stay where my company was suffered rather than prized," said she.

"So you were for trying fortune alone?"

"Better that than with an unwilling defender," said she.

"Behold your injustice!" I cried. "For, rather than lose you, I have faced all, even drowning!" And I laughed.

Her eyes were fixed on my face, but she did not speak. I believe she feared to ask me the question that was in her dark eyes. But at last she murmured:

"Why do you speak of tricks? Simon, why do you laugh?"

"Why, since by a trick you left me—indeed I cannot believe it was no trick."

"I swear it was no trick!"

"I warrant it was. And thus by a trick I have contrived to thwart it."

"By a trick?"

"Most assuredly. Am I a man to drown with half a mile's swimming in smooth water?" Again I laughed.

She leant forward and spoke in an agitated voice, yet imperiously.

"Tell me the truth. Were you indeed in danger and distress?"

"Not a whit," said I composedly. "But you wouldn't wait for me."

Slowly came her next question.

"It was a trick, then?"

"And crowned with great success," said I.

"All a trick?"

"Throughout," I answered.

Her face grew set and rigid, and, if it might be, yet paler than before. I waited for her to speak, but she said nothing. She drew away the cloak that she had offered me, and, wrapping it about her shoulders, withdrew to the stern of the boat. I took her place, and laid hold of the oars.

"What's your pleasure now, madame?" I asked.

"What you will," she said briefly.

I looked at her; she met my gaze with a steady regard. I had expected scorn, but found grief and hurt. Accused by the sight, I wrapped myself in a cold flippancy.

"There is small choice," said I. "The beach is there, and that we have found not pleasant. Calais is yonder, where certainly we must not go. To Dover then? Evening falls, and if we go gently it will be dark before we reach the town."

"Where you will. I care not," said Barbara, and she folded her cloak so about her face that I could see little more of her than her eyes and her brows. Here at length was my triumph, as sweet as such joys are; malice is their fount and they smack of its bitterness. Had I followed my heart, I would have prayed her pardon. A sore spirit I had impelled her, my revenge lacked justice. Yet I would not abase myself, being now in my turn sore and therefore obstinate. With slow strokes I propelled the boat towards Dover town.

For half an hour I rowed; dusk fell, and I saw the lights of Dover. A gentler mood came on me. I rested an instant, and, leaning forward, said to Barbara:

"Yet I must thank you. Had I been in peril, you would have saved me."

No answer came.

"I perceived that you were moved by my fancied danger," I persisted.

Then she spoke clearly, calmly, and coldly.

"I wouldn't have a dog drown under my eyes," said she. "The spectacle is painful."

I performed such a bow as I could, sitting there, and took up my oars again. I had made my advance; if such were the welcome, no more should come from me. I rowed slowly on, then lay on my oars awhile, waiting for darkness to fall. The night came, misty again and chill. I grew cold as I waited (my clothes were but half-dry), and would gladly have thumped myself with my hands. But I should have seemed to ask pity of the statue that sat there, enveloped in the cloak, with closed eyes and pale unmoved face. Suddenly she spoke.

"Are you cold, sir?"

"Cold? I am somewhat over-heated with rowing, madame," I answered. "But, I pray you, wrap your cloak closer round you."

"I am very well, I thank you, sir."

Yet cold I was, and bitterly. Moreover I was hungry and somewhat faint. Was Barbara hungry? I dared not ask her lest she should find a fresh mockery in the question.

When I ventured to beach the boat a little way out of Dover, it was quite dark, being hard on ten o'clock. I offered Barbara my hand to alight, but she passed it by unnoticed. Leaving the boat to its fate, we walked towards the town.

"Where are you taking me?" asked Barbara.

"To the one person who can serve us," I answered. "Veil your face, and it would be well that we shouldn't speak loud."

"I have no desire to speak at all," said Barbara.

I would not tell her whither she went. Had we been friends, to bring her there would have taxed my persuasion to the full; as our affairs stood, I knew she would lie the night in the street before she would go. But if I got her to the house, I could keep her. But would she reach the house? She walked very wearily, faltering in her step and stumbling over every loose stone. I put out my arm to save her once, but she drew away from it, as though I had meant to strike her.

At last we came to the narrow alley; making a sign to Barbara, I turned down it. The house was in front of me; all was quiet, we had escaped detection. Why, who should seek for us? We were at Calais with King Louis, at Calais where we were to be married!

Looking at the house, I found the upper windows dark; there had been the quarters of Phineas Tate, and the King had found him others. But below there was a light.

"Will it please you to wait an instant, while I go forward and rouse my friend? I shall see then whether all is safe."

"I will wait here," answered Barbara, and she leant against the wall of the alley which fronted the house. In much trepidation I went on and knocked with my knuckles on the door. There was no other course; yet I did not know how either of them would take my action—the lady within or the lady without, she whom I asked for succour or she in whose cause I sought it.

My entry was easy; a man-servant and a maid were just

within, and the house seemed astir. My request for their mistress caused no surprise; the girl opened the door of the room. I knew the room and gave my name. A cry of pleasure greeted it, and a moment later Nell herself stood before me.

"From the Castle or Calais, from Deal or the devil?" she cried. In truth she had a knack of telling you all she knew in a sentence.

"Why, from half-way between Deal and the devil," said I. "For I have left Monmouth on one side and M. de Perrencourt on the other, and am come safe through."

"A witty Simon! But why in Dover again?"

"For want of a friend, mistress. Am I come to one?"

"With all my heart, Simon. What would you?"

"Means to go to London."

"Now Heaven is kind! I go there myself in a few hours. You stare. In truth, it's worth a stare. But the King commands. How did you get rid of Louis?"

I told her briefly. She seemed barely to listen, but looked at me with evident curiosity, and, I think, with some pleasure.

"A brave thing!" she cried. "Come, I'll carry you to London. Nobody shall touch you while you're hid under the hem of my petticoat. It will be like old times, Simon."

"I have no money," said I.

"But I have plenty. For the less the King comes, the more he sends. He's a gentleman in his apologies." Her sigh breathed more contentment than repining.

"So you'll take me with you?"

"To the world's end, Simon, and if you don't ask that, at least to London."

"But I'm not alone," said I.

She looked at me for an instant. Then she began to laugh.

"Whom have you with you?" she asked.

"The lady," said I.

She laughed still, but it seemed to me not very heartily.

"I'm glad," she said, "that one man in England thinks me a good Christian. By heaven, you do, Simon, or you'd never ask me to aid your love."

"There's no love in the matter," I cried. "We're at daggers drawn."

"Then certainly there's love in it," said Mistress Nell, nodding her pretty head in a mighty sagacious manner. "Does she know to whom you've brought her?"

"Not yet," I answered with a somewhat uneasy smile.

"How will she take it?"

"She has no other help," said I.

"Oh, Simon, what a smooth tongue is yours!" She paused, seeming, to fall into a reverie. Then she looked at me wickedly.

"You and your lady are ready to face the perils of the road?"

"Her peril is greater here, and mine as great."

"The King's pursuit, Monmouth's rage, soldiers, officers, footpads?"

"A fig for them all!"

"Another peril?"

"For her or for me?"

"Why, for both, good Simon. Don't you understand! See then!" She came near to me, smiling most saucily, and pursing her lips together as though she meant to kiss me.

"If I were vowed to the lady, I should fear the test," said I, "but I am free."

"Where is she?" asked Nell, letting my answer pass with a pout.

"By your very door."

"Let's have her in," cried Nell, and straightway she ran into the alley.

I followed, and came up with her just as she reached Barbara. Barbara leant no more against the wall, but lay huddled at the foot of it. Weariness and hunger had

Anthony Hope

overcome her; she was in a faint, her lips colourless and her eyes closed. Nell dropped beside her, murmuring low, soft consolations. I stood by in awkward helplessness. These matters were beyond my learning.

"Lift her and carry her in," Nell commanded, and, stooping, I lifted her in my arms. The maid and the man stared. Nell shut the door sharply on them.

"What have you done to her?" she cried to me in angry accusation. "You've let her go without food."

"We had none. She flung my last money into the sea," I pleaded.

"And why? Oh, hold your peace and let us be!"

To question and refuse an answer is woman's way; should it be forbidden to Nell, who was woman from crown to sole? I shrugged my shoulders and drew off to the far end of the room. For some moments I heard nothing and remained very uneasy, not knowing whether it were allowed me to look or not, nor what passed. Then I heard Barbara's voice.

"I thank you, I thank you much. But where am I, and who are you? Forgive me, but who are you?"

"You're in Dover, and safe enough, madame," answered Nell. "What does it matter who I am? Will you drink a little of this to please me?"

"No, but who are you? I seem to know your face."

"Like enough. Many have seen it."

"But tell me who you are."

"Since you will know, Simon Dale must stand sponsor for me. Here, Simon!"

I rose in obedience to the summons. A thing that a man does not feel of his own accord, a girl's eyes will often make him feel. I took my stand by Nell boldly enough; but Barbara's eyes were on mine, and I was full of fear.

"Tell her who I am, Simon," said Nell.

I looked at Nell. As I live, the fear that was in my heart was in her eyes. Yet she had faced the world and laughed to scorn all England's frowns. She understood my thought, and coloured red. Since when had Cydaria learnt to blush? Even at Hatchstead my blush had been the target for her mockery. "Tell her," she repeated angrily.

But Barbara knew. Turning to her, I had seen the knowledge take shape in her eyes and grow to revulsion and dismay. I could not tell what she would say; but now my fear was in no way for myself. She seemed to watch Nell for awhile in a strange mingling of horror and attraction. Then she rose, and, still without a word, took her way on trembling feet towards the door. To me she gave no glance and seemed to pay no heed. We two looked for an instant, then Nell darted forward.

"You mustn't go," she cried. "Where would you go? You've no other friend."

Barbara paused, took one step more, paused again.

"I shan't harm you," said Nell. Then she laughed. "You needn't touch me, if you will have it so. But I can help you. And I can help Simon; he's not safe in Dover." She had grown grave, but she ended with another laugh, "You needn't touch me. My maid is a good girl—yes, it's true—and she shall tend you."

"For pity's sake, Mistress Barbara—" I began.

"Hush," said Nell, waving me back with a motion of her hand. Barbara now stood still in the middle of the room. She turned her eyes on me, and her whisper sounded clear through all the room.

"Is it—?" she asked.

"It is Mistress Eleanor Gwyn," said I, bowing my head.

Nell laughed a short strange laugh; I saw her breast rise and fall, and a bright red patch marked either cheek.

"Yes, I'm Nelly," said she, and laughed again.

Barbara's eyes met hers.

"You were at Hatchstead?"

"Yes," said Nell, and now she smiled defiantly; but in a moment she sprang forward, for Barbara had reeled, and seemed like to faint again and fall. A proud motion of the hand forbade Nell's approach, but weakness baffled pride, and now perforce Barbara caught at her hand.

"I—I can go in a moment," stammered Barbara. "But—."

Nell held one hand. Very slowly, very timidly, with fear and shame plain on her face, she drew nearer, and put out her other hand to Barbara. Barbara did not resist her, but let her come nearer; Nell's glance warned me not to move, and I stood where I was, watching them. Now the clasp of the hand was changed for a touch on the shoulder, now the comforting arm sank to the waist and stole round it, full as timidly as ever gallant's round a denying mistress; still I watched, and I met Nell's bright eyes, which looked across at me wet and sparkling. The dark hair almost mingled with the ruddy brown as Barbara's head fell on Nell's shoulder. I heard a little sob, and Barbara moaned:

"Oh, I'm tired, and very hungry."

"Rest here, and you shall have food, my pretty," said Nell Gwyn. "Simon, go and bid them give you some."

I went, glad to go. And as I went I heard, "There, pretty, don't cry."

Well, women love to weep. A plague on them, though, they need not make us also fools.

CHAPTER XIX

A NIGHT ON THE ROAD

In a man of green age and inexperience a hasty judgment may gain pardon and none need wonder that his hopes carry him on straightway to conclusions born of desire rather than of reason. The meeting I feared had passed off so softly that I forgot how strange and delicate it was, and what were the barriers which a gust of sympathy had for the moment levelled. It did not enter my mind that they must raise their heads again, and that friendship, or even companionship, must be impossible between the two whom I, desperately seeking some refuge, had thrown together. Yet an endeavour was made, and that on both sides; obligation blunted the edge of Mistress Barbara's scorn, freedom's respect for virtue's chain schooled Nell to an unwonted staidness of demeanour. The fires of war but smouldered, the faintest puff of smoke showing only here and there. I was on the alert to avoid an outbreak; for awhile no outbreak came and my hopes grew to confidence. But then—I can write the thing no other way—that ancient devil of hers made re-entry into the heart of Mistress Gwyn. I was a man, and a man who had loved her; it was then twice intolerable that I should disclaim her dominion, that I should be free, nay, that I should serve another with a sedulous care which might well seem devotion; for the offence touching the guinea was forgotten, my mock drowning well-nigh forgiven, and although Barbara had few words for me, they were such that gratitude and friendship shone in them through the veil of embarrassment. Mistress Nell's shrewd eyes were on us, and she watched while she aided. It was in truth her interest, as she conceived, to carry Barbara safe out of Dover; but there was kindness also in her ample succour; although (ever slave to the sparkle of a gem) she seized with eager gratitude on Louis' jewelled dagger when I offered it as my share of our journey's charges, she gave full return; Barbara was seated in her coach, a good horse was provided for me, her servant found me a sober suit of clothes and a sword. Thus our strange party stole from Dover before the town was awake, Nell obeying the King's command which sent her back to London, and delighting that she could punish him for it by going in our company. I rode behind the coach, bearing myself like a serving-man until we reached open country, when I quickened pace and stationed myself by the window. Up to this time matters had gone well; if they spoke, it was of service given and kindness shown. But as the day wore on and we came near Canterbury the devil began to busy himself. Perhaps I showed some discouragement at the growing coldness of Barbara's manner, and my anxiety to warm her to greater cordiality acted as a spur on our companion. First Nell laughed that my sallies gained small attention and my compliments no return, that Barbara would not talk of our adventures of the day before, but harped always on coming speedily where her father was and so discharging me from my forced service. A merry look declared that if Mistress Quinton would not play the game another would; a fusillade of glances opened, Barbara seeing and feigning not to see, I embarrassed, yet chagrined into some return; there followed words, half-whispered, half-aloud, not sparing in

　　　　　Anthony Hope

reminiscence of other days and mischievously pointed with tender sentiment. The challenge to my manhood was too tempting, the joy of encounter too sweet. Barbara grew utterly silent, sitting with eyes downcast and lips set in a disapproval that needed no speech for its expression. Bolder and bolder came Nell's advances; when I sought to drop behind she called me up; if I rode ahead she swore she would bid the driver gallop his horses till she came to me again. "I can't be without you, Simon. Ah, 'tis so long since we were together," she whispered, and turned naughty eyes on Barbara.

Yet we might have come through without declared conflict, had not a thing befallen us at Canterbury that brought Nell into fresh temptation, and thereby broke the strained cords of amity. The doings of the King at Dover had set the country in some stir; there was no love of the French, and less of the Pope; men were asking, and pretty loudly, why Madame came; she had been seen in Canterbury, the Duke of York had given a great entertainment there for her. They did not know what I knew, but they were uneasy concerning the King's religion and their own. Yet Nell must needs put her head well out of window as we drove in. I know not whether the sequel were what she desired, it was at least what she seemed not to fear; a fellow caught sight of her and raised a cheer. The news spread quick among the idle folk in the street, and the busy, hearing it, came out of their houses. A few looked askance at our protector, but the larger part, setting their Protestantism above their scruples, greeted her gladly, and made a procession for her, cheering and encouraging her with cries which had more friendliness than delicacy in them. Now indeed I dropped behind and rode beside the mounted servant. The fellow was all agrin, triumphing in his mistress's popularity. Even so she herself exulted in it, and threw all around nods and smiles, ay, and, alas, repartees conceived much in the same spirit as the jests that called them forth. I could have cried on the earth to swallow me, not for my own sake (in itself the scene was entertaining enough, however little it might tend to edification), but on account of Mistress Barbara. Fairly I was afraid to ride forward and see her face, and dreaded to remember that I had brought her to this situation. But Nell laughed and jested, flinging back at me now and again a look that mocked my glum face and declared her keen pleasure in my perplexity and her scorn of Barbara's shame. Where now were the tenderness and sympathy which had made their meeting beautiful? The truce was ended and war raged relentless.

We came to our inn; I leapt from my horse and forestalled the bustling host in opening the coach door. The loons of townsmen and their gossiping wives lined the approach on either side; Nell sprang out, merry, radiant, unashamed; she laughed in my face as she ran past me amid the plaudits; slowly Barbara followed; with a low bow I offered my arm. Alas, there rose a murmur of questions concerning her; who was the lady that rode with Nell Gwyn, who was he that, although plainly attired, bore himself so proudly? Was he some great lord, travelling unknown, and was the lady—? Well, the conjectures may be guessed, and Mistress Quinton heard them. Her pride broke for a moment and I feared she would weep; then she drew herself up and walked slowly by with a haughty air and a calm face, so that the murmured questions fell to silence. Perhaps I also had my share in the change, for I walked after her, wearing a fierce scowl, threatening with my eyes, and having my hand on the hilt of my sword.

The host, elate with the honour of Nell's coming, was eager to offer us accommodation. Barbara addressed not a word either to Nell or to me, but followed a maid to the chamber allotted to her. Nell was in no such haste to hide herself from view. She cried for supper, and was led to a room on the first floor which overlooked the street. She threw the window open, and exchanged more greetings and banter with her admirers below. I flung my hat on the table and sat moodily in a chair. Food was brought, and Nell, turning at last from her entertainment, flew to partake of it with merry eagerness.

"But doesn't Mistress Quinton sup with us?" she said.

Mistress Quinton, it seemed, had no appetite for a meal, was shut close in her own chamber, and refused all service. Nell laughed and bade me fall to. I obeyed, being hungry in spite of my discomfort.

I was resolute not to quarrel with her. She had shewn me great friendliness; nay, and I had a fondness for her, such as I defy any man (man I say, not woman) to have escaped. But she tried me sorely, and while we ate she plied me with new challenges and fresh incitements to anger. I held my temper well in bounds, and, when I was satisfied, rose with a bow, saying that I would go and enquire if I could be of any aid to Mistress Quinton.

"She won't shew herself to you," cried Nell mockingly.

"She will, if you're not with me," I retorted.

"Make the trial! Behold, I'm firmly seated here!"

A maid carried my message while I paced the corridor; the lady's compliments returned to me, but, thanks to the attention of the host, she had need of nothing. I sent again, saying that I desired to speak with her concerning our journey. The lady's excuses returned to me; she had a headache and had sought her bed; she must pray me to defer my business till the morrow, and wished Mistress Gwyn and me good-night. The maid tripped off smiling.

"Plague on her!" I cried angrily and loudly. A laugh greeted the exclamation, and I turned to see Nell standing in the doorway of the room where we had supped.

"I knew, I knew!" she cried, revelling in her triumph, her eyes dancing in delight. "Poor Simon! Alas, poor Simon, you know little of women! But come, you're a brave lad, and I'll comfort you. Besides you have given me a jewelled dagger. Shall I lend it to you again, to plunge in your heart, poor Simon?"

"I don't understand you. I have no need of a dagger," I answered stiffly; yet, feeling a fool there in the passage, I followed her into the room.

"Your heart is pierced already?" she asked. "Ah, but your heart heals well! I'll spend no pity on you."

There was now a new tone in her voice. Her eyes still sparkled in mischievous exultation that she had proved right and I come away sore and baffled. But when she spoke of the healing of my heart, there was an echo of sadness; the hinting of some smothered sorrow seemed to be struggling with her mirth. She was a creature all compounded of sudden changing moods; I did not know when they were true, when feigned in sport or to further some device. She came near now and bent over my chair, saying gently,

"Alas, I'm very wicked! I couldn't help the folk cheering me, Simon. Surely it was no fault of mine?"

"You had no need to look out of the window of the coach," said I sternly.

"But I did that with never a thought. I wanted the air. I—"

"Nor to jest and banter. It was mighty unseemly, I swear."

"In truth I was wrong to jest with them," said Nell remorsefully. "And within, Simon, my heart was aching with shame, even while I jested. Ah, you don't know the shame I feel!"

"In good truth," I returned, "I believe you feel no shame at all."

"You're very cruel to me, Simon. Yet it's no more than my desert. Ah, if—"; she sighed heavily. "If only, Simon—," she said, and her hand was very near my hair by the back of the chair. "But that's past praying," she ended, sighing again most woefully. "Yet I have been of some service to you."

"I thank you for it most heartily," said I, still stiff and cold.

"And I was very wrong to-day. Simon, it was on her account."

"What?" I cried. "Did Mistress Quinton bid you put your head out and jest with the fellows on the pavement?"

"She did not bid me; but I did it because she was there."

I looked up at her; it was a rare thing with her, but she would not meet my glance. I looked down again.

"It was always the same between her and me," murmured Nell. "Ay, so long ago—even at Hatchstead."

"We're not in Hatchstead now," said I roughly.

"No, nor even in Chelsea. For even in Chelsea you had a kindness for me."

"I have much kindness for you now."

"Well, then you had more."

"It is in your knowledge why now I have no more."

"Yes, it's in my knowledge!" she cried. "Yet I carried Mistress Quinton from Dover."

I made no answer to that. She sighed "Heigho," and for a moment there was silence. But messages pass without words, and there are speechless Mercuries who carry tidings from heart to heart. Then the air is full of whisperings, and silence is but foil to a thousand sounds which the soul hears though the dull corporeal ear be deaf. Did she still amuse herself, or was there more? Sometimes a part, assumed in play or malice, so grows on the actor that he cannot, even when he would, throw aside his trappings and wash from his face the paint which was to show the passion that he played. The thing takes hold and will not be thrown aside; it seems to seek revenge for the light assumption and punishes the bravado that feigned without feeling by a feeling which is not feint. She was now, for the moment if you will, but yet now, in earnest. Some wave of recollection or of fancy had come over her and transformed her jest. She stole round till her face peeped into mine in piteous bewitching entreaty, asking a sign of fondness, bringing back the past, raising the dead from my heart's sepulchre. There was a throbbing in my brain; yet I had need of a cool head. With a spring I was on my feet.

"I'll go and ask if Mistress Barbara sleeps," I stammered. "I fear she may not be well attended."

"You'll go again? Once scorned, you'll go again, Simon? Well, the maid will smile; they'll make a story of it among themselves at their supper in the kitchen."

The laugh of a parcel of knaves and wenches! Surely it is a small thing! But men will face death smiling who run wry-faced from such ridicule. I sank in my chair again. But in truth did I desire to go? The dead rise, or at least there is a voice that speaks from the tomb. A man tarries to listen. Well if he be not lost in listening!

With a sigh Nell moved across the room and flung the window open. The loiterers were gone, all was still, only the stars looked in, only the sweet scent of the night made a new companion.

"It's like a night at Hatchstead," she whispered. "Do you remember how we walked there together? It smelt as it smells to-night. It's so long ago!" She came quickly towards me and asked "Do you hate me now?" but did not wait for the answer. She threw herself in a chair near me and fixed her eyes on me. It was strange to see her face grave and wrung with agitation; yet she was better thus, the new timidity became her marvellously.

There was a great clock in the corner of the old panelled room; it ticked solemnly, seeming to keep time with the beating of my heart. I had no desire to move, but sat there waiting; yet every nerve of my body was astir. Now I watched her every movement, took reckoning of every feature, seemed to read more than her outward visage showed and to gain knowledge of her heart. I knew that she tempted me, and why. I was not a fool, to think that she loved me; but she was set to conquer me, and with her there was no price that seemed high when the prize was victory or a whim's fulfilment.

I would have written none of this, but that it is so part and marrow of my history that without it the record of my life would go limping on one leg.

She rose and came near me again. Now she laughed, yet still not lightly, but as though she hid a graver mood.

"Come," said she, "you needn't fear to be civil to me. Mistress Barbara is not here."

The taunt was well conceived; for the most part there is no incitement that more whips a man to any madness than to lay self-control to the score of cowardice, and tell him that his scruples are not his own, but worn by command of another and on pain of her displeasure. But sometimes woman's cunning goes astray, and a name, used in mockery, speaks for itself with strong attraction, as though it held the charm of her it stands for. The name, falling from Nell's pouting lips, had power to raise in me a picture, and the picture spread, like a very painting done on canvas, a screen between me and the alluring eyes that sought mine in provoking witchery. She did not know her word's work, and laughed again to see me grow yet more grave at Barbara's name.

"The stern mistress is away," she whispered. "May we not sport? The door is shut! Why, Simon, you're dull. In truth you're as dull as the King when his purse is empty."

Anthony Hope

I raised my eyes to hers, she read the thought. She tossed her head, flinging the brown curls back; her eyes twinkled merrily, and she said in a soft whisper half-smothered in a rising laugh,

"But, Simon, the King also is away."

I owed nothing to the King and thought nothing of the King. It was not there I stuck. Nay, and I did not stick on any score of conscience. Yet stick I did, and gazed at her with a dumb stare. She seemed to fall into a sudden rage, crying,

"Go to her then if you will, but she won't have you. Would you like to know what she called you to-day in the coach?"

"I would hear nothing that was not for my ears."

"A very pretty excuse; but in truth you fear to hear it."

Alas, the truth was even as she said. I feared to hear it.

"But you shall hear it. 'A good honest fellow,' she said, 'but somewhat forward for his station.' So she said, and leant back with half-closed lids. You know the trick these great ladies have? By Heaven, though, I think she wronged you! For I'll swear on my Bible that you're not forward, Simon. Well, I'm not Mistress Quinton."

"You are not," said I, sore and angry, and wishing to wound her in revenge for the blow she had dealt me.

"Now you're gruff with me for what she said. It's a man's way. I care not. Go and sigh outside her door; she won't open it to you."

She drew near to me again, coaxing and seeking to soften me.

"I took your part," she whispered, "and declared that you were a fine gentleman. Nay, I told her how once I had come near to—Well, I told her many things that it should please you to hear. But she grew mighty short with me, and on the top came the folk with their cheers. Hence my lady's in a rage."

She shrugged her shoulders; I sat there sullen. The scornful words were whirling through my brain. "Somewhat forward for his station!" It was a hard judgment on one who had striven to serve her. In what had I shewn presumption? Had she not professed to forgive all offence? She kept the truth for others, and it came out when my back was turned.

"Poor Simon!" said Nell softly. "Indeed I wonder any lady should speak so of you. It's an evil return for your kindness to her."

Silence fell on us for awhile. Nell was by me now, her hand rested lightly on my shoulder, and, looking up, I saw her eyes on my face in mingled pensiveness and challenge.

"Indeed you are not forward," she murmured with a little laugh, and set one hand over her eyes.

I sat and looked at her; yet, though I seemed to look at her only, the whole of the room with its furnishings is stamped clear and clean on my memory. Nell moved a little away and stood facing me.

"It grows late," she said softly, "and we must be early on

the road. I'll bid you good-night, and go to my bed."

She came to me, holding out her hand; I did not take it, but she laid it for a moment on mine. Then she drew it away and moved towards the door. I rose and followed her.

"I'll see you safe on your way," said I in a low voice. She met my gaze for a moment, but made no answer in words. We were in the corridor now, and she led the way. Once she turned her head and again looked at me. It was a sullen face she saw, but still I followed.

"Tread lightly!" she whispered. "There's her door; we pass it, and she would not love to know that you escorted me. She scorns you herself, and yet when another—" The sentence went unended.

In a tumult of feeling still I followed. I was half-mad with resentment against Barbara; swearing to myself that her scorn was nothing to me, I shrank from nothing to prove to my own mind the lie that my heart would not receive.

"The door!" whispered Nell, going delicately on her toes with uplifted forefinger.

I cannot tell why, but at the word I came to a stand. Nell, looking over her shoulder and seeing me stand, turned to front me. She smiled merrily, then frowned, then smiled again with raised eye-brows. I stood there, as though pinned to the spot. For now I had heard a sound from within. It came very softly. There was a stir as of some-one moving, then a line of some soft sad song, falling in careless half-consciousness from saddened lips. The sound fell clear and plain on my ears, though I paid no heed to the words and have them not in my memory; I think that in them a maid spoke to her lover who left her, but I am not sure. I listened. The snatch died away, and the movement in the room ceased. All was still again, and Nell's eyes were fixed on mine. I met them squarely, and thus for awhile we stood. Then came the unspoken question, cried from the eyes that were on mine in a thousand tones. I could trace the play of her face but dimly by the light of the smoky lantern, but her eyes I seemed to see bright and near. I had looked for scorn there, and, it might be, amusement. I seemed to see (perhaps the imperfect light played tricks), besides lure and raillery, reproach, sorrow, and, most strange of all, a sort of envy. Then came a smile, and ever so lightly her finger moved in beckoning. The song came no more through the closed door: my ears were empty of it, but not my heart; there it sounded still in its soft pleading cadence. Poor maid, whose lover left her! Poor maid, poor maid! I looked full at Nell, but did not move. The lids dropped over her eyes, and their lights went out. She turned and walked slowly and alone along the corridor. I watched her going, yes, wistfully I watched. But I did not follow, for the snatch of song rose in my heart. There was a door at the end of the passage; she opened it and passed through. For a moment it stood open, then a hand stole back and slowly drew it close. It was shut. The click of the lock rang loud and sharp through the silent house.

Anthony Hope

CHAPTER XX

THE VICAR'S PROPOSITION

I do not know how long I stood outside the door there in the passage. After awhile I began to move softly to and fro, more than once reaching the room where I was to sleep, but returning again to my old post. I was loth to forsake it. A strange desire was on me. I wished that the door would open, nay, to open it myself, and by my presence declare what was now so plain to me. But to her it would not have been plain; for now I was alone in the passage, and there was nothing to show the thing which had come to me there, and there at last had left me. Yet it seemed monstrous that she should not know, possible to tell her to-night, certain that my shame-faced tongue would find no words to-morrow. It was a thing that must be said while the glow and the charm of it were still on me, or it would find no saying.

The light had burnt down very low, and gave forth a dim fitful glare, hardly conquering the darkness. Now, again, I was standing still, lost in my struggle. Presently, with glad amazement, as though there had come an unlooked-for answer to my prayer, I heard a light step within. The footfalls seemed to hesitate; then they came again, the bolt of the door shot back, and a crack of faint light shewed. "Who's there?" asked Barbara's voice, trembling with alarm or some other agitation which made her tones quick and timid. I made no answer. The door opened a little wider. I saw her face as she looked out, half-fearful, yet surely also half-expectant. Much as I had desired her coming, I would willingly have escaped now, for I did not know what to say to her. I had rehearsed my speech a hundred times; the moment for its utterance found me dumb. Yet the impulse I had felt was still on me, though it failed to give me words.

"I thought it was you," she whispered. "Why are you there? Do you want me?"

Lame and halting came my answer.

"I was only passing by on my way to bed," I stammered. "I'm sorry I roused you."

"I wasn't asleep," said she. Then after a pause she added, "I—I thought you had been there some time. Good-night."

She bade me good-night, but yet seemed to wait for me to speak; since I was still silent she added, "Is our companion gone to bed?"

"Some little while back," said I. Then raising my eyes to her face, I said, "I'm sorry that you don't sleep."

"Alas, we both have our sorrows," she returned with a doleful smile. Again there was a pause.

"Good-night," said Barbara.

"Good-night," said I.

She drew back, the door closed, I was alone again in the passage.

Now if any man—nay, if every man—who reads my history, at this place close the leaves on his thumb and call Simon Dale a fool, I will not complain of him; but if he be moved to fling the book away for good and all, not enduring more of such a fool as Simon Dale, why I will humbly ask him if he hath never rehearsed brave speeches for his mistress's ear and found himself tongue-tied in her presence? And if he hath, what did he then? I wager that, while calling himself a dolt with most hearty honesty, yet he set some of the blame on her shoulders, crying that he would have spoken had she opened the way, that it was her reticence, her distance, her coldness, which froze his eloquence; and that to any other lady in the whole world he could have poured forth words so full of fire that they must have inflamed her to a passion like to his own and burnt down every barrier which parted her heart from his. Therefore at that moment he searched for accusations against her, and found a bitter-tasting comfort in every offence that she had given him, and made treasure of any scornful speech, rescuing himself from the extreme of foolishness by such excuse as harshness might afford. Now Barbara Quinton had told Mistress Nell that I was forward for my station. What man could, what man would, lay bare his heart to a lady who held him to be forward for his station?

These meditations took me to my chamber, whither I might have gone an hour before, and lasted me fully two hours after I had stretched myself upon the bed. Then I slept heavily; when I woke it was high morning. I lay there a little while, thinking with no pleasure of the journey before me. Then having risen and dressed hastily, I made my way to the room where Nell and I had talked the night before. I did not know in what mood I should find her, but I desired to see her alone and beg her to come to some truce with Mistress Quinton, lest our day's travelling should be over thorns. She was not in the room when I came there. Looking out of window I perceived the coach at the door; the host was giving an eye to the horses, and I hailed him. He ran in and a moment later entered the room.

"At what hour are we to set out?" I asked.

"When you will," said he.

"Have you no orders then from Mistress Gwyn?"

"She left none with me, sir."

"Left none?" I cried, amazed.

A smile came on his lips and his eyes twinkled.

"Now I thought it!" said he with a chuckle. "You didn't know her purpose? She has hired a post-chaise and set out two hours ago, telling me that you and the other lady would travel as well without her, and that, for her part, she was weary of both of you. But she left a message for you. See, it lies there on the table."

A little packet was on the table; I took it up. The innkeeper's eyes were fixed on me in obvious curiosity and amusement. I was not minded to afford him more entertainment than I need, and bade him begone before I opened the packet. He withdrew reluctantly. Then I unfastened Nell's parcel. It contained ten guineas wrapped in white paper, and on the inside of the paper was written in a most laborious awkward scrawl (I fear the execution of it gave poor Nell much pains), "In pay for your dagger. E.G." It was all of her hand I had ever seen; the brief message seemed to speak a sadness in her. Perhaps I deluded myself; her skill with the pen would not serve her far. She had gone, that was the sum of it, and I was grieved that she had gone in this fashion.

With the piece of paper still in my hands, the guineas also still standing in a little pile on the table, I turned to find Barbara Quinton in the doorway of the room. Her air was timid, as though she were not sure of welcome, and something of the night's embarrassment still hung about her. She looked round as though in search for somebody.

"I am alone here," said I, answering her glance.

"But she? Mistress—?"

"She's gone," said I. "I haven't seen her. The innkeeper tells me that she has been gone these two hours. But she has left us the coach and—" I walked to the window and looked out. "Yes, and my horse is there, and her servant with his horse."

"But why is she gone? Hasn't she left—?"

"She has left ten guineas also," said I, pointing to the pile on the table.

"And no reason for her going?"

"Unless this be one," I answered, holding out the piece of paper.

"I won't read it," said Barbara.

"It says only, 'In pay for your dagger.'"

"Then it gives no reason."

"Why, no, it gives none," said I.

"It's very strange," murmured Barbara, looking not at me but past me.

Now to me, when I pondered over the matter, it did not seem altogether strange. Yet where lay the need to tell Mistress Barbara why it seemed not altogether strange? Indeed I could not have told it easily, seeing that, look at it how you will, the thing was not easy to set forth to Mistress Barbara. Doubtless it was but a stretch of fancy to see any meaning in Nell's mention of the dagger, save the plain one that lay on the surface; yet had she been given to conceits, she might have used the dagger as a figure for some wound that I had dealt her.

"No doubt some business called her," said I rather lamely. "She has shown much consideration in leaving her coach for us."

"And the money? Shall you use it?"

"What choice have I?"

Barbara's glance was on the pile of guineas. I put out my hand, took them up, and stowed them in my purse; as I did this, my eye wandered to the window. Barbara followed my look and my thought also. I had no mind that this new provision for our needs should share the fate of my last guinea.

"You needn't have said that!" cried Barbara, flushing;

although, as may be seen, I had said nothing.

"I will repay the money in due course," said I, patting my purse.

We made a meal together in unbroken silence. No more was said of Mistress Nell; our encounter in the corridor last night seemed utterly forgotten. Relieved of a presence that was irksome to her and would have rendered her apprehensive of fresh shame at every place we passed through, Mistress Barbara should have shown an easier bearing and more gaiety; so I supposed and hoped. The fact refuted me; silent, cold, and distant, she seemed in even greater discomfort than when we had a companion. Her mood called up a like in me, and I began to ask myself whether for this I had done well to drive poor Nell away.

Thus in gloom we made ready to set forth. Myself prepared to mount my horse, I offered to hand Barbara into the coach. Then she looked at me; I noted it, for she had not done so much for an hour past; a slight colour came into her cheeks, she glanced round the interior of the coach; it was indeed wide and spacious for one traveller.

"You ride to-day also?" she asked.

The sting that had tormented me was still alive; I could not deny myself the pleasure of a retort so apt. I bowed low and deferentially, saying, "I have learnt my station. I would not be so forward as to sit in the coach with you." The flush on her cheeks deepened suddenly; she stretched out her hand a little way towards me, and her lips parted as though she were about to speak. But her hand fell again, and her lips shut on unuttered words.

"As you will," she said coldly. "Pray bid them set out."

Of our journey I will say no more. There is nothing in it that I take pleasure in telling, and to write its history would be to accuse either Barbara or myself. For two days we travelled together, she in her coach, I on horseback. Come to London, we were told that my lord was at Hatchstead; having despatched our borrowed equipage and servant to their mistress, and with them the amount of my debt and a most grateful message, we proceeded on our road, Barbara in a chaise, I again riding. All the way Barbara shunned me as though I had the plague, and I on my side showed no desire to be with a companion so averse from my society. On my life I was driven half-mad, and had that night at Canterbury come again—well, Heaven be thanked that temptation comes sometimes at moments when virtue also has attractions, or which of us would stand? And the night we spent on the road, decorum forbade that we should so much as speak, much less sup, together; and the night we lay in London, I spent at one end of the town and she at the other. At least I showed no forwardness; to that I was sworn, and adhered most obstinately. Thus we came to Hatchstead, better strangers than ever we had left Dover, and, although safe and sound from bodily perils and those wiles of princes that had of late so threatened our tranquillity, yet both of us as ill in temper as could be conceived. Defend me from any such journey again! But there is no likelihood of such a trial now, alas! Yes, there was a pleasure in it; it was a battle, and, by my faith, it was close drawn between us.

The chaise stopped at the Manor gates, and I rode up to the door of it, cap in hand. Here was to be our parting.

"I thank you heartily, sir," said Barbara in a low voice, with a bow of her head and a quick glance that would not dwell on my sullen face.

"My happiness has been to serve you, madame," I returned. "I grieve only that my escort has been so irksome to you."

"No," said Barbara, and she said no more, but rolled up the avenue in her chaise, leaving me to find my way alone to my mother's house.

I sat a few moments on my horse, watching her go. Then with an oath I turned away. The sight of the gardener's cottage sent my thoughts back to the old days when Cydaria came and caught my heart in her butterfly net. It was just there, in the meadow by the avenue, that I had kissed her. A kiss is a thing lightly given and sometimes lightly taken. It was that kiss which Barbara had seen from the window, and great debate had arisen on it. Lightly given, yet leading on to much that I did not see, lightly taken, yet perhaps mother to some fancies that men would wonder to find in Mistress Gwyn.

"I'm heartily glad to be here!" I cried, loosing the Vicar's hand and flinging myself into the high arm-chair in the chimney corner.

My mother received this exclamation as a tribute of filial affection, the Vicar treated it as an evidence of friendship, my sister Mary saw in it a thanksgiving for deliverance from the perils and temptations of London and the Court. Let them take it how they would; in truth it was inspired in none of these ways, but was purely an expression of relief, first at having brought Mistress Barbara safe to the Manor, in the second place, at being quit of her society.

"I am very curious to learn, Simon," said the Vicar,

drawing his chair near mine, and laying his hand upon my knee, "what passed at Dover. For it seems to me that there, if at any place in the world, the prophecy which Betty Nasroth spoke concerning you—"

"You shall know all in good time, sir," I cried impatiently.

"Should find its fulfilment," ended the Vicar placidly.

"Are we not finished with that folly yet?" asked my mother.

"Simon must tell us that," smiled the Vicar.

"In good time, in good time," I cried again. "But tell me first, when did my lord come here from London?"

"Why, a week ago. My lady was sick, and the physician prescribed the air of the country for her. But my lord stayed four days only and then was gone again."

I started and sat upright in my seat.

"What, isn't he here now?" I asked eagerly.

"Why, Simon," said my good mother with a laugh, "we looked to get news from you, and now we have news to give you! The King has sent for my lord; I saw his message. It was most flattering and spoke of some urgent and great business on which the King desired my lord's immediate presence and counsel. So he set out two days ago to join the King with a large train of servants, leaving behind my lady, who was too sick to travel."

I was surprised at these tidings and fell into deep consideration. What need had the King of my lord's counsel, and so suddenly? What had been done at Dover would not be opened to Lord Quinton's ear. Was he summoned as a Lord of Council or as his daughter's father? For by now the King must know certain matters respecting my lord's daughter and a humble gentleman who had striven to serve her so far as his station enabled him and without undue forwardness. We might well have passed my lord's coach on the road and not remarked it among the many that met us as we drew near to London in the evening. I had not observed his liveries, but that went for nothing. I took heed of little on that journey save the bearing of Mistress Barbara. Where lay the meaning of my lord's summons? It came into my mind that M. de Perrencourt had sent messengers from Calais, and that the King might be seeking to fulfil in another way the bargain whose accomplishment I had hindered. The thought was new life to me. If my work were not finished—. I broke off; the Vicar's hand was on my knee again.

"Touching the prophecy—" he began.

"Indeed, sir, in good time you shall know all. It is fulfilled."

"Fulfilled!" he cried rapturously. "Then, Simon, fortune smiles?"

"No," I retorted, "she frowns most damnably."

To swear is a sin, to swear before ladies is bad manners, to swear in talking to a clergyman is worst of all. But while my mother and my sister drew away in offence (and I hereby tender them an apology never yet made) the Vicar only smiled.

"A plague on such prophecies," said I sourly.

"Yet if it be fulfilled!" he murmured. For he held more by that than by any good fortune of mine; me he loved, but his magic was dearer to him. "You must indeed tell me," he urged.

My mother approached somewhat timidly.

"You are come to stay with us, Simon?" she asked.

"For the term of my life, so far as I know, madame," said I.

"Thanks to God," she murmured softly.

There is a sort of saying that a mother speaks and a son hears to his shame and wonder! Her heart was all in me, while mine was far away. Despondency had got hold of me. Fortune, in her merriest mood, seeming bent on fooling me fairly, had opened a door and shown me the prospect of fine doings and high ambitions realised. The glimpse had been but brief, and the tricky creature shut the door in my face with a laugh. Betty Nasroth's prophecy was fulfilled, but its accomplishment left me in no better state; nay, I should be compelled to count myself lucky if I came off unhurt and were not pursued by the anger of those great folk whose wills and whims I had crossed. I must lie quiet in Hatchstead, and to lie quiet in Hatchstead was hell to me—ay, hell, unless by some miracle (whereof there was but one way) it should turn to heaven. That was not for me; I was denied youth's sovereign balm for ill-starred hopes and ambitions gone awry.

The Vicar and I were alone now, and I could not but humour him by telling what had passed. He heard with rare enjoyment; and although his interest declined from its zenith so soon as I had told the last of the prophecy, he listened to the rest with twinkling eyes. No comment did he make, but took snuff frequently. I, my tale done, fell again into meditation. Yet I had been fired by the rehearsal of my own story, and my thoughts were less dark in hue. The news concerning Lord Quinton stirred me afresh. My aid might again be needed; my melancholy was tinted with pleasant pride as I declared to myself that it should not be lacking, for all that I had been used as one would not use a faithful dog, much less a gentleman who, doubtless by no merit of his own but yet most certainly, had been of no small service. To confess the truth, I was so persuaded of my value that I looked for every moment to bring me a summons, and practised under my breath the terms, respectful yet resentful, in which I would again place my arm and sword at Barbara's disposal.

"You loved this creature Nell?" asked the Vicar suddenly.

"Ay," said I, "I loved her."

"You love her no more?"

"Why, no," I answered, mustering a cool smile. "Folly such as that goes by with youth."

"Your age is twenty-four?"

"Yes, I am twenty-four."

"And you love her no longer?"

"I tell you, no longer, sir."

The Vicar opened his box and took a large pinch.

"Then," said he, the pinch being between his finger and thumb and just half-way on the road to his nose, "you love some other woman, Simon."

He spoke not as a man who asks a question nor even as one who hazards an opinion; he declared a fact and needed no answer to confirm him. "Yes, you love some other woman, Simon," said he, and there left the matter.

"I don't," I cried indignantly. Had I told myself a hundred times that I was not in love to be told by another that I was? True, I might have been in love, had not—

"Ah, who goes there?" exclaimed the Vicar, springing nimbly to the window and looking out with eagerness. "I seem to know the gentleman. Come, Simon, look."

I obeyed him. A gentleman, attended by two servants, rode past rapidly; twilight had begun to fall, but the light served well enough to show me who the stranger was. He rode hard and his horse's head was towards the Manor gates.

"I think it is my Lord Carford," said the Vicar. "He goes to the Manor, as I think."

"I think it is and I think he does," said I; and for a single moment I stood there in the middle of the room, hesitating, wavering, miserable.

"What ails you, Simon? Why shouldn't my Lord Carford go to the Manor?" cried the Vicar.

"Let him go to the devil!" I cried, and I seized my hat from the table where it lay.

The Vicar turned to me with a smile on his lips.

"Go, lad," said he, "and let me not hear you again deny my propositions. They are founded on an extensive observation of humanity and—"

Well, I know not to this day on what besides. For I was out of the house before the Vicar completed his statement of the authority that underlay his propositions.

CHAPTER XXI

THE STRANGE CONJUNCTURE OF TWO
GENTLEMEN

I have heard it said that King Charles laughed most
heartily when he learnt how a certain gentleman had
tricked M. de Perrencourt and carried off from his
clutches the lady who should have gone to prepare for the
Duchess of York's visit to the Court of France. "This
Uriah will not be set in the forefront of the battle," said
he, "and therefore David can't have his way." He would
have laughed, I think, even although my action had
thwarted his own schemes, but the truth is that he had so
wrought on that same devotion to her religion which,
according to Mistress Nell, inspired Mlle. de Querouaille
that by the time the news came from Calais he had little
doubt of success for himself although his friend M. de
Perrencourt had been baffled. He had made his treaty, he
had got his money, and the lady, if she would not stay, yet
promised to return. The King then was well content, and
found perhaps some sly satisfaction in the defeat of the
great Prince whose majesty and dignity made any reverse
which befell him an amusement to less potent persons. In
any case the King laughed, then grew grave for a moment
while he declared that his best efforts should not be
wanting to reclaim Mistress Quinton to a sense of her

duty, and then laughed again. Yet he set about reclaiming her, although with no great energy or fierceness; and when he heard that Monmouth had other views of the lady's duty, he shrugged his shoulders, saying, "Nay, if there be two Davids, I'll wager a crown on Uriah."

It is easy to follow a man to the door of a house, but if the door be shut after him and the pursuer not invited to enter, he can but stay outside. So it fell out with me, and being outside I did not know what passed within nor how my Lord Carford fared with Mistress Barbara. I flung myself in deep chagrin on the grass of the Manor Park, cursing my fate, myself, and if not Barbara, yet that perversity which was in all women and, by logic, even in Mistress Barbara. But although I had no part in it, the play went on and how it proceeded I learnt afterwards; let me now leave the stage that I have held too long and pass out of sight till my cue calls me again.

This evening then, my lady, who was very sick, being in her bed, and Mistress Barbara, although not sick, very weary of her solitude and longing for the time when she could betake herself to the same refuge (for there is a pride that forbids us to seek bed too early, however strongly we desire it) there came a great knocking at the door of the house. A gentleman on horseback and accompanied by two servants was without and craved immediate audience of her ladyship. Hearing that she was abed, he asked for Mistress Barbara and obtained entrance; yet he would not give his name, but declared that he came on urgent business from Lord Quinton. The excuse served, and Barbara received him. With surprise she found Carford bowing low before her. I had told her enough concerning him to prevent her welcome being warm. I would have told her more, had she afforded me the opportunity. The imperfect knowledge that she had caused her to accuse him rather of a timidity in face of powerful rivals than of any deliberate design to set his love below his ambition and to use her as his tool. Had she known all I knew she would not have listened to him. Even now she made some pretext for declining conversation that night and would have withdrawn at once; but he stayed her retreat, earnestly praying her for her father's sake and her own to hear his message, and asserting that she was in more danger than she was aware of. Thus he persuaded her to be seated.

"What is your message from my father, my lord?" she asked coldly, but not uncivilly.

"Madame, I have none," he answered with a bluntness not ill calculated. "I used the excuse to gain admission, fearing that my own devotion to you would not suffice, well as you know it. But although I have no message, I think that you will have one soon. Nay, you must listen." For she had risen.

"I listen, my lord, but I will listen standing."

"You're hard to me, Mistress Barbara," he said. "But take the tidings how you will; only pay heed to them." He drew nearer to her and continued, "To-morrow a message will come from your father. You have had none for many days?"

"Alas, no," said she. "We were both on the road and could send no letter to one another."

"To-morrow one comes. May I tell you what it will say?"

"How can you know what it will say, my lord?"

"I will stand by the event," said he sturdily. "The coming of the letter will prove me right or wrong. It will bid your mother and you accompany the messenger—"

"My mother cannot—"

"Or, if your mother cannot, you alone, with some waiting-woman, to Dover."

"To Dover?" cried Barbara. "For what purpose?" She shrank away from him, as though alarmed by the very name of the place whence she had escaped.

He looked full in her face and answered slowly and significantly:

"Madame goes back to France, and you are to go with her."

Barbara caught at a chair near her and sank into it. He stood over her now, speaking quickly and urgently.

"You must listen," he said, "and lose no time in acting. A French gentleman, by name M. de Fontelles, will be here to-morrow; he carries your father's letter and is sent to bring you to Dover."

"My father bids me come?" she cried.

"His letter will convey the request," answered Carford.

"Then I will go," said she. "I can't come to harm with him, and when I have told him all, he won't allow me to go to France." For as yet my lord did not know of what had befallen his daughter, nor did my lady, whose sickness made her unfit to be burdened with such troublesome matters.

"Indeed you would come to no harm with your father, if you found your father," said Carford. "Come, I will tell you. Before you reach Dover my lord will have gone from there. As soon as his letter to you was sent the King made a pretext to despatch him into Cornwall; he wrote again to tell you of his journey and bid you not come to Dover till he sends for you. This letter he entrusted to a messenger of my Lord Arlington's who was taking the road for London. But the Secretary's messengers know when to hasten and when to loiter on the way. You are to have set out before the letter arrives."

Barbara looked at him in bewilderment and terror; he was to all seeming composed and spoke with an air of honest sincerity.

"To speak plainly, it is a trick," he said, "to induce you to return to Dover. This M. de Fontelles has orders to bring you at all hazards, and is armed with the King's authority in case my lord's bidding should not be enough."

She sat for a while in helpless dismay. Carford had the wisdom not to interrupt her thoughts; he knew that she was seeking for a plan of escape and was willing to let her find that there was none.

"When do you say that M. de Fontelles will be here?" she asked at last.

"Late to-night or early to-morrow. He rested a few hours in London, while I rode through, else I shouldn't have been here before him."

"And why are you come, my lord?" she asked.

"To serve you, madame," he answered simply.

She drew herself up, saying haughtily,

"You were not so ready to serve me at Dover."

Carford was not disconcerted by an attack that he must have foreseen; he had the parry ready for the thrust.

"From the danger that I knew I guarded you, the other I did not know." Then with a burst of well-feigned indignation he cried, "By Heaven, but for me the French King would have been no peril to you; he would have come too late."

She understood him and flushed painfully.

"When the enemy is mighty," he pursued, "we must fight by guile, not force; when we can't oppose we must delay; we must check where we can't stop. You know my meaning: to you I couldn't put it more plainly. But now I have spoken plainly to the Duke of Monmouth, praying something from him in my own name as well as yours. He is a noble Prince, madame, and his offence should be pardoned by you who caused it. Had I thwarted him openly, he would have been my enemy and yours. Now he is your friend and mine."

The defence was clever enough to bridle her indignation. He followed up his advantage swiftly, leaving her no time to pry for a weak spot in his pleading.

"By Heaven," he cried, "let us lose no time on past troubles. I was to blame, if you will, in execution, though not, I swear, in intention. But here and now is the danger, and I am come to guard you from it."

"Then I am much in your debt, my lord," said she, still

doubtful, yet in her trouble eager to believe him honest.

"Nay," said he, "all that I have, madame, is yours, and you can't be in debt to your slave."

I do not doubt that in this speech his passion seemed real enough, and was the more effective from having been suppressed till now, so that it appeared to break forth against his will. Indeed although he was a man in whom ambition held place of love, yet he loved her and would have made her his for passion's sake as well as for the power that he hoped to wield through her means. I hesitate how to judge him; there are many men who take their colour from the times, as some insects from the plants they feed on; in honest times they would be honest, in debauched they follow the evil fashion, having no force to stand by themselves. Perhaps this lord was one of this kidney.

"It's an old story, this love of mine," said he in gentler tones. "Twice you have heard it, and a lover who speaks twice must mourn once at least; yet the second time I think you came nearer to heeding it. May I tell it once again?"

"Indeed it is not the time—" she began in an agitated voice.

"Be your answer what it may, I am your servant," he protested. "My hand and heart are yours, although yours be another's."

"There is none—I am free—" she murmured. His eyes were on her and she nerved herself to calm, saying, "There is nothing of what you suppose. But my disposition towards you, my lord, has not changed."

He let a moment go by before he answered her; he made it seem as though emotion forbade earlier speech. Then he said gravely,

"I am grieved from my heart to hear it, and I pray Heaven that an early day may bring me another answer. God forbid that I should press your inclination now. You may accept my service freely, although you do not accept my love. Mistress Barbara, you'll come with me?"

"Come with you?" she cried.

"My lady will come also, and we three together will seek your father in Cornwall. On my faith, madame, there is no safety but in flight."

"My mother lies too sick for travelling. Didn't you hear it from my father?"

"I haven't seen my lord. My knowledge of his letter came through the Duke of Monmouth, and although he spoke there of my lady's sickness, I trusted that she had recovered."

"My mother cannot travel. It is impossible."

He came a step nearer her.

"Fontelles will be here to-morrow," he said. "If you are here then—! Yet if there be any other whose aid you could seek—?" Again he paused, regarding her intently.

She sat in sore distress, twisting her hands in her lap. One there was, and not far away. Yet to send for him crossed her resolution and stung her pride most sorely. We had parted in anger, she and I; I had blamed my share in the quarrel bitterly enough, it is likely she had spared herself no more; yet the more fault is felt the harder comes its acknowledgment.

"Is Mr Dale in Hatchstead?" asked Carford boldly and bluntly.

"I don't know where he is. He brought me here, but I have heard nothing from him since we parted."

"Then surely he is gone again?"

"I don't know," said Barbara.

Carford must have been a dull man indeed not to discern how the matter lay. There is no better time to press a lady than when she is chagrined with a rival and all her pride is under arms to fight her inclination.

"Surely, or he could not have shewn you such indifference—nay, I must call it discourtesy."

"He did me service."

"A gentleman, madame, should grow more, not less, assiduous when he is so happy as to have put a lady under obligation."

He had said enough, and restrained himself from a further attack.

"What will you do?" he went on.

"Alas, what can I do?" Then she cried, "This M. de Fontelles can't carry me off against my will."

"He has the King's commands," said Carford. "Who will resist him?"

She sprang to her feet and turned on him quickly.

"Why you," she said. "Alone with you I cannot and will not go. But you are my—you are ready to serve me. You will resist M. de Fontelles for my sake, ay, and for my sake the King's commands."

Carford stood still, amazed at the sudden change in her manner. He had not conceived this demand and it suited him very ill. The stroke was too bold for his temper; the King was interested in this affair, and it might go hard with the man who upset his plan and openly resisted his messenger. Carford had calculated on being able to carry her off, and thus defeat the scheme under show of ignorance. The thing done, and done unwittingly, might gain pardon; to meet and defy the enemy face to face was to stake all his fortune on a desperate chance. He was dumb. Barbara's lips curved into a smile that expressed wonder and dawning contempt.

"You hesitate, sir?" she asked.

"The danger is great," he muttered.

"You spoke of discourtesy just now, my lord—"

"You do not lay it to my charge?"

"Nay, to refuse to face danger for a lady, and a lady whom a man loves—you meant that, my lord?—goes by another name. I forgive discourtesy sooner than that other thing, my lord."

His face grew white with passion. She accused him of cowardice and plainly hinted to him that, if he failed her, she would turn to one who was no coward, let him be as discourteous and indifferent as his sullen disposition made him. I am sorry I was not there to see Carford's face. But he was in the net of her challenge now, and a bold front alone would serve.

"By God, madame," he cried, "you shall know by to-morrow how deeply you wrong me. If my head must answer for it, you shall have the proof."

"I thank you, my lord," said she with a little bow, as though she asked no more than her due in demanding that he should risk his head for her. "I did not doubt your answer."

"You shall have no cause, madame," said he very boldly, although he could not control the signs of his uneasiness.

"Again I thank you," said she. "It grows late, my lord. By your kindness, I shall sleep peacefully and without fear. Good-night." She moved towards the door, but turned to him again, saying, "I pray your pardon, but even hospitality must give way to sickness. I cannot entertain you suitably while my mother lies abed. If you lodge at the inn, they will treat you well for my father's sake, and a message from me can reach you easily."

Carford had strung himself to give the promise; whether he would fulfil it or not lay uncertain in the future. But for so much as he had done he had a mind to be paid. He came to her, and, kneeling, took her hand; she suffered him to kiss it.

"There is nothing I wouldn't do to win my prize," he said,

fixing his eyes ardently on her face.

"I have asked nothing but what you seemed to offer," she answered coldly. "If it be a matter of bargain, my lord—"

"No, no," he cried, seeking to catch again at her hand as she drew it away and with a curtsey passed out.

Thus she left him without so much as a backward glance to presage future favour. So may a lady, if she plays her game well, take all and promise nothing.

Carford, refused even a lodging in the house, crossed in the plan by which he had reckoned on getting Barbara into his power, driven to an enterprise for which he had small liking, and left in utter doubt whether the success for which he ran so great a risk would profit him, may well have sought the inn to which Barbara commended him in no cheerful mood. I wager he swore a round oath or two as he and his servants made their way thither through the dark and knocked up the host, who, keeping country hours, was already in his bed. It cost them some minutes to rouse him, and Carford beat most angrily on the door. At last they were admitted. And I turned away.

For I must confess it; I had dogged their steps, not able to rest till I saw what would become of Carford. Yet we must give love his due; if he takes a man into strange places, sometimes he shows him things worth his knowing. If I, a lovesick fool, had watched a rival into my mistress's house and watched him out of it with devouring jealousy, ay, if I had chosen to spend my time beneath the Manor windows rather than in my own comfortable chair, why, I had done only what many who are now wise and sober gentleman have done in their time. And if once in that same park I had declared my heart broken for the sake of another lady, there are revolutions in hearts as in states, and, after the rebels have had their day, the King comes to his own again. Nay, I have known some who were very loyal to King Charles, and yet said nothing hard of Oliver, whose yoke they once had worn. I will say nought against my usurper, although the Queen may have come to her own again.

Well, Carford should not have her. I, Simon Dale, might be the greatest fool in the King's dominions, and lie sulking while another stormed the citadel on which I longed to plant my flag. But the victor should not be Carford. Among gentlemen a quarrel is easily come by; yokels may mouth their blowsy sweetheart's name and fight openly for her favour over their mugs of ale; we quarrel on the state of the Kingdom, the fall of the cards, the cut of our coats, what you will. Carford and I would find a cause without much searching. I was so hot that I was within an ace of summoning him then and there to show by what right he rode so boldly through my native village; that offence would serve as well as any other. Yet prudence prevailed. The closed doors of the inn hid the party from my sight, and I went on my way, determined to be about by cockcrow, lest Carford should steal a march.

But as I went I passed the Vicar's door. He stood on the threshold, smoking his long pipe (the good man loved Virginia and gave his love free rein in the evening) and gazing at the sky. I tried to slink by him, fearing to be questioned; he caught sight of my figure and called me to him; but he made no reference to the manner of our last parting.

"Whither away, Simon?" he asked.

"To bed, sir," said I.

"It is well," said he. "And whence?"

"From a walk, sir."

His eyes met mine, and I saw them twinkle. He waved the stem of his pipe in the air, and said,

"Love, Simon, is a divine distemper of the mind, wherein it paints bliss with woe's palate and sees heaven from hell."

"You borrow from the poets, sir," said I surlily.

"Nay," he rejoined, "the poets from me, or from any man who has or has had a heart in him. What, Simon, you leave me?" For I had turned away.

"It's late, sir," said I, "for the making of rhapsodies."

"You've made yours," he smiled. "Hark, what's that?"

As he spoke there came the sound of horse's hoofs. A moment later the figures of two mounted men emerged from the darkness. By some impulse, I know not what, I ran behind the Vicar and sheltered myself in the porch at his back. Carford's arrival had set my mind astir again, and new events found ready welcome. The Vicar stepped out a pace into the road with his hand over his eyes, and peered at the strangers.

"What do you call this place, sir?" came in a loud voice from the nearer of the riders. I started at the voice; it had struck on my ears before, and no Englishman owned it.

"It is the village of Hatchstead, at your service," answered the Vicar.

"Is there an inn in it?"

"Ride for half a mile and you'll find a good one."

"I thank you, sir."

I could hold myself in no longer, but pushed the Vicar aside and ran out into the road. The horsemen had already turned their faces towards the inn, and walked along slowly, as though they were weary. "Good-night," cried the Vicar—whether to them or to me or to all creation I know not. The door closed on him. I stood for an instant, watching the retreating form of the man who had enquired the way. A spirit of high excitement came on me; it might be that all was not finished, and that Betty Nasroth's prophecy should not bind the future in fetters. For there at the inn was Carford, and here, if I did not err, was the man whom my knowledge of French had so perplexed in the inn at Canterbury.

And Carford knew Fontelles. On what errand did they come? Were they friends to one another or foes? If friends, they should find an enemy; if foes, there was another to share their battle. I could not tell the meaning of this strange conjuncture whereby the two came to Hatchstead; yet my guess was not far out, and I hailed the prospect that it gave with a fierce exultation. Nay I laughed aloud, but first knew that I laughed when suddenly M. de Fontelles turned in his saddle, crying in French to his servant:

"What was that?"

"Something laughed," answered the fellow in an alarmed voice.

"Something? You mean somebody."

"I know not, it sounded strange."

I had stepped in under the hedge when Fontelles turned, but his puzzle and the servant's superstitious fear wrought on my excitement. Nothing would serve me but to play a jest on the Frenchman. I laughed again loudly.

"God save us!" cried the servant, and I make no doubt he crossed himself most piously.

"It's some madman got loose," said M. de Fontelles scornfully. "Come, let's get on."

It was a boy's trick—a very boy's trick. Save that I set down everything I would not tell it. I put my hands to my mouth and bellowed:

"*Il vient!*"

An oath broke from Fontelles. I darted into the middle of the road and for a moment stood there laughing again. He had wheeled his horse round, but did not advance towards me. I take it that he was amazed, or, it may be, searching a bewildered memory.

"*Il vient!*" I cried again in my folly, and, turning, ran down the road at my best speed, laughing still. Fontelles made no effort to follow me, yet on I ran, till I came to my mother's house. Stopping there, panting and breathless, I cried in the exuberance of triumph:

"Now she'll have need of me!"

Certainly the thing the Vicar spoke of is a distemper. Whether divine or of what origin I will not have judged by that night's prank of mine.

"They'll do very well together at the inn," I laughed, as I flung myself on my bed.

CHAPTER XXII

THE DEVICE OF LORD CARFORD

It is not my desire to assail, not is it my part to defend, the reputation of the great. There is no such purpose in anything that I have written here. History is their judge, and our own weakness their advocate. Some said, and many believed, that Madame brought the young French lady in her train to Dover with the intention that the thing should happen which happened. I had rather hold, if it be possible to hold, that a Princess so gracious and so unfortunate meant innocently, and was cajoled or overborne by the persuasions of her kinsmen, and perhaps by some specious pretext of State policy. In like manner I am reluctant to think that she planned harm for Mistress Barbara, towards whom she had a true affection, and I will read in an honest sense, if I can, the letter which M. de Fontelles brought with him to Hatchstead. In it Madame touched with a light discretion on what had passed, deplored with pretty gravity the waywardness of men, and her own simplicity which made her a prey to their devices and rendered her less useful to her friends than she desired to be. Yet now she was warned, her eyes were open, she would guard her own honour, and that of any who would trust to her. Nay, he himself, M. de Perrencourt, was penitent (even as was the Duke of

Monmouth!), and had sworn to trouble her and her friends no more. Would not then her sweet Mistress Barbara, with whom she vowed she had fallen so mightily in love, come back to her and go with her to France, and be with her until the Duchess of York came, and, in good truth, as much longer as Barbara would linger, and Barbara's father in his kindness suffer. So ran the letter, and it seemed an honest letter. But I do not know; and if it were honest, yet who dared trust to it? Grant Madame the best of will, where lay her power to resist M. de Perrencourt? But M. de Perrencourt was penitent. Ay, his penitence was for having let the lady go, and would last until she should be in his power again.

Let the intent of the letter he carried be what it might, M. de Fontelles, a gentleman of courage and high honour, believed his business honest. He had not been at Dover, and knew nothing of what had passed there; if he were an instrument in wicked schemes, he did not know the mind of those who employed him. He came openly to Hatchstead on an honourable mission, as he conceived, and bearing an invitation which should give great gratification to the lady to whom it was addressed. Madame did Mistress Quinton the high compliment of desiring her company, and would doubtless recompense her well for the service she asked. Fontelles saw no more and asked no more. In perfect confidence and honesty he set about his task, not imagining that he had been sent on an errand with which any man could reproach him, or with a purpose that gave any the right of questioning his actions. Nor did my cry of "*Il vient*" change this mood in him. When he collected his thoughts and recalled the incident in which those words had played a part before, he saw in them the challenge of someone who had perhaps penetrated a State secret, and was ill-affected towards the King and the King's policy; but, being unaware of any

Anthony Hope

connection between Mistress Barbara and M. de Perrencourt, he did not associate the silly cry with the object of his present mission. So also, on hearing that a gentleman was at the inn (Carford had not given his name) and had visited the Manor, he was in no way disquieted, but ready enough to meet any number of gentlemen without fearing their company or their scrutiny.

Gaily and courteously he presented himself to Barbara. Her mother lay still in bed, and she received him alone in the room looking out on the terrace. With a low bow and words of deference he declared his errand, and delivered to her the letter he bore from Madame, making bold to add his own hopes that Mistress Quinton would not send him back unsuccessful, but let him win the praise of a trustworthy messenger. Then he twirled his moustaches, smiled gallantly, and waited with all composure while she read the letter. Indeed he deserves some pity, for women are wont to spend much time on reasoning in such a case. When a man comes on a business which they suspect to be evil, they make no ado about holding him a party to it, and that without inquiring whether he knows the thing to which he is setting his hand.

Barbara read her letter through once and a second time; then, without a word to Fontelles, aye, not so much as bidding him be seated, she called a servant and sent him to the inn to summon Carford to her. She spoke low, and the Frenchman did not hear. When they were again alone together, Barbara walked to the window, and stood there looking out. Fontelles, growing puzzled and ill at ease, waited some moments before he ventured to address her; her air was not such as to encourage him; her cheek was reddened and her eyes were indignant. Yet at last he plucked up his courage.

"I trust, madame," said he, "that I may carry the fairest of answers back with me?"

"What answer is that, sir?" she asked, half-turning to him with a scornful glance.

"Yourself, madame, if you will so honour me," he answered, bowing. "Your coming would be the answer best pleasing to Madame, and the best fulfilment of my errand."

She looked at him coolly for a moment or two, and then said,

"I have sent for a gentleman who will advise me on my answer."

M. de Fontelles raised his brows, and replied somewhat stiffly,

"You are free, madame, to consult whom you will, although I had hoped that the matter needed but little consideration."

She turned full on him in a fury.

"I thank you for your judgment of me, sir," she cried. "Or is it that you think me a fool to be blinded by this letter?"

"Before heaven—" began the puzzled gentleman.

"I know, sir, in what esteem a woman's honour is held in your country and at your King's Court."

"In as high, madame, as in your country and at your Court."

"Yes, that's true. God help me, that's true! But we are not at Court now, sir. Hasn't it crossed your mind that such an errand as yours may be dangerous?"

"I had not thought it," said he with a smile and a shrug. "But, pardon me, I do not fear the danger."

"Neither danger nor disgrace?" she sneered.

Fontelles flushed.

"A lady, madame, may say what she pleases," he remarked with a bow.

"Oh, enough of pretences," she cried. "Shall we speak openly?"

"With all my heart, madame," said he, lost between anger and bewilderment.

For a moment it seemed as though she would speak, but the shame of open speech was too great for her. In his ignorance and wonder he could do nothing to aid her.

"I won't speak of it," she said. "It's a man's part to tell you the truth, and to ask account from you. I won't soil my lips with it."

Fontelles took a step towards her, seeking how he could assuage a fury that he did not understand.

"As God lives—" he began gravely. Barbara would not give him opportunity.

"I pray you," she cried, "stand aside and allow me to pass. I will not stay longer with you. Let me pass to the door, sir. I'll send a gentleman to speak with you."

Fontelles, deeply offended, utterly at a loss, flung the door open for her and stood aside to let her pass.

"Madame," he said, "it must be that you misapprehend."

"Misapprehend? Yes, or apprehend too clearly!"

"As I am a gentleman—"

"I do not grant it, sir," she interrupted.

He was silent then; bowing again, he drew a pace farther back. She stood for a moment, looking scornfully at him. Then with a curtsey she bade him farewell and passed out, leaving him in as sad a condition as ever woman's way left man since the world began.

Now, for reasons that have been set out, Carford received his summons with small pleasure, and obeyed it so leisurely that M. de Fontelles had more time than enough in which to rack his brains for the meaning of Mistress Barbara's taunts. But he came no nearer the truth, and was reduced to staring idly out of the window till the gentleman who was to make the matter plain should arrive. Thus he saw Carford coming up to the house on foot, slowly and heavily, with a gloomy face and a nervous air. Fontelles uttered an exclamation of joy; he had known Carford, and a friend's aid would put him right with this hasty damsel who denied him even the chance of self-defence. He was aware also that, in spite of his outward devotion to the Duke of Monmouth, Carford was in reality of the French party. So he was about to run out and welcome him, when his steps were stayed by the sight of Mistress Barbara herself, who flew to meet the new-comer with every sign of eagerness. Carford saluted her, and the pair entered into conversation on the terrace, Fontelles watching them from the window. To his fresh amazement, the interview seemed hardly less fierce than his own had been. The lady appeared to press some course on her adviser, which the adviser was loth to take; she insisted, growing angry in manner; he, having fenced for awhile and protested, sullenly gave way; he bowed acquiescence while his demeanour asserted disapproval, she made nothing of his disapproval and received his acquiescence with a scorn little disguised. Carford passed on to the house; Barbara did not follow him, but, flinging herself on a marble seat, covered her face with her hands and remained there in an attitude which spoke of deep agitation and misery.

"By my faith," cried honest M. de Fontelles, "this matter is altogether past understanding!"

A moment later Carford entered the room and greeted him with great civility. M. de Fontelles lost no time in coming to the question; his grievance was strong and bitter, and he poured out his heart without reserve. Carford listened, saying little, but being very attentive and keeping his shrewd eyes on the other's face. Indignation carried Fontelles back and forwards along the length of the room in restless paces; Carford sat in a chair, quiet and wary, drinking in all that the angry gentleman said. My Lord Carford was not one who believed hastily in the honour and honesty of his fellow-men, nor was he prone to expect a simple heart rather than a long head; but soon he perceived that the Frenchman was in very truth ignorant of what lay behind his mission, and that Barbara's usage of him caused genuine and not assumed offence. The revelation set my lord a-thinking.

"And she sends for you to advise her?" cried Fontelles. "That, my friend, is good; you can advise her only in one fashion."

"I don't know that," said Carford, feeling his way.

"It is because you don't know all. I have spoken gently to her, seeking to win her by persuasion. But to you I may speak plainly. I have direct orders from the King to bring her and to suffer no man to stop me. Indeed, my dear lord, there is no choice open to you. You wouldn't resist the King's command?"

Yet Barbara demanded that he should resist even the King's command. Carford said nothing, and the impetuous Frenchman ran on:

"Nay, it would be the highest offence to myself to hinder me. Indeed, my lord, all my regard for you could not make me suffer it. I don't know what this lady has against me, nor who has put this nonsense in her head. It cannot be you? You don't doubt my honour? You don't taunt me when I call myself a gentleman?"

He came to a pause before Carford, expecting an answer to his hot questions. He saw offence in the mere fact that Carford was still silent.

"Come, my lord," he cried, "I do not take pleasure in seeing you think so long. Isn't your answer easy?" He assumed an air of challenge.

Carford was, I have no doubt, most plagued and perplexed. He could have dealt better with a knave than with this fiery gentleman. Barbara had demanded of him that he should resist even the King's command. He might escape that perilous obligation by convincing Fontelles himself that he was a tool in hands less honourable than his own; then the Frenchman would in all likelihood abandon his enterprise. But with him would go Carford's hold on Barbara and his best prospect of winning her; for in her trouble lay his chance. If, on the other hand, he quarrelled openly with Fontelles, he must face the consequences he feared or incur Barbara's unmeasured scorn. He could not solve the puzzle and determined to seek a respite.

"I do not doubt your honour, sir," he said. Fontelles bowed gravely. "But there is more in this matter than you know. I must beg a few hours for consideration and then I will tell you all openly."

"My orders will not endure much delay."

"You can't take the lady by force."

"I count on the aid of my friends and the King's to persuade her to accompany me willingly."

I do not know whether the words brought the idea suddenly and as if with a flash into Carford's head. It may have been there dim and vague before, but now it was clear. He paused on his way to the door, and turned back with brightened eyes. He gave a careless laugh, saying,

"My dear Fontelles, you have more than me to reckon with before you take her away."

"What do you mean, my lord?"

"Why, men in love are hard to reason with, and with fools in love there is no reasoning at all. Come, I'm your friend, although there is for the moment a difficulty that keeps us apart. Do you chance to remember our meeting at Canterbury?"

"Why, very well."

"And a young fellow who talked French to you?" Carford laughed again. "He disturbed you mightily by calling out—"

"'*Il vient!*'" cried Fontelles, all on the alert.

"Precisely. Well, he may disturb you again."

"By Heaven, then he's here?"

"Why, yes."

"I met him last night! He cried those words to me again. The insolent rascal! I'll make him pay for it."

"In truth you've a reckoning to settle with him."

"But how does he come into this matter?"

"Insolent still, he's a suitor for Mistress Quinton's hand."

Fontelles gave a scornful shrug of his shoulders; Carford, smiling and more at ease, watched him. The idea promised well; it would be a stroke indeed could the quarrel be shifted on to my shoulders, and M. de Fontelles and I set by the ears; whatever the issue of that difference, Carford stood to win by it. And I, not he, would be the man to resist the King's commands.

"But how comes he here?" cried Fontelles.

"The fellow was born here. He is an old neighbour of Mistress Quinton."

"Dangerous then?"

It was Carford's turn to shrug his shoulders, as he said,

"Fools are always dangerous. Well, I'll leave you. I want to think. Only remember; if you please to be on your guard against me, why, be more on your guard against Simon Dale."

"He dares not stop me. Nay, why should he? What I propose is for the lady's advantage."

Carford saw the quarrel he desired fairly in the making. M. de Fontelles was honest, M. de Fontelles was hot-tempered, M. de Fontelles would be told that he was a rogue. To Carford this seemed enough.

"You would do yourself good if you convinced him of that," he answered. "For though she would not, I think, become his wife, he has the influence of long acquaintance, and might use it against you. But perhaps you're too angry with him?"

"My duty comes before my quarrel," said Fontelles. "I will seek this gentleman."

"As you will. I think you're wise. They will know at the inn where to find him."

"I will see him at once," cried Fontelles. "I have, it seems, two matters to settle with this gentleman."

Carford, concealing his exultation, bade M. de Fontelles

do as seemed best to him. Fontelles, declaring again that the success of his mission was nearest his heart, but in truth eager to rebuke or chasten my mocking disrespect, rushed from the room. Carford followed more leisurely. He had at least time for consideration now; and there were the chances of this quarrel all on his side.

"Will you come with me?" asked Fontelles.

"Nay, it's no affair of mine. But if you need me later—" He nodded. If it came to a meeting, his services were ready.

"I thank you, my lord," said the Frenchman, understanding his offer.

They were now at the door, and stepped out on the terrace. Barbara, hearing their tread, looked up. She detected the eagerness in M. de Fontelles' manner. He went up to her at once.

"Madame," he said, "I am forced to leave you for a while, but I shall soon return. May I pray you to greet me more kindly when I return?"

"In frankness, sir, I should be best pleased if you did not return," she said coldly, then, turning to Carford, she looked inquiringly at him. She conceived that he had done her bidding, and thought that the gentlemen concealed their quarrel from her. "You go with M. de Fontelles, my lord?" she asked.

"With your permission, I remain here," he answered.

She was vexed, and rose to her feet as she cried,

"Then where is M. de Fontelles going?"

Fontelles took the reply for himself.

"I am going to seek a gentleman with whom I have business," said he.

"You have none with my Lord Carford?"

"What I have with him will wait."

"He desires it should wait?" she asked in a quick tone.

"Yes, madame."

"I'd have sworn it," said Barbara Quinton.

"But with Mr Simon Dale—"

"With Simon Dale? What concern have you with Simon Dale?"

"He has mocked me twice, and I believe hinders me now," returned Fontelles, his hot temper rising again.

Barbara clasped her hands, and cried triumphantly,

"Go to him, go to him. Heaven is good to me! Go to Simon Dale!"

The amazed eyes of Fontelles and the sullen enraged glance of Carford recalled her to wariness. Yet the avowal (O, that it had pleased God I should hear it!) must have its price and its penalty. A burning flush spread over her face and even to the border of the gown on her neck. But she was proud in her shame, and her eyes met theirs in a level gaze.

To Fontelles her bearing and the betrayal of herself brought fresh and strong confirmation of Carford's warning. But he was a gentleman, and would not look at her when her blushes implored the absence of his eyes.

"I go to seek Mr Dale," said he gravely, and without more words turned on his heel.

In a sudden impulse, perhaps a sudden doubt of her judgment of him, Barbara darted after him.

"For what purpose do you seek him?"

"Madame," he answered, "I cannot tell you."

She looked for a moment keenly in his face; her breath came quick and fast, the hue of her cheek flashed from red to white.

"Mr Dale," said she, drawing herself up, "will not fear to meet you."

Again Fontelles bowed, turned, and was gone, swiftly and eagerly striding down the avenue, bent on finding me.

Barbara was left alone with Carford. His heavy frown and surly eyes accused her. She had no mind to accept the part of the guilty.

"Well, my lord," she said, "have you told this M. de Fontelles what honest folk would think of him and his errand?"

"I believe him to be honest," answered Carford.

"You live the quieter for your belief!" she cried contemptuously.

"I live the less quiet for what I have seen just now," he retorted.

There was a silence. Barbara stood with heaving breast, he opposite to her, still and sullen. She looked long at him, but at last seemed not to see him; then she spoke in soft tones, not as though to him, but rather in an answer to her own heart, whose cry could go no more unheeded. Her eyes grew soft and veiled in a mist of tears that did not fall. (So I see it—she told me no more than that she was near crying.)

"I couldn't send for him," she murmured. "I wouldn't send for him. But now he will come, yes, he'll come now."

Carford, driven half-mad by an outburst which his own device had caused, moved by whatever of true love he had for her, and by his great rage and jealousy against me, fairly ran at her and caught her by the wrist.

"Why do you talk of him? Do you love him?" he said from between clenched teeth.

She looked at him, half-angry, half-wondering. Then she said,

"Yes."

"Nell Gwyn's lover?" said Carford.

Her cheek flushed again, and a sob caught her voice as it came.

"Yes," said she. "Nell Gywn's lover."

"You love him?"

"Always, always, always." Then she drew herself near to him in a sudden terror. "Not a word, not a word," she cried. "I don't know what you are, I don't trust you; forgive me, forgive me; but whatever you are, for pity's sake, ah, my dear lord, for pity's sake, don't tell him. Not a word!"

"I will not speak of it to M. de Fontelles," said Carford.

An amazed glance was followed by a laugh that seemed half a sob.

"M. de Fontelles! M. de Fontelles! No, no, but don't tell Simon."

Carford's lips bent in a forced smile uglier than a scowl.

"You love this fellow?"

"You have heard."

"And he loves you?"

The sneer was bitter and strong. In it seemed now to lie Carford's only hope. Barbara met his glance an instant, and her answer to him was,

"Go, go."

"He loves you?"

"Leave me. I beg you to leave me. Ah, God, won't you

leave me?"

"He loves you?"

Her face went white. For a while she said nothing; then in a calm quiet voice, whence all life and feeling, almost all intelligence, seemed to have gone, she answered,

"I think not, my lord."

He laughed. "Leave me," she said again, and he, in grace of what manhood there was in him, turned on his heel and went. She stood alone, there on the terrace.

Ah, if God had let me be there! Then she should not have stood desolate, nor flung herself again on the marble seat. Then she should not have wept as though her heart broke, and all the world were empty. If I had been there, not the cold marble should have held her, and for every sweetest tear there should have been a sweeter kiss. Grief should have been drowned in joy, while love leapt to love in the fulness of delight. Alas for pride, breeder of misery! Not life itself is so long as to give atonement to her for that hour; though she has said that one moment, a certain moment, was enough.

CHAPTER XXIII

A PLEASANT PENITENCE

There was this great comfort in the Vicar's society that, having once and for all stated the irrefutable proposition which I have recorded, he let the matter alone. Nothing was further from his thoughts than to argue on it, unless it might be to take any action in regard to it. To say the truth, and I mean no unkindness to him in saying it, the affair did not greatly engage his thoughts. Had Betty Nasroth dealt with it, the case would doubtless have been altered, and he would have followed its fortune with a zest as keen as that he had bestowed on my earlier unhappy passion. But the prophecy had stopped short, and all that was of moment for the Vicar in my career, whether in love, war, or State, was finished; I had done and undergone what fate declared and demanded, and must now live in gentle resignation. Indeed I think that in his inmost heart he wondered a little to find me living on at all. This attitude was very well for him, and I found some amusement in it even while I chafed at his composed acquiescence in my misfortunes. But at times I grew impatient, and would fling myself out of the house, crying "Plague on it, is this old crone not only to drive me into folly, but to forbid me a return to wisdom?"

Anthony Hope

In such a mood I had left him, to wander by myself about the lanes, while he sat under the porch of his house with a great volume open on his knees. The book treated of Vaticination in all its branches, and the Vicar read diligently, being so absorbed in his study that he did not heed the approach of feet, and looked up at last with a start. M. de Fontelles stood there, sent on from the inn to the parsonage in the progress of his search for me.

"I am called Georges de Fontelles, sir," he began.

"I am the Vicar of this parish, at your service, sir," returned the Vicar courteously.

"I serve the King of France, but have at this time the honour of being employed by his Majesty the King of England."

"I trust, sir," observed the Vicar mildly, "that the employment is an honour."

"Your loyalty should tell you so much."

"We are commanded to honour the King, but I read nowhere that we must honour all that the King does."

"Such distinctions, sir, lead to disaffection and even to rebellion," said Fontelles severely.

"I am very glad of it," remarked the Vicar complacently.

I had told my old friend nothing of what concerned Barbara; the secret was not mine; therefore he had nothing against M. de Fontelles; yet it seemed as though a good quarrel could be found on the score of general principles. It is strange how many men give their heads for them and how few can give a reason; but God provides every man with a head, and since the stock of brains will not supply all, we draw lots for a share in it. Yes, a pretty quarrel promised; but a moment later Fontelles, seeing no prospect of sport in falling out with an old man of sacred profession, and amused, in spite of his principles, by the Vicar's whimsical talk, chose to laugh rather than to storm, and said with a chuckle:

"Well, kings are like other men."

"Very like," agreed the Vicar. "In what can I serve you, sir?"

"I seek Mr Simon Dale," answered Fontelles.

"Ah, Simon! Poor Simon! What would you with the lad, sir?"

"I will tell that to him. Why do you call him poor?"

"He has been deluded by a high-sounding prophecy, and it has come to little." The Vicar shook his head in gentle regret.

"He is no worse off, sir, than a man who marries," said Fontelles with a smile.

"Nor, it may be, than one who is born," said the Vicar, sighing.

"Nor even than one who dies," hazarded the Frenchman.

"Sir, sir, let us not be irreligious," implored the Vicar, smiling.

The quarrel was most certainly over. Fontelles sat down by the Vicar's side.

"Yet, sir," said he, "God made the world."

"It is full as good a world as we deserve," said the Vicar.

"He might well have made us better, sir."

"There are very few of us who truly wish it," the Vicar replied. "A man hugs his sin."

"The embrace, sir, is often delightful."

"I must not understand you," said the Vicar.

Fontelles' business was proceeding but slowly. A man on an errand should not allow himself to talk about the universe. But he was recalled to his task a moment later by the sight of my figure a quarter of a mile away along the road. With an eager exclamation he pointed his finger at me, lifted his hat to the Vicar, and rushed off in pursuit. The Vicar, who had not taken his thumb from his page, opened his book again, observing to himself, "A gentleman of some parts, I think."

His quarrel with the Vicar had evaporated in the mists of speculation; Fontelles had no mind to lose his complaint against me in any such manner, but he was a man of ceremony and must needs begin again with me much as he had with the Vicar. Thus obtaining my opportunity, I cut across his preface, saying brusquely:

"Well, I am glad that it is the King's employment and not M. de Perrencourt's."

He flushed red.

"We know what we know, sir," said he. "If you have anything to say against M. de Perrencourt, consider me as his friend. Did you cry out to me as I rode last night?"

"Why, yes, and I was a fool there. As for M. de Perrencourt—"

"If you speak of him, speak with respect, sir. You know of whom you speak."

"Very well. Yet I have held a pistol to his head," said I, not, I confess, without natural pride.

Fontelles started, then laughed scornfully.

"When he and Mistress Quinton and I were in a boat together," I pursued. "The quarrel then was which of us should escort the lady, he or I, and whether to Calais or to England. And although I should have been her husband had we gone to Calais, yet I brought her here."

"You're pleased to talk in riddles."

"They're no harder to understand than your errand is to me, sir," I retorted.

He mastered his anger with a strong effort, and in a few words told me his errand, adding that by Carford's advice he came to me.

"For I am told, sir, that you have some power with the lady."

I looked full and intently in his face. He met my gaze

unflinchingly. There was a green bank by the roadside; I seated myself; he would not sit, but stood opposite to me.

"I will tell you, sir, the nature of the errand on which you come," said I, and started on the task with all the plainness of language that the matter required and my temper enjoyed.

He heard me without a word, with hardly a movement of his body; his eyes never left mine all the while I was speaking. I think there was a sympathy between us, so that soon I knew that he was honest, while he did not doubt my truth. His face grew hard and stern as he listened; he perceived now the part he had been set to play. He asked me but one question when I had ended:

"My Lord Carford knew all this?"

"Yes, all of it," said I. "He was privy to all that passed."

Engaged in talk, we had not noticed the Vicar's approach. He was at my elbow before I saw him; the large book was under his arm. Fontelles turned to him with a bow.

"Sir," said he, "you were right just now."

"Concerning the prophecy, sir?"

"No, concerning the employment of kings," answered M. de Fontelles. Then he said to me, "We will meet again, before I take my leave of your village." With this he set off at a round pace down the road. I did not doubt that he went to seek Mistress Barbara and ask her pardon. I let him go; he would not hurt her now. I rose myself from the green bank, for I also had work to do.

"Will you walk with me, Simon?" asked the Vicar.

"Your pardon, sir, but I am occupied."

"Will it not wait?"

"I do not desire that it should."

For now that Fontelles was out of the way, Carford alone remained. Barbara had not sent for me, but still I served her, and to some profit.

It was now afternoon and I set out at once on my way to the Manor. I did not know what had passed between Barbara and Carford, nor how his passion had been stirred by her avowal of love for me, but I conjectured that on learning how his plan of embroiling me with Fontelles had failed, he would lose no time in making another effort.

Fontelles must have walked briskly, for I, although I did not loiter on the road, never came in sight of him, and the long avenue was empty when I passed the gates. It is strange that it did not occur to my mind that the clue to the Frenchman's haste was to be found in his last question; no doubt he would make his excuses to Mistress Quinton in good time, but it was not that intention which lent his feet wings. His errand was the same as my own; he sought Carford, not Barbara, even as I. He found what he sought, I what I did not seek, but what, once found, I could not pass by.

She was walking near the avenue, but on the grass behind the trees. I caught a glimpse of her gown through the leaves and my quick steps were stayed as though by one of the potent spells that the Vicar loved to read about. For

Anthony Hope

a moment or two I stood there motionless; then I turned and walked slowly towards her. She saw me a few yards off, and it seemed as though she would fly. But in the end she faced me proudly; her eyes were very sad and I thought that she had been weeping; as I approached she thrust something—it looked like a letter—into the bosom of her gown, as if in terror lest I should see it. I made her a low bow.

"I trust, madame," said I, "that my lady mends?"

"I thank you, yes, although slowly."

"And that you have taken no harm from your journey?"

"I thank you, none."

It was strange, but there seemed no other topic in earth or heaven; for I looked first at earth and then at heaven, and in neither place found any.

"I am seeking my Lord Carford," I said at last.

I knew my error as soon as I had spoken. She would bid me seek Carford without delay and protest that the last thing in her mind was to detain me. I cursed myself for an awkward fool. But to my amazement she did nothing of what I looked for, but cried out in great agitation and, as it seemed, fear:

"You mustn't see Lord Carford."

"Why not?" I asked. "He won't hurt me." Or at least he should not, if my sword could stop his.

"It is not that. It is—it is not that," she murmured, and

flushed red.

"Well, then, I will seek him."

"No, no, no," cried Barbara in a passion that fear—surely it was that and nothing else—made imperious. I could not understand her, for I knew nothing of the confession which she had made, but would not for the world should reach my ears. Yet it was not very likely that Carford would tell me, unless his rage carried him away.

"You are not so kind as to shield me from Lord Carford's wrath?" I asked rather scornfully.

"No," she said, persistently refusing to meet my eyes.

"What is he doing here?" I asked.

"He desires to conduct me to my father."

"My God, you won't go with him?"

For the fraction of a moment her dark eyes met mine, then turned away in confusion.

"I mean," said I, "is it wise to go with him?"

"Of course you meant that," murmured Barbara.

"M. de Fontelles will trouble you no more," I remarked, in a tone as calm as though I stated the price of wheat; indeed much calmer than such a vital matter was wont to command at our village inn.

"What?" she cried. "He will not—?"

"He didn't know the truth. I have told him. He is an honourable gentleman."

"You've done that also, Simon?" She came a step nearer me.

"It was nothing to do," said I. Barbara fell back again.

"Yet I am obliged to you," said she. I bowed with careful courtesy.

Why tell these silly things. Every man has such in his life. Yet each counts his own memory a rare treasure, and it will not be denied utterance.

"I had best seek my Lord Carford," said I, more for lack of another thing to say than because there was need to say that.

"I pray you—" cried Barbara, again in a marked agitation.

It was a fair soft evening; a breeze stirred the tree-tops, and I could scarce tell when the wind whispered and when Barbara spoke, so like were the caressing sounds. She was very different from the lady of our journey, yet like to her who had for a moment spoken to me from her chamber-door at Canterbury.

"You haven't sent for me," I said, in a low voice. "I suppose you have no need of me?"

She made me no answer.

"Why did you fling my guinea in the sea?" I said, and paused.

"Why did you use me so on the way?" I asked.

"Why haven't you sent for me?" I whispered.

She seemed to have no answer for any of these questions. There was nothing in her eyes now save the desire of escape. Yet she did not dismiss me, and without dismissal I would not go. I had forgotten Carford and the angry Frenchman, my quarrel and her peril; the questions I had put to her summed up all life now held.

Suddenly she put her hand to her bosom, and drew out that same piece of paper which I had seen her hide there. Before my eyes she read, or seemed to read, something that was in it; then she shut her hand on it. In a moment I was by her, very close. I looked full in her eyes, and they fled behind covering lids; the little hand, tightly clenched, hung by her side. What had I to lose? Was I not already banned for forwardness? I would be forward still, and justify the sentence by an after-crime. I took the hanging hand in both of mine. She started, and I loosed it; but no rebuke came, and she did not fly. The far-off stir of coming victory moved in my blood; not yet to win, but now to know that win you will sends through a man an exultation, more sweet because it is still timid. I watched her face—it was very pale—and again took her hand. The lids of her eyes rose now an instant, and disclosed entreaty. I was ruthless; our hearts are strange, and cruelty or the desire of mastery mingled with love in my tightened grasp. One by one I bent her fingers back; the crushed paper lay in a palm that was streaked to red and white. With one hand still I held hers, with the other I spread out the paper. "You mustn't read it," she murmured. "Oh, you mustn't read it." I paid no heed, but held it up. A low exclamation of wonder broke from me. The scrawl that I had seen at Canterbury now met me

again, plain and unmistakable in its laborious awkward-
ness. "In pay for your dagger," it had said before. Were
five words the bounds of Nell's accomplishment? She had
written no more now. Yet before she had seemed to say
much in that narrow limit; and much she said now.

There was long silence between us; my eyes were intent
on her veiled eyes.

"You needed this to tell you?" I said at last.

"You loved her, Simon."

I would not allow the plea. Shall not a thing that has
become out of all reason to a man's own self thereby
blazon its absurdity to the whole world?

"So long ago!" I cried scornfully.

"Nay, not so long ago," she murmured, with a note of
resentment in her voice.

Even then we might have fallen out; we were in an ace of
it, for I most brutally put this question:

"You waited here for me to pass?"

I would have given my ears not to have said it; what
availed that? A thing said is a thing done, and stands for
ever amid the irrevocable. For an instant her eyes flashed
in anger; then she flushed suddenly, her lips trembled, her
eyes grew dim, yet through the dimness mirth peeped out.

"I dared not hope you'd pass," she whispered.

"I am the greatest villain in the world!" I cried. "Barbara, you had no thought that I should pass!"

Again came silence. Then I spoke, and softly:

"And you—is it long since you—?"

She held out her hands towards me, and in an instant was in my arms. First she hid her face, but then drew herself back as far as the circle of my arm allowed. Her dark eyes met mine full and direct in a confession that shamed me but shamed her no more; her shame was swallowed in the sweet pride of surrender.

"Always," said she, "always; from the first through all; always, always." It seemed that though she could not speak that word enough.

In truth I could scarcely believe it; save when I looked in her eyes, I could not believe it.

"But I wouldn't tell you," she said. "I swore you should never know. Simon, do you remember how you left me?"

It seemed that I must play penitent now.

"I was too young to know—" I began.

"I was younger and not too young," she cried. "And all through those days at Dover I didn't know. And when we were together I didn't know. Ah, Simon, when I flung your guinea in the sea, you must have known!"

"On my faith, no," I laughed. "I didn't see the love in that, sweetheart."

"I'm glad there was no woman there to tell you what it

meant," said Barbara. "And even at Canterbury I didn't know. Simon, what brought you to my door that night?"

I answered her plainly, more plainly than I could at any other time, more plainly, it may be, than even then I should:

"She bade me follow her, and I followed her so far."

"You followed her?"

"Ay. But I heard your voice through the door, and stopped."

"You stopped for my voice; what did I say?"

"You sung how a lover had forsaken his love. And I heard and stayed."

"Ah, why didn't you tell me then?"

"I was afraid, sweetheart."

"Of what? Of what?"

"Why, of you. You had been so cruel."

Barbara's head, still strained far as could be from mine, now drew nearer by an ace, and then she launched at me the charge of most enormity, the indictment that justified all my punishment.

"You had kissed her before my eyes, here, sir, where we are now, in my own Manor Park," said Barbara.

I took my arms from about her, and fell humbly on

my knee.

"May I kiss so much as your hand?" said I in utter abasement.

She put it suddenly, eagerly, hurriedly to my lips.

"Why did she write to me?" she whispered.

"Nay, love, I don't know."

"But I know. Simon, she loves you."

"It would afford no reason if she did. And I think—"

"It would and she does. Simon, of course she does."

"I think rather that she was sorry for—"

"Not for me!" cried Barbara with great vehemence. "I will not have her sorry for me!"

"For you!" I exclaimed in ridicule. (It does not matter what I had been about to say before.) "For you! How should she? She wouldn't dare!"

"No," said Barbara. One syllable can hold a world of meaning.

"A thousand times, no!" cried I.

The matter was thus decided. Yet now, in quiet blood and in the secrecy of my own soul, shall I ask wherefore the letter came from Mistress Gwyn, to whom the shortest letter was no light matter, and to let even a humble man go some small sacrifice? And why did it come to Barbara and not to me? And why did it not say "Simon, she loves you," rather than the words that I now read, Barbara permitting me: "Pretty fool, he loves you." Let me not ask; not even now would Barbara bear to think that it was written in pity for her.

"Yes, she pitied you and so she wrote; and she loves you," said Barbara.

I let it pass. Shall a man never learn wisdom?

"Tell me now," said I, "why I may not see Carford?"

Her lips curved in a smile; she held her head high, and her eyes were triumphant.

"You may see Lord Carford as soon as you will, Simon," said she.

"But a few minutes ago—" I began, much puzzled.

"A few minutes!" cried Barbara reproachfully.

"A whole lifetime ago, sweetheart!"

"And shall that make no changes?"

"A whole lifetime ago you were ready to die sooner than let me see him."

"Simon, you're very—He knew, I told him."

"You told him?" I cried. "Before you told me?"

"He asked me before," said Barbara.

I did not grudge her that retort; every jot of her joy was joy to me, and her triumph my delight.

"How did I dare to tell him?" she asked herself softly. "Ah, but how have I contrived not to tell all the world? How wasn't it plain in my face?"

"It was most profoundly hidden," I assured her. Indeed from me it had been; but Barbara's wit had yet another answer.

"You were looking in another face," said she. Then, as the movement of my hands protested, remorse seized on her, and catching my hand she cried impulsively, "I'll never speak of it again, Simon."

Now I was not so much ashamed of the affair as to demand that utter silence on it; in which point lies a difference between men and women. To have wandered troubles our consciences little, when we have come to the right path again; their pride stands so strong in constancy as sometimes (I speak in trembling) even to beget an oblivion of its falterings and make what could not have been as if it had not. But now was not the moment for excuse, and I took my pardon with all gratitude and with full allowance of my offence's enormity.

Then we determined that Carford must immediately be sought, and set out for the house with intent to find him. But our progress was very slow, and the moon rose in the skies before we stepped out on to the avenue and came in sight of the house and the terrace. There was so much to tell, so much that had to slough off its old seeming and take on new and radiant apparel—things that she had understood and not I, that I had caught and she missed, wherein both of us had gone astray most lamentably and now stood aghast at our own sightlessness. Therefore never were our feet fairly in movement towards the house but a sudden—"Do you remember?" gave them pause again: then came shame that I had forgotten, or indignation that Barbara should be thought to have forgotten, and in both of these cases the need for expiation, and so forth. The moon was high in heaven when we stepped into the avenue and came in sight of the terrace.

On the instant, with a low cry of surprise and alarm, Barbara caught me by the arm, while she pointed to the terrace. The sight might well turn us even from our engrossing interchange of memories. There were four men on the terrace, their figures standing out dense and black against the old grey walls, which seemed white in the moonlight. Two stood impassive and motionless, with hands at their sides; at their feet lay what seemed bundles of clothes. The other two were in their shirts; they were opposite one another, and their swords were in their hands. I could not doubt the meaning; while love held me idle, anger had lent Fontelles speed; while I sought to perfect my joy, he had been hot to avenge his wounded honour. I did not know who were the two that watched unless they were servants; Fontelles' fierce mood would not stand for the niceties of etiquette. Now I could recognise the Frenchman's bearing and even see Carford's face, although distance hid its expression. I was amazed and at a loss what to do. How could I stop them and by what right? But then Barbara gave a little sob and whispered:

"My mother lies sick in the house."

It was enough to loose my bound limbs. I sprang forward and set out at a run. I had not far to go and lost no time; but I would not cry out lest I might put one off his guard and yet not arrest the other's stroke. For the steel flashed, and they fought, under the eyes of the quiet servants. I was near to them now and already wondering how best to interpose, when, in an instant, the Frenchman lunged, Carford cried out, his sword dropped from his hand, and he fell heavily on the gravel of the terrace. The servants rushed forward and knelt down beside him. M. de Fontelles did not leave his place, but stood, with the point of his naked sword on the ground, looking at the man who had put an affront on him and whom he had now chastised. The sudden change that took me from love's pastimes to a scene so stern deprived me of speech for a moment. I ran to Fontelles and faced him, panting but saying nothing. He turned his eyes on me: they were calm, but shone still with the heat of contest and the sternness of resentment. He raised his sword and pointed with it towards where Carford lay.

"My lord there," said he, "knew a thing that hurt my honour, and did not warn me of it. He knew that I was made a tool and did not tell me. He knew that I was used for base purposes and sought to use me for his own also. He has his recompense."

Then he stepped across to where the green bank sloped down to the terrace and, falling on one knee, wiped his blade on the grass.

CHAPTER XXIV

A COMEDY BEFORE THE KING

On the next day but one M. de Fontelles and I took the road for London together. Carford lay between life and death (for the point had pierced his lung) at the inn to which we had carried him; he could do no more harm and occasion us no uneasiness. On the other hand, M. de Fontelles was anxious to seek out the French Ambassador, with whom he was on friendly terms, and enlist his interest, first to excuse the abandonment of his mission, and in the second place to explain the circumstances of his duel with Carford. In this latter task he asked my aid since I alone, saving the servants, had been a witness of the encounter, and Fontelles, recognising (now that his rage was past) that he had been wrong to force his opponent to a meeting under such conditions, prayed my testimony to vindicate his reputation. I could not deny him, and moreover, though it grieved me to be absent from Quinton Manor, I felt that Barbara's interests and my own might be well served by a journey to London. No news had come from my lord, and I was eager to see him and bring him over to my side; the disposition of the King was also a matter of moment and of uncertainty; would he still seek to gain for M. de Perrencourt what that exacting gentleman required, or would he now abandon the struggle in which his instruments had twice failed him? His Majesty should now be returning from Dover, and I made up my mind to go to Court and learn from him the worst and the best of what I might look for. Nay, I will not say that the pure desire to see him face to face had not weight with me; for I believed that he had a liking for me, and that I should obtain from him better terms in my own person than if my cause were left in the hands of those who surrounded him.

When we were come to London (and I pray that it be observed and set down to my credit that, thinking there was enough of love-making in this history, I have spared any narrative of my farewell to Barbara, although on my soul it was most moving) M. de Fontelles at once sought the Ambassador's, taking my promise to come there as soon as his summons called, while I betook myself to the lodging which I had shared with Darrell before we went to Dover. I hoped to find him there and renew our friendship; my grudge was for his masters, and I am not for making an enemy of a man who does what his service demands of him. I was not disappointed; Robert opened the door to me, and Darrell himself sprang to his feet in amazement at the sound of my name. I laughed heartily and flung myself into a chair, saying:

"How goes the Treaty of Dover?"

He ran to the door and tried it; it was close-shut.

"The less you say of that, the safer you'll be," said he.

"Oho," thought I, "then I'm not going to market empty-handed! If I want to buy, it seems that I have something to sell." And smiling very good-humouredly I said:

Anthony Hope

"What, is there a secret in it?"

Darrell came up to me and held out his hand.

"On my life," said he, "I didn't know you were interested in the lady, Simon, or I wouldn't have taken a hand in the affair."

"On my life," said I, "I'm obliged to you. What of Mlle. de Querouaille?"

"She has returned with Madame."

"But will return without Madame?"

"Who knows?" he asked with a smile that he could not smother.

"God and the King," said I. "What of M. de Perrencourt?"

"Your tongue's hung so loose, Simon, that one day it'll hang you tight."

"Enough, enough. What then of Phineas Tate?"

"He is on board ship on his way to the plantations. He'll find plenty to preach to there."

"What? Why, there's never a Papist sent now! He'll mope to death. What of the Duke of Monmouth?"

"He has found out Carford."

"He has? Then he has found out the Secretary also?"

"There is indeed a distance between his Grace and my

lord," Darrell admitted.

"When rogues fall out! A fine saying that, Darrell. And what of the King?"

"My lord tells me that the King swears he won't sleep o' nights till he has laid a certain troublesome fellow by the heels."

"And where is that same troublesome fellow?"

"So near me that, did I serve the King as I ought, Robert would now be on his way with news for my Lord Arlington."

"Then His Majesty's sentiments are mighty unkind towards me? Be at peace, Darrell. I am come to London to seek him."

"To seek him? Are you mad? You'll follow Phineas Tate!"

"But I have a boon to ask of the King. I desire him to use his good offices with my Lord Quinton. For I am hardly a fit match for my lord's daughter, and yet I would make her my wife."

"I wonder," observed Darrell, "that you, Simon, who, being a heretic, must go to hell when you die, are not more careful of your life."

Then we both fell to laughing.

"Another thing brings me to London," I pursued. "I must see Mistress Gwyn."

He raised his hands over his head.

"Fill up the measure," said he. "The King knows you came to London with her and is more enraged at that than all the rest."

"Does he know what happened on the journey?"

"Why, no, Simon," smiled Darrell. "The matter is just that. The King does not know what happened on the journey."

"He must learn it," I declared. "To-morrow I'll seek Mistress Gwyn. You shall send Robert to take her pleasure as to the hour when I shall wait on her."

"She's in a fury with the King, as he with her."

"On what account?"

"Already, friend Simon, you're too wise."

"By Heaven, I know! It's because Mlle. de Querouaille is so good a Catholic?"

Darrell had no denial ready. He shrugged his shoulders and sat silent.

Now although I had told Barbara that it was my intention to ask an audience from the King, I had not disclosed my purpose of seeing Mistress Nell. Yet it was firm in my mind—for courtesy's sake. Of a truth she had done me great service. Was I to take it as though it were my right, with never a word of thanks? Curiosity also drew me, and that attraction which she never lost for me, nor, as I believe, for any man whose path she crossed. I was sure of myself, and did not fear to go. Yet memory was not dead in me, and I went in a species of excitement, the ghost of old feelings dead but not forgotten. When a man has loved, and sees her whom he loves no more, he will not be indifferent; angry he may be, or scornful, amused he may be, and he should be tender; but it will not be as though he had not loved. Yet I had put a terrible affront on her, and it might be that she would not receive me.

As I live, I believe that but for one thing she would not. That turned her, by its appeal to her humour. When I came to the house in Chelsea, I was conducted into a small ante-chamber, and there waited long. There were voices speaking in the next room, but I could not hear their speech. Yet I knew Nell's voice; it had for me always—ay, still—echoes of the past. But now there was something which barred its way to my heart.

The door in front of me opened, and she was in the room with me. There she was, curtseying low in mock obeisance and smiling whimsically.

"A bold man!" she cried. "What brings you here? Art not afraid?"

"Afraid that I am not welcome, yet not afraid to come."

"A taunt wrapped in civility! I do not love it."

"Mistress Nell, I came to thank you for the greatest kindness—"

"If it be kindness to help you to a fool!" said Mistress Nell. "What, besides your thanks to me, brings you to town?"

I must forgive her the style in which she spoke of Barbara. I answered with a smile:

"I must see the King. I don't know his purposes about me. Besides, I desire that he should help me to my—fool."

"If you're wise you'll keep out of his sight." Then she began to laugh. "Nay, but I don't know," said she. Then with a swift movement she was by me, catching at my coat and turning up to me a face full of merriment. "Shall we play a comedy?" she asked.

"As you will. What shall be my part?"

"I'll give you a pretty part, Simon. Your face is very smooth; nay, do not fear, I remember so well that I needn't try again. You shall be this French lady of whom they speak."

"I the French lady! God forbid!"

"Nay, but you shall, Simon. And I'll be the King. Nay, I say, don't be afraid. I swear you tried to run away then!"

"Is it not prescribed as the best cure for temptation?"

"Alas, you're not tempted!" she said with a pout. "But there's another part in the comedy."

"Besides the King and Mademoiselle?"

"Why, yes—and a great part."

"Myself by chance?"

"You! No! What should you do in the play? It is

I—I myself."

"True, true. I forgot you, Mistress Nell."

"You did forget me, Simon. But I must spare you, for you will have heard that same charge of fickleness from Mistress Quinton, and it is hard to hear it from two at once. But who shall play my part?"

"Indeed I can think of none equal to it."

"The King shall play it!" she cried with a triumphant laugh, and stood opposite to me, the embodiment of merry triumph. "Do you catch the plot of my piece, Simon?"

"I am very dull," I confessed.

"It's your condition, not your nature, Simon," Nell was so good as to say. "A man in love is always dull, save to one woman, and she's stark-mad. Come, can you feign an inclination for me, or have you forgot the trick?"

At the moment she spoke the handle of the door turned. Again it turned and was rattled.

"I locked it," whispered Nell, her eyes full of mischief.

Again, and most impatiently, the handle was twisted to and fro.

"Pat, pat, how pat he comes!" she whispered.

A last loud rattle followed, then a voice cried in anger, "Open it, I bid you open it."

"God help us!" I exclaimed in sad perplexity. "It's the King?"

"Yes, it's the King, and, Simon, the piece begins. Look as terrified as you can. It's the King."

"Open, I say, open!" cried the King, with a thundering knock.

I understood now that he had been in the other room, and that she had left his society to come to me; but I understood only dimly why she had locked the door, and why she now was so slow in opening it. Yet I set my wits to work, and for further aid watched her closely. She was worth the watching. Without aid of paints or powders, of scene or theatre, she transformed her air, her manner, ay, her face also. Alarm and terror showed in her eyes as she stole in fearful fashion across the room, unlocked the door, and drew it open, herself standing by it, stiff and rigid, in what seemed shame or consternation. The agitation she feigned found some reality in me. I was not ready for the thing, although I had been warned by the voice outside. When the King stood in the doorway, I wished myself a thousand miles away.

The King was silent for several moments; he seemed to me to repress a passion which, let loose, might hurry him to violence. When he spoke, he was smiling ironically, and his voice was calm.

"How comes this gentleman here?" he asked.

The terror that Nell had so artfully assumed she appeared now, with equal art, to defy or conquer. She answered him with angry composure.

"Why shouldn't Mr. Dale be here, Sir?" she asked. "Am I to see no friends? Am I to live all alone?"

"Mr Dale is no friend of mine—"

"Sir—" I began, but his raised hand stayed me.

"And you have no need of friends when I am here."

"Your Majesty," said she, "came to say farewell; Mr Dale was but half an hour too soon."

This answer showed me the game. If he had come to bid her farewell—why, I understood now the parts in the comedy. If he left her for the Frenchwoman, why should she not turn to Simon Dale? The King bit his lip. He also understood her answer.

"You lose no time, mistress," he said, with an uneasy laugh.

"I've lost too much already," she flashed back.

"With me?" he asked, and was answered by a sweeping curtsey and a scornful smile.

"You're a bold man, Mr Dale," said he. "I knew it before, and am now most convinced of it."

"I didn't expect to meet your Majesty here," said I sincerely.

"I don't mean that. You're bold to come here at all."

"Mistress Gwyn is very kind to me," said I. I would play my part and would not fail her, and I directed a timid yet amorous glance at Nell. The glance reached Nell, but on its way it struck the King. He was patient of rivals, they said, but he frowned now and muttered an oath. Nell broke into sudden laughter. It sounded forced and unreal. It was meant so to sound.

"We're old friends," said she, "Simon and I. We were friends before I was what I am. We're still friends, now that I am what I am. Mr Dale escorted me from Dover to London."

"He is an attentive squire," sneered the King.

"He hardly left my side," said Nell.

"You were hampered with a companion?"

"Of a truth I hardly noticed it," cried Nelly with magnificent falsehood. I seconded her efforts with a shrug and a cunning smile.

"I begin to understand," said the King. "And when my farewell has been said, what then?"

"I thought that it had been said half an hour ago," she exclaimed. "Wasn't it?"

"You were anxious to hear it, and so seemed to hear it," said he uneasily.

She turned to me with a grave face and tender eyes.

"Didn't I tell you here, just now, how the King parted from me?"

I was to take the stage now, it seemed.

"Ay, you told me," said I, playing the agitated lover as best I could. "You told me that—that—but I cannot speak before His Majesty." And I ended in a most rare confusion.

"Speak, sir," he commanded harshly and curtly.

"You told me," said I in low tones, "that the King left you. And I said I was no King, but that you need not be left alone." My eyes fell to the ground in pretended fear.

The swiftest glance from Nell applauded me. I would have been sorry for him and ashamed for myself, had I not remembered M. de Perrencourt and our voyage to Calais. In that thought I steeled myself to hardness and bade conscience be still.

A long silence followed. Then the King drew near to Nell. With a rare stroke of skill she seemed to shrink away from him and edged towards me, as though she would take refuge in my arms from his anger or his coldness.

"Come, I've never hurt you, Nelly!" said he.

Alas, that art should outstrip nature! Never have I seen portrayed so finely the resentment of a love that, however greatly wounded, is still love, that even in turning away longs to turn back, that calls even in forbidding, and in refusing breathes the longing to assent. Her feet still came towards me, but her eyes were on the King.

"You sent me away," she whispered as she moved towards me and looked where the King was.

"I was in a temper," said he. Then he turned to me, saying "Pray leave us, sir."

Anthony Hope

I take it that I must have obeyed, but Nell sprang suddenly forward, caught my hand, and holding it faced the King.

"He shan't go; or, if you send him away, I'll go with him."

The King frowned heavily, but did not speak. She went on, choking down a sob—ay, a true sob; the part she played moved her, and beneath her acting there was a reality. She fought for her power over him and now was the test of it.

"Will you take my friendships from me as well as my—? Oh, I won't endure it!"

She had given him his hint in the midst of what seemed her greatest wrath. His frown persisted, but a smile bent his lips again.

"Mr Dale," said he, "it is hard to reason with a lady before another gentleman. I was wrong to bid you go. But will you suffer me to retire to that room again?"

I bowed low.

"And," he went on, "will you excuse our hostess' presence for awhile?"

I bowed again.

"No, I won't go with you," cried Nell.

"Nay, but, Nelly, you will," said he, smiling now. "Come, I'm old and mighty ugly, and Mr Dale is a strapping fellow. You must be kind to the unfortunate, Nelly."

She was holding my hand still. The King took hers. Very

slowly and reluctantly she let him draw her away. I did what seemed best to do; I sighed very heavily and plaintively, and bowed in sad submission.

"Wait till we return," said the King, and his tone was kind.

They passed out together, and I, laughing yet ashamed to laugh, flung myself in a chair. She would not keep him for herself alone; nay, as all the world knows, she made but a drawn battle of it with the Frenchwoman; but the disaster and utter defeat which had threatened her she had averted, jealousy had achieved what love could not, he would not let her go now, when another's arms seemed open for her. To this success I had helped her. On my life I was glad to have helped her. But I did not yet see how I had helped my own cause.

I was long in the room alone, and though the King had bidden me await his return, he did not come again. Nell came alone, laughing, radiant and triumphant; she caught me by both hands, and swiftly, suddenly, before I knew, kissed me on the cheek. Nay, come, let me be honest; I knew a short moment before, but on my honour I could not avoid it courteously.

"We've won," she cried. "I have what I desire, and you, Simon, are to seek him at Whitehall. He has forgiven you all your sins and—yes, he'll give you what favour you ask. He has pledged his word to me."

"Does he know what I shall ask?"

"No, no, not yet. Oh, that I could see his face! Don't spare him, Simon. Tell him—why, tell him all the truth—every word of it, the stark bare truth."

"How shall I say it?"

"Why, that you love, and have ever loved, and will ever love Mistress Barbara Quinton, and that you love not, and will never love, and have never loved, no, nor cared the price of a straw for Eleanor Gwyn."

"Is that the whole truth?" said I.

She was holding my hands still; she pressed them now and sighed lightly.

"Why, yes, it's the whole truth. Let it be the whole truth, Simon. What matters that a man once lived when he's dead, or once loved when he loves no more?"

"Yet I won't tell him more than is true," said I.

"You'll be ashamed to say anything else?" she whispered, looking up into my face.

"Now, by Heaven, I'm not ashamed," said I, and I kissed her hand.

"You're not?"

"No, not a whit. I think I should be ashamed, had my heart never strayed to you."

"Ah, but you say 'strayed'!"

I made her no answer, but asked forgiveness with a smile. She drew her hand sharply away, crying,

"Go your ways, Simon Dale, go your ways; go to your Barbara, and your Hatchstead, and your dulness, and your righteousness."

"We part in kindness?" I urged.

For a moment I thought she would answer peevishly, but the mood passed, and she smiled sincerely on me as she replied:

"Ay, in all loving-kindness, Simon; and when you hear the sour gird at me, say—why, say, Simon, that even a severe gentleman, such as you are, once found some good in Nelly. Will you say that for me?"

"With all my heart."

"Nay, I care not what you say," she burst out, laughing again. "Begone, begone! I swore to the King that I would speak but a dozen words to you. Begone!"

I bowed and turned towards the door. She flew to me suddenly, as if to speak, but hesitated. I waited for her; at last she spoke, with eyes averted and an unusual embarrassment in her air.

"If—if you're not ashamed to speak my name to Mistress Barbara, tell her I wish her well, and pray her to think as kindly of me as she can."

"She has much cause to think kindly," said I.

"And will therefore think unkindly! Simon, I bid you begone."

She held out her hand to me, and I kissed it again.

"This time we part for good and all," said she. "I've loved

you, and I've hated you, and I have nearly loved you. But it is nothing to be loved by me, who love all the world."

"Nay, it's something," said I. "Fare you well."

I passed out, but turned to find her eyes on me. She was laughing and nodding her head, swaying to and fro on her feet as her manner was. She blew me a kiss from her lips. So I went, and my life knew her no more.

But when the strict rail on sinners, I guard my tongue for the sake of Nelly and the last kiss she gave me on my cheek.

CHAPTER XXV

THE MIND OF M. DE FONTELLES

As I made my way through the Court nothing seemed changed; all was as I had seen it when I came to lay down the commission that Mistress Gwyn had got me. They were as careless, as merry, as shameless as before; the talk then had been of Madame's coming, now it was of her going; they talked of Dover and what had passed there, but the treaty was dismissed with a shrug, and the one theme of interest, and the one subject of wagers, was whether or how soon Mlle. de Querouaille would return to the shores and the monarch she had left. In me distaste now killed curiosity; I pushed along as fast as the throng allowed me, anxious to perform my task and be quit of them all as soon as I could. My part there was behind me; the prophecy was fulfilled, and my ambitions quenched. Yet I had a pleasure in the remaining scene of the comedy which I was to play with the King; I was amused also to see how those whom I knew to be in the confidence of the Duke of York and of Arlington eyed me with mingled fear and wariness, and hid distrust under a most deferential civility. They knew, it seemed, that I had guessed their secrets. But I was not afraid of them, for I was no more their rival in the field of intrigue or in their assault upon the King's favour. I longed to say to them,

Anthony Hope

"Be at peace. In an hour from now you will see my face no more."

The King sat in his chair, alone save for one gentleman who stood beside him. I knew the Earl of Rochester well by repute, and had been before now in the same company, although, as it chanced, I had never yet spoken with him. I looked for the King's brother and for Monmouth, but neither was to be seen. Having procured a gentleman to advise the King of my presence, I was rewarded by being beckoned to approach immediately. But when he had brought me there, he gave me no more than a smile, and, motioning me to stand by him, continued his conversation with my Lord Rochester and his caresses of the little dog on his lap.

"In defining it as the device by which the weak intimidate the strong," observed Rochester, "the philosopher declared the purpose of virtue rather than its effect. For the strong are not intimidated, while the weak, falling slaves to their own puppet, grow more helpless still."

"It's a just retribution on them," said the King, "for having invented a thing so tiresome."

"In truth, Sir, all these things that make virtue are given a man for his profit, and that he may not go empty-handed into the mart of the world. He has stuff for barter; he can give honour for pleasure, morality for money, religion for power."

The King raised his brows and smiled again, but made no remark. Rochester bowed courteously to me, as he added:

"Is it not as I say, sir?" and awaited my reply.

"It's better still, my lord," I answered. "For he can make these bargains you speak of, and, by not keeping them, have his basket still full for another deal."

Again the King smiled as he patted his dog.

"Very just, sir, very just," nodded Rochester. "Thus by breaking a villainous bargain he is twice a villain, and preserves his reputation to aid him in the more effectual cheating of his neighbour."

"And the damning of his own soul," said the King softly.

"Your Majesty is Defender of the Faith. I will not meddle with your high office," said Rochester with a laugh. "For my own part I suffer from a hurtful sincerity; being known for a rogue by all the town, I am become the most harmless fellow in your Majesty's dominions. As Mr Dale here says—I have the honour of being acquainted with your name, sir—my basket is empty and no man will deal with me."

"There are women left you," said the King.

"It is more expense than profit," sighed the Earl. "Although indeed the kind creatures will most readily give for nothing what is worth as much."

"So that the sum of the matter," said the King, "is that he who refuses no bargain however iniquitous and performs none however binding—"

"Is a king among men, Sir," interposed Rochester with a low bow, "even as your Majesty is here in Whitehall."

"And by the same title?"

Anthony Hope

"Ay, the same Right Divine. What think you of my reasoning, Mr Dale?"

"I do not know, my lord, whence you came by it, unless the Devil has published a tract on the matter."

"Nay, he has but circulated it among his friends," laughed Rochester. "For he is in no need of money from the booksellers since he has a grant from God of the customs of the world for his support."

"The King must have the Customs," smiled Charles. "I have them here in England. But the smugglers cheat me."

"And the penitents him, Sir. Faith, these Holy Churches run queer cargoes past his officers—or so they say;" and with another bow to the King, and one of equal courtesy to me, he turned away and mingled in the crowd that walked to and fro.

The King sat some while silent, lazily pulling the dog's coat with his fingers. Then he looked up at me.

"Wild talk, Mr Dale," said he, "yet perhaps not all without a meaning."

"There's meaning enough, Sir. It's not that I miss."

"No, but perhaps you do. I have made many bargains; you don't praise all of them?"

"It's not for me to judge the King's actions."

"I wish every man were as charitable, or as dutiful. But— shall I empty my basket? You know of some of my bargains. The basket is not emptied yet."

I looked full in his face; he did not avoid my regard, but sat there smiling in a bitter amusement.

"You are the man of reservations," said he. "I remember them. Be at peace and hold your place. For listen to me, Mr Dale."

"I am listening to your Majesty's words."

"It will be time enough for you to open your mouth when I empty my basket."

His words, and even more the tone in which he spoke and the significant glance of his eyes, declared his meaning. The bargain that I knew of I need not betray nor denounce till he fulfilled it. When would he fulfil it? He would not empty his basket, but still have something to give when he dealt with the King of France. I wondered that he should speak to me so openly; he knew that I wondered, yet, though his smile was bitter, he smiled still.

I bowed to him and answered:

"I am no talker, Sir, of matters too great for me."

"That's well. I know you for a gentleman of great discretion, and I desire to serve you. You have something to ask of me, Mr Dale?"

"The smallest thing in the world for your Majesty, and the greatest for me."

"A pattern then that I wish all requests might follow. Let me hear it."

"It is no more than your Majesty's favour for my efforts to

Anthony Hope

win the woman whom I love."

He started a little, and for the first time in all the conversation ceased to fondle the little dog.

"The woman whom you love? Well, sir, and does she love you?"

"She has told me so, Sir."

"Then at least she wished you to believe it. Do I know this lady?"

"Very well, sir," I answered in a very significant tone.

He was visibly perturbed. A man come to his years will see a ready rival in every youth, however little other attraction there may be. But perhaps I had treated him too freely already; and now he used me well. I would keep up the jest no longer.

"Once, Sir," I said, "for a while I loved where the King loved, even as I drank of his cup."

"I know, Mr Dale. But you say 'once.'"

"It is gone by, Sir."

"But, yesterday?" he exclaimed abruptly.

"She is a great comedian, Sir; but I fear I seconded her efforts badly."

He did not answer for a moment, but began again to play with the dog. Then raising his eyes to mine he said:

"You were well enough; she played divinely, Mr Dale."

"She played for life, Sir."

"Ay, poor Nelly loves me," said he softly. "I had been cruel to her. But I won't weary you with my affairs. What would you?"

"Mistress Gwyn, Sir, has been very kind to me."

"So I believe," remarked the King.

"But my heart, Sir, is now and has been for long irrevocably set on another."

"On my faith, Mr Dale, and speaking as one man to another, I'm glad to hear it. Was it so at Canterbury?"

"More than ever before, Sir. For she was there and—"

"I know she was there."

"Nay, Sir, I mean the other, her whom I love, her whom I now woo. I mean Mistress Barbara Quinton, Sir."

The King looked down and frowned; he patted his dog, he looked up again, frowning still. Then a queer smile bent his lips and he said in a voice which was most grave, for all his smile,

"You remember M. de Perrencourt?"

"I remember M. de Perrencourt very well, Sir."

"It was by his choice, not mine, Mr Dale, that you set out for Calais."

"So I understood at the time, Sir."

"And he is believed, both by himself and others, to choose his men—perhaps you will allow me to say his instruments, Mr Dale—better than any Prince in Christendom. So you would wed Mistress Quinton? Well, sir, she is above your station."

"I was to have been made her husband, Sir."

"Nay, but she's above your station," he repeated, smiling at my retort, but conceiving that it needed no answer.

"She's not above your Majesty's persuasion, or, rather, her father is not. She needs none."

"You do not err in modesty, Mr Dale."

"How should I, Sir, I who have drunk of the King's cup?"

"So that we should be friends."

"And known what the King hid?"

"So that we must stand or fall together?"

"And loved where the King loved?"

He made no answer to that, but sat silent for a great while. I was conscious that many eyes were on us, in wonder that I was so long with him, in speculation on what our business might be and whence came the favour that gained me such distinction. I paid little heed, for I was seeking to follow the thoughts of the King and hoping that I had won him to my side. I asked only leave to lead a quiet life with her whom I loved, setting bounds at once to my ambition and to the plans which he had made concerning her. Nay, I believe that I might have claimed some hold over him, but I would not. A gentleman may not levy hush-money however fair the coins seem in his eyes. Yet I feared that he might suspect me, and I said:

"To-day, I leave the town, Sir, whether I have what I ask of you or not; and whether I have what I ask of you or not I am silent. If your Majesty will not grant it me, yet, in all things that I may be, I am your loyal subject."

To all this—perhaps it rang too solemn, as the words of a young man are apt to at the moments when his heart is moved—he answered nothing, but looking up with a whimsical smile said,

"Tell me now; how do you love this Mistress Quinton?"

At this I fell suddenly into a fit of shame and bashful embarrassment. The assurance that I had gained at Court forsook me, and I was tongue-tied as any calf-lover.

"I—I don't know," I stammered.

"Nay, but I grow old. Pray tell me, Mr Dale," he urged, beginning to laugh at my perturbation.

For my life I could not; it seems to me that the more a man feels a thing the harder it is for him to utter; sacred things are secret, and the hymn must not be heard save by the deity.

The King suddenly bent forward and beckoned. Rochester was passing by, with him now was the Duke of Monmouth. They approached; I bowed low to the Duke, who returned my salute most cavalierly. He had small

Anthony Hope

reason to be pleased with me, and his brow was puckered. The King seemed to find fresh amusement in his son's bearing, but he made no remark on it, and, addressing himself to Rochester, said:

"Here, my lord, is a young gentleman much enamoured of a lovely and most chaste maiden. I ask him what this love of his is—for my memory fails—and behold he cannot tell me! In case he doesn't know what it is that he feels, I pray you tell him."

Rochester looked at me with an ironical smile.

"Am I to tell what love is?" he asked.

"Ay, with your utmost eloquence," answered the King, laughing still and pinching his dog's ears.

Rochester twisted his face in a grimace, and looked appealingly at the King.

"There's no escape; to-day I am a tyrant," said the King.

"Hear then, youths," said Rochester, and his face was smoothed into a pensive and gentle expression. "Love is madness and the only sanity, delirium and the only truth; blindness and the only vision, folly and the only wisdom. It is—" He broke off and cried impatiently, "I have forgotten what it is."

"Why, my lord, you never knew what it is," said the King. "Alone of us here, Mr Dale knows, and since he cannot tell us the knowledge is lost to the world. James, have you any news of my friend M. de Fontelles?"

"Such news as your Majesty has," answered Monmouth.

"And I hear that my Lord Carford will not die."

"Let us be as thankful as is fitting for that," said the King. "M. de Fontelles sent me a very uncivil message; he is leaving England, and goes, he tells me, to seek a King whom a gentleman may serve."

"Is the gentleman about to kill himself, Sir?" asked Rochester with an affected air of grave concern.

"He's an insolent rascal," cried Monmouth angrily. "Will he go back to France?"

"Why, yes, in the end, when he has tried the rest of my brethren in Europe. A man's King is like his nose; the nose may not be handsome, James, but it's small profit to cut it off. That was done once, you remember—"

"And here is your Majesty on the throne," interposed Rochester with a most loyal bow.

"James," said the King, "our friend Mr Dale desires to wed Mistress Barbara Quinton."

Monmouth started violently and turned red.

"His admiration for that lady," continued the King, "has been shared by such high and honourable persons that I cannot doubt it to be well founded. Shall he not then be her husband?"

Monmouth's eyes were fixed on me; I met his glance with an easy smile. Again I felt that I, who had worsted M. de Perrencourt, need not fear the Duke of Monmouth.

"If there be any man," observed Rochester, "who would

love a lady who is not a wife, and yet is fit to be his wife, let him take her, in Heaven's name! For he might voyage as far in search of another like her as M. de Fontelles must in his search for a Perfect King."

"Shall he not have her, James?" asked the King of his son.

Monmouth understood that the game was lost.

"Ay, Sir, let him have her," he answered, mustering a smile. "And I hope soon to see your Court graced by her presence."

Well, at that, I, most inadvertently and by an error in demeanour which I now deplore sincerely, burst into a short sharp laugh. The King turned to me with raised eyebrows.

"Pray let us hear the jest, Mr Dale," said he.

"Why, Sir," I answered, "there is no jest. I don't know why I laughed, and I pray your pardon humbly."

"Yet there was something in your mind," the King insisted.

"Then, Sir, if I must say it, it was no more than this; if I would not be married in Calais, neither will I be married in Whitehall."

There was a moment's silence. It was broken by Rochester.

"I am dull," said he. "I don't understand that observation of Mr Dale's."

"That may well be, my lord," said Charles, and he turned to Monmouth, smiling maliciously as he asked, "Are you as dull as my lord here, James, or do you understand what Mr Dale would say?"

Monmouth's mood hung in the balance between anger and amusement. I had crossed and thwarted his fancy, but it was no more than a fancy. And I had crossed and thwarted M. de Perrencourt's also; that was balm to his wounds. I do not know that he could have done me harm, and it was as much from a pure liking for him as from any fear of his disfavour that I rejoiced when I saw his kindly thoughts triumph and a smile come on his lips.

"Plague take the fellow," said he, "I understand him. On my life he's wise!"

I bowed low to him, saying, "I thank your Grace for your understanding."

Rochester sighed heavily.

"This is wearisome," said he. "Shall we walk?"

"You and James shall walk," said the King. "I have yet a word for Mr Dale." As they went he turned to me and said, "But will you leave us? I could find work for you here."

I did not know what to answer him. He saw my hesitation.

"The basket will not be emptied," said he in a low and cautious voice. "It will be emptied neither for M. de Perrencourt nor for the King of France. You look very hard at me, Mr Dale, but you needn't search my face so closely. I will tell you what you desire to know. I have had my price, but I do not empty my basket." Having said this, he sat leaning his head on his hands with his eyes cast up at me from under his swarthy bushy brows.

There was a long silence then between us. For myself I do not deny that youthful ambition again cried to me to take his offer, while pride told me that even at Whitehall I could guard my honour and all that was mine. I could serve him; since he told me his secrets, he must and would serve me. And he had in the end dealt fairly and kindly with me.

The King struck his right hand on the arm of his chair suddenly and forcibly.

"I sit here," said he; "it is my work to sit here. My brother has a conscience, how long would he sit here? James is a fool, how long would he sit here? They laugh at me or snarl at me, but here I sit, and here I will sit till my life's end, by God's grace or the Devil's help. My gospel is to sit here."

I had never before seen him so moved, and never had so plain a glimpse of his heart, nor of the resolve which lay beneath his lightness and frivolity. Whence came that one unswerving resolution I know not; yet I do not think that it stood on nothing better than his indolence and a hatred of going again on his travels. There was more than that in it; perhaps he seemed to himself to hold a fort and considered all stratagems and devices well justified against the enemy. I made him no answer but continued to look at him. His passion passed as quickly as it had come, and he was smiling again with his ironical smile as he said to me:

"But my gospel need not be yours. Our paths have

crossed, they need not run side by side. Come, man, I have spoken to you plainly, speak plainly to me." He paused, and then, leaning forward, said,

"Perhaps you are of M. de Fontelles' mind? Will you join him in his search? Abandon it. You had best go to your home and wait. Heaven may one day send you what you desire. Answer me, sir. Are you of the Frenchman's mind?"

His voice now had the ring of command in it and I could not but answer. And when I came to answer there was but one thing to say. He had told me the terms of my service. What was it to me that he sat there, if honour and the Kingdom's greatness and all that makes a crown worth the wearing must go, in order to his sitting there? There rose in me at once an inclination towards him and a loathing for the gospel that he preached; the last was stronger and, with a bow, I said:

"Yes, Sir, I am of M. de Fontelles' mind."

He heard me, lying back in his chair. He said nothing, but sighed lightly, puckered his brow an instant, and smiled. Then he held out his hand to me, and I bent and kissed it.

"Good-bye, Mr Dale," said he. "I don't know how long you'll have to wait. I'm hale and—so's my brother."

He moved his hand in dismissal, and, having withdrawn some paces, I turned and walked away. All observed or seemed to observe me; I heard whispers that asked who I was, why the King had talked so long to me, and to what service or high office I was destined. Acquaintances saluted me and stared in wonder at my careless acknowledgment and the quick decisive tread that carried me to the door. Now, having made my choice, I was on fire to be gone; yet once I turned my head and saw the King sitting still in his chair, his head resting on his hands, and a slight smile on his lips. He saw me look, and nodded his head. I bowed, turned again, and was gone.

Since then I have not seen him, for the paths that crossed diverged again. But, as all men know, he carried out his gospel. There he sat till his life's end, whether by God's grace or the Devil's help I know not. But there he sat, and never did he empty his basket lest, having given all, he should have nothing to carry to market. It is not for me to judge him now; but then, when I had the choice set before me, there in his own palace, I passed my verdict. I do not repent of it. For good or evil, in wisdom or in folly, in mere honesty or the extravagance of sentiment, I had made my choice. I was of the mind of M. de Fontelles, and I went forth to wait till there should be a King whom a gentleman could serve. Yet to this day I am sorry that he made me tell him of my choice.

CHAPTER XXVI

I COME HOME

I have written the foregoing for my children's sake that they may know that once their father played some part in great affairs, and, rubbing shoulder to shoulder with folk of high degree, bore himself (as I venture to hope) without disgrace, and even with that credit which a ready brain and hand bring to their possessor. Here, then, I might well come to an end, and deny myself the pleasure of a last few words indited for my own comfort and to please a greedy recollection. The children, if they read, will laugh. Have you not seen the mirthful wonder that spreads on a girl's face when she comes by chance on some relic of her father's wooing, a faded wreath that he has given her mother, or a nosegay tied with a ribbon and a poem attached thereto? She will look in her father's face, and thence to where her mother sits at her needle-work, just where she has sat at her needle-work these twenty years, with her old kind smile and comfortable eyes. The girl loves her, loves her well, but—how came father to write those words? For mother, though the dearest creature in the world, is not slim, nor dazzling, nor a Queen, nor is she Venus herself, decked in colours of the rainbow, nor a Goddess come from heaven to men, nor the desire of all the world, nor aught else that father calls her in the poem. Indeed, what father wrote is something akin to what the Squire slipped into her own hand last night; but it is a strange strain in which to write to mother, the dearest creature in the world, but no, not Venus in her glory nor the Queen of the Nymphs. But though the maiden laughs, her father is not ashamed. He still sees her to whom he wrote, and when she smiles across the room at him, and smiles again to see her daughter's wonder, all the years fade from the picture's face, and the vision stands as once it was, though my young mistress' merry eyes have not the power to see it. Let her laugh. God forbid that I should grudge it her! Soon enough shall she sit sewing and another laugh.

Carford was gone, well-nigh healed of his wound, healed also of his love, I trust, at least headed off from it. M. de Fontelles was gone also, on that quest of his which made my Lord Rochester so merry; indeed I fear that in this case the scoffer had the best of it, for he whom I have called M. de Perrencourt was certainly served again by his indignant subject, and that most brilliantly. Well, had I been a Frenchman, I could have forgiven King Louis much; and I suppose that, although an Englishman, I do not hate him greatly, since his ring is often on my wife's finger and I see it there without pain.

It was the day before my wedding was to take place; for my lord, on being informed of all that had passed, had sworn roundly that since there was one honest man who sought his daughter, he would not refuse her, lest while he waited for better things worse should come. And he proceeded to pay me many a compliment, which I would repeat, despite of modesty, if it chanced that I remembered them. But in truth my head was so full of his daughter that there was no space for his praises, and his well-turned eulogy (for my lord had a pretty flow of words) was as sadly wasted as though he had spoken it to the statue of Apollo on his terrace.

I had been taking dinner with the Vicar, and, since it was not yet time to pay my evening visit to the Manor, I sat with him a while after our meal, telling him for his entertainment how I had talked with the King at Whitehall, what the King had said, and what I, and how my Lord Rochester had talked finely of the Devil, and tried, but failed, to talk of love. He drank in all with eager ears, weighing the wit in a balance, and striving to see, through my recollection, the life and the scene and the men that were so strange to his eyes and so familiar to his dreams.

"You don't appear very indignant, sir," I ventured to observe with a smile.

We were in the porch, and, for answer to what I said, he pointed to the path in front of us. Following the direction of his finger I perceived a fly of a species with which I, who am a poor student of nature, was not familiar. It was villainously ugly, although here and there on it were patches of bright colour.

"Yet," said the Vicar, "you are not indignant with it, Simon."

"No, I am not indignant," I admitted.

"But if it were to crawl over you—"

"I should crush the brute," I cried.

"Yes. They have crawled over you and you are indignant. They have not crawled over me, and I am curious."

"But, sir, will you allow a man no disinterested moral emotion?"

"As much as he will, and he shall be cool at the end of it," smiled the Vicar. "Now if they took my benefice from me again!" Stooping down, he picked up the creature in his hand and fell to examining it very minutely.

"I wonder you can touch it," said I in disgust.

"You did not quit the Court without some regret, Simon," he reminded me.

I could make nothing of him in this mood and was about to leave him when I perceived my lord and Barbara approaching the house. Springing up, I ran to meet them; they received me with a grave air, and in the ready apprehension of evil born of a happiness that seems too great I cried out to know if there were bad tidings.

"There's nothing that touches us nearly," said my lord. "But very pitiful news is come from France."

The Vicar had followed me and now stood by me; I looked up and saw that the ugly creature was still in his hand.

"It concerns Madame, Simon," said Barbara. "She is dead and all the town declares that she had poison given to her in a cup of chicory-water. Is it not pitiful?"

Indeed the tidings came as a shock to me, for I remembered the winning grace and wit of the unhappy lady.

"But who has done it?" I cried.

"I don't know," said my lord. "It is set down to her husband; rightly or wrongly, who knows?"

A silence ensued for a few moments. The Vicar stooped and set his captive free to crawl away on the path.

"God has crushed one of them, Simon," said he. "Are you content?"

"I try not to believe it of her," said I.

In a grave mood we began to walk, and presently, as it chanced, Barbara and I distanced the slow steps of our elders and found ourselves at the Manor gates alone.

"I am very sorry for Madame," said she, sighing heavily. Yet presently, because by the mercy of Providence our own joy outweighs others' grief and thus we can pass through the world with unbroken hearts, she looked up at me with a smile, and passing her arm, through mine, drew herself close to me.

"Ay, be merry, to-night at least be merry, my sweet," said I. "For we have come through a forest of troubles and are here safe out on the other side."

"Safe and together," said she.

"Without the second, where would be the first?"

"Yet," said Barbara, "I fear you'll make a bad husband; for here at the very beginning—nay, I mean before the beginning—you have deceived me."

"I protest—!" I cried.

"For it was from my father only that I heard of a visit you paid in London."

I bent my head and looked at her.

"I would not trouble you with it," said I. "It was no more than a debt of civility."

"Simon, I don't grudge it to her. For I am, here in the country with you, and she is there in London without you."

"And in truth," said I, "I believe that you are both best pleased."

"For her," said Barbara, "I cannot speak."

For a long while then we walked in silence, while the afternoon grew full and waned again. They mock at lovers' talk; let them, say I with all my heart, so that they leave our silence sacred. But at last Barbara turned to me and said with a little laugh:

"Art glad to have come home, Simon?"

Verily I was glad. In body I had wandered some way, in mind and heart farther, through many dark ways, turning and twisting here and there, leading I knew not whither, seeming to leave no track by which I might regain my starting point. Yet, although I felt it not, the thread was in my hand, the golden thread spun here in Hatchstead when my days were young. At length the hold of it had tightened and I, perceiving it, had turned and followed. Thus it had brought me home, no better in purse or station than I went, and poorer by the loss of certain dreams that haunted me, yet, as I hope, sound in heart and soul. I looked now in the dark eyes that were, set on me as though there were their refuge, joy, and life; she clung to me as though even still I might leave her. But the last fear fled, the last doubt faded away, and a smile came in radiant serenity on the lips I loved as, bending down, I whispered:

"Ay, I am glad to have come home."

But there was one thing more that I must say. Her head fell on my shoulder as she murmured:

"And you have utterly forgotten her?"

Her eyes were safely hidden. I smiled as I answered, "Utterly."

See how I stood! Wilt thou forgive me, Nelly?

For a man may be very happy as he is and still not forget the things which have been. "What are you thinking of, Simon?" my wife asks sometimes when I lean back in my chair and smile. "Of nothing, sweet," say I. And, in truth, I am not thinking; it is only that a low laugh echoes distantly in my ear. Faithful and loyal am I—but, should such as Nell leave nought behind her?

Anthony Hope

ABOUT THE AUTHOR

Sir Anthony Hope Hawkins, better known as Anthony Hope, (February 9, 1863 – July 8, 1933) was a British novelist, born in London, and best remembered today for his short novel The Prisoner of Zenda (1894), set in the fictional kingdom of Ruritania, a prequel The Heart of Princess Osra (a collection of short stories set in 18C Ruritania) (1896) and a sequel Rupert of Hentzau (1898). His first novel was A Man of Mark (1890), and one of his most well-known works during his lifetime was The Dolly Dialogues (1894), published in the Westminster Gazette.

After being educated at Marlborough College and Balliol College (where he was President of the Oxford Union), he trained as a lawyer and barrister, being called to the Bar in 1877. He practised as a lawyer until 1894; he started writing full time after Zenda's success, completing many other novels and plays, including Sophy of Kravonia (1906), in a similar vein. He was knighted in recognition of his contribution to British propaganda efforts during World War I.

He published an autobiographical book, Memories and Notes, in 1927.

There is a blue plaque on his house in Bedford Square, London.

Choose from Thousands of 1stWorldLibrary Classics By

A. M. Barnard
Ada Leverson
Adolphus William Ward
Aesop
Agatha Christie
Alexander Aaronsohn
Alexander Kielland
Alexandre Dumas
Alfred Gatty
Alfred Ollivant
Alice Duer Miller
Alice Turner Curtis
Alice Dunbar
Allen Chapman
Alleyne Ireland
Ambrose Bierce
Amelia E. Barr
Amory H. Bradford
Andrew Lang
Andrew McFarland Davis
Andy Adams
Angela Brazil
Anna Alice Chapin
Anna Sewell
Annie Besant
Annie Hamilton Donnell
Annie Payson Call
Annie Roe Carr
Annonaymous
Anton Chekhov
Archibald Lee Fletcher
Arnold Bennett
Arthur C. Benson
Arthur Conan Doyle
Arthur M. Winfield
Arthur Ransome
Arthur Schnitzler
Arthur Train
Atticus
B.H. Baden-Powell
B. M. Bower
B. C. Chatterjee
Baroness Emmuska Orczy
Baroness Orczy
Basil King
Bayard Taylor
Ben Macomber
Bertha Muzzy Bower
Bjornstjerne Bjornson

Booth Tarkington
Boyd Cable
Bram Stoker
C. Collodi
C. E. Orr
C. M. Ingleby
Carolyn Wells
Catherine Parr Traill
Charles A. Eastman
Charles Amory Beach
Charles Dickens
Charles Dudley Warner
Charles Farrar Browne
Charles Ives
Charles Kingsley
Charles Klein
Charles Hanson Towne
Charles Lathrop Pack
Charles Romyn Dake
Charles Whibley
Charles Willing Beale
Charlotte M. Braeme
Charlotte M. Yonge
Charlotte Perkins Stetson
Clair W. Hayes
Clarence Day Jr.
Clarence E. Mulford
Clemence Housman
Confucius
Coningsby Dawson
Cornelis DeWitt Wilcox
Cyril Burleigh
D. H. Lawrence
Daniel Defoe
David Garnett
Dinah Craik
Don Carlos Janes
Donald Keyhoe
Dorothy Kilner
Dougan Clark
Douglas Fairbanks
E. Nesbit
E. P. Roe
E. Phillips Oppenheim
E. S. Brooks
Earl Barnes
Edgar Rice Burroughs
Edith Van Dyne
Edith Wharton

Edward Everett Hale
Edward J. O'Biren
Edward S. Ellis
Edwin L. Arnold
Eleanor Atkins
Eleanor Hallowell Abbott
Eliot Gregory
Elizabeth Gaskell
Elizabeth McCracken
Elizabeth Von Arnim
Ellem Key
Emerson Hough
Emilie F. Carlen
Emily Bronte
Emily Dickinson
Enid Bagnold
Enilor Macartney Lane
Erasmus W. Jones
Ernie Howard Pie
Ethel May Dell
Ethel Turner
Ethel Watts Mumford
Eugene Sue
Eugenie Foa
Eugene Wood
Eustace Hale Ball
Evelyn Everett-green
Everard Cotes
F. H. Cheley
F. J. Cross
F. Marion Crawford
Fannie E. Newberry
Federick Austin Ogg
Ferdinand Ossendowski
Fergus Hume
Florence A. Kilpatrick
Fremont B. Deering
Francis Bacon
Francis Darwin
Frances Hodgson Burnett
Frances Parkinson Keyes
Frank Gee Patchin
Frank Harris
Frank Jewett Mather
Frank L. Packard
Frank V. Webster
Frederic Stewart Isham
Frederick Trevor Hill
Frederick Winslow Taylor

Friedrich Kerst
Friedrich Nietzsche
Fyodor Dostoyevsky
G.A. Henty
G.K. Chesterton
Gabrielle E. Jackson
Garrett P. Serviss
Gaston Leroux
George A. Warren
George Ade
Geroge Bernard Shaw
George Cary Eggleston
George Durston
George Ebers
George Eliot
George Gissing
George MacDonald
George Meredith
George Orwell
George Sylvester Viereck
George Tucker
George W. Cable
George Wharton James
Gertrude Atherton
Gordon Casserly
Grace E. King
Grace Gallatin
Grace Greenwood
Grant Allen
Guillermo A. Sherwell
Gulielma Zollinger
Gustav Flaubert
H. A. Cody
H. B. Irving
H.C. Bailey
H. G. Wells
H. H. Munro
H. Irving Hancock
H. R. Naylor
H. Rider Haggard
H. W. C. Davis
Haldeman Julius
Hall Caine
Hamilton Wright Mabie
Hans Christian Andersen
Harold Avery
Harold McGrath
Harriet Beecher Stowe
Harry Castlemon
Harry Coghill
Harry Houidini

Hayden Carruth
Helent Hunt Jackson
Helen Nicolay
Hendrik Conscience
Hendy David Thoreau
Henri Barbusse
Henrik Ibsen
Henry Adams
Henry Ford
Henry Frost
Henry James
Henry Jones Ford
Henry Seton Merriman
Henry W Longfellow
Herbert A. Giles
Herbert Carter
Herbert N. Casson
Herman Hesse
Hildegard G. Frey
Homer
Honore De Balzac
Horace B. Day
Horace Walpole
Horatio Alger Jr.
Howard Pyle
Howard R. Garis
Hugh Lofting
Hugh Walpole
Humphry Ward
Ian Maclaren
Inez Haynes Gillmore
Irving Bacheller
Isabel Cecilia Williams
Isabel Hornibrook
Israel Abrahams
Ivan Turgenev
J.G.Austin
J. Henri Fabre
J. M. Barrie
J. M. Walsh
J. Macdonald Oxley
J. R. Miller
J. S. Fletcher
J. S. Knowles
J. Storer Clouston
J. W. Duffield
Jack London
Jacob Abbott
James Allen
James Andrews
James Baldwin

James Branch Cabell
James DeMille
James Joyce
James Lane Allen
James Lane Allen
James Oliver Curwood
James Oppenheim
James Otis
James R. Driscoll
Jane Abbott
Jane Austen
Jane L. Stewart
Janet Aldridge
Jens Peter Jacobsen
Jerome K. Jerome
Jessie Graham Flower
John Buchan
John Burroughs
John Cournos
John F. Kennedy
John Gay
John Glasworthy
John Habberton
John Joy Bell
John Kendrick Bangs
John Milton
John Philip Sousa
John Taintor Foote
Jonas Lauritz Idemil Lie
Jonathan Swift
Joseph A. Altsheler
Joseph Carey
Joseph Conrad
Joseph E. Badger Jr
Joseph Hergesheimer
Joseph Jacobs
Jules Vernes
Julian Hawthrone
Julie A Lippmann
Justin Huntly McCarthy
Kakuzo Okakura
Karle Wilson Baker
Kate Chopin
Kenneth Grahame
Kenneth McGaffey
Kate Langley Bosher
Kate Langley Bosher
Katherine Cecil Thurston
Katherine Stokes
L. A. Abbot
L. T. Meade

L. Frank Baum
Latta Griswold
Laura Dent Crane
Laura Lee Hope
Laurence Housman
Lawrence Beasley
Leo Tolstoy
Leonid Andreyev
Lewis Carroll
Lewis Sperry Chafer
Lilian Bell
Lloyd Osbourne
Louis Hughes
Louis Joseph Vance
Louis Tracy
Louisa May Alcott
Lucy Fitch Perkins
Lucy Maud Montgomery
Luther Benson
Lydia Miller Middleton
Lyndon Orr
M. Corvus
M. H. Adams
Margaret E. Sangster
Margret Howth
Margaret Vandercook
Margaret W. Hungerford
Margret Penrose
Maria Edgeworth
Maria Thompson Daviess
Mariano Azuela
Marion Polk Angellotti
Mark Overton
Mark Twain
Mary Austin
Mary Catherine Crowley
Mary Cole
Mary Hastings Bradley
Mary Roberts Rinehart
Mary Rowlandson
M. Wollstonecraft Shelley
Maud Lindsay
Max Beerbohm
Myra Kelly
Nathaniel Hawthrone
Nicolo Machiavelli
O. F. Walton
Oscar Wilde

Owen Johnson
P.G. Wodehouse
Paul and Mabel Thorne
Paul G. Tomlinson
Paul Severing
Percy Brebner
Percy Keese Fitzhugh
Peter B. Kyne
Plato
Quincy Allen
R. Derby Holmes
R. L. Stevenson
R. S. Ball
Rabindranath Tagore
Rahul Alvares
Ralph Bonehill
Ralph Henry Barbour
Ralph Victor
Ralph Waldo Emmerson
Rene Descartes
Ray Cummings
Rex Beach
Rex E. Beach
Richard Harding Davis
Richard Jefferies
Richard Le Gallienne
Robert Barr
Robert Frost
Robert Gordon Anderson
Robert L. Drake
Robert Lansing
Robert Lynd
Robert Michael Ballantyne
Robert W. Chambers
Rosa Nouchette Carey
Rudyard Kipling
Saint Augustine
Samuel B. Allison
Samuel Hopkins Adams
Sarah Bernhardt
Sarah C. Hallowell
Selma Lagerlof
Sherwood Anderson
Sigmund Freud
Standish O'Grady
Stanley Weyman
Stella Benson
Stella M. Francis

Stephen Crane
Stewart Edward White
Stijn Streuvels
Swami Abhedananda
Swami Parmananda
T. S. Ackland
T. S. Arthur
The Princess Der Ling
Thomas A. Janvier
Thomas A Kempis
Thomas Anderton
Thomas Bailey Aldrich
Thomas Bulfinch
Thomas De Quincey
Thomas Dixon
Thomas H. Huxley
Thomas Hardy
Thomas More
Thornton W. Burgess
U. S. Grant
Upton Sinclair
Valentine Williams
Various Authors
Vaughan Kester
Victor Appleton
Victor G. Durham
Victoria Cross
Virginia Woolf
Wadsworth Camp
Walter Camp
Walter Scott
Washington Irving
Wilbur Lawton
Wilkie Collins
Willa Cather
Willard F. Baker
William Dean Howells
William le Queux
W. Makepeace Thackeray
William W. Walter
William Shakespeare
Winston Churchill
Yei Theodora Ozaki
Yogi Ramacharaka
Young E. Allison
Zane Grey